Lynne Graham was born in N
has been a keen romance reade
She is very happily married, to
husband who has learned to cook since she started to write! Her five children keep her on her toes. She has a very large dog, which knocks everything over, a very small terrier, which barks a lot, and two cats. When time allows, Lynne is a keen gardener.

USA TODAY bestselling, RITA®-nominated and critically acclaimed author **Caitlin Crews** has written more than one hundred books and counting. She has a Master's and a PhD in English Literature, thinks everyone should read more category romance, and is always available to discuss her beloved alpha heroes. Just ask! She lives in the Pacific Northwest with her comic book artist husband, she is always planning her next trip, and she will never, ever, read all the books in her 'to-be-read' pile. Thank goodness.

Also by Lynne Graham

The Baby the Desert King Must Claim
Two Secrets to Shock the Italian

Cinderella Sisters for Billionaires miniseries

The Maid Married to the Billionaire
The Maid's Pregnancy Bombshell

Also by Caitlin Crews

A Billion-Dollar Heir for Christmas
Wedding Night in the King's Bed
Her Venetian Secret

The Teras Wedding Challenge collection

A Tycoon Too Wild to Wed

Discover more at millsandboon.co.uk.

BILLION-DOLLAR BABIES

LYNNE GRAHAM

CAITLIN CREWS

MILLS & BOON

First published in Great Britain 2024
by Mills & Boon, an imprint of HarperCollins*Publishers* Ltd,
1 London Bridge Street, London, SE1 9GF

www.harpercollins.co.uk

HarperCollins*Publishers*, Macken House, 39/40 Mayor Street Upper,
Dublin 1, D01 C9W8, Ireland

ISBN: 978-0-263-32014-5

07/24

This book contains FSC™ certified paper
and other controlled sources to ensure responsible forest management.

For more information visit www.harpercollins.co.uk/green.

Printed and Bound in the UK using 100% Renewable Electricity
at CPI Group (UK) Ltd, Croydon, CR0 4YY

BABY WORTH BILLIONS

LYNNE GRAHAM

MILLS & BOON

CHAPTER ONE

RAJ BELANGER, the richest man in the world, was in a reasonably good mood as his helicopter landed on the roof of the Diamond Club in London.

After all, the exclusive club, a sanctuary for him and other people of immense wealth, was his personal creation. Lazlo, the manager, greeted him quietly at the door and ushered him indoors to the welcome quiet of the private members' club. The classical décor of marble columns and high ceilings matched with muted colours and the ultimate in opulent comfort was satisfying to Raj's critical gaze. And within the refined safe harbour of the Diamond Club, there were no paparazzi or celebrity spotters. The staff were rigorously vetted and trained. Every member enjoyed a private suite and the catering and business facilities were as international as the clientele.

Encountering an appreciative appraisal from Lazlo's female assistant manager, Raj looked away, his dark golden eyes reflecting irritation at the height, build and dark good looks that had always attracted too much attention to him. Six feet four inches tall, he was a lean, powerful, strikingly handsome man, who despised vanity. He stayed fit for the sake of his health and stamina. He believed that what was inside an individual was a great deal more important than their outer shell. Beauty faded, but without disease, intelligence survived. A former child prodigy of unequalled brilliance and a legendary entrepreneur in the fast-moving tech world, Raj had strong opinions and few people dared to argue with him.

His British lawyer, Marcus Bateman, awaited him in his private suite. A small, grey-haired man, he had an astute brain and shrewd business sense. As breakfast was set out for them, Raj made small talk because he never discussed private matters when there were potential witnesses present. Once they were alone, he broached the issue that had troubled him for longer than he would have cared to admit: the plight of his orphaned niece, Phoenix Petronella Pansy Belanger.

Four months earlier, Raj had lost his last surviving relative, his brother, Ethan. Ethan and his wife, Christabel, had died in a car crash. A cocaine-fuelled car crash. The nanny looking after their ten-month-old baby girl had immediately contacted social services, keen to hand over responsibility for her charge and find a new placement.

'Have you changed your mind about seeking custody?' Marcus enquired quietly.

'No, if Christabel's half-sister is deemed a suitable parent for the child, I have no objection,' Raj declared levelly. 'As a single man, I would be the wrong guardian for a little girl. The life I lead is wholly unsuited to childrearing, nor would I even know where to begin in that task.'

The older man nodded, aware that Raj had been subjected to a dysfunctional environment from when he was an infant until he was finally emancipated from that regime by his mother's desertion of his father. Raj's own disturbing experiences would make it almost impossible for him to relate to an ordinary child. In truth, Raj had never known what it was to be ordinary. He had been hothoused and home-schooled and had won a handful of advanced degrees from the world's leading universities long before he became a teenager.

It was in the normal affection and social stakes that Raj had lost out most. He had been raised without warmth or friends and with parents whose sole focus had been on developing his exceptional intellect. When his mother had given birth to Ethan, however, Raj had been naïvely thrilled by the prospect of a kid brother. Protected from their father's malign influence, Ethan had been raised with everything that Raj had been denied. He had been cuddled and encouraged, loved and praised even when he hadn't deserved it and yet, much to Raj's dismay and surprise, Ethan had somehow matured into an appalling failure. Had his brother been spoilt? Had the umbrella of cash provided by Raj's wealth caused Ethan's expectations to range too high? Had the unfair comparisons made between the two brothers cruelly damaged Ethan's ego and backbone?

Raj had done everything within his power to support his brother as an adult, particularly after his mother's demise. Sadly, Ethan had failed to rise to the challenge of the many opportunities he had been offered.

Indeed, Ethan had proved to be weak, lazy and dishonest, although his disloyal and greedy wife, Christabel, had been the worst of the two. Raj had met his niece only once at the christening font when she had been a red-faced and screaming little bundle and he had had an accidental glimpse of her once in the hall of his brother's home. Further meetings after that had proved problematical because neither Christabel nor Ethan had liked social occasions with young children present. The baby had been kept very much in the background of their lives and Raj suspected that she had seen more of the nanny than she had ever seen of her parents.

'Miss Barker, the child's aunt, has agreed to allow you to visit your niece,' Marcus told him cheerfully. 'I took the liberty of consulting your PA and organising an access visit for next week.'

Raj thrust his breakfast plate away and thanked him. 'But I gather that the foolish woman is still refusing to accept any money from me?' he murmured flatly.

'She remains determined to raise the little girl without your financial help,' Marcus confirmed. 'It's admirable in the circumstances.'

'Irrational,' Raj overruled impatiently. 'I will address the issue when I meet her next week.'

'Bear in mind that Miss Barker is not in need of money. She's a successful artist in her own right. Arguing with her could cause resentment and make it more difficult for you to retain access to your niece. In a few months the adoption will be ratified by the court,' Marcus warned gravely.

Raj compressed his lips. He foresaw no difficulty in dealing with Sunshine Barker. Had he believed that she bore the smallest resemblance to her late sister, Christabel, he would have felt forced to dispute her application to adopt their niece. But he had had Sunshine's life extensively researched and she was as different from the unscrupulous and calculating Christabel as it was possible to be. She lived in a country cottage and embraced the rural life right down to the extent of foraging in the local woods for cooking supplies. She was educated, creative, bohemian, a messy blonde in Moses sandals with a string of rescue animals. But she was also well respected in her community and well liked.

Raj did not see her as a challenge.

Sunny had dropped her contact lens and she couldn't find it, although in the process of feeling delicately over the floor and below furniture she had discovered a hairbrush and a brooch that she had thought she had lost. In frustration she fumbled for her spectacles on the nightstand by the bed but she had evidently mislaid them as well, which was unfortunate when she was virtually blind as a bat without them. They would turn up, sooner or later, she consoled herself, screening a yawn as she brushed her mane of blonde hair with the retrieved and now dusted brush.

She was tired, naturally, she was. Just yesterday she had had Pansy stay overnight for only the second time and now her niece would actually be living with her round the clock. Even so, she was still being vetted as an adoptive parent by the social services and another orgy of cleaning and tidying awaited her because, while nobody expected her to live in a perfect household, a slovenly one wouldn't be acceptable either.

It was just unfortunate that Sunny hadn't yet had time to complete her renovation of her late grandmother's cottage. She had had the bathroom and kitchen gutted soon after her grandmother's demise six months ago, but the walls still rejoiced in ancient chintzy wallpaper and her own clutter was now layered over both her mother's and her gran's cherished bits and pieces. She was looking forward to plain painted walls, but the original pine floors were a little cold and hard for a baby who was starting to walk, so she had put down fluffy rugs for her niece's benefit. Eventually, she would get the house fully sorted but, right now, Pansy's care, comfort and contentment were her main priorities.

And now this wretched insurance assessor was coming to view the barn, which had been damaged by a storm ten days earlier. She suppressed a sigh, relieved that her niece was down for her nap and that she had contrived to dress in her version of an office worker's clothing for what she viewed as a formal meeting. It was true that the skirt was a little tight…too many bacon sandwiches when she was short of time and energy, and possibly too many chocolate treats at the railway stations she had hung around in while she was commuting back and forth to London on a daily basis to get properly acquainted with her niece at her foster home. Familiar guilt at her poor food choices trickled through her. And the long-sleeved top felt a little neat too over her bountiful bosom. Sunny much preferred loose garments in soft, misty colours like the plants she adored.

The bell went in three short hasty bursts. *Three!* Good to know upfront that she was about to deal with an impatient person, indifferent to the presence of pets and a baby in the household. Bear, her Great Dane–wolfhound mix, loosed a bone-chilling howl, making her grateful that she had no close neighbours. Barefoot, she sped to the door, afraid that tardiness might affect her claim.

A very tall male towered over her. She focused on a shirt button visible between the edges of a suit jacket and then a tie and was relieved that she had put on the skirt and top.

'So, you're…er…whatever. If you would give me just two minutes, I'll slip on my shoes and take you round to inspect the barn…'

The shoes she had intended to wear were still in the bedroom but her trusty welly boots were by the wall and she thrust her feet into them instead. 'These will do,' she said with a wide smile, skimming a glance up and up…and up. 'My goodness, you're very tall.'

'You are…petite,' Raj selected with unusual tact, although he was really wondering why on earth she wanted him to inspect her barn.

He was transfixed by her because she was such a mess. Her skirt was lopsided and unbuttoned at her tiny waist, above which swelled the sort of splendid feminine bounty that Raj generally only saw in his fantasies. The ugly orange top looked like something dragged out of a charity shop and the skirt was covered with animal hair. A faint shudder of distaste slivered through him but his dark gaze stayed welded to the huge smile lighting up her face. She was gorgeous, undersized and over-endowed in curves it was true, but still undeniably gorgeous. She had the most amazing tumbling fall of long wavy golden hair and violet eyes the colour of a flower, not a person, he adjusted. Coloured contact lenses? No, she didn't seem the type and she had yet to even look him in the face.

'Do you have any identification?' she asked him, something Raj had never ever been asked before.

His hair was dark, well, she was almost certain of that but he was only a blurred vision of size. He was way too tall and broad and kind of intimidating in stature. If you were the sort of woman who *was* intimidated by large men, that was…and she was *not*.

She didn't recognise him? Raj was amazed. She had not been at the christening or the wedding. However, he had somehow assumed that she had been at the double funeral. Admittedly though, there had been a huge turnout for the funeral, and he had not met her then, probably because he had been surrounded by people too eager to speak to him and ensure that he noticed their presence and remembered their names. He should've made a point of meeting her that day, he castigated himself. Unfortunately, he had kept his distance from the group of Christabel's friends, many of whom had been taking selfies and photos and generally conducting themselves as though they were attending some glitzy event, rather than a tragic interment.

Suppressing a sigh, he withdrew his passport and extended it. Sunny Barker had the tiniest fingers he had ever seen on an adult. He was hugely entertained by the whole process as she squinted uneasily down at the passport. She was irredeemably scatty, badly needing to be organised by someone. She would drive a control freak of his type insane, he reflected absently.

Sunny peered down at the passport but it was just a blur and she thought it was a very odd means of identification to show her. Hadn't his insurance firm given him an identity card with a logo? Evidently not and that was scarcely his fault. It was not as though she were inviting him *inside* her home, she reminded herself soothingly.

'Your barn?' he prompted with rare indecision, willing to play along to be reasonable and reluctant to embarrass her, which would only increase the awkwardness of their first meeting.

'Come this way,' Sunny urged, squeezing out past him—really, he did take up an awful lot of doorstep space—to lead him down the path and round the corner of the house into what had once been a farmyard.

Bear gambolled along by her side, giving the visitor a very wide berth. Bert peered out and snarled from beneath a shrub they were passing. Bear backed away. Bert advanced, threat in every line of his tiny body.

'Stop it, Bert!' Sunny scolded. 'You're being a bully.'

Raj glanced in disbelief at the tiniest dog he had ever seen outside a handbag. The giant dog was terrified of the tiny one. He wondered why he was being shown the barn. He wondered why he was with this strange woman, who didn't even recognise who he was. Did he expect everyone to know him at first glance? Sort of, he acknowledged uneasily. And Sunny Barker was his former sister-in-law's sibling, shouldn't she recognise him? Have taken some interest in his presence in the family tree? Even if they had never enjoyed a formal introduction?

'So, here's the barn. As you can see a giant branch fell on the roof and messed it up a little.'

'More than a little,' Raj countered, studying the poorly maintained structure, automatically foreseeing any insurance firm's likely response to such a claim but stifling his urge to issue a warning. Instead, he viewed the very tall horse staring out at him over the stable door. 'Who's this?'

'Muffy. She's a Clydesdale,' Sunny told him, suddenly full of animation, delighted, it seemed, by his presumed interest. 'She was very upset about the roof tiles falling and the rain coming in.'

Raj contemplated the misnamed horse, who didn't look as though she would stir into life for anything less than a hurricane. 'She seems content.'

'She's very easy-going…but I need the roof fixed. She's elderly,' Sunny whispered, as if the horse might be shy about her age being bandied about in public. 'She needs a nice dry stall.'

'Why are you showing me your barn?' Raj chose to ask abruptly, watching as she petted the horse, the movement drawing the top tighter over the ample swell of her breasts while he wondered why he was even looking.

Anyone would be forgiven for thinking that he was a teenager who had never seen breasts before! For goodness' sake, he was a sophisticated male with four mistresses in different cities. He took care of his sexual needs in the same efficient way that he took care of everything else in his life. He focused on privacy and practicality. He could be in London, New York, Paris or Tokyo and he could lift the phone and visit any one of his mistresses. Reminding himself of those facts did nothing to prevent his intense gaze from sliding from the generous thrust of her breasts to the curve of her perky and curvy bottom as she bent over the door and then angled those violet eyes up to open very wide on him. Unforgettable, beautiful eyes.

'Why are you asking me that? You're an insurance assessor,' Sunny told him in surprise.

'No, I'm not. I'm Raj Belanger and your niece is also *my* niece and I've arrived on a prearranged visit to see her…'

'You're coming to visit *next* week,' Sunny informed him with confidence. 'Same day, pretty much the same time but definitely *next* week.'

'I think you'll find you're incorrect in that conviction. My staff rarely make mistakes,' Raj asserted drily just as the shaggy Great Dane bolted from behind his owner to flee behind Raj in a determined effort to escape the domineering, aggressive chihuahua.

Disconcerted by the sudden pandemonium, Raj suffered a glancing blow to the back of his legs and skated forward, belatedly discovering that the surface below him was slippery and giving his soles no purchase as he was thrown off balance. He fell back heavily into the mud and lifted himself even faster to stare down at his soiled hands in disgust.

'I am so sorry…' Sunny whispered, urging him by the elbow back towards the house, thinking that the bigger people were, the harder they fell, but she had never seen anyone look quite so appalled by a little mud. 'Come this way, so that you can wash.'

She had been about to tell him that he had arrived on the right day but in the wrong week, only it seemed unkind to make that comment just at that moment. Was this man truly Pansy's uncle? The richer than Croesus guy? She was appalled at the reception she had given him. Of course, he had been quiet. He had been wondering what on earth she was talking about but had been too polite to say so.

Raj was already using his phone with angry stabs of a muddy finger, speaking into it in another language in curt tones of command. He was kind of bossy and he had a short fuse, Sunny decided as she got him back through the front door and spread open the bathroom door to the soundtrack of Pansy wailing for attention. 'You'll want to…er…freshen up and I'll bring you a towel.'

Yanking fresh towels in haste from the laundry press, she laid them on the hamper by the door and tried not to notice that he had clearly fallen into a puddle because his suit trousers were wet and mired. Poor man, as prone to accidents as the rest of humanity in spite of all his wretched money, she reflected ruefully, ashamed that she had had so many unkind, biased thoughts about him in recent weeks. A male who apparently believed that he could *bribe* her to take *better* care of his niece, apparently incapable of understanding that she most wanted to be a mother to Pansy and simply love her. And there would be no price tag involved in that process.

Someone was knocking on the door again. She sped to answer it, wanting to go and lift Pansy but determined to take care of everything at once. Another formally dressed male handed her a suit in a zipped clothing bag. 'For Mr Belanger,' he told her.

She wondered where he had come from and how he had arrived with her so quickly but she was flustered now and she raced back to thrust the bag at her visitor and swiftly closed the bathroom door on him again to go to her niece's room. Pansy was standing up bouncing at the side of the cot. With her mop of blonde curls and big blue eyes, she was incredibly cute and she lifted her little chubby arms to be lifted as soon as she saw her aunt.

'Yes, my precious. Aunty was late,' she confided softly, sweeping the soft warm weight of the toddler up into her arms and hugging her close. 'Time for your snack…right?'

Raj surveyed the modern washing facilities with intense relief as he stripped. He had enjoyed disturbing glimpses of other rooms en route to the bathroom. And everything was flowery or patterned and there was clutter on every available surface. The cottage was a hoarder's dream and he could see that the knick-knacks were creeping in to despoil the bathroom as well. A line of pottery flower sculptures adorned with improbably sparkly fairies marched along the window sill and he raised his brows.

Raj liked order, reason and discipline in every space he occupied. Everything, outside the arts, had to be functional in his world. He stepped into the shower because he was soaked through to the skin and the hot water soothed him even if the soap's strange grittiness did not. He was in Sunny's home, accepting her hospitality, and it would be strange not to expect differences, he reminded himself. *She* was different, after all. *Very* different, he conceded thoughtfully.

Towelling dry and feeling rather more like himself, he got dressed again in the fresh suit and put the discarded one in the empty bag. After a moment's hesitation, he lifted the discarded towels and placed them on top of the laundry hamper. For the first time in many years, he was making an effort to be scrupulously polite.

'Mr Belanger?' Sunny called as soon as she heard the bathroom door open. 'We're in the kitchen!'

Raj breathed in deep, like a male girding his belt before battle, and, pausing to acknowledge the threat of the low doorway, he ducked his proud dark head and strode on into the kitchen where bunches of wizened foliage hung down from the rafters. His attention, however, shifted straight to Sunny and her welcoming smile before almost apprehensively moving to the child seated in the toddler high chair. A pretty little girl waved her toast at him happily while slurping clumsily out of a toddler cup.

'Sit down at the table and make yourself at home,' Sunny urged expansively. 'I know you haven't had much contact with Pansy—'

'Pansy?' Raj interrupted in surprise. 'I thought she was called Phoenix. And any official documents I've seen on her refer to her as Phoenix.'

'Apparently your brother preferred Pansy and told the nanny to use that name,' Sunny told him. 'And the social worker in charge of her case decided that was best because she already recognises her name. The other two names are a bit…fancy.'

'Interesting,' Raj remarked, duly informed. He had thought the names a mouthful as well but prided himself on being too diplomatic to express that opinion.

'Coffee or tea? I have a lovely soothing herbal tea.'

Raj didn't believe he needed soothing. 'Coffee for me, black, no sugar, thank you. And call me Raj. In a loose sense, we are members of the same family,' he opined.

Warmed by that unexpected acknowledgement of a family link, Sunny poured the coffee, set it in front of him and slid over a plate of biscuits. 'Help yourself.'

Raj scanned the biscuits that had what looked like real flowers set into the dough. They were very decorative. He breathed in deep and selected one.

Sunny laid a knife on the plate. 'They're all edible flowers but if you don't like the look of them, feel free to scrape them off,' she said lightly.

Raj ignored the knife and chewed the biscuit, which

tasted surprisingly good. He watched Sunny lift his niece from her chair, clean her up carefully and then begin playing with her.

'Who's a beautiful girl, then?' she asked the baby, who was in the air chortling with glee, bare feet kicking up.

As Sunny turned her face up to look at the child, her expression shone with love and warmth and happiness. It was exactly what Raj had hoped to see in the woman who wanted to mother his orphaned niece and he was pleased and relieved in equal parts. 'What made you decide that you wanted to adopt her?' he heard himself ask.

'I'm unlikely to have children of my own. I have a… medical condition,' she admitted uncomfortably. 'And there was Pansy alone without parents and she's my own flesh and blood. It was an instant decision. I only wish Christabel had allowed me to visit her more often and then I would have been more familiar to Pansy when I came back into her life. Instead, I had to get to know her as a stranger.'

'Why didn't your sister allow you to visit your niece?' Raj enquired with a frown.

'Well, my half-sister and I weren't close. She was eight years older and then we grew up apart.'

'That's right. I seem to remember Christabel mentioning that her mother died and her father remarried and divorced.'

'And then last year, my grandmother, who owned this house, died and left it to me because this is where I grew up. Gran was terminally ill,' Sunny explained.

'Christabel took me to court to claim a share of the house's worth after my grandmother passed away and I'm afraid she was furious when I won the case. It also emptied my savings account, though.'

Raj frowned because he had read about the case in her background file. Her late sister had been remarkably avaricious, he mused, because, after marrying Ethan, she had not known what it was to be short of money.

'May I ask why you *didn't* want to adopt Pansy?' Sunny prompted.

'I believe that you have more to offer her,' he said quietly. 'I have no wife and no real desire for offspring. I wouldn't know where to begin raising a little girl and I would be reluctant to leave her in the care of a nanny all the time. My lifestyle would not be suitable for a young child.'

'You know your own mind and capabilities best,' Sunny conceded lightly. 'Speaking for myself, I'm grateful that I wasn't in competition with you.'

'Were I, at any stage, to consider you an inappropriate guardian, I *would* challenge you for custody. I should be candid on that score,' Raj incised, delivering that warning without hesitation.

Temper sizzled through Sunny at that arrogant statement. Although *he* had no desire to take personal responsibility for his niece, he expected to sit in judgement over *her* parental skills. With difficulty, she stifled her resentment, determined not to get on bad terms with such a powerful male. 'I'm happy that you have enough interest in Pansy to visit her. She won't have a father but, hopefully, she'll have a favourite uncle.'

'That's generous of you, although I expect to be only an occasional visitor.'

In a sudden movement, Sunny broke off listening to his well-modulated drawl and sped across the kitchen to pounce on the spectacles reflecting the light coming through the windows. 'I've been looking for these everywhere!' she gasped in satisfaction as she unfurled them and fixed them to her nose. 'I lose them so easily that I always keep three pairs on the go.'

'There are pairs of spectacles sitting on the hallstand and also on the bathroom window sill,' Raj disclosed to her astonishment.

And Sunny was amazed by his observational powers and also struck almost dumb by her first proper look at him. She had seen his picture once in a newspaper and had thought that he was an attractive man if a little grim and grave of expression. But in the flesh, she learned that Raj Belanger had much greater impact on her as a woman. He had stunning even features, high cheekbones, an aristocratic nose and a wide full mouth. His face was further blessed by very dark, intense eyes surrounded by dense inky lashes. Gorgeous, simply gorgeous eyes.

'You're staring at me,' Raj said sardonically.

'I'm sorry. You just look much more handsome in person than you do in a newspaper when you're always looking forbidding,' she mumbled. 'And you don't look at all like Ethan.'

Dark colour scored the line of Raj's high cheekbones. 'You don't really think before you speak…do you?' he countered.

'It's a habit of mine. I'm sorry for getting so personal and embarrassing you.' Now equipped with her spectacles, Sunny, with cheeks burning fire-engine red, studied the calendar on her wall and her slight shoulders dropped. 'And I owe you another apology. You were expected today and the insurance assessor *is* coming next week. My only excuse is that I've been getting ready for Pansy to come home and I've been very busy.'

Raj waved a forgiving hand, grateful that they were off the topic of his appearance and her barn. Did he look forbidding as she had termed it? It was true that he didn't smile very much. Yet wasn't it strange that Sunny made him want to smile because she amused him? She was all out there like an advertising hoarding while he was the exact opposite, generally keeping his feelings to himself and of a much more introverted nature.

'Let's move into the sitting room so that you can start getting acquainted with Pansy,' Sunny suggested, lifting the plate of biscuits and his coffee and her own tea onto a tray.

Raj vaulted upright, feeling as though he were being managed and disliking the unfamiliar sensation. He watched Pansy toddle somewhat clumsily in her aunt's wake, very much like a miniature drunk struggling still to find her balance.

He was smiling when he followed the duo into the cluttered sitting room where piles of books, potted plants and, in one corner, an actual log made the small space seem even smaller. He sank down into an armchair. He studied Sunny, who was gazing owlishly at him from behind her spectacles. That blue-violet shade of eyes had a luminous quality, he decided. His attention lingered.

'Why does Pansy not know you either?' Sunny asked just as Raj was about to ask out of sheer curiosity why there was a log on the floor.

'I generally only saw my brother and your sister at adult social occasions. I entertained them at my London home but they always left the baby at home,' he explained. 'Your sister said that she needed a break from being a mother. Why weren't you at the wedding or the christening?'

'Christabel had a simply huge guest list of important people she had to invite and I didn't make the cut and our grandmother wasn't well enough,' Sunny said without chagrin. 'I did understand. She and Ethan led very glamorous lives in comparison to ours.'

As Sunny brought a plastic container of toys out and Pansy began noisily tossing everything within it out, Raj relaxed a little because he was not immediately being challenged with the task of getting to know a young child. 'Where do you do your painting?' he asked curiously.

'In the sunroom behind the kitchen. The light's good there. I usually get up at the crack of dawn to paint. But I'll have to adapt my schedule to suit Pansy now.'

Encountering a narrowed glance from his dark eyes, which flamed gold in the sunny room, Sunny could feel her self-consciousness rise exponentially. There was something very intense about Raj Belanger. She didn't know whether it was the raw, restive masculine energy he emanated or the demanding potency of his dark gaze. But there was definitely an unnerving quality to being in his powerful presence. She could feel her nipples tightening inside her bra and a faint uncomfortable clenching in her pelvis. She went rigid, suddenly registering that what she was feeling in his radius was not simple tension but pure sexual attraction. It had been so long since she had experienced such a reaction to a man that she was sharply disconcerted by it.

'I'd like to see your work,' Raj declared, breaking free of the odd spell she cast over him to withdraw his gaze from her. What the hell was the matter with him? In denial of the stirring hardness at his groin, he turned his handsome dark head away to watch the large black cat pad from behind the potted plants, where he had evidently been sunning himself, to claw at the log. 'Who's this?'

'Miracle…the only survivor of a litter who died, a bit like Bear. Bear's mother rejected him at birth. I brought him home to see if I could feed him and keep him alive and, as you can see, he survived.' At the sound of his name, the big dog approached her and pushed against her knee affectionately before lying down, the very picture of relaxation.

As Pansy saw the cat, she let out a squeal of excitement and reached out her arms. The cat sprang off the log and ran out of the room and Sunny laughed. 'Miracle already knows to stay out of her reach. Bert stays in his basket in the kitchen. Hopefully he'll be adopted this week. A lady is coming to see him. He needs a home where there are no other pets or children.

'I'll show you the studio,' Sunny added, rising up, allowing her niece once again to toddle in her wake.

He followed them into the sunroom, a large unexpectedly clear space dominated by an artist's easel and a side table stained with paint and littered with sketches, photos and brushes.

'It's not finished yet,' she explained as he looked over her shoulder at the watercolour.

'*Anthriscus sylvestris* aka cow parsley,' Raj murmured, amazed by the detail she had already brought into being.

'Or Queen Anne's lace, which sounds much more romantic,' Sunny pointed out. 'Although that's actually a different plant known as wild carrot.'

'What do you work from?'

'Sometimes photos, sometimes the actual plant, sometimes both. You know the Latin names.'

'Yes. It was a hobby when I was younger. I liked the precision of Latin plant names.'

Sunny stepped away from the canvas, surprised by the intensity of his scrutiny when she had expected him to show only a cursory interest in her work.

Raj loved the watercolour. It was so real he felt as though he could reach into the picture to touch the delicate lace blooms and it was a much more scientifically accurate presentation than he had expected from her. 'Let me buy it,' he suggested suddenly.

'I can paint you another one but I can't give you *this* one,' Sunny declared in a surprised rush. 'It's the last of a series I've done for a big botanical book that's soon to be published and I'm tied by contract to hand it over.'

'Who would ever know that you gave this one to me and another to them?' Raj asked drily.

'I would know and that's not how I work with my clients,' she retorted crisply.

'I'll commission you for another,' he responded curtly, dissatisfied by her reluctance to cater to his request, a response that he had never met with before. 'Am I allowed to ask why you won't agree to me providing financial support for my niece?'

Disconcerted by that sudden change of subject, Sunny hovered uneasily, her heart-shaped face troubled as she struggled to put her convictions together in a hurry. 'I don't want Pansy to be so spoiled that she no longer follows her dreams or strives to achieve something of her own in life. Ethan was like that. He knew he could have virtually anything he wanted because you would buy it for him or make it happen for him, and it only made him impossible to please and it stifled any natural drive he had.'

Raj gazed down at her in complete shock, colour slowly receding below his naturally olive complexion. Nobody had subjected him to such blunt speech or censure since childhood. He was stunned by her lack of tact and her daring in mentioning his late brother in such terms.

'Who do you think you are to speak of my brother in such a manner?' he shot at her in a sudden burst of anger.

It wasn't a shout; he raised his voice only a little

but his intonation was raw and the atmosphere was tense. Pansy was standing by the window, and her little face crumpled and she loosed an uncertain sob. Sunny reached down to lift and comfort her niece. 'I think it's time you left,' she said tautly.

Firm mouth compressed, Raj did not require encouragement to take his leave. He was outraged by what she had said about Ethan. She seemed impervious to the awareness that, as the giver of that money, Raj would not accept being blamed for having encouraged Ethan's faults. He had simply done his utmost to find some field that interested his brother into making an effort and the sad truth was that he had failed. Leaving Ethan to sink alone had been too much to ask of Raj's conscience. Every time he had failed with Ethan, he had tried again…and again.

He strode to the front door and opened it, breathing in slow and deep. 'I will see you next month,' he announced. 'Same day, same time…if it suits you.'

'It suits,' she conceded, white as a sheet as she watched him stride down the path and heard a vehicle engine start up and then another engine, indicating that more than one car had accompanied him to the meeting, but any cars were hidden from view by her high hedge.

Listening to the cars recede into the distance, Sunny groaned out loud. Oh, what had she done, speaking so candidly on such a private, personal and decidedly hurtful topic? Of course, he had taken offence when he had done his utmost to settle his brother into a secure position! And she had only got to know Ethan through his visits with Christabel before their wedding, because there had been little contact after that date. She should have more carefully chosen her words, lied if necessary, she reasoned unhappily, rather than risk antagonising Pansy's uncle by referring to his sibling like that. Instead, she had waded in, careless of the wound she might be inflicting, and she was ashamed. Yes, she had spoken her true feelings, but honesty was not always the best policy.

CHAPTER TWO

'IT'S NOT LIKE you to make a personal call at my home,' Raj told his British lawyer in surprise, two weeks later. 'Has some catastrophe occurred?'

Marcus chuckled and extended the large wrapped tube he was carrying. 'It's for you…from Sunny Barker, I understand. As she doesn't know where you live or have your phone number, she asked us to see that you received it and her letter.'

Raj tensed as he accepted the tube. 'Letter?'

Marcus moved forward to settle an envelope on Raj's tidy desk.

Raj ripped open the envelope with scant ceremony and pulled out the single sheet. He was stunned to realise it was an apology and a generous one, even if her wording made his wide sensual mouth compress. Had she really needed to tell him that she was sorry she had hurt his feelings? He wasn't an adolescent boy in therapy. No, she didn't have tact but what she did have was the sort of honesty that Raj had never met with before and decided integrity. It wasn't a grovelling apology either. She didn't disclaim the views she had voiced, merely acknowledged that she should have had more sensitivity and that such 'unkindness' was not the norm for her.

Raj opened the tube and, with great care, drew out the coiled watercolour within, a sizzling smile flashing across his mouth as he unfurled it to see the painting she had refused to sell to him. He carried it over to the window to check that it was not a copy, but no, she had done what she had said she would not do and had given him the original because he remembered some tiny marks at the edge.

'That relationship is progressing well, I assume,' Marcus gathered.

'We had a…difference of opinion at our first meeting,' Raj admitted reluctantly.

Marcus raised his brows in surprise. 'That must have been interesting.'

Raj nodded. He was already wondering where he could obtain a scratching post for a cat. It would get rid of that unseemly log. She had offered an olive branch. Raj was keen to be equally generous because he wasn't proud of his own behaviour. He became exasperated but rarely did he ever lose his temper and yet he had almost lost it with Pansy's aunt. He had brooded over that anomaly ever since that incident. Sunny Barker had unsettled him and he didn't like it. He had had to resist having the last word by making a second visit. That would be childish and he was never childish. Furthermore, any reopening of that controversial topic would have entailed discussing his relationship with his brother and he had no intention of violating his own privacy to that extent.

* * *

Clutching Pansy to her bosom like a magic talisman, Sunny clambered clumsily out of the helicopter onto the tarmac before being guided across to the private jet. *One* of his jets, she reminded herself dizzily, not his personal one, just simply one of a fleet. She couldn't comprehend that level of wealth. It was simply too overwhelming but, if she wanted to support her niece having a relationship with her rich uncle, common sense told her that she had to suck it up.

Raj had responded handsomely to her gift of the painting he had admired by inviting her and Pansy out to his home in Italy on the Amalfi coast. They were both trying to forge a familial relationship for a child's sake and she didn't want to screw that up a *second* time, especially not when the social worker in charge of her adoption application was delighted that she was making that effort with Raj. That had brought home to her as nothing else could have done that she was stuck with Raj Belanger in their lives. Stuck with a guy who set her teeth on edge with his arrogant, far too clever ways.

The jet interior was amazing. As soon as she stepped onboard a woman in a uniform asked to take Pansy. 'I'm Maria. I'm the nanny engaged to give you a break, Miss Barker,' she was informed.

Afraid her mouth was dropping open at such an announcement, Sunny watched her niece being carried to the rear of the cabin. Pansy was sociable and quite happy with people who were equally friendly. Recalling the complete lack of contact between Raj and his niece on his previous visit, Sunny felt guilty for throwing him out of her home. She had never done anything of that nature in her life before but that was, unhappily, a result of his effect on her. And why was that?

She *knew*, of course she did. In some weird way, Raj reminded her of the male who had once been the love of her life: Jack. Jack had been tall and broad too, the *very* masculine, outspoken type. For once, Sunny allowed herself to take those painful, youthful memories out. Jack, who had told her he loved her, had dumped her the day after she told him that children were an unlikely possibility in her life. They hadn't been lovers, for she had been only seventeen, but she and Jack had grown up together, had been childhood sweethearts. Even now, she still had to see Jack every week at church, where they acknowledged each other with a distant nod as he settled his wife and many children into their family pew.

'It means you're not really a proper woman any more,' seventeen-year-old Jack had told her, striving to justify his decision. 'I'm sorry but I want kids in my future, *my own kids*, not adopted ones or surrogate ones…or however you were hoping to *trick* me into marrying you!'

So, that had been that, the bitter end of a rosy adolescent idyll, but Sunny hadn't put herself out there to be hurt again. She had a fatal flaw and she had accepted it, made her peace with it, but she wasn't ever going to place herself again in a position where a man could dismiss and belittle her as Jack had. The burst appendix that had almost killed her at the age of twelve had wrecked her fertility prospects and there was nothing anyone could do about that reality. No matter how much that truth hurt, she had to live with it. She never had got the chance to tell Jack that she had got that same news from her poor mother only the night before she told him. Petra Barker had lacked the courage to make that truth known to her daughter *before* she reached seventeen.

Wiping her brain clean of those memories of disillusionment and pain, Sunny studied the botanical and animal magazines being brought to her with amusement. Yes, Raj already knew better than to bless her with fashion journals. Really, he was too clever for his own good, she reflected wryly. Did he think she hadn't guessed that he must have had her investigated by some private security firm? Raj Belanger was not the type likely to leave anything to chance and she was not stupid.

An opulent limo collected her from the jet and bore them off to their destination. A huge mansion that could have been a palace awaited her and Pansy at the end of a long imposing drive, guarded by giant wrought-iron gilded gates and security personnel.

Sunny refused to be impressed. Raj inhabited another world, that was all. Money was money and it didn't necessarily make people any happier. She based that assumption on Ethan and Christabel's visits before their marriage when family ties had still been acknowledged. Their only conversation had related heavily to Ethan's misfortunes in business, Christabel's supposed sacrifices and complaints, their possessions and the famous celebrities they socialised with. Listening had made Sunny want to shout that they were two very lucky people and why couldn't they appreciate their health, youth, attractiveness and good fortune in being gainfully employed? After all, it was much more than many people had.

Sunny bent down to let Pansy put her feet to the ground in her first proper shoes and she wondered if Raj would notice that his niece's ability to walk had hugely improved. She was urged through the imposing front entrance into a vast space filled with marble, glittering crystal chandeliers and art works on plinths. There was absolutely nothing welcoming about it. It was an environment that could only influence and intimidate. Raj stood in the middle of it, looking about as friendly and as remote as a towering dark monolith on the moon. Pansy shrank against Sunny's legs, her little body trembling.

'Raj…' Sunny said simply. 'What a beautiful home you have…'

But that wasn't really what she thought, Raj guessed, because her expressions were easily read. Presumably she hadn't expected him to welcome her into a grass hut built in the wilderness, so why wasn't she questioning her own unreasonable responses? he wondered. She was biased against him. The money? Was that truly the only stumbling block between them?

It wasn't even as though *she* tried to fit in anywhere. She was wearing a sort of hippy throwback outfit in a soft blue colour that was so loose and shapeless that an elephant could have climbed inside it with her. He wondered what *that* was about and then questioned why he was wondering. After all, he had only dragged her all the way to Italy because it would be good for Sunny to appreciate that she would not be the only one calling the shots in the future. She was a damned managing woman and she needed that reminder. And, last but not least, he had fabulous gardens here that he assumed she would enjoy.

'You're in ideal time for lunch on the terrace,' he announced. 'I hope your journey was comfortable.'

'It was perfect. You make everything perfect,' she conceded, out of breath as he cupped her elbow with one hand to steer her out of the giant hall. 'But you haven't said hello to Pansy yet.'

'How can I say hello to a baby?' Raj enquired brusquely.

Ignoring that response, Sunny dropped down into a crouch and spoke to the child. Pansy waved her hand at him. 'You see...she can say hello!'

'No, she can't, because she can't actually talk yet,' Raj pointed out grittily, dropping very reluctantly down to say softly, 'Hello, Pansy...'

''Lo,' the baby said distinctly, taking him very much aback with that ability.

'Hello, Pansy,' Raj murmured, a sudden smile of acceptance flashing across his firm lips.

Sunny watched in satisfaction because he had finally taken notice of the sole reason she was in Italy: her niece. But, my goodness, that smile of his was remarkable head-on, transforming his far too serious features into a darkly handsome face filled with a disturbing amount of charisma and sex appeal. A little tremor slivered through Sunny's taut frame, infiltrating places she didn't like to think about too much. It was physical desire and she fought that response to the last ditch.

He swept them out onto a tiled terrace with a magnificent outlook over beautifully maintained gardens.

'May I?' Maria, the young woman in a nanny's uniform who had been onboard the jet stepped forward and bent down to engage Pansy with a toy. Sunny released the child's hand and watched without surprise as her niece was conveyed down to the high chair sited at the far end of an extremely long table. *This* was how Raj worked with children in his vicinity, Sunny recognised. See a child, provide care and corral it where it could cause the least possible disruption. It was disheartening and it didn't leave her much room to work on his detachment. Unaware of her exclusion from adult company, Pansy waved at her aunt cheerfully and giggled.

'She seems to be a happy little creature,' Raj remarked with satisfaction.

'She is, and wonderfully adaptable because she takes interest in everything and everybody,' Sunny commented as pleasingly decorative salad starters arrived for them. 'I believe she's intelligent, may even take after you.'

'God forbid!' Raj cut in with an undeniable shudder of alarm at such a possibility.

'No, I didn't mean that I believe she could aspire to your level, only that she shows all the signs of being reasonably bright,' Sunny disclaimed in haste.

The tension in his broad shoulders and set features eased. 'I misunderstood,' he conceded, finally lifting his knife and fork to begin eating.

'What caused your…er…consternation?' she asked, curiosity alight in her vivid gaze.

'You would have to sign a non-disclosure agreement before I could answer that question,' Raj stated calmly. 'What little of my life can be kept private, I guard fiercely. I'm discreet and careful in my personal life.'

Sunny's eyes were wide and she nodded slowly in comprehension and agreement. 'I can understand that.'

Only what would remain with her for far longer was the emotional pain that had briefly shadowed his haunted dark eyes. She reckoned that his distrust of others possibly dated back to when he had been young and vulnerable. How many people he had had faith in had betrayed him back then? He was an extraordinary male in every way, who had probably paid a steep price for his brilliance, success and wealth, who had suffered in spite of it or maybe even because of it. She knew that reams of gossip and rumour accompanied his every move in public, but had never paused to imagine what it might be like living in such a goldfish bowl of constant attention.

'I'll sign one,' she conceded ruefully, recognising the necessity in his case.

Raj treated her to a slow-burning smile of approval that lit up her every pulse point and raised goose bumps on her arms. Heat flushed her cheeks, a warmth of awareness she could not suppress. Self-conscious, she concentrated on her meal, only to be surprised when barely a few minutes later a document arrived on the table and a pen was extended to her.

'Standard stuff,' he told her, flicking the fat document with a long forefinger in dismissal. 'But since you're likely to be in my life for years, I was hoping you would agree to an NDA as it makes life smoother and makes it easier for me to relax with you.'

Sunny rested back in her chair and skimmed through the document, aware of the older man at her elbow, presumably present to act as a witness. Feeling even a little pressured, she wondered if she should ask to take the document home with her and then she just lifted the pen and signed, foreseeing no future day when she would wish to reveal anything personal about Raj Belanger because she had always respected other people's boundaries.

Raj was stunned by the ease with which she had signed the NDA. People usually quibbled over terms, holding out to the last minute, invariably awaiting a financial reward for their signature, but Sunny had done none of those things, had sought nothing for her own advantage. All of a sudden Raj was in an unusually good mood, although he was thinking that Sunny needed a good legal advisor to protect her, which was an unusual thought for him around a woman. He didn't understand why but he knew the second thought that assailed him was that, *now*, he could kiss her.

Lust, he assumed, although lust had never dug such talon claws of need into him before. Indeed, he had believed that possibly he was not the most sexually rapacious of men until Sunny had strolled her messy but gorgeous self into his radius. And only then had he appreciated that something about this particular woman lit him up into a positive bonfire of sexual hunger. He had not gone a single day without thinking about her since that first meeting.

'So, I gather that now you will feel free to tell me why you believe a high IQ is a…a *burden*?' Sunny prompted over the main course.

'Not to everyone but it was in my case,' Raj asserted. 'My father was a brilliant and famous professor of psychology at Oxford when he met my mother, Clara. She was his brightest student and he seduced her at the age of eighteen.'

'I thought there were rules about that sort of thing.'

'Even then, there were. He resigned and returned to Hungary, and he took her with him while at the same time taking advantage of her ample trust fund. He used her, just as he eventually used me. She was already pregnant, and she had no family, nobody more mature to warn her that he was an abuser,' he admitted with distaste. 'But she looked up to him, admired him, believed he would know best about how to raise a child.'

Sunny winced, sensing she was unlikely to enjoy what he was on the brink of telling her.

'He, on the other hand, merely wanted a guinea pig for a science experiment on which he planned to write a book. *I* was that experiment from birth and he took copious notes on my every failure and achievement. I was raised in isolation, and I was only ever rewarded for the very best educational results,' Raj imparted levelly. 'I never played, I never had fun, my mother wasn't allowed to comfort or hold me. My father believed that the more I was deprived of, the more I would shine to try and please my parents.'

'Oh, dear,' Sunny whispered, pushing away her plate, her appetite killed by his confidences. Her empathetic brain was filled with horror at all that he had been denied as a child and her heart overflowed for him.

'I don't want your compassion, Sunny,' Raj told her warningly, recognising the glimmer of tears in her beautiful eyes. 'I only told you because I can sense your dissatisfaction with my attitude towards our niece. But you need to know first-hand that I *can't* play with her, *can't* show her affection when I have not the first idea of how to do such things…and that is why *you* will meet those needs for her that I lack the capacity to fulfil.'

'Of course, after such cruelty, you're going to think that, *feel* that way…' Sunny framed, luminous violet eyes swimming with an amount of emotion that somewhat unnerved him as she leant closer to him.

'But you can be fixed,' she told him, even more disturbingly, as though he were a broken kettle.

Her floral scent washed over him, soft and warm like her and, oh, so alluring on some level he didn't recognise. She was so close that he could count the three tiny freckles on the bridge of her delicate little nose and dwell on the soft full swell of her pink unadorned lips. Raj went hard as a rock, his sex pushing hard against his zip, a dangerously aggressive response for a male who had always believed that he could take or deny sexual impulses.

'I don't *want* to be fixed, Sunny,' he confided gruffly, almost laughing at that terminology. 'I've done tons of therapy and I am who I am and content with it.'

Sunny reached for the large hand braced tensely on the tabletop and clasped it tenderly and fervently between her own, little fingers smoothing over his taut fingers, thumbs caressing his wrist. 'But I can *teach* you how to play with her, how to show affection, and I'm more than ready to make that effort for both of you,' she swore vehemently.

'All I want to do right at this moment is kiss you,' Raj admitted darkly, fighting off the urge with difficulty.

Sunny blinked, finding it impossible to concentrate when he shot off topic to that extent. 'Why on earth would you want to do that?' she gasped in bewilderment, encountering mesmeric dark eyes that paralysed her where she sat.

'May I?' he stressed.

Shock claimed Sunny that he should be as attracted to her as she very much was to him. It had not crossed her mind once that that attraction could be reciprocal, but the knowledge of it now shone in the smile she gave him. 'If you think it would make you more comfortable with me.'

A very large hand reached out slowly as though he was afraid of spooking her. Long fingers stroked even more slowly down her neck to twine into her mane of golden hair and she stopped breathing, could literally feel herself stop breathing as if the earth had without warning screamed to a halt on its axis. She looked up at him with huge violet eyes.

'*Breathe*, Sunny,' Raj instructed hoarsely, enchanted by her reaction. 'Breathe before you pass out.'

CHAPTER THREE

SUNNY BREATHED JUST before Raj bent his dark head and covered her mouth with his.

And once again the world stopped dead, while her heart hammered and her body went off on a slew of discovery she had long since forgotten about. Nerve cells awakened from a lengthy slumber and a visceral response gripped her, heated energy pushing up from her pelvis and spreading like a dangerously contagious infection through the rest of her. Her nipples peaked with painful immediacy while a clenching sensation pulsed at the heart of her.

Raj tasted her as though she were the finest wine and he was determined to savour every tiny drop of it. His lips coasted back and forth over hers, coaxing them open, and then he was in and *she* was tasting him and every sense spun dizzily on a roller coaster of sensual discovery. His lips were soft and firm and the flavour of mint and man and the very scent of him left her light-headed. The first tiny dip of his tongue into her mouth was a revelation of skill because every inch of her responded with explosive force. As his hand closed round the back of her head in a possessive grip to pull her even closer, she was so overwhelmed by the sheer passion he had unleashed inside her that she yanked herself forcibly back from him.

Raj blinked slowly, allowing the world that had vanished to flood back in. That single taste of her had had the same effect on him as a rocket firing off and he had never felt anything that powerful with a woman before. Predictably, he instantly wanted more of it, *all* of it, all of *her*. Hard as a rock and unsated, he breathed in and out slowly, thoroughly tantalised by the revelation that there could actually be more to sex than he had always assumed.

Sunny rested a trembling hand down on the table to steady herself. She had never felt anything like that with a man before, not even with Jack, and it had shaken her inside out. But Sunny always looked before she leapt and she was immediately aware that she and Raj inhabited very different worlds and that he was Pansy's uncle, would always be Pansy's uncle. 'Well, that was—'

'Exhilarating,' Raj incised confidently, searching her hectically flushed face and the luminosity of her stunned gaze with satisfaction, knowing with certainty that she had been as affected as he was. No, she couldn't hide that from him and he liked that, no, he *loved* that. There was nothing studied or deliberately seductive or calculating about Sunny; she was simply Sunny. And he had never had that confidence with any other woman in his bed.

'Yes, well—' Sunny began jerkily.

'We'll spend tonight together on my yacht,' Raj decided, thrusting back his chair and rising to his full intimidating height. 'Let me show you the herb gardens now…'

Lord of all that he surveys, Sunny reflected, but thankfully not Lord of her as well. It was ironic that she had first wanted to laugh when he'd said that they would spend the night on his yacht *together* because Raj was making grand assumptions based on what was obviously the norm for him. One kiss and he assumed consent and agreement had been reached? That she would just fall into his bed immediately because he said so? Did she blame him for that? Or other women who had evidently gone to him far too easily?

As Raj reached out a hand to her to guide her down the flight of stone steps that led to the gardens, Pansy let out an ear-splitting screech and Maria scooped her up to try and quiet her. Pansy, however, fought the young woman, her arms stretching out for her aunt and a stifled sob escaping her. Sunny turned back and hurried along the terrace to reclaim her niece. Pansy lurched into her arms as though the poor nanny had been trying to steal her and, soothing her, Sunny walked her back to Raj, the nanny following.

'She's friendly with everyone but not surprisingly, after recent experiences, she doesn't like me disappearing from sight in a strange place,' she explained quietly.

As a party of four rather than a party of two, they crossed the lawn. Raj's gaze had chilled and no longer glowed warm burnished bronze. Tough luck, Raj, Sunny thought, *she* comes first. Able to have Sunny close by, however, Pansy relaxed again and chased a ball.

'We need to talk about this…er…night on your yacht.' Sunny broached the subject with all the awkwardness of a young woman unused to such discussions, but one who had already grasped that, with Raj, subtle deflections wouldn't work. If left to reach the wrong conclusions, Raj would happily power forward on his own steamy assumptions.

'What's there to talk about?' Raj countered dismissively. 'We're attracted to each other, strongly attracted. Let's keep this simple.'

Sunny moistened her taut lower lip. 'But it's *not* simple. It's not as though we're dating.'

'I don't date.' Somehow, Raj managed to imbue that last word with distaste.

'Neither do I, as a rule, but I also don't jump into bed with strangers.'

Raj said something in another language that had the ring of a bitten-off curse word. 'I am *not* a stranger to you.'

'You're enough of a stranger to me that I have no intention of getting intimate with you. And what about the need for us to maintain a good ongoing relationship for Pansy's sake? Have you thought of how us getting involved could mess that up?' Sunny demanded succinctly, accompanying him below a rose-clad arch into a very private expanse, bounded by tall hedges. There she paused, enchanted by the vista of a lush, blooming herb garden with gravel paths and geometric beds.

'Oh, this is heavenly…' Sunny whispered, drifting away from him to explore as though she had seen some earthly vision of paradise and could see nothing else.

Unaccustomed to being forgotten about and disconcerted by her use of that particular argument on his niece's behalf, Raj wanted to yank her back to listen to him talk some common sense into her and he withstood that urge only with difficulty. He stalked after her, incensed by his rare failure to get his point across.

'So, I have to date you to have sex with you?' Raj loomed over her, blocking out the glorious sunlight.

'Don't be silly. That's not what I said,' Sunny replied. 'And if you're only interested in having sex with my body rather than *me*, just forget the notion.'

Raj breathed in so deep and long that she was vaguely surprised he didn't rise into the air with the pressure on his lungs. 'I don't understand.'

'Are you single?' Sunny asked.

'Of course I am!'

Sunny tipped her head back to look at him. That violet gaze, some dangerous mix of pale blue and grey, rested on him with a remarkably sceptical quality. 'Are you seriously telling me that there are no other women of any kind in your life?'

Intelligence warned Raj to lie but he had never lied to any woman who shared his bed, had never allowed the smallest chance of a misunderstanding to occur. The women who entertained his leisure hours knew that they had a limited shelf life and that his interest eventually waned. He got bored quickly, always had, always would. He didn't get attached in any way. Sex was just another outlet, a harmless diversion and was usually no more important to him.

Sunny watched faint colour edge his high cheekbones and her heart sank because she had hoped that she was wrong and that there genuinely *weren't* any other women in his life.

'There are women…but not in the dating sense,' he framed with as much delicacy as he could contrive, hoping that she left the subject there.

Sunny's brows climbed as she continued to stare at him. 'Hookers?'

Raj was embarrassed, and he didn't think he had ever been so embarrassed in his life, and he couldn't credit that she could be digging to that extent or even that he was allowing her to do so. 'No…now let's leave.'

'Escorts?' Sunny cut in, startling him afresh.

'No.' Raj stared down into her feverishly curious face and was startled to find himself on the brink of wholly inappropriate laughter. 'Mistresses.'

Her brow furrowed. 'More than one?'

Raj was done. He didn't even understand why he had answered her nosy questions. He jerked his chin in silent confirmation because no way was she getting one more word out of him.

'OK…' Sunny wandered away from him as though he hadn't spoken and began rhapsodising over a fall of lavender and the way the light falling on it created waving shadows.

She lived on another plane, an artistic plane, Raj acknowledged in frustration. At that moment he felt as though he had just had his insides dug out with a rusty spoon and he didn't know why that was so, yet she was sufficiently unaffected to admire the vegetation. That was why he didn't enjoy that comparison.

Sunny bent down to sniff the lavender and break off a piece and rub it between her fingers. Her eyes were still stinging with unshed tears. Mistresses in the plural. Well, at least he was honest about it, but it meant that *she* could never be with him.

'You don't seem surprised.' Raj hovered nearby, uncertain as to why he was reopening the wretched subject when he refused to discuss it any further with her. He only knew that he needed a response from her.

Sunny scrambled upright again, blinking rapidly. 'I'm not. It's practical, efficient…the sort of arrangement I would've expected from you,' she framed in a stiff undertone. 'Sorry, I pried.'

'You didn't. You asked and I chose to answer.' Raj reached for her hand but she tugged it away from him. 'What's wrong?'

'We shouldn't get close. We should work on being just friends…but not friends with benefits,' she hastened to point out in sudden mortification. 'I'm not the mistress type and I don't share, so, believe me, we're at a dead end here.'

Sunny was telling him that he couldn't have her, but Raj could not accept that refusal because he had never once met a situation he couldn't conquer or twist to his advantage. 'You don't share, so as well as dating you're talking about something exclusive as well,' he recapped with a frown of disbelief. 'That's not achievable, so we will have to compromise.'

'No more, Raj,' Sunny interposed gently. 'You know that you have no intention of compromising in any way and that you only expect *me* to compromise. I won't. I'm as stubborn as a pig when it comes to what's right for me…and for Pansy.'

'How do you presume to know me so well?'

Sunny gazed up at him, her own bewilderment at her conviction mirrored in her bright eyes. 'I honestly don't know how, but I do know that you're a very strong character and that you'll persist unless I'm firm.'

'*Firm?* I'm not a child, Sunny.'

No, she thought, he could do a lot more damage to her than a child ever could. But he was, indisputably, a raging storm of a male, accustomed to getting his own way and capable of manipulation beyond her worst expectations. Gut instincts served her well and that was truly how she saw him. He was dangerous to her peace of her mind and stability and her niece needed a strong and steady parent.

And yet, on another level, she could still barely believe that Raj Belanger, with all the many options he must have, could actually want *her*. It was not as if she were a supermodel or some sleek socialite or sophisticate.

'We don't have anything in common,' she pointed out quietly.

'We have passion,' Raj countered with immense assurance. 'What more would we need?'

'If I have to spell out what more, we would be a disaster...and anyway...' Sunny stood tall and lifted her chin '... I don't want this. I'm happy with my life as it is.'

'You haven't had me in your life before.'

Sunny dealt him a reproachful glance. 'This subject is closed.'

Raj laughed in genuine pleasure at that response. Pansy surged up to his knees chasing her ball and, without thought, he scooped up the ball and lifted it above his head.

'No…throw it along the ground low or she won't see it!' Sunny whisper-hissed at him.

Raj rolled the ball between the flower beds and Pansy giggled and ran after it. 'She's much better on her feet,' he remarked.

Sunny smiled up at him. 'Yes, she's all change every day at the moment, moving from being a baby into being a real little personality.'

Her smile had the effect of making him smile and it irritated him because he was not pleased with her. She had handed him an ultimatum and Raj did not react well to ultimatums. In addition, she would now be chary of getting on the yacht in case he was taking them there for some nefarious purpose. Further irritation laced his big powerful frame. That particular problem, however, would be easily solved, he acknowledged as he pulled out his phone and made a quick call.

Sizing up the other issues, he questioned why he was trying to mix business with pleasure for the first time in his adult life. He never made that mistake. True, Sunny and his niece were not business, but they did not fall into the other category either. In fact, they had a category all of their own, somewhat filling that gaping space left by Ethan, that *family* space, he reasoned. Craving Sunny for pleasure was a messy, complicated desire. He compressed his firm lips. Logic warned him to suppress his hunger for her. But he didn't feel logical about Sunny. It wasn't rational or convenient to want her. There was simply something about her, some indefinable quality that called to him…*still* called to him even when she infuriated him. And it struck him as ridiculous that he, the ultimate cold-blooded, rational male, should appear, even in the trivial pursuit of sex, to have less common sense than eccentric Sunny.

He surveyed her and his niece. Sunny was kneeling in the gravel, showing a flower to Pansy, tickling her chin with it, laughing at the child's little giggle. The hippy dress already had grass stains and tracks from dusty gravel and she couldn't have cared less. Messy but somehow appealing for all that. Golden hair shining in the sunlight, luscious pink mouth pouting as she teased Pansy, her ever-ready smile beaming out. Warmth, he labelled, that was what she emanated like a forcefield. Warmth and acceptance and a kind of joy in ordinary life that was utterly fresh and new to him.

Sunny strolled back to the giant fancy house where they enjoyed fancy desserts and coffee on the terrace. It was downright magical with the fabulous view, the glorious weather, the food and the sheer glamour of it all, Sunny conceded, and it was exactly as Raj had probably planned it. The way she suspected Raj planned *everything.* There it was, that ridiculous belief that she knew how his brilliant mind worked. When he wanted something, he knew how to get it, never mind how unscrupulous his methods might be. After all, she was fairly sure that her visit had been planned as a long, slow seduction over lunch and drinks and glorious herbs in the sunshine. She might be naïve and inexperienced, but she was far from stupid.

'Tell me about Christabel as a child,' Raj asked her.

'Her mother died when she was quite young. She

was eight when I was born, so I have very few memories of her because she was always away modelling or acting and my father was away with her,' Sunny confided. 'From what my mother told me, our father viewed Christabel as a superstar from the moment she won her first beautiful baby competition, which was before Mum's time with Dad. By the time they married, Christabel's star quality was Dad's sole interest. He gave up work to chaperone her when she started modelling in Paris at the age of fourteen and then she was starring in that TV soap opera that made her name.'

'You're giving me a different take on your sister. She was *pushed* into the public eye as a kid?'

'I think she was and our father acted as her manager. I only know that Mum felt as though our father married her to give Christabel a mother and then decided that he didn't need her or have time for a wife as well. She felt excluded. When Mum fell pregnant with me, Dad asked her to get a termination because he said they couldn't afford another child and that was the last straw for her,' Sunny admitted. 'They staggered along for another couple of years and then my gran was grieving so hard for my grandfather that Mum moved in with her. It was supposed to be temporary but it became permanent and my parents got a divorce in the end.'

'And what about your relationship with your father?' Raj prompted.

'It never really got off the ground. He visited a few times when I was a baby and then he passed away, so I didn't really know him, except through my relatives' opinions.'

'You were worth so much more than Christabel. She was as shallow as an envelope.'

Sunny winced. 'Maybe our father *made* her that way and taught her only to value her worth through her beauty and fame and earnings.'

'You always have that compassionate take,' Raj groaned as though she was paining him.

'None of us are perfect,' she argued. 'All of us have faults. You can't just judge people from afar.'

Raj groaned again. 'That's straight out of the Bible stuff…of course, you go to church.'

'Was it accurate, that investigation you had done on me?' Sunny enquired with unmistakeable amusement in her luminous gaze.

'Yes and no. The facts were correct, but the report didn't even catch a flavour of you as an individual,' Raj asserted without concern that she had guessed that he had had a private security firm check her out in advance of their first meeting.

She appreciated his honesty and was tempted to ask what flavour she was in reality, but bit her tongue instead lest he assume that she was flirting with him and digging for a potential compliment.

Later, they climbed into a motorboat to be taken out to the yacht, *Belanger I*, in the bay and she breathed in slowly, calming herself. Nothing was going to happen between her and Raj because an adult discussion had killed that possibility stone dead. What was wrong with her that, instead of relief, she was experiencing disappointment?

The truth was that Raj had wanted more and so had

she, but common sense had prevailed. For the first time in years she had wanted a man and that recognition still shook her. She had shut down that part of herself after the disillusionment served by Jack. Jack had hurt her so badly at such a delicate age when she was still finding herself and she had gone through university specialising in turning potential boyfriends into mates, platonic mates. Yes, there had been presentable men back then, but none who had tempted her to try again.

Sunny shot a guilty glance at Raj as the breeze ruffled his luxuriant black hair above his bold bronzed, hard profile. A frisson of awareness ran through her, lighting her up inside like a shower of fireworks in the dusk skies, and she shivered. Almost instantly, Raj noted that shiver and stepped closer, peeling off his suit jacket and draping it round her, the silky warmth of the lining engulfing her arms and dropping to her knees, big hands resting briefly on her shoulders to steady her, and her tummy flipped as though she were on a roller-coaster ride. The scent of the jacket, of *him*, engulfed her, an indefinable scent that was just him: warm, male, laced with the faintest scent of cologne, and it felt so intimate that she shivered again.

Raj wrapped both arms round her. 'You're really cold. I'm sorry.'

Involuntarily, she encountered a look of surprise from Maria because it was a hot day and the breeze was slight. Her face burned even hotter. Raj made her feel horribly like an infatuated teenage girl.

Off the boat onto the massive yacht that she hadn't even had sufficient concentration to appreciate from a distance, she returned his jacket to him with a muffled thanks and took her niece's hand in hers to climb the stairs facing them.

'I'll carry her. The steps are too steep for her little legs,' Raj intervened and swept up Pansy without hesitation, bending down to murmur, 'Unfortunately, although your legs aren't much longer, I can't carry *both* of you…'

Reddening afresh, Sunny hastened upward and reached the top step to find a woman looking down at them all with a huge, bright smile. 'Welcome onboard,' she said in slightly accented English.

'Sunny, meet Bambina Barelli. She's an Italian *contessa* and a good friend.'

'I don't use the title these days, Raj…and no need for an introduction to this little girl!' The brunette reached for the child in Raj's arms with enthusiasm. 'You're Pansy, aren't you?'

And Pansy chuckled when, for the very first time, her aunt wished she would scream and act distant with a stranger. The meanness of that thought hit Sunny's conscience hard. Unhappily for Sunny though, Raj's 'good friend' Bambina was absolutely gorgeous, supermodel gorgeous with long swishy black hair, perfect features, almond-shaped dark eyes and legs that looked incredible in a short gold cocktail frock with diamonds glittering at her throat and ears. Sunny felt sick, her stomach swirling with nausea.

CHAPTER FOUR

'I NEED TO get changed,' Sunny framed, chin at an angle, eyes veiled.

'The stewardess will show you to your cabins...' Raj nodded to the hovering staff and watched Sunny, Maria and Pansy depart at speed. He frowned. He had assumed she would be relieved at Bambina's appearance but, if anything, the brunette had put her on her guard. *Az Isten szerelmere*, he thought in the Hungarian that had been his first language.

Sunny was like a string of computer code he couldn't interpret or guide in the most sensible direction. Weirdly rebellious against the norm that was what he deemed to be the average female response.

Their little group was shown into adjoining cabins. Pansy's rejoiced in a cot for a princess adorned in stupid drapes that would be dangerous for a toddler and Sunny and the nanny combined in silent agreement to remove the hazards.

'This is another...world,' Maria almost squealed in English, dark eyes wide and bright with excitement. 'And the opportunity of a lifetime. My mama will not believe that I was on board Raj Belanger's yacht with La Bambina as a guest!'

'She's a famous lady?' Sunny queried tightly.

And it flooded out of Maria. La Bambina was the Italian equivalent of a celebrity aristocrat from the very top drawer of Italian rich and famous people. She was never out of the gossip columns and as famous for her discarded husbands and lovers as her fashion sense. So, obviously, one of Raj's cohort of mistresses. What else could the woman be? Was she onboard his yacht to show Sunny what she had missed out on achieving? Well, so much for that loser game.

Once Pansy had had her supper, been bathed and tucked into the princess cot, Sunny went to change for dinner. No, she didn't have some gold cocktail dress tucked into a designer closet. She had an embroidered corset top with beads and long swirly skirt of equally handcrafted and beaded glory. It was very bohemian but she was comfortable in it, even if she did think that the neckline showed a little too much cleavage.

Go, Sunny, she instructed herself as she looked in the mirror, feeling horribly short-changed by nature, which hadn't endowed her with long legs or small, pert boobs or that slender designer silhouette that all models possessed. She was short and pretty dumpy when it came to designer comparisons. Indeed, just then it seemed a matter of wonder to Sunny that Raj should ever have looked at her with lustful intent.

Raj stalked forward to greet her in the huge salon, which acted as a reception area on the yacht. Sunny felt hugely self-conscious because she hadn't made use of the beauty salon appointment offered to her to have her hair and her make-up, and whatever else she dreamt of, done, but Maria had snatched up the opportunity. Sunny, however, was au naturel, the way she always was, and she refused to change herself to fit, to seek to embrace some perfected specimen of herself to try and copy the same quality as La Bambina, because that would be a no hopers' game. She couldn't do it. She wasn't classically beautiful or perfectly built in that tall, slender way to show off the latest fashions.

And then, with all that very much in her mind, Raj came to her and said, 'You look amazing in that outfit.'

Sunny almost laughed because it was so ridiculous a comment in such company. 'Thanks,' she said politely.

Raj thought it was an unexpectedly gorgeous dress, but then, it really didn't matter what she wore when he only wanted her out of it. But there it was and at least the garment showed off her magnificent bosom The display of those peachy opulent slopes of feminine flesh turned him on. He couldn't help it with her, she was just *her*, but she dressed as if she were enormous and he had to remember that.

Idly he wondered who was responsible for that. Christabel, who had been built like a toothpick, or other relatives, who might also have enjoyed a different shape? Or the boyfriends, who hadn't appeared in the investigative report because none had been visible, past or present. Even so, Raj refused to credit that a woman with Sunny's tiny but highly desirable body shape and gorgeous face had been noticed by only him. *Of course*, there had been men, but she had been discreet with her private life, he reflected grimly, wondering why that awareness of her past should bother him, because the one thing he had never ever been with women was possessive.

Drinks were served. La Bambina hovered round Raj like a shadow, always within reach, almost slavish in her desire to please. Sunny watched as the brunette ferried drinks to him, ignoring the servers available, instead stationing herself at Raj's elbow, ever ready, it seemed, to rush and attend to his every request. And if anything, it made Sunny realise how she and Raj would never suit, even in the short term. She wasn't the type to wait on her man as if he were some god. That was a fact. Why accepting that truth distressed her, she refused to recognise. In Raj's world, women seemed worryingly lower level, catering to the big guy distinguishable by his wealth and power. But then, that was her making judgements based on slender evidence, she scolded herself.

Of course, La Bambina was one of his mistresses. What else could she be?

There were little touches that Sunny was hyper-aware of occurring between the couple. The brunette would brush his shoulder, his elbow, truly any part of him that was decently within reach, nothing jarring or too intimate but still little feminine hints that this guy belonged to her in an intimate way. Raj, however, didn't touch Bambina once, but then Sunny suspected that he was by nature an undemonstrative male.

They went into dinner in another shockingly opulent saloon and the dishes were out-of-this-world tasty but Sunny was pushed to eat a few mouthfuls, in spite of her healthy appetite. Beside her, Maria was agog, drinking in every aspect of her surroundings, and Raj rose in her estimation by not having barred the nanny, a paid employee, from the meal. Even so, Sunny found that she couldn't take her attention off Raj, accepting little titbits La Bambina passed him as if they were lovers of long-standing familiarity. And obviously they *were…*

'I thought you would enjoy this…' Raj announced over the coffee when they had all moved into another reception area and he reached for her as though she were his partner, hand on her elbow to bring her up out of her seat and forward, which won her a huge disconcerted glance from La Bambina, which she might have enjoyed in any other mood because the brunette had pretty much ignored both her and the nanny, concentrating her energies and her chatter purely on Raj.

It was a Monet, one of the waterlily series and, of course, as an artist, Sunny had noticed it the moment they had entered, but there it hung on the wall without fanfare or any special staging, giving her merely a hint of what Raj's riches could acquire.

'It's truly amazing,' she whispered frankly, leaning in nearer than she had ever been able to get to a museum exhibit. 'Simply being able to be this close to a masterpiece is a huge thrill.'

His black brows lifted in surprise. 'You don't show that.'

'My appreciation is expressed quietly,' she murmured softly.

'I have another painting onboard that you would like,' he began, but La Bambina appeared beside them and started to gush about the Monet, reeling off all the facts that any amateur art enthusiast might have shared, not all accurate either, but Sunny made no comment, smiling politely and curling her nails into her palms until they bit like talons. It was an unfamiliar feeling for her.

She felt sick with jealousy and it horrified her. After all, even Jack, married at twenty-one with a baby proudly on the way, had not inspired her with that sin. That development had not been unexpected. Jack might have loved her but love hadn't been enough. Jack had decided that he wanted kids, above all, and her impairment had ensured that he went after that goal like a bullet out of a gun. It was a cause of rather bitter amusement that Raj would want a fertile lover about as much as he would want a needy, demanding woman in his bed. Raj had no idea of sharing a future or a life with her, and her feelings of jealousy, inspired by his gorgeous sidekick, Bambina, were foolish, because she very much doubted that he saw the brunette as much more important to him.

Maria was sharing her cabin with Pansy and had been dismayed when Sunny had suggested they swop accommodation, anxiously pointing out that she had been hired to look after Sunny's niece and needed to do her job. Sunny returned to her cabin alone, changed into a cool cotton slip of a nightdress and donned her robe. Then she paced restlessly, attention falling on the call button she had been urged to use to request service, only she didn't think using it after midnight would be very considerate of the crew.

She wished she were in her studio, within reach of a way to divert her buzzing energy into something positive. Frowning, she left her cabin without further deliberation. What was the matter with her?

Yes, it had been a jarring experience to finally meet a male, who attracted her and realise that she couldn't have him. But life was full of jarring, wounding experiences, she reminded herself irritably as she walked up to the upper decks where public spaces abounded. A father who had no interest in her had been the first of hers, a sister who had never accepted her as a sister had been the next, followed by Jack and then, one by one, the deaths of everyone she loved. Pansy, she conceded, was the single most wonderful thing that had ever happened to her, so why was she pining for a male she barely knew?

'Miss Barker?' A steward appeared in the doorway of the saloon, startling her. 'Can I get you anything?'

'I'd love a cup of tea,' she said a little chokily. 'Is it OK to go outside?'

In answer he rammed open doors leading out onto a deck for her while reciting all the many different teas available onboard. 'English tea,' she selected, the slight breeze catching the dampness on her face.

The *Belanger I* wasn't sailing anywhere until she and Pansy left for their flight home in the morning. And then it was cruising…where? Well, she had no idea, no idea when they would see Raj again either. Possibly in a month's time? She would have to steel herself for monthly visits but at least then she wouldn't be struggling not to think about what he was doing with Bambina in his bedroom as she was thinking tonight. Her face burned, her eyes, however, stung and she dashed angrily at them as her tea arrived on a handsome tray. Honestly, the way she was carrying on and making a meal of her little disappointment was ridiculous. Anyone could be forgiven for thinking that she had fallen in love with the guy at first sight!

Blinking rapidly, she sipped her tea, fighting to calm herself. She wasn't accustomed to dealing with such a crazy surge of emotions and if Jack hadn't brought them out of her, what was it that made Raj different? And then what was her worst nightmare at that moment happened. Raj stepped out onto the deck to join her. Raj, more casually clad than had been his wont to date, well-worn jeans hugging his long strong thighs and slim hips, a shirt partially unbuttoned to display a slice of bronzed masculine chest.

'Raj…' she mumbled weakly, horrendously unprepared and conscious of her less than pristine appearance because she hadn't believed anyone else, other than possibly the crew, would be up and about at one in the morning.

He dropped down into an athletic crouch in front of the cushioned seat she was trying to sink into unnoticed, subjecting her to the full onslaught of those intense intelligent dark eyes of his. 'What's wrong?'

'Nothing's wrong!' she exclaimed, wincing at the defensive squeak of her reaction.

Her face was streaked with tears and he hated the fragile vulnerability he saw etched there in her evasive gaze, hated it as much as he would have hated knowing that he was responsible for her plight. When the steward had mentioned that she was up and seemed troubled, he had leapt straight out of bed. He didn't know why, didn't know why it even mattered to him, because she and whatever might be upsetting her were none of his business.

He leant forward and with his thumb rubbed away a tear still wet on her cheekbone. 'You've been crying. I wouldn't be a good host if I didn't ask why.'

'You're a very good host, Raj. I'm just up here having my own little personal pity party and thank you, but there's nothing anyone can do to help.'

Raj vaulted upright again and dropped down into the seat beside her. 'I don't believe that.'

'Won't Bambina be looking for you?' Sunny asked quietly, trying to make the question sound casual. 'It's the middle of the night.'

His level black brows drew together. 'Why would she be looking for me in the middle of the night?' He paused and then he just as suddenly barked out a laugh. 'You can't have thought… *Bambina?*' he gasped. 'Me with her? Are you joking? She'd be a stage five clinger if I opened my bedroom door!'

The shock of that unchoreographed and utterly unexpected statement of denial sank through Sunny like a shock wave and did nothing immediate to fix her anxious mood. 'But, I mean, I thought you were…together.'

'Never,' Raj declared bluntly. 'She often acts as my hostess when I'm in Italy. That is why she was on board this evening. I thought you would feel safer.'

'Safer?' Sunny stressed in bewilderment. 'Why would I have needed her here to feel safer?'

Now it was Raj's turn to study her in confusion. 'Once I'd made my interest clear and you had said no, I believed you would feel nervous of spending the night on my yacht without another woman around.'

'Like a *ch-ch-chaperone*?' Sunny stammered with difficulty while the most colossal giggle built and built inside her tight chest. 'But Maria is here.'

'Staff don't count the same way,' he pointed out, watching her face grow pink and taut and her lift a hand up to cram it against her soft pink lips.

Sunny went into a choking burst of coughing and turned her head away and down. No, she couldn't laugh and risk offending him when he had taken every precaution possible to ensure that she felt *safe* with him. 'Raj… I feel safe with you even after saying no,' she framed unevenly. 'I don't think you would do anything I didn't want you to do.'

'Good to know,' he murmured drily. 'But you still haven't told me why you were crying. I'm probably not the best person around for a therapy session but it seems like I'm the only one available right now.'

Sunny snatched in a deep breath. 'I was thinking about the people in my life who aren't here any more and feeling sad. Sometimes I do that and have a wallow but it's no reason for anyone else to worry about me.'

'But *I* don't like you feeling sad,' Raj told her levelly.

'I'll try never to do it around you again,' she swore on the edge of another inappropriate giggle, all desire to cry fully quenched now.

'Who do you miss the most?' he asked quietly.

'Mum,' she admitted tightly, her eyes dismaying her with a sudden prickle of more impending moisture, making her blink. 'She walked back late from a friend's one evening and got hit by a car. It was so sudden. She was like a bright light in our lives and then she was just…*gone*. My grandmother was devastated. She didn't expect her daughter to pass before she did. A lot of people loved her even if my father didn't.'

Sunny was disconcerted as a pair of hands slid beneath her slumped body and scooped her up and onto Raj's lap and she turned questioning violet eyes up to Raj.

'You were crying again and I'm trying to comfort you. Don't expect me to be good at it. I don't know how,' he concluded bluntly.

Her hand came up to cradle one side of his lean, darkly handsome face, small fingers stroking his stubbled jawline in a soothing motion. 'But you're trying and that's what counts.'

'Does it?' he breathed unconvinced, instinctively leaning his jaw into her soft palm and rubbing it.

And Sunny didn't even think about it, she just stretched up and kissed him, not an ardent kiss, merely a soothing brush of lips. Raj, however, had a different intent. The tip of his tongue snaked out to stab her lips apart and gain access and, within seconds, soothing turned into volatile and passionate. A little gasp sounded low in her throat as her head spun with the intoxication of that close contact with him. Her whole body felt as though it were lighting up with euphoria and her heart was hammering so hard, it seemed to be racing through her very veins.

'Is this a yes or a no?' Raj rumbled against her, sounding very much like a grizzly bear struggling with speech.

It was a moment of truth, voiced, perhaps unfortunately, when Sunny's blissed-out gaze was welded to intense dark eyes that glowed bronze, and her hands rose of their own volition to rest on his big shoulders as if to steady herself in an unsafe world. 'I can't think when you kiss me,' she objected.

'Either you want to have sex with me…or you don't,' Raj breathed, clearly out of patience, of which she suspected he had very little.

But something in that blunt, impatient declaration made Sunny smile and laugh, absolute certainty rippling through her in that same moment. Yes, it was a big step to decide to have sex for the very first time, but she also felt that it was past time she stopped walling herself off from ordinary life because Jack had let her down. His life had moved on but hers had in many ways stayed static and that shamed her pride in her own strength of mind. The right guy just hadn't come along, or possibly she had not been ready to recognise him, but Raj was different, Raj with his banked-down intensity, restless energy and his wonderful way of looking at her as though she were the only woman in the world.

'Yes,' she murmured tautly. 'My answer is yes but, bearing in mind your lifestyle, it can only ever be *one* night.'

Long fingers tugged up her chin, intense dark eyes assailing hers. 'Why?'

'Because that is the only thing that makes sense for us. We'll get this crazy attraction out of our systems and go back to normal,' she told him with determination.

'I'm not sure I work that way.'

'I think you'll find out that I was just a crazy notion.'

A reluctant laugh was wrenched from him. 'But why would you want to think that of yourself?'

'I could be wrong but I doubt it.'

Speech fled as he crushed her parted lips hungrily beneath his again and pounding excitement infiltrated her as well.

The excitement was new to her, refreshingly, shockingly new, and it seemed to sweep away everything else. She knew that there were other women in the background of his life, but she didn't think she needed to concern herself with that reality if he and she were to be together only one night and never again. She could make her peace with that decision, accepting that it was an imperfect solution but that it was the best she could come up with that allowed both of them to continue leading their own lives as they wanted.

Raj sprang upright, still holding her in his arms. 'You're a continual surprise to me.'

'You should put me down.'

'Why? I like carrying you,' Raj confided, gazing down at her with avid dark eyes as he stalked across the reception area and up steps. 'Maybe I'm scared you'll run away.'

'I'm not an inconsistent woman.'

'You've changed your mind twice today and it could

happen again. Of course, you are free to change y mind at any time,' he assured her with studious gravi y.

'I unnerve you,' Sunny guessed in dismay.

Raj's sensual lips compressed. 'There's just a tiny touch of chaos about you. It's unnerving but it's also fascinating…in an odd way.'

They were inside a very large, dimly lit bedroom. The night skies were visible through the glass roof high above. He settled her down with care on the rumpled bed and hit a button to send a cover over the roof above, sealing them into greater darkness and privacy.

'I should warn you,' Sunny said, pushing herself up on her elbows, 'I haven't done this before. I'm a virgin.'

His black brows pleated in unconcealed surprise.

'Sorry about that,' she mumbled in the silence that stretched.

Raj frowned uneasily. 'You're as rare as a unicorn and I'm a man who enjoys rarity. But I can't understand why you would still be that innocent.'

'I was just never tempted enough to get into it physically with anyone…until you.'

'But I'm not offering you a relationship.'

'I'm not looking for one. Oh, is that what's worrying you? That I might not know what I'm doing? Or that I might attach expectations to you afterwards?' Sunny smiled with rueful amusement. 'Trust me. I know what I'm doing and I'm not in a place where I could have a relationship either.'

The tension in his lean strong face evaporated, his misgivings about becoming her first lover quelled.

And Sunny laughed as he came down to her, long

fingers tracing her cheekbones, his eyes brilliant with hunger, a predatory smile curving his shapely mouth. He lifted her back into his arms and kissed her senseless. A stirring heat awakened in her pelvis and her nipples prickled and tightened. He leant back to slide her out of her robe and yanked his shirt off over his head with one hand in an easy movement.

Looking at him, she felt her mouth run dry. He was all solid muscle sheathed in sleek olive skin, a muscled six-pack and the fabled vee carving down to his hips coming into view as he stood up to unbutton his jeans. His attraction was visceral in its masculinity. Black hair tousled, he returned to her and pulled her back to him, framing her face with his big hands, ravishing her soft lips with raw passion before laying her back against the pillows.

'I want to fall on you like a starving wolf,' he growled, tugging at the nightdress that still shielded her from him and extracting her from it with determination. 'That's how ravenous you make me.'

He bent his head over the lush curve of her breasts, hands rising to cup her plump flesh, mouth darting down to tug insistently at the swollen tips. Her fingers came down on his wide shoulders, delved into his thick black hair as she twisted, breathless, at the sweet surge of response arrowing up between her legs. Little sounds escaped her and self-consciousness never came to claim her because she had never wanted anything in that moment as much as she wanted Raj. It was intimate and sensual, two things she had never allowed herself to experience, and what she was feeling now when he touched her was overwhelming.

Slowly he worked his path down over her shapely curves, lingering wherever he wished. He discovered with an appreciative laugh how she reacted when he kissed the pulse in her neck and plucked at the tender skin there with the edge of his teeth. Her hips writhed as he concentrated on the damp pink lips between her thighs. She learned minute by minute to want more, indeed to want more so fiercely that she had to resist the temptation to try and persuade him to go faster.

He traced her with long skilled fingers that made her tremble. He circled her clitoris with the most terrifying restrained delicacy and then lowered his head there to explore her with his mouth and his tongue until she was thrashing and squirming in a feverish delirium of arousal. The slow, agonising build-up to that level of excitement was almost more than she could bear. Her back arched and her lips opened on a gasp as the waves of sensation drove her up to a height and pushed her over it into a shattering climax.

Wrung out in the aftermath, Sunny gazed up at him with a heart that was still pounding and a body that was still singing.

'And now for the main event,' Raj teased with a dark edge to his deep voice, rearranging her with sure hands when she was certain that she was so relaxed she would flop if he freed her. Protection, he reminded himself, marvelling that he had almost overlooked that necessity and then recalling that Sunny couldn't get pregnant and throwing the idea of precautions to the four winds.

'Just get it over with,' Sunny whispered ruefully,

because she had never ever expected much from her first experience of sex.

'Wrong mindset.' Raj slid between her parted thighs and nudged his hard, velvety length against her tender entrance. 'It will be better than that.

'You don't know but you *should.* We're dynamite together,' Raj continued with blazing confidence as he shifted his lean hips and slowly eased into her.

Raj gazed down at her with immense satisfaction because he already felt as though he had waited for her...*for ever.* She lifted his day, she brightened his often gloomy horizon, and of course she was saying all that stuff about one night only but he didn't believe a word of it. She played safe, she *always* played safe. He had recognised that in her at their very first meeting. Sunny kept herself safe from change by living in her little cocoon of rural anonymity and he threatened all that with his alternative outlook.

Sunny shimmied her hips a little in invitation as she felt him invade her all too eager body. A quiver travelled up her spine before dispelling into other more sensitive places, anticipation rising in a swooshing tide of hunger. He lifted her legs and spread her wider, seated himself deeper and pushed and there was a brief, bearable sting of pain that made her brow furrow as she waited for worse to come, but it didn't come. That was that, that little pang of discomfort, and all her worst expectations had failed to pan out.

Raj emitted a stifled groan. 'You're so tight...and you feel so good.'

Relieved of her concern, Sunny shifted up into the

glorious heat and weight of him, finally surrendering to the experience, and all resistance fled as he sank harder and faster into the liquid heat of her. Excitement curled at the heart of her, sensation spreading out in a slow, breathtaking ripple that engulfed her body and her senses. He was stretching her, holding her and all those feelings seemed to coalesce in a starburst of intense emotion and feeling that stoked the heat at her core. As he took her with increasingly relentless strokes, all thought ceased and she became a creature of reaction instead. And her response climbed and climbed to magnificent heights before he pushed her over the peak a second time and the drowning sweet pleasure took over again.

'We're amazing together,' Raj husked, rolling over and still retaining a grip on her to tug her into a cooler stretch of the bed.

Sunny stilled for a brief moment but she had heard how it went on a one-night stand and from what she had understood a woman should not hang around afterwards. She pulled away. 'I'll get going now,' she said flatly.

'I want you to stay,' Raj decreed.

'But there's a sort of etiquette to these occasions… I understand,' she told him anxiously. 'Staying on isn't the thing.'

Raj shifted across the bed and closed both arms round her. 'I don't want you to leave.'

Sunny was surprised and Raj was even more surprised when those words escaped him, he who always slept alone, who hated women who tried to linger. But somehow Sunny put him in pursuit mode and that was an entirely new experience for him. Was she being elusive as part of a deliberate act? As that cynical suspicion filtered in, he flipped over to lean over her and met wide, troubled eyes, empty of any calculation other than the fastest route to the exit.

'Raj… I—'

'Stay,' he told her with emphasis.

Sunny froze, only losing her tension when he reached for her again. 'I'm not used to this,' she admitted awkwardly.

Raj loosened his hold on her. 'Relax with me,' he suggested.

'I can't… I'm not used to sharing this kind of intimacy,' she muttered unhappily. 'What if Pansy needs me during the night?'

Raj reached for the phone and spoke into it. 'There. You can be reached now.'

'You mean…you actually told people that I'm here with *you*?' Sunny gasped in horror. 'Where's your discretion?'

'You killed it. Go to sleep,' he urged.

And somehow, she did, yielding to the exhaustion of travel and unexpected events and more emotions than she knew how to handle. She drifted off, only to waken at some timeless stage of the night with Raj asking her if it was all right.

'What's all right?'

'Sex without protection,' he framed in an urgent undertone. 'I'm tested every month and I haven't been with anyone since we met. You said you can't get pregnant, so…? I've never had unprotected sex.'

'Go ahead,' she whispered, shimmying her hips back to his and his arousal with sensual pleasure.

And he did and it was slow and astonishingly exciting as his hands glided over her with wondrous expertise, tantalising and arousing until her head was falling back and she was in a paradise of intense sensation and then he was there exactly where she needed him to be. Hard and urgent and demanding and by the time he finished she was drifting off to sleep again, utterly ignoring his suggestion that she join him in the shower. A step too far, she was tempted to tell him, but she felt way too lazy and still too inhibited to subject herself to that test. Tomorrow was a new day, a moving-on day, she reminded herself doggedly, wondering why Raj wasn't acting as standoffish in the aftermath as she had naïvely expected.

CHAPTER FIVE

RAJ WAKENED LATER than was his wont, in an empty bed, and he immediately frowned.

Why had Sunny not wakened him? Most particularly after they had shared such an astonishing night together. Had he been the sort of guy who suffered from a fragile ego, he could have felt slighted. But there was nothing fragile about Raj's ego, particularly when he was recalling a sleepless night of passion such as he had never before enjoyed. She had wanted him as much as he had wanted her, he reflected with confidence as he strode into the shower. But even so, he was already recalling those admittedly glorious moments of unprotected sex and tensing over them. He had got carried away. He would address that potential problem before she flew back to the UK.

Of course, Sunny had got up early to be available for their niece, he assumed, content to forgive her on that score alone. A child's needs *should* take precedence over the adults' desires. He could only wish that he had enjoyed the nurture of a mother like that. Unfortunately, fate had cursed him with a weak, cowardly mother, one enthralled for years by a cruel, manipulative man. Only Clara's second pregnancy had inspired and strengthened her enough to walk out on Raj's father. Pansy, however, would only ever enjoy the blessing of Sunny and all the love and attention Sunny could shower on the child.

In her cabin, Sunny finished packing her overnight bag, having already attended to Pansy's. Every too quick movement jarred her still tender body with muscular aches and faint little pangs in parts never before used with such thoroughness. She smiled to herself. It had been one magical, unforgettable night, she savoured, grateful that she had had the courage to take up the opportunity rather than remaining controlled by a better-buried past. There would be an aftermath of sadness eventually for what could *not* be in the future, she conceded ruefully, but then that was life, always giving with one hand and then taking with the other. In the meantime, it was only human to be wondering if it was normal to make love that many times in the space of a few hours. Raj had been…insatiable. There was no other word for his hunger for her and she had felt empowered by her apparent desirability. Only that was a shallow, superficial thing, she acknowledged, shamefaced, and not something she could reasonably feel proud of attracting.

As a crew member came to collect their luggage, she was informed that Raj had asked to see her in his office. Leaving Pansy with Maria, who was planning to take the child out onto the deck to see the school of dolphin whose presence they had been alerted to by the attendant, Sunny followed the same man into a lift that whisked her up to the top deck. Her cheeks were hot at the prospect of seeing Raj again. Tiptoeing out of his cabin at dawn had been an easy escape but one that now had to be paid for with the awkward first meeting she had earlier ducked.

'Good morning, Sunny,' Raj greeted her with an expansive smile of welcome. 'I expected to have breakfast with you and Pansy, but you sneaked off early without rousing me.'

Raj looked magnificent in a pale linen suit, more casual in cut than she was accustomed to seeing on him, although nothing could diminish his height and breadth or the taut, fit definition of his musculature below the dark blue open-necked shirt he sported. That very thought made her face warm again and fired an uneasy clenching sensation low in her pelvis, making her shift in her seat.

'I thought it was easier for us both my way,' she confided unevenly, breathing challenged by his proximity as he directed her down into a comfortable armchair graced with a panoramic view of the Italian coast and the sea. A faint hint of his designer cologne flared her nostrils and made her even stiffer. 'You've got the most amazing office environment to enjoy up here.'

A knock sounded on the door and a tray arrived.

'Soothing camomile tea,' Raj announced, dark eyes gleaming with amusement.

'And coffee for you. The tea would have been a healthier option but just ignore me when I preach,' she told him.

'We were rather bold last night,' Raj remarked. 'I sincerely hope that there isn't any chance of a child coming from that boldness.'

Sunny froze. 'None whatsoever. I'm infertile,' she assured him, pale as a ghost at having to repeat what was soothing news to him but a painful recollection for her.

Raj relaxed his guard. 'I would like you to extend your stay onboard,' he stated with the utmost casualness.

Dismay lit Sunny's strained eyes and she lowered her lashes. 'I'm afraid I can't. I have to get back to my studio and my animals.'

'I can fix all that,' Raj pointed out, smooth as ice, bronzed eyes wandering over her at his leisure, his gaze heating her up wherever it lingered, swelling her breasts inside her bra, creating a damp heat between her thighs, which she pressed together hard. 'I'll have your art supplies flown out or new supplies obtained. I will organise care for your livestock. You won't need to worry about anything.'

Sunny breathed in slow and deep. 'But I *want* to go home,' she said tightly. 'I've really enjoyed this very glamorous trip and your hospitality. It's been a treat and I mean that. I'm very grateful.'

'Did the sex qualify as a treat or merely as an aspect of my hospitality?' Raj derided.

Sunny paled at his tone and the tension that had hardened his lean, darkly handsome features to granite. 'That's not a fair comment. We both knew and accepted what last night was.'

'I know what you said but I didn't believe you or accept what you said or even agree with it,' Raj admitted boldly.

'Oh, dear,' Sunny mumbled uneasily. Shaken by that unvarnished warning of intent, she slowly sipped her tea in its bone china monogrammed cup, the saucer rattling a little as her hand trembled. 'You should've said all that to me last night.'

'What guy would when he wants a woman? I didn't believe you meant it because your decision doesn't make any sense.'

'It makes *perfect* sense,' Sunny sliced in a little louder, determined to be heard. 'We have different values, different lifestyles. One night was self-indulgent but comparatively harmless in the long term. It ended it, no hard feelings.'

'Newsflash… I've got hard feelings!' Raj shot back at her rawly.

'There's nothing I can do about that except wish that I hadn't made the decision to stay with you last night,' Sunny replied curtly. 'It's not as if it's a rejection. It's simply rational and practical. And we shouldn't be confusing this relationship for Pansy's benefit. We're her uncle and her aunt. We are not lovers.'

'That's not a matter of concern while she is still so young!' Raj interposed fiercely. 'I wanted you last night. I want you now. I'm not a changeable individual. You cannot switch off a response like that, and that you believe you can only proves how out of your depth you are!'

'I didn't say it would be *easy* to switch off again,'

Sunny objected as she set down the tea and stood up, feeling intimidated by the fact that he was still standing. 'But that's the price for the freedom we enjoyed last night. If we continued some sort of affair, it would get messy. You wouldn't like messy and I refuse to break my own rules.'

'You're not a teenager with a curfew any more, Sunny,' Raj said very drily. 'You can make your own rules.'

'Not about accepting your other women, not about the basic truth that we couldn't work in any field because we are so different,' she protested and then she paused, and, recognising the shielded detachment in his cool bronzed gaze, she suddenly threw up her hands in frustration. 'Oh, why am I even bothering trying to explain when you're not listening…? Just as you *refused* to listen to me last night. If you don't want to hear something, you ignore it. If you don't like it, you ignore it. Well, maybe that works in your world and people feel forced to accept your point of view as supreme, but it doesn't work in mine and it never will!'

'Have you anything else to say?' Raj enquired glacially. 'Or are you done shouting at me?'

'I was not shouting!' Sunny fired back at him furiously.

'You are definitely shouting,' Raj informed her gently, watching her pace in front of him, another one of her all-enveloping shapeless dresses flapping around her ankles. 'And I have a very low tolerance for being shouted at.'

'Oh, shut up!' Sunny loosed at him in ferocious annoyance at that measured declaration. 'Nobody has ever got me as mad as you get me! You stand there giving forth like Moses off the Mount but you're not going to get away with doing it to me!'

'And I won't allow you to sidle away from the truth,' Raj countered, stepping between her and the door. 'Is that how you work, Sunny? All charm and appeal until someone dares to challenge you? And then, you *run away*? That's not how I work.'

'You're being difficult,' Sunny protested.

'But isn't that what you expected from me?' Raj tossed back, still acting as a very effective block between her and the exit. 'I won't allow you to run away from what you refuse to face.'

'I don't refuse to face anything!' Sunny flung at him angrily.

'I'm sorry but you *do*,' Raj countered with grave intent. 'You don't want this attraction because it doesn't meet your requirements…whatever they may be!'

'Like mistresses in every port of call…like *that's* normal!' Sunny exclaimed in a total fury exceeding anything she had ever felt before. She was outraged that Raj was daring to behave as though he were a single guy able to be with her alone. 'Yeah, sorry about those normal requirements of mine, but actually they're fairly basic…if you *can* tune into the regular expectations of the average woman, which I'm not sure you can.'

Raj stalked forward a step. 'And what are those expectations?'

'The expectations you're determined not to hear,' Sunny slung back at him vehemently. 'I don't *share*! Would you agree to share me with another man?'

A muscle pulled tight at the corner of his unsmiling mouth. 'Of course not.'

'There you are, then,' Sunny said softly, the anger leaving her in a relieving surge as she realised that she had finally found an argument that he respected. 'You're looking at what you offered me and you wouldn't accept that for yourself. Is that sexism? Hypocrisy? I don't know. What I *do* know is that I won't accept *less* than you evidently would.'

Raj gritted his even white teeth. He wasn't accustomed to being outdone in a dispute but he could not, at that moment, come up with a reasonable response and that infuriated him. He was neither sexist, nor hypocritical. The world he lived in had taught him to adapt to certain unavoidable changes. He wanted sex like any young, healthy male but if he didn't want his bedroom exploits and secrets spread across the tabloids for public consumption, he had to take specific steps to protect himself. And that had inevitably led to the mistress solution, women who accepted that sex was basically all that he required from them. Only Sunny did not fit into that category.

'I understand that this is a negotiation,' he returned levelly.

Sunny stared back at him in shock at that assurance. 'That's *not* what this is.'

'What else can it be? You tell me what you will not accept. I may or may not choose to meet your terms.'

'You've been in business for far too long,' Sunny argued unhappily. 'Relationships do not fall into the business realm.'

Raj gave her a very wry smile, lips turning up at the corner in acknowledgement of their directly opposed viewpoints. 'Sunny…' he murmured gently. 'I have never *been* in a relationship with a woman.'

Sunny was aghast. 'But that's not possible.'

'It is perfectly possible in my sphere. The women… it is only physical. There is no relationship. Barely any conversation…' His smile became pained. 'Then again, I am a male with few words and sharing my thoughts feels unnatural. They give me sex. I give them a comfortable lifestyle. It is an exchange at the most basic level and nothing more.'

And it was one of those odd moments that she experienced with Raj when she wanted to wrap her arms round him and point out that he never stopped talking with her. Only then did it occur to her that he had already had something different with her from what he had had with others of her sex and her heart still gave a painful tug. 'Raj,' she sighed helplessly.

'It's much more with you.'

'Yes, I get that,' she muttered, suddenly thrown on the back foot again, unable to see how they could possibly go in that direction.

'Last night…was special,' Raj volunteered as she came into his radius on her wandering path to the door. 'You are the first woman I have trusted in many years. I had unprotected sex with you. I have never before even contemplated taking such a risk with a woman but you are different. You… I trust.'

'Yes,' she whispered shakily, overwhelmed by that claim, secretly delighted by it.

'You, I want,' Raj completed, reaching out to close his big hands gently over her arms and draw her close.

The scent of him was like an aphrodisiac in the air as Sunny drew it in. She had spent the night in his arms, a night such as she had never dreamt of having, and every moment of it had been precious to her. For the very first time that morning, she relaxed, drawn by the heat and reassuring solidity of his lean, powerful physique.

'And you want me too,' Raj completed tautly.

'But I want more of you than you're willing to give,' Sunny chimed in helplessly.

Raj lifted her up to him and crushed her parted lips beneath his and she could feel her own body thrum and pulse like an engine suddenly switched on. Her head fell back as he sent his tongue delving between her readily parted lips to explore further. A quiver of hunger rippled through her and, that fast, she wanted him again and it was an inexpressible need in the situation they were in. Shaken by the experience, torn in two by it, she pulled herself back and stepped away, her lovely face flushed and troubled.

'We can't do this. I should go and be with Pansy.'

'Your mind is closed to me, closed to any solution that does not agree with yours.'

'That is as may be, Raj…but I'm free to have my own opinion and protect myself.'

His brilliant dark eyes rested on her and hardened. 'Of course, but you insult me when you imply that I would harm you in any way.'

A rueful smile curved Sunny's reddened mouth. 'You wouldn't do it deliberately, but you don't look at the whole picture and you would do it without intending to,' she responded quietly.

And she accompanied him down onto the deck where Pansy was racing about in pursuit of an electronic cat that purred and made squeaky noises.

'I don't give her advanced toys of that sort,' Sunny confided. 'I prefer the basic stuff.'

'Don't restrict her to what you played with as a child,' Raj advised. 'The world has moved on, as must we to stay relevant.'

On the flight back home on the private jet, Sunny was exhausted. Pansy slumbered beside her and, eventually, Sunny drifted off as well. After all, she hadn't slept much the previous night and she was emotionally drained in a way she had never experienced before. Raj wound her up and more feelings than she had known she even possessed came surging up out of her to create an inner turmoil that scared her.

The first thing she noticed when she drove into the yard was that her barn had been repaired. How could that be possible? She climbed out and released Pansy before standing back to get a proper look at the barn. Before she'd left, she had only reached the stage of requesting quotes from local builders. Unfortunately, the insurance company had already indicated that they were not prepared to pay for the whole job because the barn rafters were rotten. Since she was still recovering from the recent stresses of the court case on her bank account, she had planned to go for the best repair job she could afford and hope the building came through

par, possibly in need of some kind of tonic to help her shake off the bug.

'You are pregnant,' Dr Smyth informed her quietly.

Shock engulfed Sunny in a dizzy wave of disbelief. 'But I was told that wasn't possible when I was seventeen and I've always believed that I would be childless,' she admitted.

'I don't presume to criticise the doctor who told you that.'

'No, it was actually my mother who told me that I would never have a child,' Sunny interrupted, wanting to be fair.

'You were only twelve when you had surgery after a ruptured appendix. Your reproductive organs were damaged but you were fortunate to have a skilled surgeon in the aftermath,' the older man explained. 'Evidently, the repairs he undertook and the healing that took place in your young and healthy body were successful. And here you are now…'

'Yes,' Sunny agreed, wrenched between delight and horror at the truth that she was receiving. What she had assumed was impossible was, after all, possible. And the news shook her inside out and upside down.

Good grief, how could she ever tell Raj? She had assured him that it was safe to have sex without precautions and she had been wrong. Miraculously, she had conceived, but she was not naïve enough to assume that Raj would react to her announcement in the same way. Raj would be appalled and her heart sank at the prospect of telling him…

CHAPTER SIX

SUNNY SHIFTED POSITION in the opulent limousine on the drive to Ashton Hall while absently wondering why Raj's staff had warned her to bring her passport, because they were not on this occasion leaving England.

Pansy was dozing, replete after her lunch before their departure. Maria was playing some game on her phone. She had been in the limo when it arrived to collect them, and Sunny couldn't help but be impressed by the fact that Raj had recognised that continuity of care was important for their niece's stability. Particularly, she reflected anxiously, when their every meeting with Raj seemed to happen at a different place. It had been six weeks since they had been together on his yacht, six weeks since they had talked face-to-face.

But none of that mattered now, none of the differences, none of the disagreements, she reminded herself firmly. Time had moved on for them both. Raj had his life with his other women and she had her life with Pansy and a future baby. Utterly detached, those lifestyles, she acknowledged. But…a *baby*, a joy that she had believed would never be hers, and Raj had given her that baby. Unknowingly, without intent, she conceded, that daring rush of joy draining away again into guilt and shame. Raj would never have given her that baby by intent and that truth mattered *so* much.

The limousine turned down a long leafy lane and pulled off onto a gravelled frontage to align with a jewel of a Georgian country property.

'Oh, wow!' the nanny gasped in delight. 'Working for Mr Belanger is so exciting!'

Sunny scanned the opulent vehicles already parked and the helicopters on the front lawn and thought instead that Raj was exceptionally busy. And hadn't she known that already when his staff had had to cancel his visit a fortnight earlier and remake it? Raj worked and travelled and that was his chosen way of living, because nobody could say that he worked simply to earn when he already had more money than he could use in a dozen lifetimes. No, Raj moved on to the next challenge in the science and development field, always ahead of the crowd. He used his brilliance, kept himself gainfully occupied in the world of profit and expansion, probably as he had been taught as a child, and he continually prospered and triumphed. So, why did a part of her feel sorry for Raj's inability to relax and pause to smell the roses? It was a nonsense to think that way about a male who was so phenomenally successful.

Their arrival was a repeat of their previous arrival in Italy. Staff hovered uncertainly and then Raj came striding out and Sunny's heart stopped dead and then hammered in a dangerously staccato beat because, my word, she thought in the same moment, he was beautiful. Incredibly tall, well built and superbly sophisticated, sheathed in a formal black business suit that accentuated his black hair and very dark eyes.

Pansy, unimpressed by that detachment of his, whooped and scurried forward to greet him without hesitation, reaching his knees to embrace his legs and there was the change. A smile spread across his lean, darkly handsome face like a tide and he grinned down at his niece in welcome, delighted by her enthusiasm, not yet understanding that he was the only male in Pansy's world and already undeniably special to the little girl. He scooped her up into his arms.

''Lo, Unc,' Pansy managed, a little hand reaching up to his face to touch his nose. 'Noz…eye…' she told him, keen to show off her latest learning before fumbling to a halt at his lips, forgetting that word.

'Hello, Pansy,' Raj said cheerfully. 'That's mouth… *mouth*,' he sounded out with care.

And Sunny just melted inside herself because she saw the effort he was making, the natural way he was ready and willing to interreact with their niece at the most basic level. It had only taken a little encouragement for him to stop being so self-conscious and fearful of rejection. And she could never ever air that conviction because to voice it would injure his pride. But she could see how easily he could react to having a child of his own and it hurt that she was so convinced that he would never ever offer that warmth to *their* child. An unplanned, unsought child, an accident…a *mistake*.

Raj freed Pansy as soon as she squirmed for freedom. He strode across the echoing marble hall with its chequerboard black and white floor to focus on

Sunny instead. She was dressed once again in a flowing purple garment that screened all possible view of her shapely curves. And he didn't care because he now knew what lay under all that screening fabric and it was entirely his to enjoy, his to appreciate and he was, he conceded, a male very much into the concept of *his* woman only showing herself to him in private.

She was smiling, that smile lighting up her beautiful face, sunlight flooding in to gleam across the golden tumble of her hair, and he was thoroughly entranced by the prospect of the weekend ahead. Sunny…all to himself. He went hard as a rock, shifting position to accommodate that instantaneous surge of physical hunger. He felt like a teenager again. He couldn't wait, he genuinely would struggle to wait to be alone with her, finally freed from all other concerns. Just him and Sunny, just exactly as he'd planned weeks ago even if he had had to wait longer than he had hoped to see her again…

'Sunny,' he murmured softly. 'It feels like for ever since I saw you last and I'm afraid I'm about to ask you to wait yet again for me. My business conference is still current. An important person was delayed and, as a result, we are running late and my time frame has changed.'

'That's fine,' Sunny hastened to assure him as he gathered both her restive hands in his and just held them. Swoon, she was thinking dizzily, not having expected such an enthusiastic reception after their last meeting. She had been mistaken, she allowed guiltily. Clearly Raj did not hold spite. Evidently, she and

Pansy got a clean sheet for every visit and that was heart-warming, particularly after what had happened between them. Instantly she relaxed on that belief, colliding with those very dark, so intense eyes of his and feeling the heat rise below her skin. He had stunning eyes and she only had to meet those eyes to remember them on her before dawn as he sank into her hard and deep and gave her the most breathtaking pleasure she had ever known.

'I've organised a tour of the house and grounds to keep you occupied and later, we're having dinner together.' With a wave of his hand, he signalled an older man. 'This is Stuart, who manages the estate here at Ashton Hall.'

'I really wasn't expecting… I mean, if you're busy, and you obviously are.'

'Right at this moment,' Raj husked, staring down at her with hungry dark eyes, 'you are the most important person.'

Sunny was stunned into silence by that announcement. Did he mean that literally? Were they at odds again in the understanding stakes? Had he assumed, because Raj was very prone to assuming stuff that suited him, that because she had fallen into his bed so easily, she would be willing to do so again? Or was she being fanciful? Imagining more than he meant? Maybe he was simply smoothing over and moving past the intimacy of that night on his yacht? Or being charming? Trying to relax her?

It was hard to tell with Raj. He wasn't like other people. He didn't always make reasonable deductions from what she saw as fact. He was quite likely to make up his own story of how he wanted things to happen inside his own complex head. And that worried her, seriously worried her because she didn't want to end up arguing with him again and increasing the tension.

But friction was inevitable, she reminded herself unhappily. She had to tell him this weekend that she was pregnant. He deserved to know that truth from the first. That wasn't something she could deny or conceal and she wanted to be fair and open with him because he would definitely prefer that approach.

Stuart showed them up an elegant staircase into bedrooms and reception areas, letting drop that all the conference visitors would be leaving and that only she and Pansy were spending the weekend. Pansy and Maria were soon ensconced in a comfortable nursery filled with new toys. Sunny was shown into a spacious bedroom where her case already awaited her. Leaving it untouched, she continued the tour with Stuart and Pansy, walking downstairs again to admire a pillared ballroom and a gracious library and other grand reception rooms before moving outside to take in the view.

A rolling green lawn ran up to the edge of a fenced park and beyond that she could see a herd of deer grazing at the edge of dense woodland. It was peaceful and beautiful and she allowed Stuart to show her where the walled garden was before telling him that they would find their own way back. A priority for her was to let her niece enjoy a closer look at the deer.

That was achieved but the peace and quiet didn't last long because Pansy's whoops of excitement sent the herd leaping away at speed, a development that her niece found even more thrilling. After that, she headed for the walled garden where she dawdled near any promising plants with her camera and took pictures while Pansy scampered about, revelling in her freedom.

When they returned to the house, Stuart offered to have Pansy's supper brought to the nursery and she agreed. It was time to get Pansy into the bath and into her pyjamas for bed. By the time all that was accomplished, Sunny was ready to dress for dinner. When she returned to her allotted room, she found a dress hanging in a garment bag outside the wardrobe. It carried a note from Raj: 'Please wear this for me.'

Sunny frowned and extracted it from the bag. It was layered, long and stretchy and the sort of soft blue shade she liked. What on earth strange idea had Raj taken into his handsome head? Buying a *dress* for her? And how did she refuse without causing offence? And didn't she have a big enough challenge to surmount with her unexpected pregnancy? Honey, she recalled her mother saying, was always better received than vinegar.

Showered and her usual minimal make-up applied—well, possibly rather more than usual—she donned the dress. It moulded her curves more than she liked but she appreciated the floaty upper layer and it did fit amazingly well. She might as well enjoy the sight of her waist while she still had it, she thought forlornly, because nature would soon be thickening it up. And how was Raj likely to feel about that? Well, what did that matter, considering that that night had been a one-off? Even so, nervous tension made her antsy.

Stuart knocked on the door to tell her that Raj was waiting for her downstairs.

Her heart was beating very fast when she reached the hall where Raj awaited her. He looked amazing, sleek and sophisticated in an exquisitely tailored dark suit that moulded his broad shoulders and faithfully outlined his long, powerful legs. 'We're a little late but it's a clear night for flying.'

'Flying?' she stressed in astonishment.

'Tonight, we're doing something special for dinner,' Raj informed her, walking her down the shallow steps and round the side of the house to a helicopter.

'But Pansy—'

'Maria knows that we'll be back tomorrow morning and she will be able to get in contact with us at any time,' Raj asserted. 'I've thought of everything.'

Reckoning that it was hard to combat such a claim and remain strictly polite, Sunny bundled up her skirts and began to clamber awkwardly into the helicopter, but a pair of hands settled to her hips for Raj to lift her in. Flustered, she settled in a seat and utilised the headphones she was handed. Why the heck were they doing something *special* for dinner? What was that about? Her frown deepened.

'You really are the most frustrating man I've ever met,' she told him roundly before the pilot lifted the heavy craft into the air.

Raj merely smiled. He wanted her to enjoy herself. In fact, he was determined that she should enjoy herself every moment that she was with him. He had phoned her several times over the past six weeks, ostensibly to ask after his niece, but the previous week he had noticed that Sunny seemed out of sorts, not her usual upbeat self, and it had bothered him. She needed a little fun in her life and, although he considered himself to be one of the world's most serious and least fun-loving guys, he was convinced that he could dig deep and surprise and please her.

'Paris?' she checked in wonder as the limousine powered them through the busy well-lit city streets and she peered out at the magnificent buildings. 'Just for dinner?'

'Just for dinner. I'm taking you to one of my hotels.'

'It's like being Cinderella for the night.'

'I'm no fairy godmother…nor am I a Prince Charming,' Raj proclaimed with a shudder.

A magnificent hotel dazzling with the combined light of crystal chandeliers and blazing windows awaited them. Raj swept her in through the front doors, past glittering groups of people sporting evening wear and opulent jewellery, and straight into a mirrored lift. As the doors closed on the view, she registered in horror that everyone seemed to be staring at *her*.

'Why was everyone looking at me? Do I look that strange?'

'No, of course, you don't look strange. It's my fault that people are staring,' Raj assured her in exasperation. 'The only women I'm ever seen in public with are employees. Obviously, you are not an employee and that makes you a source of interest.'

And some of the interest could be in the highly identifiable dress she wore, fresh off the catwalk and designed by the season's hottest designer, Stevie Carteret. He had seen the dress in a newspaper and had thought it looked exactly like something that Sunny would like. It was sort of floaty and enveloping but the wispy top layer was transparent and the close fit of the dress beneath showed off Sunny's glorious curves.

Sunny studied their reflection in one of the mirrors. They were the odd couple, Raj so tall, her barely reaching his chest. But even that glimpse of him, his square jawline blue black with stubble because he hadn't shaved again, his wide sculpted mouth relaxed, made her heartbeat quicken, her breath catch in her throat, that warm curling sensation of sensual familiarity spread like temptation through her pelvis.

'I'm surprised you're taking me out in public,' she confided breathlessly as he guided her out of the lift and straight across an opulent hallway into an incredibly elegant reception area.

'In today's world it's wiser to show you off occasionally rather than try to hide you. Hiding anyone merely invites speculation and suspicion. I learned that a long time ago.'

'What is this place?' she asked as he closed his big hand over hers and led her out onto a balcony set with a table for two and a waiter hovering in readiness.

'It's my penthouse apartment on the top floor. It's convenient and fully serviced without the need for further staff.'

'It's also very beautiful,' Sunny savoured, standing by the wrought-iron railing to admire the view and note the boats chugging down the river far below them, boats crammed with tourists admiring the historic city by night, their cameras flashing, their bright chatter floating softly upward.

Raj placed his hands either side of hers where they were braced on the rail and then slowly eased his hands over hers. 'I thought you would like it.'

Insanely conscious of the heat of his big body at her back, Sunny laughed and quivered with awareness and a weakening yearning to simply lean back into him. 'I do but I'm also wondering how many times you've been here and you've been so lost in work that you didn't even take the time to appreciate the beauty.'

Raj grinned, drinking in the faint coconut scent drifting up from her hair. 'That's why you're here,' he told her shamelessly. 'To keep me grounded…to show me everything I fail to notice around me.'

The warmth of him was spreading through her like a dangerous drug, lighting up pathways she had worked hard to shut down again weeks earlier. Raj, for that one sultry night, had been an indulgence, but the whole point of an indulgence was that it should be a very, very occasional treat because to repeat indulgences too often was to be self-destructive. And Sunny reminded herself that she was much too sensible for that sort of behaviour, particularly when she was pregnant.

Champagne was being uncorked by the waiter and Sunny thought fast and told a hurried lie. 'I'm on these tablets right now that mean I shouldn't touch alcohol.

I don't want to be a party pooper but I would rather not drink.'

'Not a problem.' Raj waved away the champagne and suggested that they sit down and start their meal.

'Sorry about that,' Sunny muttered as she sipped her water, still feeling ashamed of the lie she had told to conceal her condition. He would understand later but this seemingly special dinner, staged high above the grandeur of the river Seine, was neither the right moment nor the right place in which to make such a very personal and private announcement.

'Don't apologise on my behalf, because I seldom drink. My father was a heavy drinker. I suspect he was an alcoholic and that that powered his violent temper and his mistreatment of my mother and me,' he intoned grimly. 'If *that* is in my genes, I should be careful.'

They ate delicious starters and embarked on the main course. Why, Sunny was wondering, did this appear to be a meal that was celebrating something? She was bemused. It felt as though she had missed some crucial line of dialogue at some stage, ensuring that everything after it seemed oddly out of sync. She drank the fruit juice that was brought to her and concentrated on her tender steak. When the dessert arrived, she toyed with hers.

Raj closed a hand over hers. 'Come closer.'

Sunny's eyes opened very wide. 'Er...why?' she mumbled.

Raj's gaze welded to the generous swell of her firm breasts and then up to her soft pink luscious mouth. 'I want to hold you,' he said frankly. 'Obviously.'

Obviously? Since when was that requirement obvious? He dismissed the waiter, said he'd call for coffee and reached for Sunny. He was so strong that he literally lifted her out of her chair to bring her down on his spread thighs with a growly sound of satisfaction that reverberated through his chest. 'That's better. Now watch the fireworks,' he told her.

What fireworks? she almost asked, but a split second later fireworks were shooting up into the night sky and bursting into brilliant multicoloured flowers in the most breathtaking display. 'Those are so pretty...they even have pastel ones. Pansy would adore this.'

'We'll do this with her another time.'

Sunny rested back in his arms, shocked that she had settled there without argument, but he felt so good and he made her feel so safe. 'You knew the fireworks would be on,' she guessed.

'I put them on for you,' Raj corrected.

Sunny twisted on his lap and awkwardly peered at his hard profile. 'But why would you do that?'

'Because I felt like it...and because you can be very slow on the uptake, Sunny,' he spelt out softly, his mouth dropping down to a sensitive spot on her nape and dallying there until tiny little quivers of response were running through her like a river in full flood. 'Something I'm only now finding out.'

'What are you saying?' Sunny almost whispered.

Expelling his breath in a measured hiss, Raj thrust his chair back and lifted her again, lowering her to the floor to stand before him. 'This whole evening...you *still* haven't got the message?' he breathed almost incredulously.

'What message?' she asked, held captive by dark eyes flaming gold like a tiger's.

'There are now *no* other women in my life,' Raj imparted with precision. 'That term was what we negotiated…and now we have a deal, signed, sealed and delivered.'

Sunny was shattered. She stood there, anxious lavender-blue eyes locked to him in dawning comprehension. 'I told you that relationships don't come under the deal heading.'

Raj groaned out loud. 'And I told you I'd never had a relationship before. But you and I…*that's* a deal. It took me longer than I expected to settle the mistresses and remove them from my life but I haven't been with any of them since I met you, so that's exclusive, right?' A questioning ebony brow lifted.

'Right,' she agreed limply, because she truly could not think of anything else to say when he had stunned her stupid and her legs felt like cotton-wool supports because she had never ever envisaged being in the situation he had now placed her in. 'I can't believe you went to all that trouble for me.'

'I want you. And when I want something as much as I want you I will do whatever it takes to make it happen.'

'Obviously,' she said shakily. 'But I really wasn't expecting this development. I agreed to be with you for *one* night, not anything like this!'

'Understandably, I made certain assumptions of my own,' Raj fielded.

'Oh, that doesn't surprise me in the slightest!' Sunny flung back at him, breathless with lingering shock and disbelief. She had tried to keep him at a distance. She had put up barriers but Raj had rolled over the top of her barriers like an enemy tank. Entirely off his own bat, he had shelved his mistresses in apparent favour of her alone.

But how could that possibly work in the future? Eventually, he would get tired of her, of course he would, and then everything with Pansy would become horribly awkward because, in the aftermath, neither of them was likely to want to see the other.

'And what about when we break up again? How is that likely to affect Pansy?' Sunny demanded.

Raj groaned. 'Why is Sunny the optimist considering worst-case scenarios here? We're adults, we'll remain civil and it won't have the smallest effect on our niece.'

Sunny breathed in deep and slow, calming, composing herself.

'This isn't a game, Sunny. I don't play games. What I like about you is that you're honest with me about what you want, what you expect, and I will *try* to deliver,' Raj told her with roughened sincerity. 'But I'll get it wrong sometimes. I hate failure but it's human to fail. I like perfect the best and, so far, this evening has been perfect.'

Only it wouldn't be perfect any more if she practised that honesty he liked so much about her. Everything would fall apart in the instant she admitted that she had conceived his child. He wouldn't see the miracle that she saw, no, he would see a betrayal of trust, because she had naïvely assured him that she couldn't get pregnant. Only she hadn't known that there even *could* be a risk of that development.

She was torn in two at the prospect of having to tell him. No, not at this moment when he was smiling, when he had got rid of the other women in his life to make a special place for her, when he had put on flowery fireworks purely for her benefit. How could she allow him to have surrendered so much for a reward like that? He wouldn't see their unborn child as a reward. Raj viewed life and people through a different lens.

'And now it's about to get even more perfect,' Raj concluded, vaulting upright with a slashing wicked smile that made her heart pound. He scooped her up into his arms with ease and strode back indoors, ignoring her gasp of surprise as he strode through double doors into a bedroom fit for a queen. Her troubled gaze flicked over gleaming contemporary furniture, lamplit pools of privacy and the biggest bed she had ever seen draped in white linen. Through the windows she could see the fireworks still throwing up colourful blossoms. She would tell him about the baby in the morning, she decided, when things were calm again and he was in a more receptive mood.

'I've been thinking of this moment multiple times a day for weeks,' Raj confided as he knelt down on one knee and flipped her shoes off with the utmost casualness.

'I never even got to thank you for the dress,' Sunny exclaimed, suddenly shy at the prospect of being stripped naked, wondering if he would notice the subtle differences that were already changing her body. Her breasts were larger, and, goodness knew, she hadn't needed nature's help there, and there was a very faint curve now to her tummy, which had previously been flat.

'I saw a picture of it and it was *you*,' Raj told her, dropping his jacket where he stood, yanking off his tie, all action and impatience now that what he saw as the formalities had all been taken care of.

Yet Sunny seemed to still be in shock because she was as yet showing him none of the relief and satisfaction he had somehow expected. He had embraced celibacy for many weeks for her, had focused on the goal and that goal was acquiring Sunny at any cost. And even before he dared to lay a finger on her, he knew that she was worth it, he knew that she wanted to be with him because he was the man that he was, because she *cared*, and he had never had that before. She didn't want him to take her out and show her off, she didn't want the public recognition that could drive normal people to insanity, she didn't want the money and all that it could buy, she only wanted *him*. And in Raj's world, that made her a pearl beyond price.

CHAPTER SEVEN

SUNNY WATCHED RAJ haul off his shirt, revealing his magnificent, bronzed torso, not to mention all the pure, defined lines of his pecs and abs. He was in superb physical condition and she knew that one of these days there would be a sketch pad in her hand and she would be drawing him in charcoal, shading in the angles and the hollows of his lean, athletic body. He was beautiful, from his sharp as diamond cheekbones to his deep-set dark golden eyes and the sensually alluring curve of his lips…and he wanted her, *her*, she reflected in sheer wonderment.

Nobody had ever wanted her enough to make sacrifices for her…except, perhaps, her mother, she conceded ruefully. Refusing to terminate her pregnancy, Sunny's mother had protected the child that her husband didn't want, the child that Sunny's father had feared might cost money that he saw as more properly belonging to her half-sister Christabel's needs. But that sacrifice had pretty much cost her mother her marriage, although her mother had been clear that that marriage had been on the rocks by then owing to her father's complete absorption in Christabel and his management of her career.

And then there had been Jack, who had turned his back on the love he'd said he had for her to find a fertile woman who could give him the children he craved. Fortunately for his wife, she had had no problems falling pregnant, but how would he have reacted if conception had not been that easy? Raj, on the other hand, hadn't seen her as being less of a woman because she had believed that she was infertile, but then he had never hoped to have children with her anyway. Only, how would he feel now when she finally confessed the truth? In despair, she banished that hovering black cloud of fear and dissension from her mind to concentrate on the present.

Shedding his trousers, Raj came down on the bed beside her and flipped her over to run down the zip on her dress before proceeding to extract her from it with single-minded intent. As she tumbled back against the pillows, he smoothed her rumpled hair and studied her with satisfaction. The smooth slopes of her firm breasts were cradled in blue silk and lace.

'It's almost a crime to take this off you,' he husked, reaching under her for the clasp to detach the bra. 'You have to know that you look amazing…all that smooth glowing skin.'

'I must've got the sun in Italy.'

'How? You were clothed from head to foot,' he scoffed.

And she smiled secretively, wondering if there was truth in that old chestnut about a pregnancy glow. The bra was trailed off and she succumbed to her shyness, wrenching back the smooth sheet to scram its cover.

'You're no fun,' Raj complained, amused by her bashfulness, cupping her cheek in one large hand to ravish her mouth hungrily with his while he tossed the sheet back, and then long fingers strolled across her hip down to the silk-clad triangle covering her mons.

Sunny quivered as he skated a fingertip over the most sensitive spot of all and pervasive heat began to rise between her legs. He traced an achingly tender nipple with the edge of his teeth and she shuddered, suddenly on fire for him, arms reaching up to pull him closer.

'I like it when you lose control of that prim nature,' he growled.

'I'm not prim.'

'It's not a bad thing, not a criticism. I'm more accustomed to the opposite trait and I'm not a fan of that either. I only need you to be yourself with me.'

'I don't know how to be anything else.'

While she was gazing up into his stunning eyes, he tugged up her knees and disposed of her last garment before shimmying down the bed with lithe grace and sliding between her thighs.

He traced her seam with the tip of his tongue and then moved on with fervour to explore all that lay between. She gasped and arched and he held her down, his hands firm on her hips while he subjected her to the most merciless onslaught of pleasure she had ever experienced. And then the pace slowed as he circled her clitoris and even before he slid a finger into the molten depths of her she was moaning and crying out as a climax took her by storm, shaking her body with waves of drowning bliss.

'You're really quick at that,' Raj remarked with unwelcome amusement.

'You're too good at it.'

'I've only done that with you…at least since I was seduced and taught the basics by an older woman when I was fourteen.'

She frowned. 'That was too young.'

'I was too young for most of the things I was surrounded by at university. It was inevitable that some young woman would wonder what the kid nerd would be like in bed, and I was curious enough to accept the invitation,' he admitted.

'Wrong, all the same.'

'I was a lonely kid. Any kind of interaction with another student meant something to me.'

'I hate the idea of that.' Sunny explored his parted lips with her own, slowly, delicately, until Raj took over, delving deep, twining his tongue with hers over and over until hunger began to engulf her again.

Strong and sure, he came down on her, lifting her legs, pushing against her where she was most tender. He entered her with a raw groan of pleasure, stretching her tight walls, seating himself deep, and then he began to move. Her heart hammering, she arched up to him, struggling to contain the raw excitement sending flames of feverish impatience hurtling through her. He settled into a rhythm, shifted, changed his angle, drove her a little insane while the pressure mounted and tightened inside her. And then, in the midst of that heated desperate climb to satisfaction, he turned her over, pulled her up on her knees and pounded back into her with relentless energy. Just as suddenly she reached that peak and he pushed her over it. She stifled a scream in the padded headboard, her heart racing so fast that she was convinced she would stop breathing there and then. With a deep groan of fulfilment, he pulled back from her.

'OK?' Raj tugged her back down into the bed, spread her limp body out and tugged the sheet over her. 'I'll want you again soon but you're tired. Nap for a while.'

Tired? She felt as though her entire body had been wired and then somebody had yanked out all the wires that made her limbs work. She was a boneless, weightless doll but her conscience was heavier than lead at the same time. She would tell him about the baby in the morning.

'What are you thinking about?' she asked him abstractedly.

His brow furrowed. 'The fireworks were naff. I would have preferred to use synchronised drones but I would've needed a lot of them and getting permission in an urban area like this would have been a major headache…'

Ask a man, get an answer, she thought ruefully. 'I loved the fireworks.'

'I'll run a bath for you,' Raj announced with sudden energy, vaulting out of the bed and striding through one of the doors.

Gushing water sounded and then she heard him

using his phone, talking fast in fluent French. A little while later someone rang a bell. Raj strode through the bedroom, a towel wrapped round his lean waist, and strode back again, a giant box in his arms. 'The bath's almost ready,' he told her, waking her up on the very edge of sleep.

A little while later, Raj scooped her out of the bed and carried her into the bathroom. Giant gilded impressive candelabra filled with candles flamed all around a sunken bath with a steaming surface covered with rose petals and flowers. It was as magnificent as a film stage set and it took her breath away. He set her down and guided her down the steps into the bath.

'Do you really like this sort of nonsense?' he enquired critically half under his breath.

'Oh…yes,' she admitted, sinking happily into the warm water.

'Sorry it took so long. They had to get me candles and holders and all that jazz,' he complained.

'It was truly worth it. Thank you,' she whispered weakly, shaken by the effort he had made on her behalf.

Raj smiled and her heart squeezed inside her tight chest. She was falling in love with him and she knew she couldn't control her emotions around him. He was everything she had ever dreamt of but nothing that she had ever expected to find. In action he had a sort of hurricane effect, all bristling energy and determination, but underneath the seething impatience and exasperation with the world's difficulties was an absolutely wonderful guy.

'You're amazing,' she said softly as he walk[illegible] out of the bathroom.

Raj stopped dead and wheeled round to look [illegible] at her with hard dark eyes. 'I don't do soppy, Sunny. I don't have those feelings to give. I've never felt them for anyone.'

Well, that was telling her, but taking that onboard after the evening they had shared was still a challenge. The glorious fireworks, the intimacy, the fabulous bath? Nothing special in his estimation, it seemed. And didn't that fact just give her an even more huge gulf to cross with him in the morning when she finally told him that she had conceived?

Sunny blew out the candles one by one, made use of the towelling robe on offer and moved back into the bedroom. Raj was seated by the television watching the business news in front of a trolley of food.

'You're eating again?' she teased, having decided to ignore that crack that he didn't do soppy. Not a denial worth taking seriously, she thought, not when she'd had the flowery fireworks and the equally flowery candlelit bath.

'Being with you makes me hungry.' He sprang upright and simply reached for her in the same motion, lifting her up into his arms and settling down again with her as if such behaviour were perfectly normal.

'Is that an achievement?' she whispered helplessly.

'It hasn't happened before.' Yanking over the trolley with one relaxed foot, Raj reached for a plate and passed it to her, offering her selections, pushing his own favourite snacks. 'You're a healthy eater.'

'And you're surprised?'

'Nothing about you surprises me.'

Oh, just you wait until tomorrow, she reflected unhappily, thinking of the baby on board without his awareness and that seemed wrong to her, that she still hadn't told him, that she was holding off on that ground-breaking news for the right moment. And in truth there *was* no right moment for that kind of news. Her surprise was likely to stretch far beyond anything he had envisaged and breach his trust and relaxation in her company. Once he knew, everything would change in his attitude and *that* was why she was staying silent, she acknowledged ruefully. She would happily live in their little cocoon of togetherness for a few hours more before she let reality in to burst the bubble.

He laid a gift-wrapped parcel onto her lap when she had finished snacking. 'I picked it up in Geneva. It struck me as the sort of thing that you'd like.'

'You shouldn't keep buying me stuff…' she muttered uncomfortably, removing the wrapping paper with care to expose a leather folder. Opening it up, she discovered that it was a travelling sketchbook, one side holding the paper, the other the pencils. 'But this is perfect and so compact too. I'll be able to take it out and about with me. Thanks, but no more gifts, please.'

She fell asleep, only rousing when he slotted her into the cool bed, unwrapping her from the robe, ignoring her drowsy protests.

'You're a very restful woman to be with,' he told her.

'Because I keep on falling asleep?'

'No, because you don't feel the need to fill every silence with idle chatter.'

With a sleepy chuckle she burrowed into her pillows, luxuriating in the heat of him at her back. He wasn't holding her, certainly wasn't spooning her, but he was close and that was enough.

A light trail of kisses down her sensitive spine brought her to wakefulness. 'Hmm…' she framed. 'What time is it?'

'Dawn, best time of the day.'

'I'll take your word for it,' she mumbled, smothering a yawn.

His mouth explored the smooth slope of her shoulder and she squirmed back into the hard heat of his aroused physique. 'Oh… I should shower first.'

'No. You smell of me. I love that,' he growled, closing her into his arms, his big hands glancing across her sensitive nipples and unerringly tracing a fiery path to the damp heat at her core. 'I want you.'

Sunny parted her thighs in silent consent for him to continue and a roughened laugh coursed through his chest. He lifted her leg and sank into her with delicious strength and a soundless sigh escaped her parted lips. He went slow and deep and the excitement climbed through her pliant body in surge after surge until her heart was hammering and little moans were wrenched from her throat. It happened for both of them simultaneously. He slammed into her receptive channel one last time and her body shattered like glass into a writhing orgasm as he reached completion with her.

'Shower or bath?'

'Shower…but you keep your mittens off me,' she warned, suddenly recalling what still lay ahead of her and yet unable to regret a moment of the time they had spent together, lost in intimacy. At least she would have some memories to revisit after she had depth-charged their togetherness out of existence with the announcement she was about to make.

'No choice but to do so if we want to make it back early for Pansy,' he reminded her.

Reality felt as though it had a tight grip round her throat. She slid straight out of bed, grabbed up the robe, pushed her arms into the sleeves and reached the bathroom in record time. Within minutes she was showering, shampooing her hair, working out exactly what she would say to him over breakfast. She tugged on her jeans, wincing at the struggle she had to get the zip up. She completed the outfit with a multicoloured filmy loose blouse and stuck her feet into ballet flats.

Rain was pattering softly down on the balcony when she emerged and saw a table laid for breakfast in the main reception area. She breathed in deep and slow. As soon as they were alone, she murmured quietly, 'I have something important to tell you but I want to ask you to let me do the talking. Please don't rush into judgement. This isn't a scam or a con or anything that really requires your concern. Please don't interrupt me and please contain your reactions and allow yourself time to think in private about what I tell you. First and foremost, we have Pansy to consider and we need a good working relationship to achieve that. Angry words or accusations won't be soon forgotten, so that's why I'm asking you to take a deep breath and say nothing for now.'

His ebony brows had pleated. His lean strong face was taut. Her senses buzzed because he looked so achingly handsome. Her colour rose.

'Obviously, I'm intrigued,' he said.

'You won't be by the time I'm finished,' Sunny forecast heavily. 'When I was twelve years old I suffered a burst appendix and I almost died. Five years later, when I was seventeen, my mother informed me that I would never have children because of the damage done to my reproductive organs. At least, that is presumably what the doctor told her back then. I was shocked. So much that I had taken for granted was taken from me that night, and the next day, when I shared that news with my boyfriend, Jack, he dumped me. He had said he loved me but he wanted children and if I couldn't give him what he wanted, he didn't want me either.'

'Short-sighted.' Raj hadn't been joking when he'd said that he was intrigued. His first thought, which had sent his blood pressure rocketing, was that another man had come into her life. But he found that hard to believe. There was no reluctance in Sunny when she was with him, no sense that her loyalties were divided except when it came to their niece. And that he found perfectly acceptable. A con? A scam? What nonsense was she referring to? And why on earth was she choosing to begin with a detailed rendering of her infertility when he was already aware of her condition?

'Six weeks ago, we were together on your yacht and we were intimate without precautions. You thought it was safe. I also thought it was safe but when I went to the doctor a couple of weeks ago and had tests because I was feeling under par, I learned that I was pregnant.' Sunny rose from her chair and walked across the room. 'I was transfixed. I couldn't believe it. I argued, pointed out that it was impossible. He looked at my notes and told me that after the damage caused by my burst appendix, I had been lucky enough to have repairs carried out by a skilled surgeon…and clearly, I had healed. According to him, I should never have been told that I was infertile and that, at worst, I should only have been warned that I *might* have difficulty conceiving.'

'Sunny,' Raj began tautly, stormy dark eyes locked to her like an impending tidal wave.

'No…no, say nothing,' Sunny reminded him, actually shaking an admonitory finger at him, her voice a little shaky. 'For now, the floor is mine. Last night, you tore the ground out from under my feet. I wasn't expecting all *this*!' She stretched her arms wide to encompass their surroundings, the fireworks and the candlelit bath she would never forget. 'I was going to tell you last night. I wasn't expecting you to tell me that you had parted with the other women in your life. I assumed that, as far as you were concerned, I would be returning to simply being Pansy's aunt again. So, forgive me for not coming clean with you last night. I couldn't face it.

'Now…' Sunny spun back to him, golden hair flying round her flushed features '…let me get the factual stuff out of the way. I'm planning to have this baby and I'm very happy about it, just a little sorry that it's happened the way it has because that's unfortunate for you. You didn't get a choice but then I didn't either. We were both genuinely misled. I'm not considering a termination or adoption or any other option. I'm a strong, independent woman with decent earning power. I don't need anything from you. I don't *want* anything from you.'

'Sunny,' Raj gritted in interruption as he lost patience.

Violet eyes struck his in a heady collision. 'Keep quiet,' she warned him. 'I'm telling you everything you need to know and you should listen. This child need not change your life in any way. You won't need to acknowledge him or her or even see the child. This is *my* child, nothing whatsoever to do with you. I will never tell anyone who fathered my child. If pressured, I will say I had a regrettable one-night stand with a stranger.'

'Regrettable?' Raj growled with incredulous bite.

'Oh, don't take it personally. That's what I would say for the sake of a story that nobody would wish to question further. I don't regret that night, I *couldn't…*' Sunny's tense face suddenly lit up with a guilty smile and there was apology in her eyes as she looked at him. 'It was a wonderful night and it also gave me my heart's secret desire, so I'm never likely to complain about that.'

Raj gritted his teeth again. He saw the prospect of another deal looming in front of him. He would have to negotiate and compromise, and compromising had never come naturally to him. He liked to win. He hated losing. But then this was Sunny, hog-tying him into a remarkably sensible silence to ensure that *he* said nothing rude or unforgivable. A…*baby*. Her heart's desire, his biggest *fear*. The challenge of being a parent when he had never had a parent to respect. Not his hateful father, not the weak mother he had despised but supported out of loyalty and pity. A baby with Sunny, on the way and welcomed by her, at least.

He vaulted upright, relieved from the restraint of remaining silent. 'I don't see why this development should change anything between us,' he spelt out tautly.

Sunny moved forward, looking at him in apparent astonishment. 'But—'

'No, you've had the floor. Now it's my turn,' Raj pronounced gruffly as he locked his hands to her arms and pulled her unexpectedly close. 'There's nothing more to say on that topic for now. But I do need to ask you about hosting an event with me in ten days' time at my London base.'

'An…event?' Sunny whispered, struggling not to sound as though she was struggling with disbelief that he could simply move on and immediately leave her earth-shattering pregnancy announcement behind him.

'It's a fund-raising event for my charitable foundation. However, most of the events I throw are business related. I would appreciate your presence by my side for this one. We're a partnership now and it should be public,' he continued smoothly. 'I'll also organise a maternity wardrobe for you. It's a business expense, don't worry about it.'

Her lower lip parted from her upper in sheer awe at his detachment. He hadn't reacted at all. He had stayed silent just as she had asked and how could she complain about that? Evidently her reassurances that she required no further input from him on the issue of her pregnancy had worked a treat. So, why was she now being ridiculously perverse and wanting to know what his *true* feelings were? After all, hadn't she barred him from expressing those feelings?

'You haven't eaten much for breakfast.'

'I wasn't very hungry,' she confided. 'Nerves got the better of me.'

'Am I that intimidating?' Raj asked softly.

Sunny reddened uncomfortably. 'No, of course not, but I had worked myself up into a real tizz over things.'

'No need. I'm steady as a rock in a crisis. Lived through too many of them to be anything else,' he fielded lightly, easing her even closer while she was wondering if that word 'crisis' was a hint as to his hidden reactions to the news that he was going to become a father.

Raj shifted his hips against her and she stilled, feeling in shock the hard thrust of his arousal even through their clothes. Maybe a crisis turned him on, she thought limply.

'So, if you're not planning to eat anything more, I wondered if…?'

'You're a very demanding guy,' she muttered unevenly.

'And you can be a very demanding woman,' he told her before he dropped his head and kissed her breathless with a ravishing hunger that blew her away.

'Have we…er…got time?' she almost whispered,

me and self-consciousness holding her still and uncertain.

He hoisted her up against him and carried her back into the bedroom and began calmly divesting her of her clothes. 'Jeans are too hard to get you out of,' he complained.

'Won't wear them again,' she mumbled, still stunned by the developments taking place. 'I prefer skirts and these are too tight now.'

'Shush,' Raj hushed her with the heat and passion of his mouth on hers again and excitement raced through her like a rejuvenating drug. She sat up on the bed and began to wrench at his Brioni suit with unappreciative hands. 'You want me?'

'So much,' she said with a helpless shiver.

'I want you the same way,' Raj drawled without hesitation. 'I won't let this development come between us.'

And, half dressed, he pinned her to the bed and took her with raw passion and her climax was breathtaking. All the relief she was experiencing, all the fear she had buried drove her higher and higher and she was splintering into a million pieces when Raj finally pulled away and muttered that it was time to get to the airfield.

'Er...this maternity wardrobe,' she framed uneasily. 'I don't intend to be your newest mistress.'

'If you stand by my side, you should be wearing clothes that ensure that nobody can try to diminish your status in my life,' Raj declared squarely. 'And although it's superficial, people do judge by appearances and I will not allow you to put yourself in a lowly position.'

'So, the clothes will be more for your benefit than mine.'

'You've got it. And by the way,' Raj continued levelly, 'I don't often appear with a woman in public, unless she's an employee, and you will also be acting as my hostess, so why would anyone assume that you are merely a mistress?'

Sunny groaned. 'This sounds like an awful lot to take on…will it be worth the hassle?'

Raj froze and spun back to her as she tried to zip up her jeans again and conceal the fact that it was a struggle for her to do so. 'Am I worth it?' he shot back at her. 'You are worth it to me.'

And Sunny nodded in agreement, dazed by him, her body still singing with pleasure and a steadily mounting sense of peace. He hadn't made a four-act tragedy out of her unexpected pregnancy. He hadn't doubted that the baby was his…at least, she didn't think so. He was taking her fertility in his stride because that was Raj, who would storm on past while other people were still trying to work out what was coming next. She decided that that was a surprisingly soothing response.

They were back at Ashton Hall by mid-morning and Pansy ran across the hall to welcome her back. Scooped up into Sunny's arms, she accepted a hug and reached out a hand to Raj in greeting, grabbing at his sleeve. In response he lifted the little girl from Sunny and swung her high. The hall rang with her delighted chuckles. He suggested taking his niece down to the home farm on the Ashton estate and Sunny was impressed. He had listened when she'd told him how much Pansy enjoyed seeing animals and had already organised a suitable outing.

When they got back to the house, a fashion buyer, organised by Raj, was waiting to see her to take her measurements and consult her preferences in colour and style. The speed with which everything happened on Raj's orders left her breathless. She acquiesced, told herself that she had to adapt to a certain extent, had to at least try and fit in. Just look at how fast he had appeared to adapt to the prospect of a baby! If he could make the effort, so could she, she reasoned.

But *had* Raj adapted? Or was he simply ignoring what he had referred to as 'a development'? There was nothing personal about that attitude. It seemed as though he would accept the baby because he wanted *her* and she had made it clear that she expected nothing more from him. Who could tell what the future would bring? He was granting her the independence she had requested and how could she complain about that? Everything that happened would be her choice and surely that was reassuring?

That evening they dined in the grand dining room, just the two of them. As they went upstairs, Raj caught her hand in his as she would have veered left to her bedroom. 'I had the staff move your stuff while we ate,' he imparted. 'You sleep with me now.'

Sunny swallowed hard. 'And that's it? We don't even discuss it?' she exclaimed.

'What is there to discuss? We're together and we

have no reason to hide the fact,' he pointed out, sounding perfectly logical.

Sunny breathed in slow and deep. 'I'm starting to feel a little taken over, like my life's not mine any more,' she admitted unevenly.

Raj shot her a hard appraisal. 'You're as free as you've always been. All the choices are yours to make.'

'It's just all happening so fast. I suppose I don't like change,' she muttered uncertainly as he released her hand in the manner of a male who had forgotten he was holding it and now regretted ever touching it in the first place.

She could see him mentally stepping back from her and she hated it. She decided it wasn't the moment to take a stance, particularly not when all her belongings had been removed from the room she had been using. 'Never mind. I'm just having a bit of a wobble. I'll get over it,' she insisted, moving on by his side.

'No,' Raj said quietly. 'I think you still have to decide whether or not you want to be with me and embrace all the baggage that comes with me.'

'Right.' Sunny hovered and then followed him. 'I don't like it when you read me that accurately.'

Raj thrust open the door on a massive well-appointed bedroom. 'I've got some work to catch up on,' he said casually. 'I'll see you later.'

And he just left her there, marooned in the centre of the huge room. She wandered into the bathroom and found nothing that belonged to her, eventually discovering a second bathroom that contained her toiletries. The few clothes she had brought were stowed in a separate dressing room. Everything was separate, she realised. He liked his own space too. After a few minutes of uncertainty, she got undressed and finally climbed into the comfortable bed.

Raj was annoyed with her. She knew that. He made decisions lightning fast and expected her to react just as quickly. But that wasn't her nature. He had decided that he wanted her and had met her unwitting demands by getting rid of the other women in his life. But she hadn't known that he would be *willing* to do that, hadn't ever stopped to think what it would mean to *be* with him in a relationship because that had not seemed to be a possibility a few weeks earlier.

So, obviously, having gone to such lengths, Raj expected her to fully accept what she had got herself into and not dilly-dally on the edges of his life fussing about every new step he put in front of her. She was supposed to fall into place automatically. And did she want to do that? Did she want Raj enough to stride boldly into the unknown? Was she just a coward? Or was she trying to protect herself? After all, nobody got to control the future.

And she was already halfway to being in love with him, even if he didn't do 'soppy'. Bailing out at this stage would be foolish, especially when she would be forced to keep on seeing him, particularly when she carried his baby.

She lay alone in the bed for a long time and when he finally came to bed he was quiet and he didn't come close to her at all. She had screwed up. Maybe he had expected her to be pleased and flattered when he moved her into his bedroom. After all, it was quite a statement and it was very Raj, who would refuse to sneak around in his own house when he had nothing to hide. But that statement he had made had, ironically, divided them.

'I've decided that I'm all in,' Sunny admitted as he watched her and Pansy getting in the car to leave the next morning.

His rare smile lit up his lean, darkly handsome face. 'You won't regret it,' he swore.

CHAPTER EIGHT

'I'LL SEE YOU tonight when you arrive and I'll probably rip your clothes off in the first hour,' Raj warned her on the back of a groan. 'It's been a *very* long few days.'

Flushed and with helpless heat coiling in her pelvis like a welcome party, Sunny came off the phone again and walked back into the kitchen where Gemma was pouring tea.

'Was that Raj?' her neighbour asked.

'And you'll be seeing him tonight,' Gemma remarked. 'But it'll still be a challenge conducting a long-distance relationship. He seems to travel all over the place.'

'Yes, I'll learn as I go,' Sunny said lightly. 'And thanks again for stepping into the breach with the animals this evening. I don't mind asking you occasionally, but I don't plan to do it as regularly as this. I'll make other arrangements.'

Gemma assured her that it wasn't a problem but Sunny knew the difference between an occasional favour and a regular demand on someone's time and was determined not to continue putting the other woman out. She had acquired her animals. Her two dogs—Bert was beginning to look more and more like a permanent member of the household—and her cat and her horse, not to mention the ducks saved from certain death when they were dropped off in a box at her gate. She had taken them all in when she was a regular stay-at-home, who rarely went anywhere. They remained her responsibility, nobody else's.

She wondered what her friend would say once she realised that Sunny was pregnant. There would be a lot of gossip and curious looks and she would simply have to deal with it. There was no need to justify a baby she was over the moon to be carrying or defend herself when it was no longer unusual for a woman to choose to have a baby alone. It was, as Raj would say, merely 'a development'.

She drove herself down to London, singing nursery rhymes to Pansy and pointing out animals when the little girl got bored. Raj's London base was a massive house on the Thames. Even getting into the grounds past the security meant being checked off a list and having her car boot searched. Pansy began to grizzle, tired and hungry and fed up.

'Miss Barker…' An older woman dressed in black awaited her at the front door. 'I'm Beth, Mr Belanger's housekeeper.'

She was ushered in like visiting royalty to find that Maria was already waiting for their arrival. The nanny pounced on Pansy and grinned when Sunny told her that her niece needed food and possibly a nap. As Pansy was carried off, Sunny was shown upstairs to the master bedroom suite where she knew all her new clothes would be stored. She flicked through them, finally extracting a long gown in the finest dark blue lace. It was neatly tailored to allow a little more space over the tummy while shaping her other curves. Having previewed the dress online, she had already decided that she would wear it for Raj's event and, rummaging through her new shoe collection, she extracted a navy pair of heels in triumph.

Raj stalked in. 'You're here!' he proclaimed with satisfaction.

'I was working out what to wear tonight,' she told him while wondering how he could look so good with his black hair tousled and his jawline darkly shadowed by stubble. He looked what he was: a very powerful masculine tycoon, awash with volatile energy and buckets of raw sex appeal. Studying him, a visceral tug clenching at the heart of her, she stilled a shiver that had nothing to do with being cold.

'It's been a long week.' He raked long brown fingers through his unruly black hair. 'I didn't expect to miss you.'

Raj almost made that sound like an accusation, as if she should've been with him rather than away from him.

'I'm here now,' she parried lightly. 'Have you seen Pansy yet?'

'She waved her toast at me. She was too busy eating to give me much attention. I'll spend time with her tomorrow.'

'I'm afraid we have to leave early tomorrow morning. I have a painting commission and the buyer's in a hurry.'

Raj lifted an imperious brow. 'The buyer will have to wait.'

'No, I agreed to work with his time limit,' Sunny broke in.' It's his mother's favourite flower and it's for her birthday. I need to make a start on it tomorrow. I'm delighted that it will be finding a home with someone who will truly appreciate it.'

His shapely sexy mouth tightened. 'I'm already a keen convert. I've got a glorified weed hanging above my bed. I truly appreciate it too for all that intricate detail.'

And she finally noticed that it was her painting hanging there on the wall and she smiled with pleasure that he had given it a place in his bedroom. She moved closer, almost mesmerised by the pulsing masculine energy and charisma of him that close and the way that aura pulled her in. 'I missed you too but I can't keep on taking so much time away from home. I have to work. I have to look after my animals.'

'We'll discuss all that later,' Raj asserted. 'Right now I only want—'

'To rip my clothes off? Please don't rip anything,' she said very seriously. 'Until I take possession of my new wardrobe…thank you, by the way… I'm low on clothes that fit and most of the stuff in the new wardrobe is fancy stuff for when I'm with you.'

His big hands framed her cheekbones. 'Stop fussing. I promise there will be no ripping of any kind,' he swore very seriously as he whipped her top over her head and dropped it on the floor and went looking for the zip on her jeans.

'Why are your jeans so big?'

'To allow for expansion,' she muttered in embarrassment, rolling the elasticated waist of her maternity jeans down over her hips, mortified by his question. She might not have expanded quite enough to need actual maternity wear but her own clothing was already too tight for comfort.

He tipped up her chin and his mouth came crashing down with passionate force on hers, his tongue darting deep into the sensitive interior of her mouth, and a long shudder racked her, heat and craving infiltrating her with fresh energy.

Raj lifted her off her feet and laid her on the bed, flipping off her shoes and yanking off her jeans with scant ceremony. He surveyed her with maddening intensity. 'You are fit for this, aren't you? Maybe you're too tired or not well?' he suggested awkwardly, and it was an endearing awkwardness, as if he was unaccustomed to making such personal enquiries.

Sunny stretched up and yanked him by his tie down to her level. 'I'm ready and willing and you promised me.'

A smile slashed Raj's stubborn, wilful mouth. 'I did, didn't I?'

His hands found hers and pinned them to the bed while he kissed her with fiery hunger. The whole time she was conscious of the mobile phone buzzing in his pocket. Finally, he wrenched his lips from hers, sucked in oxygen and answered the call, speaking in brief sentences as he levered himself back off the bed. He dug the phone back in his pocket.

'I've overbooked you,' he groaned. 'We have no time for this no matter how much I want you.'

'You've overbooked *me*?' As Sunny sat up tense with incomprehension, Raj lifted her discarded garments, shook them out and set them carefully beside her. 'Get dressed,' he urged.

'Are you joking?'

'Only wish I were but you need time to dress for our guests and I also need you to come downstairs right now to look at something,' he told her ruefully.

Sunny stole a doubtful glance at the arousal tenting the fine fabric of his tailored trousers and reddened. 'You'd better close your jacket.'

'I'm sorry. I got carried away.' He sighed, shooting her a burnished dark look of hungry regret.

Sunny got dressed again in a hurry and then gasped in horror when she saw her reflection. Having tidied her mussed hair, she followed him back downstairs into an imposing drawing room. Raj settled her down in a seat. Two men lugging a chained metal security box entered and settled it at his feet before beginning to unlock it.

'It's a rare blue diamond. I wanted to see if it suited you.'

A pendant was lifted out of another internal box with reverent care and Raj swept it up to thread it round her neck. Sunny squinted down at the glittering stone.

'Look at me,' he urged.

And she did.

'I'll take it,' Raj pronounced with satisfaction.

'I can't accept this…' she hissed at him, stretching up to his ear as she began to unclasp the item.

'It's an investment,' Raj declared.

Sunny cradled the magnificent diamond nervously in the palm of her hand. 'It's the most amazing blue.'

'The boron atoms in the carbon atoms,' he explained. 'It reflects your eyes.'

'I can't accept something this valuable as a gift.'

'I want you to wear it this evening.'

'OK, but I'm not keeping it. Be warned…it'll only be round my neck on loan and as a favour to you.'

Troubled by the appearance of so evidently expensive a jewel, Sunny checked on Pansy, who was in her bath with Maria looking after her, before heading for the shower and working on her own presentation. Fully dressed and feeling very fancy, she picked her passage down the stairs in her high heels, the glorious diamond glittering below her collarbone like a breathtaking statement of wealth and exclusivity.

Raj strolled towards her, brilliant dark eyes radiating satisfaction. 'You look magnificent.'

'Thank you, but I'm starting to feel just a little too like a dress-up doll,' she confided in a low voice. 'Like I'm not really allowed to be me any more.'

Raj frowned and a photographer stepped forward to take photos of them as well as record the arrival of the most important guests. The evening was aimed at raising funds for Raj's charitable foundation and, in particular, a chain of children's hospices. Sunny recognised occasional well-known faces from the media and strove not to get self-conscious when Raj introduced her to everyone as his hostess. She saw the curiosity roused by that label and the attention commanded by the guiding hand he kept clamped to her spine. Drinks were served in the ballroom, all the catering handled by uniformed professionals. Speeches were made before the buffet was opened and it turned into a glitzy social occasion.

Raj was constantly mobbed. Beautiful women in over-the-top revealing dresses endeavoured to catch his eye and sparkle with jokes and one-liners, touching his arms, any part of him they could decently reach, striving to make a connection with him. Meanwhile, Sunny felt as though she was on display like a show pony. Her diamond pendant was repeatedly oohed and aahed over and she learned that it was a famous diamond, mined in Australia. The superb pendant began to feel like an albatross weighing down her neck. Whenever sheer curiosity prompted someone to try and get into closer conversation with her, Raj whisked her away, shielding her from everybody.

'It's nobody's business who you are,' he pointed out. 'That's private.'

'I've got nothing to be ashamed of, nothing to hide,' Sunny told him gently. 'And it's not a private event, because official photos are being taken at every turn.'

'It's my role to protect you,' Raj informed her with finality.

Sunny pictured a coffin lid slamming down on top of her. Raj would be happiest to lock her in a box and it would be *his* box, kept locked and accessible only to him. He needed to learn that she had spent a lot of time tied to home by her grandmother's declining health and, although she would willingly make that same sacrifice again, she would not make that same sacrifice of freedom or independence for any man alive. She valued her ability to do as she liked, wear what she liked, speak to whom she liked and no way would Raj be allowed to deprive her of those choices. She had been willing to make adjustments to fit in with his lifestyle but she wasn't prepared to give way to every demand and expectation.

'I've been thinking about your idea of leaving early tomorrow,' Raj mused later that evening when the last guests had departed.

'It wasn't an idea,' Sunny pointed out on the way upstairs, where she paused on the landing to step out of her shoes and carry them, flexing her pinched toes. 'It was a decision and it's already done and dusted.'

'There are *other* options,' Raj imparted as he thrust open the door of their bedroom. 'Don't close your mind to the alternatives or the solution.'

'No, there aren't any other options, not when it comes to my commissions and taking care of Pansy and my animals,' Sunny replied briskly, refusing to be drawn into a dialogue when she had no intention of changing her stance. 'I can only do those things at home.'

'I have a file for you to look over…a property file,' Raj told her, level dark eyes resting on her bemused gaze with a curious air of expectancy.

'I'm not moving anywhere. I'm staying put where I am.' Disconcerted by that new mystifying turn to the conversation, Sunny became even more tense.

'I think I could change your mind about that.' Raj swept a fat file off a nearby table and extended it to her. 'Skim over it and see. I own a lot of property and I can staff any one of them for you.'

'Well, you *would* think that you could change my mind, but you'd be wrong in this instance. My goodness, Raj, you could talk your way out of your allotted place in heaven and end up in the depths of hell out of pure obstinacy. You don't take a hint, you're relentless...quit while you're ahead!' she advised, moving her hand out of range of the file and walking into the bathroom she had been using.

She was letting herself get worked up and she told herself off for not hanging onto her cool, but Raj had the capacity to make her feel cornered and she had no intention of letting him get away with that. Grabbing up her toiletries bag, she gathered up her necessities and then paused to detach the diamond at her throat. She set it down on the dresser top and padded on into the dressing room, where she retrieved her own clothes and nightwear and fresh underwear for the next morning.

'What on earth are you doing?' Raj demanded fiercely. 'What are we arguing about?'

'You're clever enough to know the answer to that question,' Sunny replied, wrapping her possessions together into a bundle, toiletries bag clutched awkwardly below one arm as she tried to sidestep him. 'I'm not sleeping in here with you.'

'Sunny!' As she opened the door to leave, he stalked after her. 'If you walk out of here right now, I will be angry with you.'

'And if I don't walk out, I'll be guilty of murder,'

she confided tightly, hurrying down the corridor to the room she had used before.

Since she had taken off her shoes, her dress was trailing and she tripped up on the hem. She went sprawling with a gasp of fright, her belongings flying everywhere. Tears of frustration burned the backs of her eyes as she began to pick herself up again, grateful she hadn't hurt herself. A hand at her elbow, Raj levered her upright with care and crouched down to snatch up some of the stuff she had dropped as she did the same.

'This is crazy. I don't do scenes like this,' he censured.

'That's why I left your room,' Sunny said with as much dignity as she could muster, bundling everything up again.

'You could've fallen down the stairs.'

'But I *didn't*.' Sunny thrust open the door of the room she was determined to use.

Raj watched her lift her nose in the air, her chin at an angle, her spine rigid. What the hell was he supposed to have done? Frustration and impatience combined inside him, making him feel explosive.

He settled the property file down at the foot of the bed where she could browse through it once she had calmed down. Sunny dropped her clothing on the bed and carted the toiletries bag into the en suite bathroom.

'Tell me what I did,' he gritted, lounging back against the door to close it with a push of his big shoulders. 'Shouldn't I at least know what I'm supposed to have done?'

'You warned me that you hadn't been in a relationship before. I should have listened more, expected less. I feel like you're trying to take me over by stealth,' Sunny admitted unhappily. 'I'm not a business acquisition, Raj. I'm not a problem you have to cure, a breakage you have to fix. I'll never be perfect and that's fine with me but maybe it's not fine with you. Maybe you're only able to be satisfied with a sophisticate in a fancy designer dress with a whopping great diamond round her throat.'

'It was a business event and you wore a normal evening outfit. I wanted you to feel that you fitted in to improve your confidence.'

'There's nothing wrong with my confidence,' Sunny lied, unwilling to cede that she had felt more at ease during the evening because she had blended in with the other guests. 'But I have a life and I like my life as it is. I knew I would have to make allowances to fit into your life and I've done that. I'm travelling. I'm leaving my animals. I'm cutting my working hours back. I'm wearing the clothes you insisted on buying me. I even wore that diamond tonight to please you. But I'm *not* moving house for your benefit. I'm *not* prepared to keep on handing Pansy to a nanny for your benefit either!'

'Be fair, Sunny,' Raj urged. 'Maria has generally only looked after Pansy at bedtime and when you're in bed yourself. You're entitled to use an occasional babysitter when you're with her the rest of the time.'

'But when will you make compromises for my benefit?' Sunny asked boldly. 'You see, you expect me to do all the compromising. When I'm difficult, it's like a chess game with you in which you make moves to corner me.'

Raj elevated an ebony brow. 'A little dramatic…?'

'No, I'm not being dramatic!' Sunny shot back at him, her hands on her hips. 'You make everything sound so logical! The clothes, the stupid diamond, the nanny! But I don't want to change and I don't want to move house either.'

'Do you want me?' Raj asked with lethal composure. 'Let's face it, it all comes down to how much you want me. I've already changed my habits and routine for you, which is something I've never done for a woman before. This is all new for me as well. So, you don't wish to move house? If I accept that, how could I ever visit you in your current home? Where would my security team stay? How would they guard the property?'

Sunny threw up a silencing hand. 'Don't say anything more!' she gasped, stricken.

'Are you aware that Pansy, as my niece, should have a bodyguard as well?' Raj continued inexorably. 'And what about you, since you have conceived my child? Don't you realise that your security in your little rural nest could be targeted by people who would want to access my money through you? Those are harsh truths, Sunny. They may not be what you want to hear but they are reality all the same.'

Sunny had turned bone white as he spelled out those hard facts. No, she hadn't thought about security needs for any of them. But Raj had said something that had cut her in two and made it almost impossible to maintain her concentration.

Do you want me? Let's face it, it all comes down to how much you want me.

She wanted him way too much for her own peace of mind. Way too much for sanity. He already had her craving him like an addictive drug. It was too much, the way she was feeling was *too much.* All her emotions were jangling inside her and rising up in a flood from a tumultuous base.

She breathed in deep, pale and stiff as board. 'I think we should break up.'

'We're not travelling in that direction. We haven't been together long enough for you to make a logical decision on that score,' Raj decreed without hesitation.

'You can't tell me what I can and cannot do,' Sunny flung at him angrily.

'I'm not trying to do that. I'm asking you to take a deep breath and calm down.'

'Calm down? Isn't that what men always say when a woman disagrees with them?' Sunny flared, trying to thrust him out of her path to enable her to open the door behind him.

He was too big and he was as solid as a rock but once she'd registered her intent he flung up his expressive hands in exasperation and stepped out of her path. 'Think about this. Think about what you're doing and why.'

Sunny yanked open the door with positive violence and scrutinised him with fierce violet-blue eyes. 'You're dumped.'

'Seriously?' Raj elevated another expressive black brow as if she were throwing a strop about nothing.

'Just because it hasn't happened to you before doesn't mean it can't happen,' Sunny hissed and, marching back from the door, she scooped up the property file and walked back to plant it into his reluctant arms.

'Adults talk problems through, sort things out,' Raj informed her.

And she wanted to hit him. The violence coursing through her terrified her. She had a mental image of pushing him out of the door and pushing until he fell down the stairs. And then that image crumpled at the picture of him being physically hurt because that was more than she could bear in the highly emotional mood she was in. No, she didn't want to hurt him, she wanted to shut him up, bounce him out of his inhuman calm and control and make him leave.

'We can't be sorted. We're a hellish mess together.'

'We could do better than this,' Raj conceded with pronounced reluctance. 'It's a question of cooperation. Why are you so angry with me?'

Sunny gritted her teeth. 'You're trying to move me into one of your mansions!'

'Some women would be reasonably happy about that,' Raj dared to declare.

'I'm not!' she almost shrieked at him in her ire, scared of listening or believing lest he begin to talk her round.

'I could buy up all the land round you and extend your house,' Raj remarked. 'You see, I can compromise in a sensible way, but, admittedly, only when I'm forced. I am a challenging character. I acknowledge that.'

'You didn't even allow me the freedom to speak to your guests this evening!' Sunny accused, heading off on a new tack.

'My guests were too curious about you and I didn't want you to put yourself in a position where you might drop too many private facts, which could later cause you embarrassment or hurt. You are very innocent and trusting with the people that you meet. I admire that quality in you. But it makes you very vulnerable. You take an optimistic view of life, a view that is directly opposed to my own. I am more cynical, and my motivation this evening was to look after you, not to clip your wings or to stifle your natural friendliness.'

'Don't talk down to me! Go back to your own room,' Sunny hurled at him, because she already knew that Raj could undoubtedly reason himself out of anything short of murder.

'We'll talk tomorrow,' Raj breathed with finality, and he walked out, shoulders squared, back straight as a board.

No, they wouldn't be talking tomorrow, Sunny decided fiercely. She would leave at the crack of dawn, go home, move on with her life, rediscover the pleasures she had neglected since Raj had entered her life and thrown everything up in the air. Of course, she would still have to maintain his connection to Pansy and make those visits every month. And eventually the baby would presumably enter that arrangement as well, she thought abstractedly. For the first time, he had referred to the baby other than as a 'development'. And he had referred to the baby as being *his* child. Well, her baby wasn't his child, it was *hers.*

Every just bone in her body was jarred by that unkind thought and she winced for herself and got ready for bed. But some of what Raj had told her about their *security* needs lingered heavily with her. Were she, Pansy and their unborn child at risk because of their connection to the richest man in the world? Why had she not foreseen that danger for herself? Why had she been so blind about that harsh reality? Raj was right, she didn't like stuff of that nature, always shut out such frightening possibilities. Guilt folded round her that she had forced Raj to spell out the obvious. Suddenly she was appreciating that she had never been in full control of her relationship with Raj, nor would she ever be. Not when their baby's very safety could be compromised by some ghastly threat.

Seriously shaken by such thoughts but unable to see what she could possibly do to remedy the situation other than distance them all from Raj, she set her alarm for an ungodly early hour. Life without Raj, life without the excitement and the host of other responses he sparked in her. For goodness' sake, she had been on her own and perfectly happy that way for years and she would be again, she promised herself. She would bury herself in her work. She would have *two* children to raise. She still had the house to finish. Exhaustion finally plunged her into sleep.

CHAPTER NINE

GALES OF LAUGHTER greeted Sunny before she even made it into Pansy's bedroom.

It was five-thirty in the morning and faint purple shadows lay like fading bruises below Sunny's eyes. She had put on more make-up than usual because she felt like a mess and the sight of Raj down on the floor playing with their niece, who was still clad in her pyjamas, was the last thing she needed in the mood she was in. She had been hoping to leave his home without seeing him again.

Stunning dark golden eyes sought out her evasive gaze with determination. 'I wanted to see her before you left. She hasn't had her breakfast yet. Maria helped me change her…er nappy. Pansy thought that was very funny because I was fumbling and slow and she kicked me while I was trying to work out the tapes.'

'This is the best time of the day for her. She's always full of joy and nonsense,' Sunny told him unevenly, bending down to lift her niece, who had come running with a smile as soon as she'd appeared. Pansy gave her a noisy kiss and then indicated that she wanted to get down again and return to playing with Raj.

Raj was down on the floor, sheathed in faded jeans

and a T-shirt, the casual attire not screening an inch of his glorious long muscular frame. He had lined up little cars for Pansy to rearrange. 'I thought she would only like girl things but she brought the cars to me.'

'She changes her mind from one day to the next. She plays with everything. I'll get her breakfast now and… I suppose, see you next month, however we organise it,' she muttered, desperate to escape because he looked so natural down there on the floor with Pansy.

So natural and so very handsome with his high, sharply defined cheekbones, sculpted lips and hard masculine jawline, not to mention the lean, powerful body clearly defined by well-worn denim. He'd been correct when he had said he had changed, he *had* adapted. The guy she had first met in his designer suit would not have put himself forward in the same way, would not have worked at interacting with a toddler, would not have overcome his own misgivings and awkwardness to such an extent. And she respected him for the huge effort he had made and knew that she would never do anything to undermine his relationship with Pansy.

After all, he was still the man she loved, still the male she had dumped in a clumsy effort to get her own life back…only to finally register that perhaps getting her own life back would never be possible.

'I'm sorry,' she said abruptly. 'I'm sorry for some of what I said. 'I know your intentions were good.'

'Don't doubt that,' he told her with assurance. 'You need space to think.'

No, she thought ferociously, she didn't need space to

think, she needed to work out how to raise a defensive resistance, how to remain pleasant and friendly without intimacy. It was no help to have Raj there on the floor in front of her, displaying all the characteristics that she found irresistible. That quick and clever mind, that cool inescapable grasp of logic in control. And then there was the long, sleek, utterly sensual length of him, able to offer so much amazing pleasure, that pleasure, that excitement that she had never known before and therefore was so much more vulnerable to receiving.

She craved him in the most basic ways and that was a wake-up call for her to be on her guard, not to settle for superficial stuff but to hold on hard to her defences. Raj had made her crave sex. Just acknowledging that embarrassed her in his radius. Here she was, a victim of a weakness that she had never dreamt even existed. She might have ditched him but she still wanted him.

Raj departed and she got Pansy dressed for breakfast and took her downstairs but still the recollection of Raj lingered. Raj *trying*, Raj *adapting*, Raj proving that he could change, just as she *could* change, she reminded herself ruefully.

Sunny was climbing into her car, ready to leave, when Raj appeared at her window. She lowered it, mindful of a desire not to behave as though she was running away like a coward. He gazed down at her, dark as night eyes brooding, and it was so sexy that her toes curled in response. He had amazingly long lashes, amazingly penetrating dark eyes. Wake up, girl, she urged herself, striving to escape from the charismatic spell he cast.

'So, see you next month,' she said brightly, feeling like an idiot.

'Any doctor's appointments that I need to know about?' Raj enquired perfectly politely.

'Well, yes, my first ultrasound,' she confided reluctantly. 'In a couple of weeks.'

'I won't want to miss that,' Raj assured her.

'But we never talked about this…about the exact level of your involvement…if any,' she reminded him.

'Be fair. You wouldn't *let* me,' he pointed out quietly.

'I'll send you the date,' she proffered thinly, because stepping away from the intimacy, setting herself free from her longing for Raj meant going cold turkey and decreasing any closer connections.

'Don't try to shut me out,' he breathed with sudden urgency. 'This is my first child. This is *very* exciting for me.'

And she thought of that admission the whole drive home.

Exciting for me.

No, she hadn't expected that from Raj. Something so basic and yet, so life-changing, she acknowledged ruefully. Of course, he was curious. Of course, he was excited. This would be his *first* child. Pansy had softened him up, made him aware of children in so many basic ways, and now he was ready for that challenge. And she? She had tried to shut him out, without intending that, without meaning to do that to him. She had leapfrogged over all the reasons that he couldn't cut her off to pretend as though none of those things was happening.

She hadn't allowed him to talk about his feelings about the baby she had conceived. She had denied him that outlet. My word, she had been selfish, trying to shut him out from what would soon be as much his business as hers. And all so that she could redraw her boundaries for his benefit to keep him at a distance. My baby, *not* yours, my child, *none* of your business.

She had behaved badly. She had forced him into a corner by making her own assumptions as to how he would react. Yet the truth was that Raj was not the guy she had assumed he was when they first met. He was a male ever willing to grow and move on to fresh territory. Her brain could not handle that conundrum when she was so very aware that she had ditched him.

A week later, Sunny wakened to the dogs barking and Pansy crying. Wondering weakly if she could have slept in, she rolled out of bed. Her mobile phone was ringing and the doorbell was buzzing and both at the same time. Grabbing up her robe with her brow furrowed, she hurried off to deal with Pansy first.

Through the glazed front door she saw dark shadows suggesting that more than one person was crowded on her doorstep. She sped into Pansy's room to retrieve her niece. The toddler hugged close, she returned to her bedroom to answer the phone. It was Gemma.

'Sunny? I had a journalist on my doorstep yesterday asking questions about you. I sent him about his business but my neighbour told me that there's an article about you in the paper today. I'm bringing it round. It's a lot of drivel!'

Conscious of the hubbub round her front door and that people with cameras were trying to look in through her windows, Sunny retreated to the kitchen to let the dogs out. She lifted her mobile to answer it when it rang again. Raj's cool, level voice greeted her.

'I've sent help to keep the crowd of paparazzi in control…and I'll drop in later in person. Don't read the newspapers for a day or two,' Raj advised.

A knock sounded on the back door. Then it opened a mere few inches. 'Miss Barker? Mr Belanger sent me with my team. I'm Sam and we're clearing the paps from your garden back onto the road where the police will handle them if they obstruct the flow of traffic. I suggest you let the dogs back indoors again. I had to detach the little one from a man's ankle.' Bert was handed through the ajar door, little round eyes huge at the indignity, spindly legs pedalling frantically in mid-air. 'He's ferocious, isn't he?'

'Sometimes,' Sunny conceded, because Bert could also be very cuddly, but she really didn't care if he'd frightened off any unwanted intruders with cameras. As she grabbed Bert, Bear squeezed past Sam into the kitchen and sat down, relieved, it seemed, to be away from all the noise and fuss.

In twenty minutes, Sunny had changed and dressed Pansy, and contrived to freshen up in the bathroom. Then she fed the dogs, put on the kettle and gave Pansy her breakfast. By that time, Gemma was at the back door.

'My word, there's a huge number of journalists out on the road. A policeman was trying to move them on and then there are…*private* security people here helping out?' she queried in fascination. 'All suited and wearing sunglasses and those earpieces, looking like they belong in a James Bond movie.'

'They're courtesy of Raj,' Sunny confided breathlessly.

Gemma was surprised. 'But I thought that was over.'

'Evidently he'll still look out for our welfare,' Sunny said with a slight shrug.

Gemma spread a crumpled tabloid newspaper on the table. There were far more photos of Christabel than there were of Sunny. But then her late half-sister had been both glamorous and well known. In fact there was only one photo of Sunny, depicting her by Raj's side at the fund-raising event at Ashton Hall. She could have done, however, without reviewing photos of Christabel falling out of various nightclubs, obviously under the weather, and she certainly would have preferred not to see the scene of the car crash again that had taken her half-sister and brother-in-law's lives.

'They're trying to insinuate that you're a druggie too.'

'No, I think they were short of dirt to serve up, so they rehashed poor Christabel's worst moments instead. My only public profile is as an artist and you can't get much mileage out of that.'

'They're madly speculating about you and Raj… and, er, *that* diamond.'

'It was on loan. Raj did warn me that there'd be a lot of speculation.'

'Apparently, he's never shown off an actual girlfriend before and they're wondering if it's just a family connection linked to Pansy or something *more*,' Gemma proffered as Sunny speed-read through the article, catching the use of certain words to describe her that suggested she might be a little weird with her penchant for long skirts, animals and wild foraging.

'So, they know about Pansy.' Sunny sighed. 'That won't please Raj.'

'The press have probably always known about her. They just weren't interested in the poor child until you came along and developed a bond with her uncle.'

'Unca,' Pansy said on cue.

'Uncle,' Sunny corrected.

Pansy went off into her 'nose…eye…mouth' spiel.

'Look, I'll clear off now. I know you have that painting to finish. Do you want me to take the dogs with me?'

'Thanks, but there's no need while I'm here.' Sunny saw the older woman to the back door and recommended that she use the shortcut across the paddock to avoid the men with cameras.

She finished her painting while Pansy was enjoying a nap, and was getting cleaned up when she heard a helicopter overhead. She had put on a green sundress although in the autumnal cool it was a little chilly for it, but it still fitted her when so many other items had become too tight. When she heard the helicopter coming in to land, she ran outside, paused a moment to soothe Muffy, who was shifting anxiously in her stall, and then walked on out to see Raj arriving. A bunch of security men fanned out in a circle round the craft and then Raj sprang out, black hair ruffling in the breeze and so vital and so intensely masculine that she clenched her teeth together on a visceral inner tightening that had nothing to do with nerves and everything to do with desire.

He strode towards her, effortlessly elegant in a mid-grey designer suit that faithfully outlined his broad shoulders, lean hips and long powerful legs to the manner born. He looked amazing and utterly out of place in a paddock. He was metropolitan fashionable and immaculate and even as she watched cameras were lifting above the boundary hedge to catch photos of his arrival and she winced.

Raj ignored the cameras but several of his security team went running in their direction.

'You didn't need to come all this way.'

'A slight detour. I'm on my way back from Scotland. It wasn't a problem,' he countered, striding ahead of her to thrust open the back door into the kitchen. 'How are you managing all this? Have the paps been annoying you much?'

'Not with your security men keeping them away from the windows and out of the garden,' she fielded lightly. 'In fact, I actually finished my painting this morning.'

'You'll have to let me see it.' Raj sank down at the kitchen table right in front of the newspaper she had intended to cram into the recycling bin. 'I see you didn't take my advice… I can't say that surprises me.'

'Coffee?' she prompted, keen to change the subject.

Raj assented with a nod but he was too busy scrutinising the article to look back at her. In any case, she was still in his mind's eye, all soft and flowy in a simple green dress, relaxed, casual, golden hair a little rumpled. She was sort of squinting at him too, which meant that she hadn't got her contact lenses in and probably had mislaid her spectacles again. There was a tiny streak of yellow paint above her brow. He breathed in deep and slow and strove to study the newsprint instead.

'I hate the way they've associated you with Christabel. I shouldn't say it, but she was very bad news for Ethan. He was a grown man but he was easily led. He liked anything that got him high and she was much the same and when the other men came into the picture, it was almost impossible to keep him steady and sober. I tried to get him into rehab but Christabel wouldn't have it, said I had no right to interfere. And she was right, but their child was there by then and someone had to speak up and try to make a judgement call.'

Sunny had paused in making the coffee to stare at him. 'Christabel had other men?' she murmured in shock.

'I'm sorry. I assumed you would know. She wasn't exactly secretive or discreet about it. Ethan wasn't enough for her and her acting career had crashed because of the drugs. She craved attention and her lovers gave her that. I should've got him out of the marriage, but he still loved her. I could've bought her off. If I had, Ethan would still be alive…they both might be. I failed him.' Raj's dark eyes were bleak with pain and regret and her heart went out to him. 'He needed a save but

I was the wrong person to help. He resented me, so I stepped back.'

'I'm so sorry, Raj. I totally misunderstood the situation when I accused you of spoiling him by indulging him,' she whispered gruffly.

'My mother did the spoiling. Ethan was the centre of her world and when she died, he went to pieces. I had to pick up those pieces and he hated that too.'

'And where were you when all this spoiling was happening?' she asked curiously.

'Studying at one or another university, winning prizes and newspaper column inches, setting up my first companies. I didn't see much of either of them growing up, so I didn't have the chance to develop a normal sibling relationship with Ethan.'

'Someone has to be willing to accept help to *be* helped,' she mused reflectively. 'Sometimes all you can do is stand back and mind your own business. There's nothing in that newspaper article that upset me, other than the writer choosing to rehash Christabel's most public mistakes.'

'The press won't leave you alone now. That's *my* fault too. I shouldn't have shown you off at the fundraiser at Ashton.'

'You probably shouldn't have come here to see me either. That will only incite more rumours.' Sunny sighed.

Raj pushed back the chair, his lean, strong face taut. 'I won't let that keep me away from you. I want you and Pansy and the baby in my life. Surely you can understand that?'

The super-gifted male with everything had never had a proper family and quite naturally he now wanted what he had never had.

'I do understand it,' she conceded quietly.

The silent tension between them smouldered. Sunny looked away first just as Bear roamed a little too close to Bert's basket and Bert leapt out and began to bark in a passion at the larger dog.

Raj stood up. 'Stop it!' he thundered down at the chihuahua.

Bert's big round eyes bulged and he fell silent. Then he turned in his tracks and raced back into his basket.

'He only needs a firm word.'

'From a man, I suspect. His late owner was a man. Certainly, Bert doesn't listen to me like that.' Sunny viewed the little dog curled up in his basket as if he would not dream of hurling a rude challenge at another animal. He was perfectly calm.

Raj studied her with veiled eyes. They had a problem, a major problem, and he wasn't even sure that she recognised the fact. Sunny was too busy trying to stay in control of everything, including him...had he been the sort of guy willing to accept that. He believed that, fortunately for all of them, he was *not* that guy. Look at the chaos she had already created with her determined attempt to keep him out of their lives! But, if they married, he would have all three of them under his protection. Sunny, Pansy, his child. That was what needed to happen. That would fix the situation, he decided with cold logic.

'Sunny...' Raj breathed without warning. 'Marry me.'

Sunny blinked and stared incredulously back at him. 'Raj—'

'I mean it. I don't want the three of you on a sporadic visiting basis. I want you all permanently. Marriage is the logical next step forward for us and it will overcome many of the irritations currently making your life difficult. If you're my wife, I can shield you from all such annoyances. I will not have you depicted in the press as some temporary occupant in my bed, a target for insinuation and rumour. Nor do I want my child becoming a target.'

He closed his hands over hers and tugged her closer.

'You've shocked me,' she whispered truthfully, shaking her head as if to clear it of the mental fog that had engulfed her. 'I really wasn't expecting this.'

A big hand rested against her breast. 'Your heart's racing.'

Sunny tensed, wanting his fingers to stroke, cup, caress, colour flaring in her cheeks. 'It's not every day I get a marriage proposal. In fact, this is my very first.'

'So, say yes,' Raj husked softly.

'And you'll promise not to be bossy and overprotective any more?'

'I don't think you'd credit that kind of promise from me.'

The doorbell was buzzing again and she backed away with a sigh. 'That must be a real visitor,' she assumed. 'Or your security wouldn't have let them past the gate.'

She walked out to the hall and opened the front door and was completely disconcerted to find Jack Henderson on the step. Jack smiled warmly at her, something he hadn't done in her vicinity since their breakup as teenagers. 'Jack?' she whispered questioningly.

'I was worried about you in the midst of all this newspaper madness. It's not you. You like a quiet life.'

'I do, but Raj is here and I'll be fine. The fuss will die down.'

'Raj Belanger, right?' Jack checked, his mouth twisting. 'Pansy's uncle?'

'That's correct.'

'As soon as he leaves, you'll be all right.'

A strong arm closed round her taut figure from the back. 'Sunny will be leaving *with* me,' Raj decreed.

Her lashes fluttered in bewilderment. 'But—'

'When I'm here, Sunny doesn't have to worry about anything,' Raj delivered with precision. 'Thank you for the thought but she is not in need of assistance. Unlike you, I would never abandon her when life gets rough.'

Paling at that derisive challenge, Jack turned on his heel and walked back down the path.

Sunny was aghast. She twisted her head. 'How the heck could you say that to him?'

'Easily. He ran out on you when you needed support. I would never do that to you.'

CHAPTER TEN

SUNNY FOLDED HER ARMS. 'So, according to you, I'm leaving here *with* you.'

Raj shrugged a broad shoulder. 'You haven't given me an answer yet to my proposal.'

Sunny was thinking about being married to Raj. The prospect made her feel quite dizzy when what she really needed to do was to keep her feet on the ground and her brain at full functioning capacity. 'There would have to be negotiation.'

'Of course. Conditions?'

'You would have to travel less and choose one property as a family base for the sake of the children.'

'Children,' Raj stressed. 'Not a feature of life I ever expected to experience. And then you came along.'

'Yes, I came along and being with me will entail certain adjustments in your lifestyle. Children need a home and stability,' Sunny declared. 'You can't continue to flit from one property to another because children need to attend schools and enjoy recreational activities. Not only do they need a routine to thrive, they also need to socialise with other children. None of that can be achieved with a father who expects them to travel with him and who flies somewhere virtually every day.'

'Not every day,' Raj qualified with a frown. 'We'll use my London base as a home but there will be times when travel is unavoidable.'

Sunny gazed back at him. The prospect of a father for Pansy and her unborn child was a huge draw but the prospect of simply having constant access to the man she loved was the more powerful attraction.

'I appreciate that this is not romantic in the least,' Raj conceded wryly as he tugged her up against him with a gruff sound deep in his chest that reverberated through her slighter, smaller frame like a wake-up call of sensual response. He pushed her hair back from her face and claimed her soft lips with hungry, driving intensity and she shivered against him, insanely conscious of the long hard thrust of his erection and the dampness between her legs.

'That doesn't matter,' she muttered. 'You can't do romantic if you can't do love.'

'And I'm definitely not likely to be doing that,' Raj drawled impatiently.

'I just want you,' she said truthfully. 'And I want to be happy. How is this massive change in our lives going to work?'

'The good news is…you just leave it all to me. Pack what you need for twenty-four hours and everything else will be transported to you tomorrow,' Raj told her. 'Muffy can go to Ashton Hall and the dogs and the cat, of course, can be with us by this evening.'

Breathless at those ideas, Sunny whispered apologetically, 'And there's ducks down by the pond in the bottom corner of the paddock.'

Raj breathed in deep. 'Not a problem,' he declared. 'Now go and pack while I make the arrangements.'

Sunny hovered in the doorway. 'Where will we get married?'

'Ashton. It's licensed for ceremonies.'

'Could the vicar at my church do the honours? And I've friends and neighbours here who I'd like to invite,' she said quietly.

'Of course.'

Sunny stayed in the doorway. 'You shouldn't have blamed Jack for the way he treated me. He was only seventeen at the time, as was I.'

'He made you feel defective,' Raj contradicted. 'He wanted perfect and you don't get perfect in this life. He was cruel and he had years in which to think better of his treatment of you and offer his regrets. But he never *did*, did he?'

Her eyes dropped from his as she reflected on how much it would have meant to her had Jack thought better of his comments at the time. 'No, you're right, he didn't.'

'Rest assured that I will never ever expect perfect, but I will not allow those who hurt you to go unpunished,' he extended grimly. 'You're too soft, too forgiving, but that balances out my more cynical, harsh nature.'

'I'll go and pack. What about this house?'

'You've got plenty of time to decide what you want to do with it. Relax.'

'I need to organise the delivery of that painting,' she muttered distractedly. 'And no, you don't need to take charge of that too!'

'It might be easier if you put your specs on,' Raj suggested, filching the pair he had noticed abandoned beside the sink and extending them to her.

'I don't know how I ever managed without you,' Sunny framed abstractedly.

'There's a streak of paint above your left eyebrow,' Raj added helpfully. 'And you were going to pack.'

Several hours later, Sunny and Pansy landed with Raj at his London home. There had been some frantic packing. Deprived of Sunny's full attention, Pansy had thrown her first tantrum. There had been a whole lot of wailing and sobbing. Neither food nor attention had consoled her and eventually she had fallen asleep nestled close to Bear, who had been very troubled by her distress. Raj had carried his niece onto the helicopter with all the delicacy of a cat burglar, terrified of her waking up again mid-air. But, exhausted by her shenanigans, the little girl had slept and wakened to Maria's familiar face and a nursery full of toys.

Sunny, however, was greeted in the ballroom by a stylist and a wedding planner. An endless parade of models on a hastily set-up catwalk displayed wedding dresses for her examination. And she fell in love on the spot with the one that had delicate flowers embroidered all over it, of course she did. It was sleeveless and it had a detachable train, a lowish laced back and a modest tailored corset bodice that would give her all the support she required.

Careful measurements were taken. A second dress was suggested for the reception. Sunny chose a sleek elegant gown with cap sleeves and a flattering neckline that she planned to wear with comfortable ballet slippers. She spoke to the stylist about a toning wedding outfit for Pansy and then the stylist moved on to footwear. While Sunny was deliberating on the temptation of pearlised very high-heeled shoes and more traditional diamanté-encrusted sandals, Raj joined them.

'The doctor will be here in an hour.'

'What doctor?' she asked, wandering away from the fashion crew around her for some privacy.

'The obstetrician I arranged to call here this evening to see us. He'll give you your first ultrasound as I won't be in the UK next week for the one you mentioned.'

Sunny stared at him in a daze. 'That's a lot to unpack.'

'I'm trying to be helpful.' Raj had the nerve to look reproachful. 'I didn't want to miss out on the ultrasound and I want you to be checked over just to be sure everything's in order.'

'Where are you flying away to?' In spite of her attempt to make that a normal question she could hear the slight accusing note in her own voice.

'New York…and possibly, er, a little stopover in Iceland. I'll be away ten days but back in time for the wedding. I've put staff at your disposal and everyone knows you're in charge here,' Raj informed her with satisfaction. 'I have to clear the decks to get some time off to spend with you after the wedding.'

Sunny nodded, not wishing to be a nag. 'When do you leave?'

'In a couple of hours…late flight.'

She gritted her teeth. 'Yet you took me away from home.'

'By tomorrow, all your belongings will be here and you can go on just as you would at your former home.' Closing one hand over hers, he urged her back out into the hall, where they were free of an audience. 'This is for you…'

Lifting her hand, he threaded a diamond ring onto her wedding finger. It had the same blue depth as the stone in the pendant and it was equally magnificent. 'It's gorgeous,' she conceded. 'But I wanted to be with you tonight.'

Raj frowned. 'I thought being free after the wedding was more important. I'm not used to consulting anyone about my decisions. I accept that that will have to change to some extent.'

With determination, Sunny laced her beringed hand with his long clenching fingers. 'It's not a problem. But I'll miss you.'

And he grabbed her up into a passionate kiss that sent the blood drumming like mad through her veins. 'I will miss you too.'

Sunny drifted back into the ballroom to rejoin the fashion crew and make selections. Her lips were tingling from the urgency of his and her breasts were tight and her breathing uneven. She had been looking forward to a wickedly rapturous reunion and then he'd told her that he was leaving her for ten days. And that was Raj, along with the unexpected gift of a superb engagement ring and a medical check-up. Suddenly she was laughing at the sheer unexpectedness of his energetic, driven temperament, the speed with which he operated, the many levels on which he thought and planned in advance. Naturally, with all that complexity and no habit of discussing plans with others, he was bound to trip up occasionally.

There was a lot more wedding planning to be done, from the colour of the tableware to the cake to the music—already organised, she was told—and the number of guests. Hundreds, she was informed, and that was even before she added her own list of people to the invitations. For the first time, it occurred to her that she was going to be the bride in a massive showpiece of a wedding. A pregnant bride. But people didn't really worry about that these days, she reminded herself, although undoubtedly there would be some who would suspect that Raj was marrying her only because of the baby.

Only Sunny would not be one of those people. Raj wanted her and he wanted Pansy as well. She had realised that truth very quickly. He was keen to claim the family that he had never had. It was a choice he had never enjoyed before. Marrying her, she appreciated, would be something akin to a science experiment for Raj. He was greeting the opportunity with enthusiasm but would still be waiting to see how the chips fell. She and Pansy and her animals would be on trial, she decided ruefully. Ultimately, Raj would have to decide whether they added to or detracted from his untrammelled life of not committing to anything other than business. It was a grave, sobering thought to cherish before a wedding.

The obstetrician, who arrived after the fashion team had departed, was suave and charming, visibly tickled pink to be invited to take care of her pregnancy. With him came his nurse and a technician and a lot of medical equipment. Raj looked on the cavalcade with approbation.

'I want to know that you're safe, that I've taken every possible precaution with your health,' he confided.

She could not be critical of such an outlook. Yes, it annoyed her that he had gone above her head and yet, on the other hand, she was delighted that he was sufficiently interested in seeing their unborn child to arrange an ultrasound that he too could be present to enjoy. Ushered into a private reception room with a doctor, she had a comprehensive medical questionnaire to fill in and all the usual tests.

Raj joined them for a discussion of how her previous reproductive problems might play out during her current pregnancy. Raj's troubled brow cleared when the obstetrician confessed that he saw no reason for her past surgical history to influence her pregnancy in any way. Then it was time for her to lie down on the couch and the technician moved forward and the gel was rubbed over her slightly protuberant tummy.

'I'm not flat any more,' she sighed.

'That's my baby in there. You don't need to make excuses on that score,' Raj proclaimed with satisfaction.

'Would you like to know the gender? It may be possible to see now but it may also not be possible,' they were warned. 'It depends on the position of the baby in the uterus.'

The screen before them came alive and at first Sunny couldn't pick out anything but lighter spaces and darker places. Then the technician was talking them through it and she saw the tiny legs and the little arms and her heart was in her mouth and Raj was leaning forward with pronounced interest to learn that they could look forward to becoming the parents of a baby boy.

Raj closed her hand into his and grinned at her, delighted and not even trying to hide the fact. 'A boy?'

'A large boy. Miss Barker is already showing more pregnant than would have been expected at present. It's possible that a C-section may be necessary at the delivery stage, but we'll know more about that in a few months,' the obstetrician told them with assurance. 'There is no cause for concern at this time. Miss Barker is in good health, as is the baby.'

A wide smile on his sculpted lips, Raj rose from his seat and helped her off the couch as she righted her clothing. He said all that was polite, checked that a further visit was scheduled and guided Sunny back out again. 'That was…unexpectedly *very* exciting,' he admitted in evident surprise. 'Our baby, there on screen for us to see. A kind of first hello. Amazing!'

'You've never seen an ultrasound before?'

'Why would I have? I know how the tech works but I was never interested. I didn't believe that I would ever have a child. It has never been one of my goals,' Raj admitted quietly. 'But now that our son is on the way?

It's changed everything. You have enriched my life, Sunny. I can never thank you enough for that.'

Sunny paled, wishing that he had used his words in another way. As it was, she felt as though he was more excited about their child than he was about marrying her. And how could she be happy about that? After all, any woman could have given him a child and that ability did not make her either special or unique. She had lucked out in more ways than one, she thought unhappily. She had fallen accidentally pregnant by a very rich guy, who was thoroughly enjoying the experience even of her actually *being* pregnant with *his* child. But it wasn't personal. It wasn't love and maybe it was naïve of her to still want more than the romantic trappings of an engagement ring and a free hand to organise the society wedding of the year.

Raj was rich and intelligent. He wouldn't marry her in any hole-and-corner way that might suggest that he was marrying her unwillingly or only because she carried his child. No, Raj would push the boat out in public. He would also look after every aspect of her pregnancy and guard her from every ill to ensure her health and security. He would do all of that for his child…not for her in person. Her baby had somehow become more important than she was, she conceded heavily.

A little voice in her troubled brain cried out that Raj had given up his convenient mistresses for her benefit and that at that point he had had no idea that it was even possible for her to conceive. But that was sex, she reminded herself. When she had said no to Raj initially, his interest in her had grown exponentially. She had then become infinitely more desirable in her unattainability because he, primarily, was not accustomed to women saying no to him. Her conception had been a massive surprise, but it was also something new and fresh and Raj Belanger was intellectually programmed to be fascinated by anything new and fresh. Furthermore, his attitude to children had been tempered by his meetings with Pansy. Pansy had gently eased him into the idea of a paternal role.

'You're very quiet,' Raj remarked. 'I have to leave.'

'I can cope,' she said brightly, forcing a smile as Bear and Bert surged across the big hall to greet her.

Bert, however, raced straight past her to gambol round Raj's feet. 'Why's he doing that?' he demanded, stepping back in surprise from the little dog's approach.

'Evidently, he's *your* dog now. It's pretty obvious he prefers men and I'm the lady who tried and failed to rehome him with two different women, so Bert has finally found his new owner and you're stuck with him.'

'But he's an insane bully.'

'Not around you, he's not. He *listens* to you.'

'The cat doesn't. When I told him off for scratching at my desk, he stuck his nose in the air and strolled away.'

'We should've packed the log.'

'He has a scratching post.'

'He likes his log. Don't you think I tried a scratching post for him? He's choosy.'

'I'll phone you first thing in the morning when I'm

in New York,' Raj promised. 'And try to do some shopping for our honeymoon. You'll need lighter clothing.'

'Where are we going?'

'Haven't quite decided yet but there'll be sunshine and plants for you to be inspired by,' he said confidently.

The next ten days were packed tight with activity for Sunny. She had innumerable calls from friends, astonished by their wedding invitations and the identity of the man she was to marry. Only a few of them had seen that photograph of her with Raj in the newspaper but, as public knowledge of their wedding plans spread, there were a couple of articles printed about her in more serious newspapers with references to her career as a botanical artist. Mid-week, the social worker in charge of Pansy's case sent her documents to enable Raj to become part of the adoption application. And Sunny moved to Ashton Hall to get ready for the wedding.

Raj phoned her every day until he reached Iceland and that was the last she heard from him. When he had still not returned the night before the ceremony, Sunny started getting antsy. He didn't answer his phone either. The morning of the wedding she enjoyed the attentions of a make-up artist and a hairstylist but her nerves were torn by Raj's continuing absence. Surely he wouldn't jilt her at the altar? If something were truly wrong, she told herself, it probably would have been in the newspapers or someone would have contacted her, wouldn't they?

News of his late arrival was brought by her hairstylist, who reached the hall at about the same time.

Relief spread through Sunny. Attired in her gown, she descended the stairs, confident of the fact that she had never taken so much care with her appearance and that she looked her very best.

Raj watched his bride move towards him. She had never looked more beautiful than in her fairy-tale dress with its tiny beaded flowers, the diamond pendant at her throat, a simple coronet crowning her upswept hair. A tremulous smile softened her tense lips when she saw him. He gave her the bunch of simple wildflowers to carry and took her hand in his to walk her into the ballroom through their assembled guests.

'I thought you weren't going to make it,' she said breathlessly, striving to look neither to the left nor to the right at the sheer mass of people watching them. In any case, she was still reliving that first glimpse of Raj, his tall, lean, powerful frame sheathed in a morning suit of exquisite tailoring. Black hair tousled by his ever-restless fingers, stunning dark golden eyes locked to her, his strong bronzed features taut. Gorgeous, drop-dead gorgeous, and to be all hers now.

'Mechanical problems with the jet we were in, an accident in a cave with a foolhardy friend, who had to be rescued, had to reorganise our transport, smashed my phone into a wall. *Dire*,' he admitted feelingly in a measured undertone and staring out of a tall window into the sky where a faint distant whine advertised the presence of the tiny craft darting above the house. 'Those blasted press drones chasing pictures,' he added. 'It's illegal to jam them. I'd shoot them out of the sky if I could but that's not legal either.'

'Forget about them,' Sunny advised.

Her fine brows rose as they arrived with the vicar at the altar set up for the ceremony. A *cave*? What on earth had he been doing in a cave of all things? But the marriage service had begun and it was the old-style version. She was absorbed, making her vows, listening with intense amusement as Raj's innate impatience had him diving in too early with his responses. Finally they exchanged wedding rings.

Raj skimmed a brief kiss over her mouth, evidently no fan of public displays and mindful of her make-up, and she wanted to grab him by the lapels and demand that he kiss her properly, an urge that mortified her. It was done. They were married, and as that intoxicating awareness infiltrated her she was shot back to reality by Pansy finally breaking free from Maria's restraining hold and darting over to her to grab her knees through the dress. Raj swooped down to hoist the little girl up into his arms and she went straight into her 'eyes…nose…mouth' routine.

'It's just like any other day for her.' Sunny chuckled. 'She'll keep us grounded.'

'You look gorgeous in that dress,' Raj told her frankly, dark deep-set eyes caressing.

'Why couldn't you phone me?'

'Because I broke it during the caving accident and everyone else was using theirs.'

'What the heck were you doing in a cave?'

'Stag do. Caving, snow mobiles, white water rafting. Iceland. I enjoyed the first day of it. I like a physical challenge, but when that drunken idiot got hurt fooling around and had to be rescued, I felt as though I was too mature for it all.'

'So, Iceland was a stag do,' she gathered in mounting annoyance, thinking of the way she had been summarily deserted and left to handle all the wedding palaver. 'Is your friend badly hurt?'

'Broken leg and arm. He was lucky to get away that lightly,' Raj advanced.

'You should have mentioned the stag do,' she told him flatly. 'And when you were so late getting here, I thought you might not show up for the wedding, which was very inconsiderate.'

'I'm not used to explaining my every move to anyone!' Raj shot back at her without apology.

Sunny's smile was bleak as they drifted into a drinks reception and many, many congratulatory meetings from their guests. She couldn't match faces to names but she met Raj's closer friends. And all the time she was thinking that, because Raj didn't love her, he was still holding her at a distance. He hadn't shared anything with her. My goodness, had she made a terrible mistake in marrying him?

'I have to get changed for the reception,' Sunny told him, stiff with the effort of keeping up a smile.

'Not before you're photographed in that gown.' Raj signalled the photographer mingling with the crowd and whirled her off.

Thirty minutes of posing was enough for her and she fled upstairs, finding Raj on her heels as she hurried into their bedroom, still seething with anxious thoughts.

'Undo my lacing,' she urged, turning her back on him as she kicked off her high heels and shrank.

The straps slid down her shoulders as the corset loosened. With a husky groan, Raj slid his hands below the bodice to cup her breasts and chafe her straining nipples. An inarticulate cry broke from her lips as she fell back against him and he tugged the dress down so that it fell and bared her for his pleasure. 'Gorgeous,' he said thickly.

'Raj—'

'You can say no, although I'll try very hard not to mess up your hair. I'm burning up for you.' He flexed his hips against her bottom and she felt him long and hard and urgent and the warmth in her pelvis heated to boiling point.

'Going to say no,' she framed, out of patience with him. 'Sorry, but no.'

Aware of his dark stare, Sunny climbed into her other dress, sliding her feet into the comfy ballet slippers with relief.

'What's wrong?' Raj demanded.

Sunny rounded on him. 'What's *right*? You're out of touch for days, worrying me, and then you almost miss our wedding… That's how late your arrival was! I was afraid I was being jilted, which is not a thought any bride wants to have. Just because you don't love me, Raj, doesn't mean you can get away with treating me without consideration!'

Raj's lean dark features were rigid. 'That was not my intention. I believed—obviously wrongly—that you had more faith in me than to have such a fear.'

Sunny's heart sank inside her. That stripped their relationship down to the very barest bones, she thought wretchedly. A male in love would have been more sympathetic towards his bride's feelings but Raj was not in love. Raj had married her to retain access to her and Pansy and eventually his own child. For him, that had been a totally practical solution, neither romantic nor sensitive, and to look for him to show her anything more than a desire for sex was obviously foolish.

When they returned to their guests, the ballroom had been transformed for the reception and they took their seats to be served. There was only one speech, from Raj's best man. Neither of them had relatives to make speeches. While they ate they were entertained by a world-famous female singer. They cut the cake, they danced.

Pansy fell asleep in Sunny's arms. 'Either we stay the night here or we leave soon,' she warned Raj.

'I'll stay for another hour.' Raj dug out his phone. 'You can catch the helicopter with Pansy out to the yacht.'

'I should change,' Sunny said wearily.

'Why bother? You can change when you get there.' He cupped her face with long gentle fingers. 'You look tired and you shouldn't be pushing yourself too hard. It's been a long day.'

A crowd accompanied them outside. Raj helped her board and took charge of his niece to clip her into her seat before climbing back out again. Sunny screened a yawn as she put on the headphones and the helicopter rose in the air.

Raj saw the low-flying drone above first and shouted. His heart leapt into his throat as he watched the drone collide with the rotor blades. The craft lurched and spun as someone screamed and everybody around him backed off, cries of alarm filling the air. Raj felt sick. The helicopter began to drop down and pitched clumsily to one side before the pilot skilfully got it back under control and dropped it somewhat heavily down on the ground again.

Raj was the first to wrench open the doors. He grabbed Sunny, who was wide-eyed and shaking, while someone else released Pansy from her seat. Only a few feet from the craft, he wheeled to an abrupt halt and simply held Sunny. Pale as a sheet, he hugged her close and she realised that he was trembling against her.

'We'll stay the night here,' he breathed. 'I'm not letting you out of my sight again. Excuse me.'

Sunny watched him stride over to speak to the pilot and heard him thank the older man and congratulate him on their safe landing. Maria appeared to retrieve Pansy, who, amazingly, had slumbered through the entire experience.

Raj hovered over a sofa in the drawing room as a doctor checked Sunny out, satisfied that she had merely had a fright and was still in shock. He insisted she stay lying down and Raj crouched down beside her and closed one hand over hers. 'I love you,' he breathed rawly, startling her with that confession and the powerful tenderness lightening his eyes. 'And I only just realised it. How stupid is that?'

Sunny stared up at him with wide rapt eyes. 'I don't get it.'

'If it had been me that had a near-death accident, perhaps you would. I realised that my whole world was in that helicopter and that if it crashed I would lose *everything*—you, Pansy, our baby. It was the most terrifying moment of my life.'

Sunny cupped his jaw with her fingers in dawning wonderment and conviction. 'Seriously?'

'I want to wrap you in a protective cocoon and you wouldn't let me.'

'I knew I was falling in love with you that very first night on the yacht,' she told him softly. 'It was like something in me recognised you very early on. I guessed how you would react to things. You probably don't believe in them, but I think we're soulmates.'

'Soulmates.' Surprisingly, Raj liked that description. She fitted him like the missing piece of a puzzle. He no longer felt alone. He wanted to share stuff with her that he had never wanted to share with anyone. She calmed him when he was on edge, warned him when he was about to go over it. 'You see my flaws, my mistakes, and you still love me?'

'But you're the same with me,' she pointed out tenderly.

'I thought of asking you to marry me the same day that you told me that you were pregnant, but I was scared you would think I was crazy. And then you shut me out and you had the right to do that: your baby, your body.'

'This is your baby too. I was running scared. I didn't

want you to think that I was expecting anything from you and I guess I got carried away with my independent speech. Truthfully, I would always have wanted a father for my baby because I didn't really have a father of my own. My father couldn't see past Christabel to see *me*.'

'And I learned how *not* to be a father from mine, who only saw me as a scientific subject for a study that might make him famous. When you first told me you had conceived, I was terrified because I didn't think I would know *how* to be a father to a child.'

'That's why I told you that I was a superwoman, who could do it all on my own.'

'You knew?'

'Well, I had a fair idea you would be challenged.'

'And in the wrong mood, Pansy can be challenging, and I learned that I could cope the same way you do, with common sense and care. I don't feel as restless and dissatisfied with you in my life. I told you I couldn't do soppy.'

'And then you did the fireworks and the fab bath by candlelight and I thought, *Oh, yes, he can do anything he wants to do.* And you wanted to do it for me. It made me feel amazing.'

They strolled very slowly back to their wedding reception, but were so mutually absorbed that they really might as well not have bothered. That tight little pool of happiness enclosed them and closed out other people. A long time later, they went to bed and they talked and laughed and made love. The next day they travelled by road to join the yacht. Raj was set on Madagascar.

'Fabulous flora,' he promised her.

'I love you,' she told him fiercely, touched that he was always thinking of her interests, rather than his own.

'I'll love you for ever,' he swore passionately.

EPILOGUE

SIX YEARS LATER, Sunny rested back in the sunlight and contemplated her family as they played.

Pansy, a strikingly pretty little girl even at the age of seven, was presiding over the younger children in the family. She was a bossy boots and already obsessed with medicine. Since she showed every sign of having inherited her grandfather and uncle's intellect, it was likely that Pansy would eventually fulfil her ambition.

Kristof was five, pushing six, with a head of dark cropped hair and his mother's violet-blue eyes. He was a maths whizz like his father but he wanted to be a fireman. His little brother, Tamas, was three and he liked to paint on walls, if nothing else was available. He was a laid-back little boy otherwise, blond and brown-eyed. Pansy's long-desired little sister had finally been born the year before. Lili was dark and blue-eyed like her older brother Kristof and, now that she could crawl, she tried to follow Pansy everywhere. Pansy had found her little sister more of a liability than she had expected but also more fun. That was the family complete. Four children, all relatively close in age, were quite sufficient, Sunny reflected, simply grateful to have achieved the family she had always wanted without having the fertility problems she had feared would dog her.

They lived in London during the week and often spent weekends at Ashton Hall, where the children could run wild and participate in all the outdoor activities they enjoyed. Holidays invariably revolved round the yacht and visiting Raj's various properties. Sunny had discovered a very rare orchid on the Ashton estate and her painting of it now hung in the Royal Academy. She painted most days and their travels had influenced her art, for she now excelled at depicting more exotic flora than had once been to her taste. Raj, she had come slowly to recognise, had not clipped her wings. No, he had enhanced her ability to fly high and free.

She still wasn't very much into fashion and she still mislaid her specs everywhere she went. Raj still organised her but she had got used to it. She realised that she had never really known what it was to be happy until she had met him, and having found that happiness, she had at first been afraid to trust in it and had feared all the change and vulnerability that came with reaching for what she most wanted. But she had no regrets.

Raj striding out now to join their picnic, sheathed in well-worn jeans and an open shirt surveyed his family with pleasure. An elderly chihuahua, who had become like his little shadow followed his every step while Bear, who was much lazier, slumbered peacefully in the shade of the trees while keeping a careful eye on the children.

'Dad's here...*at last*,' Pansy exclaimed. 'Do you realise that Mum wouldn't let us eat until you arrived?'

Amused by that reproof, Sunny merely smiled. 'Family eats together.'

'I got stuck on the phone,' Raj sighed, dropping fluidly down beside Sunny on the rugs she had spread.

She was wearing something long and loose and swirly. It probably had a designer tag but it was still very much her style and she looked beautiful. Lili was steadily crawling towards him. Kristof, showing off, tried to execute a rugby save which sent Tamas flying and he burst into floods of overexcited tears. Sunny picked him up and planted a sandwich in his hand and he subsided before returning to the game with vigour. Lili finally reached Raj's knees and he swung her high and she giggled and giggled, her chubby little body convulsed with delight.

'If people will keep lifting her and carrying her, she'll never learn to walk,' Pansy lamented.

'She needs cuddled,' Raj countered. 'We all need cuddled now and again.'

'Mum's *always* cuddling you,' Pansy groaned in embarrassment.

Lili saw food and sat down clumsily to eat and Pansy dropped down beside her to help, pushing a toddler cup into her sibling's hand. Eventually they were all eating and quiet.

Raj poured Sunny wine and lay down beside her in the dappled sunlight. 'Tonight we will be alone in Paris,' he savoured. 'And you, my children, will have Maria and her assistants taking care of you.'

Sunny smiled even more widely because they spent their every anniversary alone in Paris and she got her fireworks and her fancy bath. Her dancing violet blue eyes met his level dark gaze in a moment of intense connection. She had never believed it possible to love anyone as much as she loved Raj. Or that anyone would ever look for her when she was absent and love her with the intensity that he did.

'Watch out…they're going to start kissing!' Pansy screwed up her face in disgust.

Raj's hand closed over Sunny's. 'Remind me again. Why did we decide we would have four of them?'

'You and Pansy needed more people to boss around.'

Her shapely body melted into the heat and hardness of his that night in Paris while she watched her fireworks from the balcony, exulting in the happiness flooding through her. 'I love you,' she murmured with her warm heart in her eyes.

He carried her back indoors to the big white linen draped bed and spread her across it with precision. He leant over her and kissed her until her heart was pounding. 'You are so loved, my precious Mrs Belanger.'

* * * * *

PREGNANT PRINCESS BRIDE

CAITLIN CREWS

MILLS & BOON

CHAPTER ONE

PRINCESS CARLIZ HAD never crashed a wedding before.

Not because she was opposed to the idea, in theory, but because she was normally inundated with entirely too many invitations to count. There was usually precious little impetus to go scrounging about for *extra* weddings to attend.

This one, of course, was different.

Her entire life depended on her ability to do what she needed to do at this wedding today, and she knew that if she was to say that to someone—anyone—they would dismiss her and call her needlessly histrionic.

But that didn't make it any less true.

This wedding would always stand as a *before* and *after* moment in her life. It was up to her to make it either a good memory or a deeply sad one, but she knew full well she would be carrying it around forever.

"No pressure, then," she muttered wryly to herself as she boarded the small, sleek watercraft she had hired for her purposes in the Marina di Pisa, tucked there at the mouth of the Arno some ten kilometers from the city famed for its leaning tower.

Carliz had approached this whole enterprise like a puzzle. She always had liked a good puzzle. And concentrating on the details of how to make it onto a private, tidal island with heaps of security, then into one of the most hyped-up ceremonies of the year when they would most certainly be attempting to keep everyone out, was far more interesting than other things she could have been concentrating on. Like how she felt about the fact that she was doing such a reckless, foolish, and deeply questionable thing in the first place.

But then, Valentino Bonaparte—sometimes called Vale by his friends, which was not how Carliz would describe herself—was the thorniest puzzle of all.

Her curse was that she was determined to solve him, one way or another.

It had been easy enough to secure a boat. She was a princess, the Italian seaside catered to tourists of all descriptions but especially rich ones, and it was nothing at all to whisk her across the stunning blue waters of this part of the Mediterranean Sea. Particularly on a lovely summer day like this. Somewhere between the island of Capraia, renowned for its anchovy fishery, and Elba, better known for the ten months it had housed the exiled Napoleon, sat a small, tidal island that Valentino's family had claimed as theirs for generations.

Carliz wrapped her hair carefully in a silk scarf and sat out in the sea air as the boat cut through the waves, not afraid to imagine herself the heroine on this journey. Bravely striding forth to do what must be done no matter the cost.

It did not matter—at the moment—that she knew that Valentino would not return the favor.

His family like to claim that they were direct descendants of Napoleon himself, but no one took this seriously.

She had once heard Valentino say at a party that he rather thought it was an overly imaginative goatherd who had become the first of *his* Bonaparte line. That was all there was on his family's island. Goats, wild oleander, and fortresses on three sides. One belonged to the famously vile Milo Bonaparte, who had raised Valentino and his illegitimate half brother, Aristide, in well-publicized and ongoing conflict. When they had turned eighteen, their father had divided all of the island in two, save the peninsula he lived on, and told his sons to prove which one of them deserved to inherit the rest when he died. Because only one of them could have the greater share.

They had each built their own grand castle on their land. At the other.

For it was well known that the two Bonaparte sons, born on either side of the blanket, had once been great friends but were now mortal enemies. Some speculated it was all down to the inheritance they each hoped to gain, though that made little sense, as both men had made themselves fabulously wealthy in their own right.

But then, Carliz knew all too well that Valentino could exist for years in a state of conflict and feel no compulsion whatever to fix it or even address it. It was like he preferred his own misery. That was another reason that she was taking the extraordinary step she was today, she told herself when the boat landed, and her men helped her alight.

That and the fact that *she* did not like misery at all.

First, though, she had to find the wedding. This was not a large island, as islands went, but it was big enough to be divided into three, each third with enough space to boast its own castle. There was ample opportunity to go to the wrong bit, and then what? She doubted private islands had taxi stands.

She hadn't thought that part through, if she was honest. If her father was still alive, he would no doubt have despaired of her recklessness. Then again, he would have done the same if Carliz had locked herself away in a convent and let the nuns lead her to a higher purpose that might well have involved less of what he'd called his younger daughter's *spiritedness*.

It had never been a compliment.

But Carliz had not gone into the nunnery. Instead, while her serious sister solemnly took the throne after their father's death and their mother had made herself into a walking, talking shrine to his memory, Carliz had done precisely what she pleased.

Because that was the point and privilege of *not* being the heir, to her mind.

Accordingly, she was the first member of her family to attend university in the whole of her tiny kingdom's history. Much less in England, surrounded by commoners. And once she'd graduated with an art degree, Carliz had flirted with the idea of an appropriately bohemian lifestyle, but she soon found that she was too royal to be taken seriously in her preferred medium. She could paint all she liked, and she really did like to paint, but no one could see past her sister's reign when they looked at her works.

Or maybe she was kidding herself, she had no talent whatever, and it was thanks entirely to her sister.

In any case, she had teased Mila—Queen Emilia to everyone else—that it was therefore her obligation and most solemn duty to become the thorn in the proverbial crown.

You can do as you like, her sister had replied in her

serene way that was not a reaction to her station. She had always been calm unto her soul. *I only ask that your scandals be entertaining, not embarrassing.*

Carliz had promised. And she always kept her word.

And thus she had sparkled her way all across Europe, from the mountain heights of their tiny little kingdom to Spain's warm beaches, across to the gleaming villas and attendant yachts of the Côte d'Azur. She had skied every hill in Switzerland. She had wandered around the palm trees and wide boulevards of Los Angeles, and spent a season of inner peace and vegan food—not good bedfellows, in her experience—tucked away in a mysterious Malibu canyon.

Your sister indulges you, her mother had said dourly at some point in all this cavorting about, perhaps when Carliz was beginning her first Parisian era. Or maybe it was the second Milan season. It was hard to recall, because it was all couture houses and nights that began after midnight and bled straight on through morning. *But sooner or later you will need to contribute in some way to the crown.*

Surely, Mother, my contribution of joie de vivre *is more than sufficient*, she had replied, not entirely facetiously. *I make Mila laugh.*

You will need to marry well, her mother had thundered at her from behind the shroud she had adopted, the better to look like an early Christian martyr midtorment. She did not laugh. Ever. *Your sister is yet without child. Even you must understand what that means. You have responsibilities, Carliz, whether you like it or not.*

And it was not that Carliz did not want responsibilities. Sometimes she thought she would be much better for them. But there was a restlessness in her. Not a recklessness, as her father had often claimed—it was a kind of yearning. It permeated everything. She was so good at a carefree laugh, a witty comment, the perfect story to set the whole party into gales of laughter. She was terrific at shifting the mood of any room she entered. It was her belief that it was that very restlessness that allowed her to do well at such things, because she was not all on the surface and she did not treat others as if they were, either.

But these were not considered gifts. They were only party tricks. Even though, as far she could tell, the job of the spare princess was to illuminate all the parties she could, her party tricks did not seem to be enough.

Carliz had indulged in vague thoughts about the sort of things she could do. She'd imagined that even though she couldn't think of something intriguing off the top of her head, she could surely find *some* way to be useful instead of merely decorative.

Besides, though she was in no rush to find herself the sort of husband her mother would consider appropriate, Carliz could admit that she was a bit bored with sparkling about hither and yon. A friend of hers suggested charity work, the typical balm for the aimless heiress, which would at least bolster goodwill.

What Carliz had found, instead, was that she truly loved it. She had worked with orphans, at home and abroad, and for the first time in her life had gotten a glimpse—a glimmer—of what it would mean to actually live a life of purpose instead of mere pomp and occasional circumstance.

But then she had met Valentino.

She stopped as she clambered up the rocky beach and

let out a breath, because even thinking about him changed the temperature. Of the air. Of the sky. Of her whole body. Even the thought of him made her…silly.

It had been like this from the moment they had met eyes. Met, then held.

Too long for comfort, composure, or anything else the least bit polite.

It had been a charity banquet in Rome. It had been a balmy night and so the banquet had been more or less outside, beneath lights strewn about in the trees and stretching between the old walls to create a ceiling in the old ruin, so that everything was cast in a warm, bright glow.

Everything except him.

He was breathtaking. Thick dark hair, a sensually stern mouth, and eyes like a faded blue sky set against his olive coloring to swoon-worthy effect.

And yet there was something ruthless in the cut of him. The blade of his nose, the slice of his cheekbones, the intense athleticism of his form that was obvious even in the exquisite bespoke suit he'd worn that night.

Carliz had felt drawn to him as surely as if he'd wrapped his arms around her and hauled her to him.

Oh, how she wished he had.

She had worn red that night. And red was how she'd felt—seared through, set alight, and made new.

She remembered catching his gaze the way she had, and then, in the next moment, finding herself in his arms. As if it had happened that way, in an instant. As if neither one of them had moved at all. As if fate had taken a hand and thrown them together, from one end of a crowded event into the center of a packed dance floor.

That was impossible. She knew that. One of them must

have moved toward the other. There must have been some understanding, some communication—but if so, it was lost to her. All she recalled was that searing glance.

She could still *feel* it. She felt it *all the time.*

And then, better still, the exquisite beauty and agony of being in his arms.

They hadn't spoken. It was too intense, too overwhelming.

And she knew this had not been in her head alone. For one, she was not given to such flights of fancy. And for another, she'd seen it on his face. That stark wonder. And something else—that same alarm she could feel in her, too, that *anything* could sweep through them like this.

Because things like this could not be real.

There was no such thing as love at first sight. Everyone knew it.

Tell me your name, he had said at last, and they had both reacted to that.

She had shivered, because his voice seemed to be a part of her already, moving deep within her, changing her and claiming her. And she had shivered again when his eyes had moved to track the goose bumps that rose up, then trailed down the line of her neck, then out across her bare shoulders.

Carliz, she had managed somehow, to say. *Princess Carliz of the Kingdom of Las Sosegadas.*

I am Valentino, he had replied.

And later, she would find herself tempted to analyze that. To suspect that he had deliberately not told her his surname and puzzle over the fact that he had also not offered her that nickname of his, but in her brighter moments she knew better. Neither one of them had been in possession of any defenses in that moment. It would have been better if they had.

It would have been easier, then and now.

After the dance had ended, he'd drawn her off the dance floor, and they had stood there, too full of each other to breathe. Too…altered.

She could remember the amazement on his face. That same wonder she could feel sparking within her. She remembered the way he'd led her through the party when he could bring himself to move, in a way that should have made a scene, given who they were, though no one afterward had remarked on it.

To her it was so obvious, this thing that had blown up between them. So blatantly sensual. So impossibly carnal.

So *right*.

When they reached the shadows outside the ruin, at last, he had backed her against the nearest remnant of a wall and looked down into her eyes.

Carliz, he had said, as if her name on his tongue was an anguish all its own. *Carliz, this is not who I am.*

She hadn't spoken. She'd felt…almost choked by the intensity of that moment. His gaze on her. Her very real sense that she had fallen off a cliff from all that she knew and there was only this freefall, now. That there was no way out. No going back. No fixing whatever this was.

No story she could tell or witticism she could offer that would make this any less than it was.

So instead, following an urge she could hardly name, she had lifted up her hands and traced those sensually harsh lines of his stunning face. She had made a soft noise when she'd touched him, when the heat of him seemed to rush through her like its own, deep roar.

His skin was scalding to the touch. His brows were a symphony, a weapon.

And when she'd moved her fingertips over that austere, demanding mouth of his, he'd opened his lips and enveloped her fingers with all of that terrible, wonderful heat. And she had learned things about herself, then.

Dark, magical things.

Too many things to name, cascading through her all at once, and all of them lessons of heat and wonder, longing and desire.

Inexorably and not nearly fast enough, one of his hands had found its way to the nape of her neck and held her there.

And she'd known he was going to kiss her.

She had felt as if she'd been waiting the whole of her life to kiss him back.

And when he'd lowered his face to hers and claimed her mouth with his, she was certain she had waited an eternity.

For then Carliz was born anew.

Because he kissed like wonder. And with one stroke of his tongue after the next, he wrote his name indelibly on her heart. She kissed him back in the same way, the heat and marvel reaching a crescendo all its own.

When he'd pulled back, they were both shaking.

And then, as she'd watched him and panted out her need and frustration that they were not *still* kissing, Valentino had stepped back. He had squeezed his eyes shut. He had rubbed his hands over his face and made a sound that she could only describe as pure anguish.

She had felt it in her own gut, like a dagger thrust in deep.

This cannot happen, he had told her.

Carliz had sighed a little. *I think it already has.*

This cannot happen, he had said again, and he had fixed the dark world of his eyes on her. *This will not happen.*

And she would never understand—to this day, she could not understand—how he had turned as sharply as he did, then walked away and left her there, as if what had happened between them was a daydream. As if it had not happened at all.

She didn't follow him that night. She couldn't. She had stayed where she was, clutching onto that wall as if without it she might topple off the planet and lose herself amongst the stars forever.

But eventually, she had gotten her legs beneath her again.

Eventually she had learned how to breathe as if breath was new.

And when she did, she went to war.

Carliz reminded herself of that now as she made her way through a bit of a hedge and found herself on a brightly lit lane, where many exquisite-looking people in fancy dress were walking along, all headed toward the grand, sprawling house on the hill above them.

Or more precisely, she realized as she slipped into the procession as demurely as possible, toward the small chapel that sat tucked in at the foot of the hill, with a view over the sea she'd only just crossed.

A pretty place for a wedding, she thought. And then she congratulated herself on how clinical that thought was, as if everything in her body didn't rise up to reject it. There were rooms in the house up above, with windows that looked straight down at the procession toward the chapel, and she couldn't help but wonder if he was there now. Watching. Waiting.

Preparing to marry a woman who wasn't her.

Carliz glanced up, then forced herself to stop. And as she walked the rest of the way, she kept her scarf as much over her face as she could and kept her gaze toward the ground, because she did not wish to be recognized. Not yet.

She had spent the past three years paparazzi-ing herself at Valentino Bonaparte. Who had not been able to avoid her entirely, though he had not touched her again. Still, every time their gazes locked it was like fireworks, and he hated her for that.

Or maybe it was that he hated that she would not let it go.

Though Carliz thought that of the two of them, she was the one who really ought to have hated him. For experiencing what she had that night, then walking away. For kissing her like that, as if no other woman would ever exist but her, and as if he could not live without her.

And then having the audacity to go ahead and do just that.

She had spent two years making the relationship she hadn't actually had with him into one of the biggest scandals in Europe. All it took was a whisper to this tabloid, an anonymous tip to another. Making sure she was spotted leaving places he had been. Making sure that it looked as if she was trying to hide from the cameras while she did it.

After all, speculation was often better than any real story could ever be.

Then he had announced his engagement to a blameless, spotless heiress of indisputably high character.

Carliz did not like to think about that particular day. It had been a dark one.

Even her sister had called, filled with sympathy and endless concern…though more because Mila was worried about what Carliz might do, Carliz was aware. Less about the state of Carliz's heart.

Not the Carliz could tell anyone about the *actual* state of her heart.

Once again, she hadn't thought things through. Everybody thought that she and Valentino had been involved in a torrid affair. Since she was chiefly known for her sparkling and not her charitable works, the narrative had tended toward praising Valentino for keeping his side of the street scrupulously clean while offering very thinly veiled jabs at Carliz for being such a mess in public.

She had thought it was all fun and games. That, at the very least, it would inspire Valentino to confront her himself.

But he had declined.

And so she didn't see him again until after his engagement. When they had both inadvertently turned up at the same birthday party for another European royal, who Valentino knew from his own time at university. Or perhaps it was from that desperately fancy club everyone knew he was a part of, so exclusive that people spoke of it in whispers—even when the people that they were speaking to had no idea it existed.

This time there had been no dancing. He was an engaged man and it was clear he did not intend there to be any scandal attached to him, or to his lovely, worthy intended who Carliz did her best not to loathe simply because *she existed.*

Nonetheless, thanks to Carliz's antics, there were entirely too many eyes watching the two of them as they came face-to-face at that party.

I hope you are satisfied with yourself, Valentino had said, a banked storm in those faded blue eyes and censure all over his face.

As satisfied as I imagine you are with yourself, she had replied, with a smile for the onlookers. *A thousand congratulations on your future happiness, Valentino.*

Saying his name to him washed through him, its own wave. She could see it. She could feel its echo inside her own bones.

That storm in his gaze had intensified.

I owe you no obligation, he had shot back. *I told you. Whatever this is, it cannot happen. I* told you *this.*

It makes no sense to me, she had said, and there was too much *feeling* in her voice. There was too much raw emotion all over her, spilling out everywhere. She knew it but she couldn't seem to keep it within.

We should never have met, he had told her, and then he had once again walked away.

Carliz had not even had to go out and drum up the headlines that had greeted her the next day. Because she'd created the monster and now it fed itself. The papers were full of speculation about their tense meeting. About their lost love.

About this untenable situation she had created for herself.

About this man who she knew full well felt as she did, but refused to accept it. And refused even further to *do* anything about it.

Carliz had resolved to get over him. To put that lightning strike of a meeting behind her and move on.

But then she'd seen him one more time.

She had not been supposed to be there. She couldn't remember the name of the event, only that it took place in a forlorn castle somewhere in England, carefully refurbished but still little more than a lonely beacon over a remote and barren landscape. Like a lighthouse standing over a rocky shore where no ships sailed.

She had come in the night before after attempting to exhaust herself with literal whirlwinds of the sort of activities that she'd used to find such fun. She'd gone on a mad tour from the Pacific Islands to Rio de Janeiro to Barcelona, all to forget about Valentino Bonaparte. She had been sandy and salty, her ears still ringing from too much music and her whole body in need of a month's rest after all of that dancing.

And so she had slept through the day and into the next night with the party already carrying on in the castle's ancient keep below. When she'd woken up she'd felt inside out and in no fit state to interact with anyone.

Carliz was very good at pulling the pieces together, no matter her actual state. She had always been good at it. A little bit of makeup and she was fine. She was well. A pretty dress and she was giddy and happy, and whatever else she was required to be at any given time.

But that night, she had felt pale with exhaustion. And not simply the kind that sleeping could cure. Her heart was too heavy. She had begun to think that he was right. That they should never have met.

If they had never met, she would never have known.

If she hadn't known, she would not have to suffer like this.

She could not, somehow, find it in her to buck up, put on her party face, and go out there where people would expect her to sparkle the way she always did.

Carliz went to her window instead to look out over the party below, and that was when she saw that he was there.

It was a glory and misery to see him, to feel that electricity—that same old lightning bolt—and yet to know that it was meaningless. She thought it was so unjust that it was possible to feel that way about someone and have it mean so little. To know, against her will, that it was possible to fall for someone like this and also to know that it was futile.

She had been so sure that she could convince him to take the chance. She had been so positive that he would come around.

Maybe the real trouble was that Carliz was not accustomed to failures. Because she did not set herself up with true challenges, perhaps. Because she did not ask much of herself. She knew that was what some would say.

Or maybe, she thought then, it was just she was heartbroken. And she would remain heartbroken. She would never be able to explain it to anyone else, because they wouldn't believe her if she told the truth and she couldn't bring herself to actually tell someone a lie. What the papers said, she couldn't control. She could only insinuate, then fail to correct their assumptions, and they had drawn their own conclusions.

But now…now she was simply going to have to live with this.

So she watched him from her window, aware that he

would not be pleased if he caught her at it. That he would prefer to pretend she did not exist at all, and if she did, that they did not recognize each other.

She was going to have to live with that, too. And maybe, someday, learn how to convince herself that she couldn't recognize him after all.

Carliz told herself that it was a farewell. His wedding was in a handful of months and that would be that. Because her scandals had only ever been entertaining, as her sister had requested. They could not involve a married man. They would not.

She couldn't even allow herself to be the fake lover of a married man. It would be too cruel to his wife. Too unnecessarily vicious when the truth was, it would only be more acrobatics around the same heartbreak.

So she stood there instead and watched him as he commanded space around him. As others flocked to him, the way they always did.

She told herself this would have to do, and then she would surrender herself to whatever her mother thought was necessary to do her duty. She saw no reason to delay the inevitable, not now.

That should have been the end of it. She was sure that it would have been.

Except as she watched, Valentino stepped away from the rest of the crowd. He stood on the edge of the keep, half in shadow, and seemed to do nothing at all but breathe.

She found herself pressed up against the window, watching him avidly, because he didn't know she was here. No one did. He didn't know she could see him, that in fact, she might be the only one at the party who could.

There was no way he could know that she was the only one who saw the way he let his eyes drift shut for the barest moment, as a look as close to grief as any she had ever seen crossed over his face.

It was the exact same look she had seen once before.

When he had stepped away from her after that kiss. In that moment before he told her that nothing could happen between them.

And in that moment, she knew. Valentino was not resigned to this course he had taken. He was not happy about his upcoming wedding.

This, tragically, meant that Carliz had no choice.

At first she'd thought it would be that very night. She'd pulled herself together, had gone downstairs, yet by the time she made it to the party he had already left. And later she'd read in the papers that they had planned it that way, the two of them. Ex-lovers, according to the tabloids, who clearly could not stand to be in the same room with each other.

If only, she had thought sourly. Instead, she was an ex-lover who had never been a lover at all, and how unfair was that?

That was when she'd begun planning this puzzle.

Carliz knew full well that this was her last chance. Her only chance. Even she could only beat her head against the same brick wall for so long. She slipped into the lovely, airy chapel with the rest of the guests, keeping her eyes demurely lowered as she took a seat in one of the pews toward the back.

Here, too, she hadn't planned exactly what she would do. She was hoping the perfect solution would come to her. She knew that there was always the option of standing up in the middle of the ceremony, assuming that was something they did here. Not that she was entirely certain that her objection would count. Besides, she couldn't help but feel that standing up like that would be seen as an act of violence, and she wasn't sure she wanted to deal with the fallout of such a dramatic scene.

On the other hand, waiting for Valentino to come to his senses hadn't worked either.

It had done the exact opposite of working, in fact.

And so she sat, feeling overly warm and more than a little bit distressed, wondering if she was *truly* prepared to put herself beyond the pale like that. It was one thing when it was nothing but a few headlines in the outrageously and notably untrue tabloids. There were people here, however. People who would watch and witness whatever it was she did here. People who would always know that Carliz de Las Sosegadas was the sort of person who would disrupt another woman's wedding.

Her sister would never forgive her. It was precisely the sort of embarrassing event that she had asked Carliz to avoid.

Carliz was not big on prayer, but she found herself casting a few missives upward, asking for a better option.

She waited and she waited. The people around her began to fidget in their seats, and the low murmur of speculation began to get louder.

Until, eventually, a door opened toward the front of the chapel and a man stepped in. She tensed, but knew in the next moment that it was not Valentino. This was a shorter man, rounder. He marched into the middle of the altar, and bowed slightly to the assembly.

"I regret to inform you all that the wedding will not

be going forward as planned," he said. "Please accept the deepest apologies for having come all this way. A fleet of boats has been called into ferry you all back to the mainland as the tide is yet high. Good day."

All around, the murmurs broke into full-throated speculation. Excited whispers became nervous laughter, and Carliz was fairly certain she could hear her name in the comments—though no one had spotted her here.

She felt a bit of shame all the same, if she was honest.

But she still didn't move, because her mind was racing. And the worst part of all was that here she was, sitting in a chapel where a wedding had just been called off and she suspected that she would be named as a reason for that decision. She couldn't argue it. She had put herself in that position and more, she had done so all by herself.

Yet inside her, she felt the faintest, tiniest, strangest little sliver of hope.

And so, when everyone else left the chapel, she followed. She held that scarf around her face, looking around to make sure that no one was monitoring her, and as the rest of the guests made their way to the water, Carliz headed to the big house on the hill—and Valentino—instead.

CHAPTER TWO

WHEN THE DOOR to his bedchamber opened without permission, Valentino Bonaparte tried to convince himself that the woman who appeared before him like an apparition was little more than a daydream, but he knew better.

Valentino was many things, many of them apparently unpardonably foolish, but he had not stooped to lying to himself. Not yet.

Though there were a great many hours left in this already cursed day. Given what had already occurred—something he would have assumed was impossible—he could not rule anything out.

"You cannot possibly be here," he told the woman who stood there in the doorway. The doorway to his bedroom, a place where she had spent entirely too much time—if only in the dreams he preferred to act as if he did not have.

She did not smile. Not quite. "And yet I am."

He turned fully around, putting his back to the window where he had stood all this while. First waiting for the guests to arrive so the task of his wedding could be completed in an orderly fashion. Then watching them all leave in the wake of his man's announcement.

There was no doubt that the world would soon know

that Valentino's deliberately provocative half brother had upped the ante by stealing his bride out from under his nose and on the day of the wedding, but he had not felt that *he* needed to announce it.

It was enough, surely, to cancel the entire affair.

And now Carliz was here. Without invitation.

As always.

He took a moment to study her as she stood there, framed by the open doorway, aware that he was responding to her the way he always did. His chest felt tight. His blood ran hot. His sex was hard.

Time did not improve his reaction to this woman. Distance did not diminish it.

She had been bothersome from the moment they'd met.

Today she was dressed in what looked like a selection of flowing scarves, including one draped over her head. As if she thought anything could conceal her. But Valentino would know her anywhere.

Carliz was drawn in regal lines, from her smooth brow to her aquiline nose to the willowy form she inhabited with a certain, specific grace that was entirely her own—and set every part of him alight. She was the sort of woman who gave the impression of being forever languid, when a closer inspection always revealed that there was nothing languid about the way she carried herself. Princess Carliz was the walking embodiment of what might happen if a lightning bolt turned itself human, wrapped itself in supple flesh, and created storms wherever she went.

He knew the way she smelt. A faint hint of spice, so faint that when he had been close to her—on two very dangerous occasions—he had wanted nothing so much as to bury his face in her neck, breathe her in until that scent was a part of him, and then find every part of her body, every secret space, where he might lose himself in her more fully.

Sometimes he dreamed that scent and woke, alone and furious all over again.

Valentino knew the way she tasted, a mad heat that he had spent years acting as if he could not recall. Or had forgotten. Or had never found compelling in the first place.

He had never had another choice. The only other option was chaos, and it was clear to him that the events of the day made it more than obvious that the role of chaos agent in the Bonaparte family was already taken.

But he remembered the way Carliz had looked at him after that ill-advised kiss, her gaze ripe with a kind of wonder, bright with stars, and impossible. That was what he knew to be true of this woman above all else.

She was impossible.

Then again, this was a day already filled with impossible things. What was one more?

"Did you do this?" he asked her quietly.

She moved further into the room, pushing the scarf that must have covered her face back so he could see the soft, burnished gleam of her hair—not quite blond, not quite red, but something that danced between the two and flirted with shades of brown besides. He could not see which of the layers she wore were wraps or scarves and which might suggest the presence of a dress—and Valentino thought he might go mad with wondering. With the way the soft fabric moved against her body, concealing more than it revealed, and yet making him hunger to see the rest.

To taste her at last. Everywhere.

He suspected she was fully aware of his reaction. That she had planned for it, in fact, and he did not want that image in his head—of Carliz gauging her own feminine power in a mirror, fully knowing what it would do to him.

It had been a point of agony for him in these past years that she knew him far better than she should. Whatever it was that had exploded between them that cursed night, she had been able to use it to her advantage. Or so it seemed to him, because he could find nothing at all advantageous in the way this woman affected him.

But he was not the sort of man who cried mercy.

"I suppose I can glean from that question that you are not the one who called off your own wedding," she was saying.

He thought she would cross to him, but instead she wandered through the room instead, and he wondered if she knew that he would never be able to sleep well in here again. Not without remembering the way she drifted so close to the end of the bed, letting her hand dance over the coverlet. Not without getting that scent of hers everywhere, like the faintest shower of cinnamon powder on everything.

Valentino would see her ghost here, forever, gazing at the art on his walls then looking past him toward the view of the rest of the island, carefully situated to show neither his father nor his brother's houses. He preferred to act as if he was the only Bonaparte here, as he was the only one concerned with the family legacy, and had built his house to make certain it seemed that way while he was here.

It was only after Carliz had taken in all these things,

all the tiny details that made up his life—a life he did not wish for her to know anything about—that she turned back to look at him once more.

Her gaze, as always, was direct. Knowing. Too steady for his own good.

Once she was gone, Valentino knew that he would be tormented by this moment. That he would spend uncountable hours seeking out her scent when it could not possibly linger here. When he would make sure the staff scoured this room to make certain it could not.

Even now, he wanted to lean closer, to inhale deeply, to reach out and put his hands on her—

Weary as he was of the virtue that had so far gotten him precisely nothing in this life, Valentino clung to it.

He did not close the space between them. Because he knew better. He did not get his hands on her, nor indulge himself by finding out what, exactly, was beneath those dancing, flowing scarves. If it was only the hint of her bare skin that he saw, every time she breathed, or if it was truly possible that any sudden movement might send all of that fabric sliding to the floor.

You do not need to know, he told himself with a clenched sort of piety.

"I did not call off the wedding," Valentino told her, before he forgot that he ought to make this a conversation and not another staring match with all of these unnecessary *other things* he did not intend to do anything about. "The bride was thoughtful enough to send a message that she would not be attending the festivities, so canceling the ceremony seemed a prudent next step."

It had not been a message, as such. It had been a report from his security detail that his bride had run off to the other side of the island, clad in her wedding dress, in the company of none other than Aristide.

Rumor has it he married her, signor, his man had informed him a shockingly short while later. Before the guests had even left the chapel.

The thought of his half brother filled him with the usual roar of fury and pain, old grudges, and worse still, those persistent memories of the friendship they'd had. Before they knew who they really were to each other. Before the truth had come out.

Before Valentino had lost not only his mother, but his inheritance. And also his relationship with the housekeeper who had been sleeping with his father all along while treating Valentino as if he was also her son. Ginevra, the housekeeper he had viewed as family.

And Aristide himself.

The friend he had considered a brother until it turned out he really *was* his brother, and that ruined everything.

On a philosophical level, Valentino had no idea why it hadn't been obvious to him from the start that Aristide would ruin even this. A wedding that should not have registered on his brother's radar, as Valentino very much doubted that matrimony interested the profligate, careless Aristide in the least.

All Aristide ever cared about was making things difficult for the brother from whom he had already taken so much.

He excelled in it.

Luckily, Valentino thought now, as he often did, *I care only and ever about one thing.*

Aristide could tarnish his own name all he liked—but Valentino embodied the family legacy. He *was* the

Bonaparte tradition, despite his father's best efforts and his brother's many antics. *He* would not tarnish.

If anything, this wedding nonsense would only make Valentino look better by contrast. The very picture of duty and quiet resignation in the face of more unsavory behavior from the usual suspects.

Really, he should thank Aristide for making the case himself so airtight. Though he knew he would not. That he would die first, in fact.

"Well," said Princess Carliz, looking at him with those curious eyes of hers that made him think of treasure chests and ancient castles, the kind of things that ran in her blood back through the ages.

"Well?" he echoed.

And it was then, as Valentino heard the edge in his own voice, that he realized two things.

One, that he had not already called to have her removed, which he would like to put down to the demands of this moment—but he could not pretend that he was emotional about this. Not in the way one might expect a jilted groom to be. He was annoyed, yes. He did not like the mess of this or the fact he knew that he would be required to do some cleanup. He also did not care to have his plans altered.

But two, and more critically, it only just now occurred to him that he and Carliz were…alone.

All alone, here in his bedchamber, where no one else would dare set foot without his express permission.

That thing in him that he had gone to such lengths to keep at bay, to keep at arm's length, to keep *away* from beat hot and hard.

"I hope you don't expect my sympathies." Carliz

looked at him with an expression he'd seen before. It was that *knowing* look of hers that he disliked intensely. Because she should not know him. She should not know a single thing about him. They were strangers. Except, of course, that was not precisely true—though it should have been. And he could not understand why it was that this woman got to him in ways no one else ever had. In ways he could not allow. "I don't know why you were marrying the poor girl in the first place."

"I can assure you that there is nothing poor about her."

Carliz waved an impatient hand. "Do not bore me with some tedious dissertation on your dynastic responsibilities, please. There is no possible way that you have heard more on that score that I have over the years. My sister's potential husband search requires a committee to splice together the perfect bloodlines that appeal to my mother's European sensibilities, my sister's refinement and consequence, and what the palace considers appropriate advertising for the next generation of the modern kingdom. If they could get away with a lab experiment and a selection of petri dishes, I believe they would."

"The bride may have had second thoughts," Valentino said, lifting his shoulder in the barest shrug. And he did not choose to ask himself why it was that he was so happy to let Carliz think he was nonchalant about this. Before she'd walked into the room, he had been as close to irate as he allowed himself to become—though always with the strictest control. He did not particularly wish to figure out why he did not want her to know that. "Luckily, I do not require lab experiments in petri dishes, only a certain level of respectability. I am sure she will be easily replaced."

"How tempting for the next figurine you tote to the altar." Carliz's voice was scathing, something she very clearly did not mind if he knew. "If only I, too, could be a nameless puzzle piece for you to move about at will, easily and often duplicated, exchanged, then soon enough forgotten."

And for the first time since he'd woken up this morning, filled with the dark resolve that had gotten him into this position in the first place and fully prepared to execute his duty no matter what, Valentino found himself feeling…something a whole lot like *good.*

There was no other way to explain the sudden lightness he could feel in him after so long holding up the weight of this heaviness he'd brought upon himself. Because despite what his wretched father had done—from parading his mistress beneath his wife's nose and thereby, eventually, causing his wife's death to all the years of pitting his legitimate son against his bastard for his own entertainment—Valentino had always been conscious of his place. Of who he was. Who he would always be, no matter what games his father played. No matter what became of his inheritance.

He was still and ever Valentino Bonaparte, the one and only true heir to his family's legacy. It was still incumbent upon him to be the Bonaparte he wished to see in the world. Not like his reckless half brother, certainly. And certainly nothing like his cruel father.

There had been others before Milo, and it was Valentino's job to make certain that there would be more after him. Men like his grandfather, dignified and reserved, and filled with distaste for the sort of person Milo had become. There had been the uncles that Milo had always hated, mostly because they didn't approve of him. There had been the older one, Vincenzo, the original heir. He had been a stalwart man in his own father's style, all that was intelligent and fair-minded. But he had died, taken abruptly when he was in his twenties, long before he'd had the chance to secure his legacy.

It was the youngest brother in the family, Bruno, who had told Valentino stories about the lost heir to the Bonaparte fortune. Uncle Bruno, who had been deeply revolted by Milo for most of his life and had renounced the family entirely when he'd moved to America and married his long-term partner. Severing all ties in his wake.

Valentino had always been keenly aware that if only the sainted Vincenzo had married and secured the family line earlier rather than later, so much of what had happened after could have been averted.

He had felt as if a clock were always ticking in him as he'd set about securing his own fortune, so that he would never, ever be dependent upon his father's cruel whims. It had been a relief to decide that he was finally ready and then to move forward as swiftly as possible. His requirements for a wife were quite simple, after all. He wanted someone practical and biddable. His mother had been neither of those things, and look at where she had ended up. His mother had been emotional. She had fancied herself in love with Milo, she had suffered for it, and Milo had used that love shamelessly.

Valentino had always been clear on that score after watching the many disasters of his family unfold before him. There would be no love where he was concerned. Love cursed whoever it touched. Love corroded and destroyed.

Love was, at best, a catastrophic disaster.

Love, apparently, was what kept Ginevra, the housekeeper of his youth and long his father's lover, still at her job tending to the original house on the estate and Milo himself even though her own son had done shockingly well for himself and should have been more than able to support her.

He could not think of a better warning against love than the two women who had actually loved a monster like Milo Bonaparte. His mother had died. Ginevra toiled on. None of them were happy, nor ever would be.

With all of that in mind, Valentino had decided that Francesca Campo fit the bill nicely. She had been so biddable that she had nearly disappeared in the middle of conversations. It was true that he had found her boring, but he had thought that was a positive.

After all, if he'd wanted a lightning bolt, he'd known right where to find one.

And right now, said lightning bolt was advancing upon him.

"Do you know why I am here?" she was demanding, with all her usual delicacy.

Which was to say, none. For a princess, she was astonishingly direct.

"Somehow I doubt it was to offer your felicitations," he murmured, watching those scarves dance and flow as she moved, damn her. "Likely that is the reason you're not invited."

"I had to sneak onto this island," she told him. "I had to crash your wedding, the only event of any significance that I have not been invited to in as long as I can recall."

"Perhaps you have confused reality and fantasy yet

again," he said coolly, though nothing in him was cool. It was all fire and the dark. The dangerous, enveloping dark. "Is it possible that you forgot, once more, that we have no relationship, you and I? Did you perhaps tell yourself a different story so often that you forgot it was a lie?"

"We might not have had the wild affair the papers think we did," she said, coming to stand directly before him, that gaze of hers trained on him. "But this is not a *lie*, Valentino. And I don't need you to tell the truth about it. I know the truth."

"What is it you think you know, *Principessa*?" he asked, though he knew better. He knew this was not a conversation he should allow. He had made certain, for years, that it could not take place. There was no reason to stop now. But he could not seem to keep himself from it. "What is it you imagine this is?"

She opened her mouth as if to answer him, but then stopped. And he knew too much about her for his own good, though he had vowed to himself that he would pretend they had never met. Still, he had found himself accidentally finding his way to articles, here and there. Not simply the usual tabloid fodder that trailed about after her, but the few actual, interesting discussions of who she was, mostly in relation to her sister, Queen Emilia of Las Sosegadas, a tiny little jewel of a kingdom tucked away in the mountains between France and Spain.

And even then, he had felt as if every sentence he'd read had been confirmation of something he already knew from their brief, electric meetings. He could see that she was clever. It was the way she looked at him, and right through him, when no one else had ever seemed particularly capable of that.

No one, that was, except his brother—but he chose not to focus on that twisted, tortuous relationship.

Carliz was beautiful, yes, but he had seen her when she was not putting on that act of hers. Not that she was *not* bright and glorious, drawing everyone near. She was all of that, but she was also more. She was not *only* that gleaming, laughing version of herself, and even though the moments they had spent together did not add up to even an hour, he had seen more of her than the whole of the world.

He told himself that was a curse, but it felt more like a blessing.

"I have a better idea," she said now, studying him. "Why don't you tell me what this is?"

"I have told you. Repeatedly." But he would do so again, because he needed to hear it too. "It is nothing. It can only be nothing. It will never be anything else."

"That does not sound like nothing." She shook her head. "And if it was really nothing, I feel certain you would already have had me removed from this room. Ejected from the grounds of your estate. Or thrown in jail like any other sad little stalker. But that's not what I am, is it?"

Valentino was surprised that there was the urge in him to agree with her. To say the unsayable things. To throw himself off a cliff, here and now. He did not know how he managed to keep himself from giving in to it. That was how strong it was. "I understand what you want me to say. But that doesn't mean I will say it."

"Of course not. Because if you said it, then you could

no longer hide away in all your denial. And then what would you do?"

And Valentino laughed. It was a rusty sound, because he was not a particularly joyful or typically amused person. He was a man of strict compartments. Only his mother and his brother had ever called him by his full name, and he liked it that way. Because now that his mother was dead, it was only his greatest enemy who called him Valentino.

To the rest of the world, he was Vale. It made things very easy for him. Anyone who called him by the nickname knew only the performance he put on, not him.

But Carliz called him Valentino. Worse, he had told her to. He had given her that name himself, when he never did such a thing. He always handed out his nickname, so he could file the people who used it into the appropriate spaces.

"I saw you in Paris not long ago," he told her. "I was there on business. You were there to make a scene."

"I would say I remember," she replied, looking unrepentant. "But that would be a lie."

"I remember well enough. You were there with the usual entourage. Taking over the restaurant, spilling out into the streets." He had not expected to see her. He had been shocked she had somehow not felt the weight of his stare, or simply *felt* his presence, and he didn't like what that said about him. "You were laughing and making merry though it was clear to me that you were empty inside."

"But have you not heard? I am always empty inside. That is one of the foremost qualities about me that people admire." She leaned closer, and he was hit with that spice and a hint of silk. “The emptier I am, the more they can imagine me however they like. It makes for a lovely sparkle, and I am nothing if not *sparkly.* Really, it is a public service.”

“I told myself I was not following you,” he said, not sure why he was telling her this. Not sure why he was admitting to this fault in his character. “I was merely walking back along the same boulevard. And you had no idea that I was there. You were simply careening this way and that in a Parisian night, heedless of your surroundings.”

“I pay a security detail a great deal of money to make certain that I can be as heedless as I like, whenever I like.” Though Carliz smiled, wryly. “It is more honest to say that the crown pays, because as my sister has pointed out many times, she would be the one called upon to pay a ransom for anything truly upsetting to befall me. Still. I was perfectly safe.” Again she studied him again. “But you were not concerned about my safety, were you?”

“You looked so lost, Carliz,” he told her, and maybe he knew she would react to that. That she would suck in a breath. “That was when I decided to forgive you for all the lies you have told about the two of us over the years. I doubt you knew any better.” He leaned in, just a little, the better to stick in the knife. “Just a lost little princess, stumbling around Europe, making messes for her sister to clean up.”

He saw something flash in her eyes, but in the next moment, she laughed. And this was not that sparkly laugh of hers that she trotted out in front of the cameras. Or for her shallow little friends’ mobile phones. This was a low sort of laugh, warm and deep.

It moved in him like the kind of fine bourbon he only allowed himself seldomly.

"It's not going to work," she told him. "I can't be shamed. Though you are welcome to try, if you like. Everyone does."

"Princess," he said from between his teeth, as if she was the one needling him when he had just sunk a knife in, deep. And on purpose. "This has been a challenging day. I am now embroiled in a scandal not of my own making and you are here, right in the middle of it. It makes me wonder what level of collusion there has been between you and my brother."

She looked intrigued by that. "I absolutely would have colluded with your brother. But I didn't think of it."

"When I leave this room I will have to pick up the pieces, yet again, from one more disaster not of my making." Valentino let out his own laugh then, but this time it was nothing but bleak. "I cannot even blame my brother. He has always behaved as badly as possible, I assume to live down to the expectations placed upon him. I cannot blame my would-be bride, for it is not as if she truly betrayed me. That would require an emotional connection we never had. But you are something else again. I find it is easy enough to blame you."

"You can blame me all you want," Carliz threw right back at him.

She stepped even closer, and now it was dangerous. They were barely a breath apart. Her scent was all around him, and he could feel her heat, too, and it would not even require a decision to reach out for her. He could simply exhale—

"Good," Valentino growled. "Because I intend to blame you for everything. Thoroughly."

"Please do," she dared him. "At last."

And maybe he needed that decision to be made, even if she was the one to make it. Either way, he finally shrugged off that leash he'd had wrapped tight around his own neck since he'd first laid eyes on her in Rome. After all this time, after letting it choke him for years, he finally just…cut the chain.

Because this day of all days, Valentino thought he might as well do the thing he was already accused of doing. He might as well have *one taste* since he had already paid for it in the press. Over and over again. And would likely continue paying for it after today.

And besides, he had always rather liked a lightning storm.

Maybe he had needed a disaster of this magnitude to admit it.

Valentino reached out and put his hands on her body, the silk of those scarves and the heat of her skin beneath. Then he drew her closer still, so that body of hers was pressed against his chest the way he woke up remembering, sometimes.

This was like that night, but much, much better.

Because when he kissed his maddening princess this time, he had no intention of stopping.

CHAPTER THREE

CARLIZ HAD SPENT a lot of time convincing herself that she'd made up… Well, everything when it came to Valentino. There had been months in there, maybe even a whole year, where she'd felt she had no choice. She'd had to convince herself that she suffered from nothing at all but an overactive imagination, or die.

Because he was marrying another woman. And she had been given absolutely no choice but to live with that.

But any doubt she might have had on that score was swept away when his mouth took hers.

Completely and utterly and immediately.

Because if anything, the taste of him was far, far better than she'd allowed herself to remember. It was the way they *fit*. It was the heat, the power, the way she could feel his mouth as if it was on every part of her.

He kissed her as if they were both drowning in the same wild sea of sensation, and he wanted it that way. He kissed her as if he was daring her to let go, to drown with him, to let this thing swallow them whole.

It was that voracious.

He was that intense.

And it was funny, after all this time, to finally get the thing she'd claimed she'd wanted all along. It was funny to push and push against the same brick wall only to have it open up like it had only been a door all along.

She felt a bit like stumbling. She felt a bit as if the way her feet gripped the floor below her was uncertain and precarious, and Carliz didn't know if she should step back and steady herself…or simply jump.

But when Valentino changed the angle of his mouth on hers, and he licked his way inside, she realized that her body had already made the decision.

Because this was *flying*.

So she twined her arms around his neck and kissed him back as if her life depended upon it. She felt as if it did.

When something in her began to shudder, low and deep, she knew that despite the things she'd told herself in that boat out on the water…she had not expected any of this to work. She had expected that she would sit there in that church, gearing herself up to make a scene but then not doing it. Because as angry and confused and heartsick she was over Valentino's marriage she might have been, she could not imagine explaining to her sister how and why she had found it necessary to ruin another woman's wedding.

So publicly.

And so, deep down, she had suspected that she would have been creeping back to her boat, hiding her face in her scarves so no one would see her tears, and then limping off to figure out what the rest of her life was supposed to look like. Now that love was dead and there was no need to worry about it any longer.

This was much better.

This was everything she had stopped hoping could

happen. His mouth on hers, his hands spearing into her hair and gripping her, hard, in a way that made every single nerve in her body bloom bright with sensation.

Inside and out and everywhere else, because she knew Valentino in a way that no one else did. She had seen the way he was described in the press. Stern. Controlled. Methodical. They were usually insults, but she knew better. She knew that when it came to this, to the fire that burned only here between the two of them, he was all of those things—but in the kind of ways that made a woman's body not quite her own.

"You are a witch," he told her, harsh and thick against the line of her neck. "You have bewitched me."

"If I knew any spells," she said, tipping her head back to give him all the access he wanted, "I would have cast them long ago. I would not have waited for your wedding day."

He growled out a sound that thrilled her, pure and simple, from the tips of her ears down to the tops of her toes.

It was an animal sound, rough and glorious. He pulled back, so that the whole of her field of vision was that face of his, those stern and sensual planes and the glittering heat that made his faded blue eyes look like whole summers. He bent slightly and swung her up into his arms, then carried her over to his bed as if she was light as a feather.

And Carliz knew her own body very well. She and her sister had been raised by a strict mother and stricter governesses who had drilled into them the importance of their royal appearance, but what was meant by that was the appearance of effortlessness. Mila had gone through periods of struggling to maintain the size that she and

the palace advisors had decided provided the be
graphs, replete with elegance and sophistication,
queen. Carliz had not struggled as hard, but then she was never going to be photographed with seventeen tons of ceremonial robes, a scepter, and the ancient crown—the wearing of which required perfect posture and an elegant form. As was clear from all the pictures of portly King Amadeo in the fifteenth century.

All of that to say that Carliz was five feet, ten inches tall and while she like to keep herself in the sort of shape that allowed for offhanded bikini wearing whenever she liked, she was not a twig.

But Valentino didn't seem to notice. He carried her as if she was tiny. As if she was a small, precious thing he could tuck in a pocket, if he wished.

It made her want to find that pocket, curl up in it, and maybe breathe for the first time in as long as she could remember.

He set her down on the edge of his bed, and then his hands were in her hair again. He tugged her head back. Then he dropped his face to her neck and he growled once more.

This time, it sounded like a warning.

"It's that scent," he muttered. "It's been driving me mad."

She wanted to say something amusing about that, but she couldn't get her mouth to work, because he knelt down before her.

In a manner she could not call the least bit supplicant.

"I…" she began, but that dark fire in his blue gaze stopped her.

"Carliz." Her name was like a command, and her whole body shivered. "It is either time, or it isn't."

She understood what he was asking without him having to ask it. It was that stark. And there were a million things she might not understand about what was happening to her or why he'd resisted it for so long, but she knew she would die if they stopped. She thought she would actually, literally die.

So she nodded, though her heart was in her throat.

And then his hands were on her thighs, sleeking their way up the inside of her legs and making her gasp. Making everything in her body seem to twist into something molten as she started leaning back, as if he needed room.

Valentino didn't look up at her, so focused was he on what he was doing. He lifted her up, sliding his hands beneath her to grip her bottom as he hauled her closer to the edge of the bed and settled there, his face *right there*—

But then it stopped mattering.

Because he put his face between her legs and he breathed in, deep. And when he breathed out again, she could feel the rush of air against the most sensitive part of her, separated from his lips by only the faint scrap of silk that she wore.

He said something then, some kind of dark oath.

"Valentino," she began.

But all he did was growl and then set his mouth on her tender flesh, sucking on her as if that silk was nothing.

And her body simply…took over. Carliz arched up on the bed, as if pulled toward the high ceilings by some cord attached to the center of her chest. Her heels found their way into the center of his back, and she couldn't tell if she was pushing herself up or keeping herself still, but it didn't seem to matter.

Because he was eating her alive. And he was taking his own sweet time doing it.

That shuddering inside her tumbled in and around itself, and everything rushed toward the place where his mouth moved, flooding her, until he made a deep noise of approval. Then he shifted her, taking the heat of his mouth away. And all she could hear was her own panting, high-pitched and breathless.

There was a tug, then another one, harder still, but she didn't understand what was happening until his fingers gripped her bottom again and spread her open like a feast. Before licking his way into her molten heat at last.

And for a long while, maybe a lifetime, there was absolutely nothing but that.

The things he knew. The way he knew them, and how he showed her. The way he licked into her, moving his chin and his jaw so that everything was sensation. Everything was fire.

Still, she had the notion that this wasn't for her at all. That her pleasure was a simple by-product of his own need to taste her like this.

Somehow that made it all even hotter.

Carliz felt everything shift inside her as he moved, as he *consumed* her. It was like a wave rising up, gathering steam, racing straight for her.

And there was a part of her that wanted to avoid it. There was a part of her that was on the verge of overwhelmed, and maybe she would even have pulled away, if only to see if she could control the heat of it, the intensity—

But he wouldn't allow it.

Valentino held her tighter. He licked in deeper.

He let his teeth scrape that proud little center of her, once. Then again—

And Carliz turned to ash.

It was a white-hot *implosion.* She heard someone scream, and her body took over, jerking into his mouth as if she was trying to ride him from below.

She could feel him shaking too. Because he was all around her, and she was holding him between her thighs, and it was only later that she would realize that the shaking she felt was his laughter. As if he couldn't believe the glory of this either.

There was nothing but that bliss.

Spitting on and on and on.

Carliz only spun back into flesh and bone when he pulled her up to sit on the edge of the bed again. His hands were on her shoulders, but it took her so long to focus on him and when she did, his mouth was in that straight, serious line. But his eyes were bright and dancing.

"Take heart, *Principessa*," he said in that low, growly voice. "This is only the beginning."

She could feel that in every single cell in her body. And every single one of them was *blazing hot.* And so she smiled, as if this kind of thing happened to her every day. "Marvelous," she said, in some approximation of *blasé*. "It would be so disappointing if, after all this, it was just…boring."

But that lassitude making her hot and sleepy and silly disappeared in an instant when his gaze changed. When it got hotter. More intent.

"I promise I will do my best," he said in that deep, dangerous way of his. "I would not wish to bore you."

It was possible that she would come to regret saying something so flippant.

That was what Carliz thought as he stopped doing whatever it was he was doing—she realized, belatedly, that it was possible he'd been intending to undress, for she was sure that he'd been wearing a full suit before and now was simply in shirtsleeves and his trousers—and looked down at her in a way that she could only call…alarming.

In that it set off every single delicious alarm inside her body in a way she had never felt before.

She had the distant thought that she'd been playing with this fire all along, and hadn't realized it. As if it had been a wee little book of matches when he was more properly a wildfire.

He looked even more stern than before. That glittering thing in his gaze was even more intense. Valentino crossed his arms as he stood there before her, positioned between her sprawled-out legs. While she slumped there with her panties torn off and her dress hiked up to her waist.

And it didn't occur to Carliz to fidget, or to cover herself. Or to do anything but gaze back at him, wide-eyed, once again feeling small and precious and more beautiful than she ever had before in the whole of her life.

"Take off your dress," he told her.

It was an order. And…she liked it.

And he knew she liked it. His brows rose, waiting for a protest or a fight or even a reply. Maybe a laugh.

But her breath was coming faster, parts of her prickling into life and making themselves known. Her breasts felt heavy against her chest and her nipples were pinched of their own accord. Her skin felt too hot, and every time she breathed, it was as if she was causing her own dress to caress her. It made her want to squirm. Maybe she did, because she felt precious and debauched all at once. And she had never been this wet.

Ever.

And, in any case, it didn't occur to her to disobey him. She pulled the dress up and over her head in one movement and threw it aside, realizing when she saw that look of approval on his face that his approval was exactly what she wanted. She sat up straighter, as if she was offering her breasts to him, and he nodded.

"That too," he said.

Carliz's hands were shaking as she fumbled with the front closure of her bra. She peeled it off her breasts, sucking in a breath as that simple little bit of motion made her react as if he'd done it. She was oversensitized. She was shivering. And yet there was not one part of her that was cold.

"Beautiful," he murmured, and there was something about his approval that delighted her. It shimmered through her, making this hotter, making her feel molten and almost too bright with it to bear.

"You are a madness in me," he told her. "You have driven me to the limits of my control, *Principessa*, and this I cannot allow."

She didn't know what that meant. But the way he looked at her, the way he studied her as she sat there, fully naked before him, made that same shimmering, shivery heat wrap her up even more.

"The things you have done require retribution," he

told her, which might have been scary if she hadn't seen that gleaming dark fire in his gaze. If she hadn't *felt* it, everywhere, as if he was still licking into her core. "Do you understand?"

"Yes," she said, though she didn't.

"Because if we are telling truths here tonight," he said, in that low, stirring way of his that she felt—again—like he was pressing the words into her skin with his tongue, "then we can admit, you and I, that the paparazzi should never have known a single thing about the two of us."

"It could be argued that they didn't. That they don't."

"Yet you will not make that argument." His eyes were stern too, then, and it made her heart ache. As if there was nothing she wouldn't do for this man's good opinion, and happily. Had that been what had motivated her all along? But no. There was also all this *fire*, the flames still licking at her as if they would never stop. They hadn't yet. "Because you know exactly what you did, Carliz. And so do I."

He moved to the bed and sat beside her, still fully clothed. And then, raising that demanding brow, he patted his thigh. "Come, then. You know as well as I do what you have earned." His eyes gleamed. "We'll start with a reminder of our sins."

For a long moment, she didn't understand. She stared at his thigh, harder than any rock beside her. Then at his face and intensity there, so all-consuming it made her wish she could simply crawl inside of him… Yet, whether she understood it or not, she couldn't stop shivering. And every single time she did, it made her wetter between her legs. It made her breasts feel heavier. It made oversensitized skin feel as if she was so raw that it might simply peel off in the next moment, leaving her brand-new and entirely his.

She didn't hate that idea.

"Carliz," Valentino said quietly. Intently. "Over my lap, please."

And then she did understand, and it slammed into her like its own explosion. Hot. Hard. Devastating.

"You… You want to…?"

"Three years." He bit off the words quietly, his eyes a bright flame. "How many tabloid stories do you think I was forced to suffer through in that period of time, thanks to you? Twenty? Forty?"

"I…" But she couldn't finish. She didn't even know what she might say.

And her heart was a trapped bird in her chest.

"Carliz."

It was the way he was looking at her. As if he fully expected her to obey him. But more, as if he needed her to. As if that was a part of this wild connection between them. As if this had been at the heart of it all along.

Carliz would have said that it couldn't have been. That there was no part of her that would ever want this kind of thing… But she wanted *him*. Her body was still tingling and shivering from what he'd already done to her. He had already proved that he knew her body far better than she did.

Her body had no qualms about any of this. Her bones felt made of nothing more than *want*.

And the fact that he wanted to spank her should have scared her. It should have turned her off immediately. If it did, she would not have cared about his approval.

She would have extricated herself from this situation, no matter what.

But if anything, she was so excited she thought she might squirm off the side of the bed altogether.

"Do not make me ask you again," he said, and though his voice was hard and his mouth so firm, there was something else in his gaze. That pale blue fire, darkening by the moment.

Carliz understood that she would follow that fire anywhere. That she already had.

That if she believed she had seen his heart from across a crowded room—and she did—she could believe this, too. That this was what needed to happen.

That these things she wanted, without knowing why, were worth chasing.

So she took that same leap of faith once more. She let herself roll toward him. Then she carefully and delicately draped herself over his lap.

He shifted as she did, putting his leg between hers in such a way that she understood she would not be able to squirm off of him. She was dangling there, completely exposed to him, unable to hide anything—even the way she kept shivering with all that expectation and wild, whirling delight.

"Count," he ordered her.

And when his palm landed on the soft flesh of her bottom, she yelped.

It was not a *delight*. It *hurt*. She tried to roll away from him only to discover that her initial impression was correct. She couldn't.

Carliz opened her mouth to complain, bitterly, but that heavy palm was on the place where it smacked her, first holding it, then rubbing it. Just slightly, until all she could feel was the heat of his hand, and somehow, that sharp spike turned into something hotter. Something that sent a kind of molten thread shooting out into other parts of her, putting her on notice.

Making her squirm again, but not because it hurt.

"Count, please," he told her. "Because if I do, I am almost certain to lose my place. And if I lose count I will, naturally, have to start over."

Carliz, who had never been spanked in her life, counted each smack that this man doled out to her. And he had not been kidding about the numbers.

He spanked her, hard. He held her in place and this time, when a wave raced toward her, she found that it was a more of *whole tide.* And soon enough, she was letting wave after wave transform her as she counted, as he spanked her and spanked her, the heat of the blows mixing with the heat inside of her, until it was something new, something impossible and unwieldy and too large to bear.

This, she thought, *is what I wanted all along.*

The connection. The intensity. The riot inside her. The implacable *rightness* of his hand, its rhythm, its cadence—never faster or slower.

As if this had been what she'd wanted from him from the start. Steady. Inexorable. Something perfect she could never have dreamed of, could never have asked for.

So she melted into him and she let the tide take her away, and when he was done, she thought he murmured something like *good girl,* which made her shudder and moan even more. And then to her surprise, he shifted that hard thigh beneath her, smoothing a hand down over the curve of her bottom until he found his way to all of that molten heat she couldn't deny. And that rigid center of a need she couldn't even believe could exist after *a spanking.*

"Now come for me, *mia principessa,*" he murmured and then he pinched her there, hard.

And everything inside of Carliz seemed to buckle. Then explode.

Wave after wave of sensation rocked through her until she was sobbing and writhing, and when he massaged her bottom it was a sharp, bright fire but made her come harder. And on and on it went, no beginning and no end, and it was impossible.

All of this was impossible.

And then, at last, he sat her up again and shrugged out of his clothes beside her.

She was dizzy, and delirious, or maybe it was simply that she was focused so intently on him it was as if they were the same person. She felt as if they were the same person, but so marvelously, magically split in two so it felt *this good* when they came together again.

When Valentino was naked, he crawled onto the bed and then hauled her up with him toward the head, laying her out beside him. She could feel everything, all at once. The soft linens at her back, even though they agitated the hot flesh of her bottom. And then him next to her, that hair-roughed chest as beautiful in its own decidedly masculine way as his face. It was too much to take in, all the beauty of that perfect male form of his. The ridged abdomen. The impossible perfection of his muscled arms. The ease and certainty in the way he rolled her beneath him and settled between her legs.

She made a soft sound, and his gaze lightened.

will feel every spank,” he told her, as if he was g her a gift. “And I give you permission to cry out uch as you need. As loudly as you want.”

Her throat was dry. “I…”

“All you need to say is thank you, Carliz,” he told her.

And so…she did.

Then, for the first time, she watched that mouth of his curve.

Deadly and beautiful and entirely hers.

And then he slammed his way inside her, and she… catapulted into another realm entirely.

Because everything was a wild flash of a sensation so intense it was something too new, too all-encompassing—

And everything was beautiful.

And it was all fused together, intertwined and tangled, until she found herself gripping onto him for dear life.

Her brain tried to pick apart the different sensations. The stinging in her bottom and that initial sharp pain inside of her that she had no time to adjust to—because he filled her, completely and utterly.

He filled her, and then he held her tight, as if getting his bearings, too.

She tried to breathe, but quickly realized that was not a priority. Not now.

Because there was too much sensation to bear, and yet she wanted all of it. There was too much sensation to handle, and yet she managed it. Somehow, she did it. She *wanted* to do it. She wanted *all* of it, all of him. She clenched a little bit, making him mutter a curse, but that made it better. She tested all that heavy heat wedged so deep inside her, and the more she did, the better it got.

Carliz took a breath, finally. And that was when he began to move.

She did the only thing she could think of to do. She clung to him. And then, when she realized he was setting a slow, deliberate pace, she matched his movements. The way she had when they'd danced in Rome.

The way she'd done, internally, when he'd spanked her.

It was all the same dance, she thought now.

And it wasn't as if any of the sensations dissipated. But somehow, they all rolled into one. And he was at the center of it, thrusting deep inside her, pulling out, then doing it again.

And again.

And he was so *big.* She felt split in half and filled almost too much, but she liked it. Because every time she thought that surely she'd reached capacity, he found some new depth. And they moved together, so she had no choice but to figure out how to do this, how to make it better and better as she went. How to wrap her legs around him. How to hold on, and arch back, so he could drop his head and take one of those hard nipples into his hot mouth.

So he could make her cry out like he was teaching her melodies to brand-new songs.

Carliz had never felt both outside her skin and more inside it than she'd ever been in her life. Filled with him, and covered in sensation from her bottom and that molten core of hers and everywhere their bodies dragged together and then apart—

And then, suddenly—inexorably—the waves began to hit. One after the next.

But he didn't stop.

He kept going, so that each wave that hit was bigger, longer, wilder.

And still he went on, until she began to think the sounds she was making really were songs, and they were lost in the same sea together, and she would be happy to drown. Just like this.

Wrecked beyond repair, but flying high all the while.

His pace changed. His movements became jerky and he rolled with her, holding her so tightly that it should have hurt, but it didn't. Carliz felt herself break wide open once more, and when she did, he shouted too.

Together, then, they tumbled end over end, one wave into the next.

And the only thought she had in her head was his name.

She didn't know how long she slept like that, but it must have been some while. When she woke, she was beneath the covers and Valentino was standing at that window again. Carliz felt a moment of cold fear that he would reset to their usual level. That they would start pretending the way they always did.

Instead, without turning around, he spoke. "I'm certain you must be hungry."

She sat up, swallowing hard when she realized that her throat was dry. There was a meal set out on the low table in front of his fireplace. And she was starving. But she didn't go to the food. She went to him instead, following an urge she'd had before yet had never indulged. Because she'd never been naked before when she'd had it. He'd never been there, wearing only a pair of trousers.

She wrapped herself around him, with her face pressed against one of the planes of muscle on his back. He started to say something, but she was still following that urge inside her, so she began to press kisses all along the smooth, hard expanse of his back. She got up on her tiptoes and pressed a kiss to the nape of his neck, then followed his spine all the way down.

And when he turned to her, there was a storm in those eyes of his. But Carliz dropped to her knees before him, put her hands on the waist of his trousers, and held his gaze as she pulled him free.

He was hard again. Bigger and bolder than she'd imagined, and she'd never thought that she would have the desire to do something like this. But this was Valentino. And she wanted nothing more than to taste him. To know him.

In every possible way.

When he didn't tell her to stop, she leaned forward and took him into her mouth.

And then, she played. She used her tongue. She experimented with suction. She licked the length of him, once and again, and got lost along the way.

But when she began to feel that ache rise inside her again, as if he was the one touching her when it was the opposite, he pulled her away.

"No," she began. "I want—"

"Too bad," he replied.

Though there was something like laughter in his eyes.

They didn't make it to the bed that time. He lifted her up in his arms, then slid her down the length of his body. He caught her thighs in his hands, holding her as she sank down over his length, until he filled her completely.

And started all over again.

It was a long time before she made it to that table in

front of the fireplace, and ate her fill. Then let him treat her like dessert.

All night long, he taught her things about her body that she was a little bit afraid no one should know. Because now that she knew these things, how could she ever go back to who she was? Who she'd been before? But she couldn't worry about that. She couldn't worry about anything.

It was the longest night of her life, and Carliz loved every moment.

And it was sometime after dawn that he tucked her beside him, anchored her with his heavy arm, and they both slept.

She woke some while later to find sun streaming in the windows and the room completely empty. More disconcerting, there was no evidence that anything had happened here. Even the bed she slept in was shockingly neat, to her eye. The tray of food they had feasted on over the course of hours had disappeared. Her dress and scarves and shoes were laid out on a chair. So neatly that it made something in her…uneasy.

Carliz spent a long time in the shower, aware that there were parts of her body she'd never felt before demanding her attention. She liked it.

Her backside ached, but the ache felt like a part of all the other marvelous things she had felt and done. So the more she was aware of her bottom, the more she was also aware of her own soft heat.

When she was dressed and somewhat pulled together, she held her shoes in her hand and padded out of the room into the grand old house she'd barely looked at yesterday while she'd been trying to find him. She knew Valentino had built it. It felt like an ancient castle, except the brilliance of it was that it wasn't, really. And so everything was modernized. Lights came on as she walked. The temperature was pleasant and perfect. It only *looked* old.

She knew enough from her own kingdom that accessible history was the kind of history people remembered. What they held dear. It was history that no one could touch or understand that people preferred to forget, then repeat.

Her own thoughts seem to sit heavy on her when she found her way to the ground floor, and discovered Valentino there.

Everything in her stilled.

He was standing in the great hall with his arms folded, his gaze trained on her as if he been waiting for her some while. And all she could think was that she had tasted every part of him now. That she knew how he *tasted.*

"I hope you're well rested," he said.

"Thank you," she replied. She waited, but he only gazed at her. "That's the most ridiculous thing you could possibly have said."

Something glittered in his gaze, but then it disappeared behind that opaque mask she knew too well. For she'd seen it too many times.

"I apologize for my intensity," he said.

Carliz stiffened. "I have not asked for an apology."

He inclined his head. "Yet I offer it all the same. I was perhaps more affected by the events of yesterday than I realized. I should not have taken them out on you."

"I think what happened between us was always going to happen," she said, carefully, as if she'd only just glanced down to find she was standing in a pile of broken glass. “Whether it was yesterday or some other day, it was inevitable.”

“I do not believe that.”

He said it so starkly. With such dreadful certainty. It made her feel…winded.

And he seemed to know it. He watched her so closely, as if he already knew every possible response she might have. “My security team found the boat you had waiting for you, and dispatched it,” he said. “Another one is available for your use, should you need it. But of course, this is a tidal island, and low tide is in one hour. If you wish, you can take a vehicle to the mainland. Or walk.”

She didn’t understand. And it had been a long time since Carliz had felt so completely out of her depth. Maybe she never had been, not like this. She couldn’t make sense of the fact that this man had made her feel so beautiful, so alive, and now she felt awkward. As if she’d misunderstood. As if she’d made this all up, all along.

“Valentino,” she began.

“You and I will never see each other again,” he told her, and he looked at her directly as he said it. There was nothing particularly opaque in his gaze, not then. It was direct. It was certain.

It was heartbreaking.

“I don’t understand,” she whispered.

“What I can tell you is what I have told you all along,” he said, and she hardly recognized his voice. Too smooth. Too controlled, when he had groaned out his pleasure against the flesh of her breasts. “This is impossible. Last night should never have happened. There is no you and I, Carliz. There never will be.”

Then, impossibly, he turned and walked away.

Though, to her shame, she didn't truly believe he was leaving her there until she heard the sound of a helicopter flying off above her.

And no one was there to see her when she let her knees buckle. When she slid down to the floor. There was no one there as witness, no one to see her cry.

That was a good thing, because she was there a long time.

But eventually, the floor grew too hard, too cold. She remembered what he'd said about the tide.

So Carliz got to her feet. She gathered up her scarves and what remained of her dignity, and she walked off that damned island, determined not to look back. Not to waver. Not to make even the faintest wish that things could be different, because they weren't.

She had been a fool, plain and simple.

And when her feet touched the mainland, she vowed there and then on the whole of Italy and Europe stretching out behind it that she was done with Valentino Bonaparte.

For good.

CHAPTER FOUR

THREE MONTHS LATER, on a late September day that was blue and cool with hints of the glorious summer that she had seen here with her own eyes in July, Carliz stood on an Italian beach at low tide and hated…everything.

Mostly herself.

Well. No. Mostly one Valentino Bonaparte, but *herself* came in a close second.

"I do not want to do this," she muttered, letting the spiteful little breeze steal her words and send them tumbling down the beach toward the village that had stood right where it was since long before there were any Bonapartes kicking about.

Or any Sosegadases, for that matter.

But there was no point in her having come back here if she wasn't going to do the thing she'd come to do, so she forced herself to start walking.

She remembered walking off the island last time all too well. The shoes she'd chosen to potentially stop a wedding had proved unequal to the task, so she'd had to do it barefoot. In the previous night's dress of scarves and mystique.

If there had ever been a walk of shame more complete, Carliz really could not imagine what it might look like.

It was almost funny, she had thought that morning as she'd walked away from all things Valentino Bonaparte, her toes cold in the wet sand and every single muscle in her body screaming out in a full-throated, brand-new voice. She had been accused of many, many a walk of shame in her day. All she really had to do was appear in public before noon and some or other walk of shame was assumed and then speculated upon. Just as any indication that she'd been so much as introduced to a man meant, to all the tabloids, that she was dating him. She'd always found it all entertaining in the extreme.

Likely, she'd discovered that day, because she'd never done the things they'd accused her of doing.

Because that walk away from Valentino's personal castle had taught her that she was not meant to be like the people who did these things on the regular. No shame to any of them, of course. She envied anyone's ability to love themselves enough that it didn't matter whether or not anyone else did.

That was not how she'd felt that day. She still couldn't really imagine putting herself in a position like that again, much less with someone else. Or with someone new. The very idea made her feel ill, then and now.

Back in July she'd tried to convince herself that it was all for the best that she'd had that long walk ahead of her, with more than enough time than anyone would need to sort these things out in their head, surely.

She'd assured herself she was emotionally sorted when she'd arrived on the shores of mainland Italy and had then turned to the actual details of rescuing herself from her own folly. It was possible that she taken her time with that rescue, despite her self-assurances. She'd called her unamused security team once she'd gotten on a train to Rome so they could meet her there. She'd spent a few days in one of her favorite spas, complete with ancient baths and mandated silence, and then a rather leisurely route back home into the mountains of Las Sosegadas.

Where Mila had been waiting with a stack of international papers the palace staff curated for her perusal and entirely too many questions about the called-off wedding of the man the whole world thought she'd had that epic affair with.

I was not invited to Valentino's wedding, Carliz had replied, calmly. But it was the sort of calm that was undercut with the kind of steel she used very rarely. Which, of course, had only made her sister's brows rise higher. *Therefore, anything that occurred there has nothing to do with me.*

It's very scandalous, Mila had replied in her usual manner, though she looked more speculative than normal. She waved her hand at the collection of papers. *Everyone is speaking of it. And, of course, as his most notable ex-girlfriend, your name is coming up. Quite a lot.*

If there was a better definition of reaping what one sowed, Carliz had already slept with him. But that she'd created an affair that hadn't happened until now, and that she would very much like to pretend had not happened at all, ran a close second.

She'd made herself shrug, though nonchalance had felt difficult to come by. *You know as well as I do that no one can control what the tabloids choose to speculate about, Mila.*

Carliz had suffered through a similar interrogation from her less sedate mother, then had taken herself off to her apartments in the palace, curled up on her bed beneath blankets she did not need for warmth, and wondered what the hell she was going to do with the rest of her life.

Slowly, she came to think that the way Valentino had chosen to reject her that terrible morning had helped. Because she had always believed that if he would just give in to the chemistry between them, he would *see*. He would *know*.

He would stop telling her that it was nothing.

And it turned out that he did see. He did know—and he still wanted nothing to do with her.

In its own way, that was really very liberating.

A few days later, when she'd grown tired of acting *perfectly fine* to her family while assuming the fetal position in private, she'd found herself in the studio space she'd long kept for herself in the palace. It was an airy room in her apartments that she hadn't so much as walked into in ages. Or even thought about. But she'd once found painting a more appropriate emotional release than, say, planting stories in tabloids.

Carliz had settled in with a sense of purpose. She'd looked through all of her half-finished canvases and she'd sat down before the one she'd loved the most, certain that at any moment, inspiration would strike and she would leap into one of those painting fevers that had used to take her over in school. She would go off on an oil paint bender that would last until the painting was done and she emerged, feeling reborn and victorious, on the other side.

But no matter how long she sat there, she never touched brush to canvas.

She looked all the colors, all the shapes, and saw Valentino. She saw the things that they had done. She felt his handprint, hard and red against her bottom.

It had taken days to fade.

She had cried—hard—when it finally had.

Carliz had been home for nearly two weeks when her mother once again brought up the subject of an appropriate husband. This time, the Queen Mother chose to do it at one of their usual weekly family dinners, just the three of them. Her Majesty the Queen, the queen mother in her typical shroud, and the normally bright and shiny Princess Carliz, who was not sure that she would ever feel sparkly or at all like herself again.

Mother, Mila had said reprovingly after a lengthy monologue on the implications of both the queen and the Princess Royal's enduring single state as well as what the appearance of a tight family unit would do to bolster support for the monarchy, her favorite topics, *can you not see that Carliz is suffering? A man she was very close to had a very well-publicized breakup and yet has been notably absent from Carliz's vicinity, so one can only assume that Carliz's affections were not returned. She needs grace, not dating advice.*

It was nearly unbearable, Carliz had thought then, her gaze on the plate before her, to have it all boiled down like that. Her sister might as well have said, *he's just not that into you.* Because it amounted to the same thing, didn't it?

She had forced herself to look up. She'd forced a smile at her sister, then had looked at her mother.

You keep going on about wanting me to marry, she'd said. *But I am quite certain that in one of the twenty thousand or so extremely boring lectures that we received as girls about our duties, responsibilities, and so on, Her Majesty the Queen herself must marry first.*

She certainly should, their mother began.

I will not be marrying for some time, Mila had said then, in that firm way that made it clear she was speaking as the queen, not as a family member. Even their mother inclined her head. Mila toyed with her wineglass. *Our father regrettably died too soon. I am too young, I think. I will need to wait some while before I can be certain that whoever marries me does not harbor any aspirations to power.*

Understandable, murmured their mother with great sympathy, because her reverence for the crown and its pronouncements knew no ceiling. Only days before she had been ranting to Carliz that Mila *must* marry, and soon, to secure her legacy.

Very well then, Carliz had said, to her own surprise, perhaps because she was tired of gazing despondently at her plate. *I suppose I might as well carry on the family legacy until Mila is ready.*

When no one had responded—an excessively unlikely occurrence with her family—she had looked up again to find the pair of them staring back at her with differing levels of shock. Mila's was tinged with curiosity, her mother's with suspicion.

I'm not joking, Carliz had clarified. *I need to do something with my life. As Mother has pointed out repeatedly, and more vocally by the day, it might as well be doing my duty to crown and country.*

And really, it hadn't been that bad. She had heard her friends from school speak of far more painful dating scenarios that they underwent simply because they were seeking a partner in life, and they didn't have an entire palace team involved to act as a buffer.

First there had been a great many meetings with the team assigned to the mission of getting the Princess Royal married. They had started off with a startlingly thorough dig through her entire life, asking all manner of impertinent questions.

I would hope, Carliz had said at one point, her manners beginning to fail her, *that the fact that I am a royal princess, sister to the queen of Las Sosegadas herself, should stand in place of whatever curriculum vitae it is you're building here.*

Indeed, huffed her mother, who had been sitting in.

Rather shockingly, Carliz had thought. It was so… supportive.

Forgive me, Your Highness, the chief aide in charge of the marriage operation had said at once. *This is not a CV, for, naturally, you do not need to sell yourself. You are the prize. We are only gathering as much information as we can to help us choose the appropriate partner for* you *to consider.* There had been the slightest, deferential pause. *And, of course, only those who complement not only* your *strengths, but the kingdom itself.*

Carliz did not mention a stern mouth and pale blue eyes. She had not allowed herself to think of such things in the light of day—though her dreams did as they pleased—and anyway, it had been clear that only she thought they complemented each other at all.

She had heard a lot about the needs of the kingdom after that. As if her family wasn't intimately and intricately linked with the kingdom in too many ways to count. As if she, herself, had not spent the whole of her life in the kingdom and of the kingdom, and therefore could not possibly understand it.

But the good news, she'd thought as she sat in all those meetings and resolutely refused to think of Valentino no matter how many potential suitors they paraded before her, was that she was *fine* as time went on.

Perfectly fine.

True, she'd felt a little gray around the edges. Some people might call that a touch of depression, but that wasn't something members of her family were permitted to suffer from, so she certainly hadn't claimed it as such. And besides, she'd had nothing at all to be depressed about. Her days had been filled with worthy appointments. In service to the queen, she'd cut ribbons to open things and had made grateful little speeches of commendation that she'd forgotten entirely the moment the words were out of her mouth. She'd smiled, she'd posed, and she'd no longer bothered to argue with the soulless wardrobe department in the palace, who were forever trying to dress her as if it were still the 1940s and there was a war on.

Carliz had assumed that the strict policy she'd taken of no longer allowing herself to dwell on anything involving Valentino Bonaparte—not her memories, not any stray mention of him in the papers, as if the man did not exist—was the reason that she often felt…unwell. Not actually *sick*. She'd just had a general sense of ongoing malaise that she'd assumed would pass.

Eventually.

Because all things passed *eventually*.

Or maybe it wouldn't, she'd found herself thinking sometime in the beginning of September. But so what? It was probably better for everyone involved, from her sister on down to the subjects who clapped so wildly when they saw her in the street, that Carliz pretend she'd never known what it was to sparkle in the first place.

Because, after all, that had always been an act.

Maybe that was the part that needed to pass, she'd thought. Maybe this was the new, improved, *mature* version of her. As September had started, the team had begun to send her out on carefully curated dates. Though, functionally, they were more like interviews. The men had already been briefed that they were being considered as potential husbands for the famous Princess Carliz. Accordingly, they were all perfectly polite. They were all blandly good-looking in the same sort of way. They all looked… *European*, she'd supposed. They all visited exquisite tailors, which they demonstrated in their sartorial choices, suggesting a certain fashion threshold was on the palace's list. They were all happy to talk at length about their pedigrees and their portfolios, while she sat and made note of which ones had receding hairlines to match their receding chins.

The better the bloodline, the more unfortunate the chin, she'd discovered.

It sounds hideous, Mila had said one evening. She'd come home from an event and Carliz had picked up the habit of their youth, slinking into her dressing chamber when she arrived home each evening so she could lounge about while Mila got ready for bed. Because it was one of the few times she was really just… Mila.

Assuming she was ever *just Mila* any longer.

Hideous is far too strong a word, Carliz had replied, curled up on the nearest chaise with a glass of wine, though she'd found she was enjoying her wine a good deal less these days than she had once. *They are all... Perfectly nice. Eminently suitable. Astonishingly adequate, I would say.*

Her sister had shaken her head. *Damned with faint praise.*

I did not think I was praising them at all, Carliz had replied, laughing. But then had sobered when her sister had trained a very steady look on her.

I understand that it is very unlikely that I will ever meet anyone, Mila had said, but very matter-of-factly. There was no hint of self-pity in her voice. *I've come to terms with that. But I really did hope that you, at least, could have that pleasure. I thought you might even fall in love.*

I love the idea of love, Carliz had said, carefully, after a moment. She thought of her half-finished canvases. She thought of a long, lonely walk on a sandbar in the sun, while the incoming tide threatened and there were hot handprints on her flesh. *I love the fantasy of it. I could read books about love, watch films about love, sing songs about love forever. But the reality is something else. And I think only fools pretend otherwise.*

Her sister had watched her a long moment, then changed the subject.

And so Carliz had gone out on her businesslike dates, debriefed with the team afterward, and had made no complaint about the men they selected. This had pleased no one, because her lack of any choices, for or against, made it impossible to winnow her suitors down to one clear winner.

Which was, the head aide was at pains to tell her, the point of the entire exercise.

I think I might just write all their names down on pieces of paper, Carliz had said on another night later in in the month, this time sitting next to Mila on the queen's favorite sofa in the small, private sitting room where she watched television programs she then pretended she'd never heard of when in public.

The better to remain mysterious, she always said.

Carliz had continued, *I'll throw them in a hat, then pick a name. Instant fiancé, problem solved, and we can all move on.*

Mila had actually turned toward her, pinning her with that look of hers. *This is really not what I want for you*, she had said quietly. And so kindly that Carliz had nearly felt the urge to cry. *I understand that you don't want to talk about this, but ever since Valentino Bonaparte's wedding failed to happen, you've been broody. Withdrawn. Words I would never use to describe you. If I didn't know better I would think you were...*

Carliz had forced out a laugh. The bitter sound of it had been unforced. *Heartbroken? Yes, Mila. Yes, I am.*

And there had been something liberating in saying that out loud. She hadn't allowed herself that. She hadn't let herself think about her *heart* at all. And here, now, she felt...thick, everywhere, as if her heart had shattered into so many pieces she'd had to grow a protective barrier to keep from bleeding out.

She hadn't said that, though. Not out loud. *I think that everyone deserves a devastating heartbreak at least once in their life. Because that's how you discover what's important. That it's not feelings that matter, but facts. And sometimes you have to learn that the hard way.*

I wasn't going to say heartbroken, Mila said quietly, her gaze still far too kind. *I was going to say pregnant.*

Out on that very same sandbar that served as the only path to Valentino's island, and only when the tide was low, Carliz stomped on.

She had obviously dismissed her sister with a roll of her eyes. But later that night, she had found herself lying wide awake, staring at the ceiling. Because not once in that entire wicked night with Valentino had either one of them even mentioned the issue of protection.

She knew why she hadn't. *She* didn't know any better.

Or at least, she did know, but she'd never been in a position like that before, where the things that she knew completely deserted her because he'd kissed her, and he'd picked her up, and then nothing was ever the same.

But that did not excuse *him*.

She'd fretted about that for days. She'd told the team that she was deep in contemplation about her next steps regarding the husband hunt. Then she'd taken herself off to one of her favorite cities, New York, where it was easier than it should have been to sneak away from her security detail, pop into a chemist's on the nearest corner, and then slip into a bathroom in the first dive bar she came to.

Carliz had taken the test there and then.

And she had nearly caused an international incident because she'd sat in that stall so long, staring at the answer she didn't want. It had been right there before her in two little lines.

Unmistakable lines.

She had stayed in an apartment down in the West Village that she normally used as a hub while she flitted about, in and out of art museums, having lunches and dinners and drinks out with any of her millions of friends who didn't know her at all.

But this trip, she just…sat there. She ordered in food from her favorite restaurants, then didn't eat it. She stared at the walls, but what she saw was that night.

Again and again, that night.

Then, worse, the morning after.

She stayed there for almost ten days, because Carliz had absolutely no idea what she was going to do next.

And now here she was.

She had considered, at length, not telling Valentino about her pregnancy at all. He certainly didn't deserve to know. Every interaction they'd had had been terrible, up to and including that night and its aftermath. In truth, the past couple of months had taught her that she should be embarrassed that she had spent so much time and energy chasing around after him. She was. Truly.

But the conclusion she'd come to, despite herself, was that while all of that was perfectly valid and she could feel about it precisely as she liked, one thing remained true. It was not and would not be the fault of the baby.

Her baby.

Because Carliz, unlike Valentino, was not made of stone and spite, she was also capable of feeling empathetic about the things she knew about his history. About the father who had carried on with the housekeeper in the house where he'd lived with his wife. So that both wife and housekeeper were pregnant by him at the same time—though the news about their sons' true relationship was not disclosed until later.

Carliz knew that she was many things, not all of them

flattering or fabulous in the least, but she'd like to think she was not cruel. If Valentino wished to treat his child the way his father had treated him, that would have to be his choice to make. She would not do that choosing for him.

She had interrogated herself on this topic all the way to Italy. Was she truly acting out of that sense of what was right? Or was she using this as an excuse to see Valentino again?

But every time she asked herself that, she thought about those final moments with him in the hall. That opaque mask he'd worn, after everything they'd done with each other all through the night.

And her stomach never failed to turn.

It did again now.

"No," she muttered. "This is not about seeing him."

She'd had the palace physician snuck in to see her when she returned home from New York. The doctor had confirmed what she already knew, that she was nearly three months along. But better yet, the baby was thriving. All was well.

You look better than I've seen you in a while, Mila had said that night at dinner.

Filled with purpose, Carliz had replied, with a smile. *At last.*

And that was true in its way. Or if she did not have *purpose*, at least she had a plan.

First she would tell Valentino. When he responded negatively, as expected, she would start to plot out the next part of her life. She had decided that she needed two possible paths forward. One, a quiet life somewhere else, where she would not embarrass her sister. She rather fancied New Zealand and a magical little town on the South Island that she had visited once, Wanaka, where all kinds of creative people lived. She could simply be a single mother with the rest of them out there in the world, she thought, and raise her child in peace.

On the other hand, if Mila was inclined toward acceptance, she would have to plan her next moves with the palace.

But Valentino was the first step.

She walked and walked, keeping ahead of the tide. And the closer she got to the island, and Valentino's house that she could see rising there on its hill, the more aware she became of her body.

Carliz told herself it was because she hadn't exercised as much as she usually did, in these last, grayish months, but she knew that wasn't quite true.

It was as if walking back across the sandbar reignited that awareness of herself that he had taught her that night. That stunning, wondrous understanding of who she really was, and what her body was truly made for, and all the astonishing things two people could do with each other.

"Including make another human," she snapped at herself, in case she was tempted to forget.

But that didn't make her breasts feel any less heavy, though not in the way they'd been heavy for the past week or so. It didn't make her feel any less thick, and not simply because her clothes didn't fit the way they'd used to.

Her body clearly remembered this island and that night, and as far as it was concerned, it was high time to get ready for more. She could feel that telltale slickness between her legs as she moved. Even her breath was shallow, as if she was already panting out all of that passion and need.

She was disgusted with herself.

Once she made it onto the island, she found herself marching down the avenue of cypress trees that led to Valentino's house. This time, there was no one else about. There was only her. And she had not worn scarves to disguise her identity, either. Carliz was dressed very simply, because this was a simple errand and nothing more. It did not call for *an outfit.* She wore a pair of jeans with an extremely stretchy waist. A pair of shoes far better suited to traipsing over the sand than the last. She wore a hat on her head to keep the sun off, because she remembered it burning her on the walk back, when she had already been more than red enough. And otherwise, she wore only a camisole beneath a roomy buttoned shirt.

Carliz thought she looked a bit like she was going on safari, though she doubted very much she would get the pleasure of hunting the particular big game she wanted today.

Just as she had three months before, she charged up the stairs cut into the side of the hill that led directly from the house's extensive gardens down to the chapel. Just as before, she marched directly up to the front door and swung it open.

But this time, she did not walk in to find the place deserted, all of the staff called off somewhere else.

This time, Valentino was standing there as if he was a statue she'd left behind in exactly the same position. Today he was at the base of the stairs, but his arms were still folded. His expression was still disapproving and otherwise, firmly opaque.

And God help her, she did not want to think about that stern mouth and all the things he could do with it. All the things that she'd been lying to herself for some while about. All the things that she would love for him to do to her again.

But she would deal with that shocking personal betrayal later.

"I believe I was very clear, Carliz, the last time we saw each other," Valentino said.

And she understood then that he had seen her coming from afar.

That he had planned this confrontation when he could instead have very simply…locked his door.

The betrayal got worse, though, because she could feel that shivering thing all over her. She hated it. And she hated him. Yet still there was something in her that was thrilled by the fact that he thought she had come back here for anything less than a good reason.

Because there was always going to be that part of her that wanted nothing more than to get naked with him again. And again.

And forever—but she shoved that treacherous thought aside.

"I cannot imagine that anyone could be more clear," she told him.

Despite herself, she took him in. She couldn't help herself. Her eyes moved all over him, looking for flaws, she told herself—but if so, she was disappointed. For there were none.

He did not look like a fallen angel, not Valentino. He looked like the sort of angel that would never dream of falling and more, would mete out retribution those who did.

And really, it would have been better for her all around if she had not thought that word, *retribution*, in his presence.

"I'm glad to see that you remain as unpleasant as ever," she continued when he did nothing but glare at her in all his disapproval. "I would have called you, as that seemed the decent thing to do, but it was made clear to me that even if I managed to obtain your phone number, it would be changed should I ever call it. Ditto your email. So here I am."

"I don't know why you cannot accept the truth of things," he said, but almost casually. Almost philosophically. "You are forcing me into a corner and I do not think you will like how I choose to step out of it."

"There is no need for you step anywhere," she told him, and it was a challenge to match his tone, but she did. "I have come a great distance—and across a vanishing sandbar, no less—to tell you something I would have much preferred to share from afar. Do you understand what I'm saying to you? I don't want to have this conversation."

"And yet here we stand."

Carliz sighed, though she would have to deal with the wound that left behind later. "After the appalling way you behaved the last time I was here, I have no wish to ever lay eyes on you again. You should congratulate yourself, Valentino. You have finally succeeded. I am entirely indifferent to you, whether you live or die, or anything else that might possibly concern you."

His brow lifted once again. Maybe as if something she'd said had landed like a weapon. Not that she should care about that.

"Carliz," he began, in a voice made entirely of warnings that her body took as dark, delicious promises—something else she would need to unpack later, when she was alone.

Later, when she knew she'd survived this.

She lifted a hand to stop him. "I'm having your baby," she said. Direct and to the point, and it did not matter what he did with that, not now it was said. "You can do with that information what you will."

And then she finally—*finally*—did the right thing.

She turned on her heel and marched to the front door, leaving him of her own volition. Something she wasn't sure she was capable of doing until she did.

Then she started for home.

CHAPTER FIVE

SHE TURNED AROUND and exited the house so quickly that, at first, Valentino was tempted to imagine that this was yet another one of his far too realistic fantasies where the troublesome Princess Carliz was concerned. He'd been plagued by them since the night of his doomed wedding. They'd so far showed no sign of abating.

Surely this was yet another indication that the woman was still haunting him—that he needed to work harder to exorcise the demon in him that was this infernal need for her. This impossible *wanting.*

He stood there as if he was a part of the statuary that lined the hall, but the way his heart was beating—much too fast and much too hard—told him otherwise. Despite his best efforts, he was not made of marble. He was all too regrettably human. And that likely meant he had not made her up.

Much less what she had come to tell him.

Before he could form a thought, much less a plan based on reason rather than the chaos of desire, he was following her.

He threw open the door she'd slammed shut behind her and was surprised to see that she was moving at a fast clip through the garden, when he would have said that

Carliz was not the sort to hit such speed. He had never seen her do anything but *glide*. And she was not *running*, exactly, but she was clearly doing her best to get away from him as fast as she could.

It was an unnerving sensation to see her moving away from him.

Valentino could not say that he liked it. At all.

Grimly, he set off after her. He had told himself—repeatedly—that he would not keep tabs on her, but he had failed in that. Almost immediately. He had found himself scouring the papers both on and offline, telling himself he was only looking to see what had become of his reputation in the wake of the wedding scandal his brother had forced upon him. Handily enough, every article or segment on the subject mentioned Carliz too. He'd steeled himself to see her out on the party circuit once again, selling her take on the scandal to the paparazzi so they could torture him with his brother's perfidy and his fiancée's shirking of her vows, but instead it was as if Carliz had fallen off the face of the earth.

It only went to show how hard she had worked in the first place, he had been forced to conclude, to make the relationship they'd never had a topic of such interest to so many.

Valentino had never thought he would miss that.

Then again, he'd also imagined that he'd have better sense than to put his hands on that woman. The woman he'd wanted from the first moment he'd seen her, but had known at a glance was not for him.

Because he knew what happened when people gave in to their wants at the expense of their responsibilities—and even their souls. He'd watched it play out before him in real time and he'd lived through the aftermath. He wa still living through the aftermath.

And now, to add to the trauma of his father's love triangle and all the pain it had caused, now Carliz haunted him too. All night, every night, and all through the day as well.

Valentino was ruined in ways he had not imagined possible.

He was a wreck of himself and it was all her fault, but he knew that he was the one to blame.

The proof of that was the fact he was chasing after her now, when he should have let her go. The way he should have done that night in Rome. He should have turned and walked away from her, not toward her. He should never have taken her in his arms. They should never have danced.

But it was too late for all of that now.

Valentino caught up to her at the base of the hill, in front of the chapel where he had not gotten married.

He reached out, then dropped his hands before he caught her by the elbow and steered her around to face him. Because nothing good came from putting his hands on Carliz.

Nothing good at all, no matter how it felt at the time.

"I beg your pardon," he said, falling into step with her and sounding far calmer than he felt, because he knew that was perhaps the only weapon he had in a situation like this. Assuming there were any weapons to be had when it seemed he'd gone and blown up his own life—as if, after all, his father's poison was not as deeply buried in him as he'd thought if that was even possible. "I could not have heard you correctly. It sounded as if you said…?"

having your child?” Carliz stopped walking e same sort of force she’d used to slam his door d her, and rocked back on her heels as if she nearly bowled herself over. She swept the wide-brimmed hat she wore off of her head and smoothed a hand over her hair, never shifting that wary, clever gaze of hers from his, its very steadiness its own affront. Or so he chose to call it, that tension inside of him. “Do you want to guess how far along I am? Go ahead. I bet you’ll get it on your first go.”

“Impossible,” he said at once.

Except…was it?

He had spent a lot of time going over that night in minute detail. And one thing that he could not remember doing, at any point, was taking a moment to handle his own protection. He had thought of that failure later, but not in terms of any potential pregnancies. More in terms of the fact that he should not have been surprised it felt so good. As if she’d been fashioned specifically for him.

Everything feels good without a condom, he’d lectured himself scathingly. That wasn’t revolutionary, it was simply a fact that men had been whining about for ages.

“Do you need me to give you a lesson on human biology?” Carliz was asking, her own voice too close to scathing for his liking, though he should have exulted in it as more evidence that she belonged far, far away from him. “It’s really very simple. If you have sex and don’t do anything to prevent pregnancy, lo and behold, a pregnancy can occur.”

“I assumed you were on the pill,” he said. Because it was the only thing he could say. It was also the truth.

But she looked back at him in the same narrow way,

with no change of expression. "Why would I be on the pill?"

"You cannot possibly depend on your lovers to protect you." He detested saying that out loud, as Valentino found he did not wish to imagine her with other men. Equally, he did not wish to ask himself why that was when he had never been at all interested in the other pursuits of his partners. "Men, as I proved myself to my shame, are not equal to the task."

He didn't like saying that, either, having prided himself his whole life on being more than the equal of any task set before him. But it was true no matter if he liked it. Or didn't like it.

Carliz shook her head, still looking at him as if there was something wrong with *him*. "Is that… Are you putting on the fact you got caught up in the heat of that moment—like anyone else would and I certainly did—as another hair shirt for you to wear?"

She made a scoffing sort of sound while he tried to take that in. A hair shirt? *Another* hair shirt? He had never been quite so Catholic, surely. But he suddenly had the urge to adjust the shirt and coat he was wearing.

He repressed it.

"Spare me, Valentino," Carliz said before he could protest her characterization of him. "Please. I wasn't on the pill because I've never had any reason to be on the pill. And I didn't ask you to use protection because it quite literally never occurred to me." She let out a bitter little laugh. "Not a mistake I intend to make twice but really, once does the trick."

And he couldn't stand this. Not just what she was saying about her pregnancy or the way she was looking at him. All this time he'd been so sure that he knew her, if against his will. This woman was irrepressible. There was nothing bleak about her.

Until now.

It was like looking at his mother all over again.

Except this time, it wasn't his father who had done this thing. It was him. He had turned into his father without even realizing it.

The very idea made him feel sick.

"You are right," he managed to get out, tersely. "I should not attempt to make this a failure of responsibility on your part. We share the blame. I apologize. I will admit that I'm surprised that a woman like you made mistakes like that, but then, I'm equally surprised that I did the same."

He was pleased with that. It was equitable. They were both adults. There was no need to descend into any puerile mudslinging when they'd both been in the same bed.

But Carliz tilted her head to one side and stared at him in a way that he found…distinctly uncomfortable.

"A woman like me," she repeated, as if they no longer spoke several of the same languages. "Do you mean a virgin, Valentino? Because I was a virgin that night. You took my virginity, as a matter of fact, and quite thoroughly. You even spanked me, and I liked it. *And then* you told me that you never wanted to see me again." Her eyes were bright in a way he'd never seen before, and there was color on her cheeks that he assumed was the bloom of her temper. "I apologize if in the middle of all of that I didn't have the time or wherewithal to give you chapter and verse on my feelings about birth control and my lack of experience overall."

He only stared at her, not sure whether he wanted to let his own temper surge, or possibly just kiss her again, and both options made him loathe himself. Carliz made a noise, somewhere between frustration and disgust.

Then she stepped around him, and carried on stomping back toward the beach and the sandbar that was still visible at this point. Though the tides were always turning, wholly uninterested in the affairs of men.

There were very few moments in Valentino's life where he had felt as if the world had been picked up and shaken from end to end like a tawdry snow globe. As if at first it stopped abruptly enough to send everyone reeling, and then everything he knew was shaken away.

The first time had been when he was twelve. And had discovered that the best friend he considered a brother was, in fact, his *actual* brother.

The second was the night his mother had died, and the understanding he hadn't wanted that night—that his father could have saved her, or at least tried to save her, but he had not. He had *chosen* to wait for the tide to go down.

This was the third.

Because if his princess had been a virgin that night, and he could not imagine why she would lie about something like that, then everything he thought he'd known about her was wrong. Or off-center, somehow.

He, who had always prided himself was wrong. Horribly, shockingly wrong.

Again, something in him whispered, like a terrible smoke winding deep inside him. The way he had been about his family and his whole damned life as a child. The way he had been about his father, who he had never liked much, but had not understood was an actual monster until that night.

He didn't know how long he stood there, but then, once again, he had to chase her down the lane in an effort to catch up.

"Let me guess," she said, her cheeks flushed with more of that hot temper he hadn't known she had, as she charged toward the beach, "now you're going to tell me that you don't believe me. You will demand that I somehow prove that I was a virgin then, when it is obviously much too late. When you know perfectly well that pain was part of the pleasure that night, because you taught me that."

"Carliz."

And he didn't mean to use that voice. He didn't think he meant it, but it was the one that she'd obeyed without thinking that night. She did again, now. She stopped dead.

And when she looked at him, there was a wariness in her gaze.

"I believe you," he told her, in a low voice that was not *that* voice, but was raw all the same. "And I did not mean to hurt you."

Something crackled through her, like that electricity that was so much a part of her spilling over. But this time, it was fused with that flushed hot temper of hers, too.

"I didn't say you hurt me," she belted out at him. "*I* wasn't hurt. *I* wasn't the one who woke up that morning and decided to be awful, pretending once again that there was nothing between us. I don't know what this is right now either." She threw out a hand toward him, and he didn't know if she meant to point at him or it was simply a decorative gesture. "Suddenly you're understanding? Suddenly you have some deep interest in my well-being that you've never shown before now? Let me guess. You're already calculating how you can use my pregnancy to your advantage. You're already wondering how you can spin it so that you once again come out on top of your brother. Whatever that looks like this month."

He hadn't been thinking that. But he couldn't deny that it was entirely likely that he would have started at any moment. Had he not been so shocked by her announcement, he likely would have convened his press people already to get them working on the appropriate stories to seed.

Still, Valentino didn't like the fact that she'd called him out on that. He didn't like it at all.

"What exactly was your plan?" he demanded. "You thought you would drop in, drop a small bomb and then… what?"

"I have a great many opportunities available to me, as a matter of fact," she told him with a certain loftiness that he assumed royals were taught at birth. "Thank you so much for asking. I spent most of the last three months looking for an appropriate husband." He must have made some kind of face at that, when he prided himself on being unreadable under all circumstances. But she laughed. "I'm sorry. Is that upsetting to you? Are you the only person alive who gets to go out and find someone to marry because they fit a checklist?"

His jaw was so tight that he was afraid he might snap a tooth, but he couldn't seem to unclench it enough to respond. She made that noise again.

Then she turned once more, and kept going.

Valentino had to stay where he was for a moment,

breathing a little more heavily than was wise, because while he did not want to think about her other lovers, he *really* did not like the idea of her married to someone else.

He found that he hated it.

But he told himself that was perfectly valid. After all, she was carrying his child.

This time when he drew up beside her she had made it to the small path that led down from the lane to the beach.

"Obviously any marriage plans you might have will have to be put on hold," he told her, possibly with a touch more severity than was called for. "I do not intend to share custody of my child, Carliz. You should know that at once."

"You've known about this child for exactly fourteen minutes," she threw back at him without even looking over his way. Then she did, even shoving that hat backward on her head to really make sure he saw the seriousness all over her face. "I will not be putting anything on hold for you. Ever again. Of that, you can be one hundred percent sure, Valentino."

"Then why did you bother to come here?" He moved closer to her than was necessary, and much closer than was wise. "Why would you tell me that you are carrying my child, the heir to my family legacy, if you intend to marry another?"

Carliz made a slight, instantly repressed movement, and he had the mad notion that what she really wanted to do was put her hands on him. He wanted that too. Badly.

Because if she put her hands on him, he knew exactly what would happen next, and he didn't care if his brother, his former fiancée—his sister-in-law, he reminded himself—his awful father, and the whole of the Italian mainland lined up to watch them.

Maybe some of that showed on his face too, because she wisely kept her hands to herself.

"You act as if I've done something to you, Valentino." The wind caught at her hair and he could see the pert impression of her nipples behind her shirt, though he knew it was not the temperature that was pinching them to attention like that. Or not only the temperature. Because the chemistry between them, as ever, was nearly all-consuming. "You act as if this is all my fault."

She blew out a breath, but before he could counter that he had not even once suggested that she'd tried to trick him, or that she was foisting another man's child on him, or even questioned her too closely on the matter—as he had heard in places like the Diamond Club that many of his peers had done from time to time—she kept on.

"Something happened between us in Rome that changed everything," she said, as if saying it was forbidden but she was doing it anyway. Her eyes got big, trained on him the way they were while the fall sunshine spilled down over her shoulders like it was as attracted to her as he was. "I'm sorry that you're too terrified of that reality to even have a conversation about it. But I'm not an idiot. I'm fully aware that neither one of us walked into that event planning for anything like *that* to happen. At any point over the past few years, you could have had an honest conversation with me about the fact that it did, but you never have. I regret how I acted in the course of those years, but I did it because I truly believed that there was something there worth fighting for. I have no idea what you were doing."

Valentino wished he couldn't hear the way her voice scratched at that. He wished he couldn't remember those years himself.

"And no," she said, raising her voice when he started to say something—though he wasn't sure if he meant to defend himself or possibly just apologize, "I don't want to hear what you have to say about it now. It exploded the night of your wedding the way it was always going to, sooner or later. There's no going back from that. But now I'm carrying a child."

She reached down to put her hand on her belly, and he had been too busy drinking in the sight of her. The fact of her, not the shape of her. The brightness all around her. The way light seemed to find her wherever she went, sunlight or lamplight alike. The way her eyes gleamed and her cheeks flushed.

Then, too, he'd been remembering the way she squirmed as she lay over his lap, sobbing first in pain and surprise, then with the pleasure of it.

But now that she put her hand on her belly, he could see that her shape had changed. That she had a notable roundness there, when before her stomach had been slightly concave. Something he would know, because he had spent a great deal of time tasting every inch of the span between her hipbones that night before moving lower.

"I never really thought about having children," she told him, still holding her belly and his gaze with the same sort of steel. "It was something I assumed I would do, somewhere down the road, because everyone does. My mother has always been going on at me about doing my duty to the family and producing potential heirs, particularly since my sister seems dead set on reigning as the

Virgin Queen of our time. Someone will have to succeed her and if it is not me, or one of my children, it will all have to go to a cousin who none of us can stand. So you see the dilemma."

"I don't."

She scowled at him. "I was going to have to have a child anyway. And I have accepted the fact that it will happen now, not later. I did not intend to have *your* child, Valentino. And that is really all I came here to tell you. The child exists. I expect nothing from you. And you can continue to play these games of denial and blame that you've been engaged in from the start, but I don't want to be involved in them anymore."

Carliz turned around again on that note, but this time with great dignity, as if she thought that might shame him. And maybe it could. Maybe it would.

But not right now.

She set off across the beach, but the tide was already coming in. Still, she was moving at a fast enough pace that if she kept it up, she should only get a little bit wet on the other side. There would likely be no compulsory swimming to make it to shore.

He watched her leave him again.

He didn't like it any better.

And once again, Valentino's heart was heaving about behind his ribs as if he'd run a marathon or two today. These had been a strange few months. There had been the fact that his brother had stolen his bride and married her, right under his nose, that he kept waiting to hit him like the betrayal it was. But he knew it wasn't going to. He was furious that his brother had spoiled his plans, that was all. He didn't really care that Aristide and Francesca were married. He only cared that they'd embarrassed him.

He only cared that he'd had to hear his father's taunts and jeers on that topic, when he had dutifully stopped by for a dinner he'd put off as long as possible. He subjected himself to one per season, so little could he tolerate anything that Milo said or did.

This time, it had been even worse than usual, but not because Milo was getting any hits in with his snide remarks about what Aristide and his *worthy* little heiress wife must be up to. But because he had been thinking of the wedding night he'd had despite misplacing his intended bride. And because that night with Carliz had left him too raw. As if she'd flayed some essential armor away from his skin without him realizing it and he didn't know how to go about replacing it.

He told himself it was irritating, nothing more.

But the truth was that he had spent far too much time remembering all the details of that night over the course of these last three months. And all the ways that she had proven herself to be absolutely perfect for him in every way.

Sexually compatible, he liked to correct himself. That was all he meant by that.

Because a truth he had come to accept a long time ago was that he had certain needs and preferences. And it was a fact that mostly, he could not allow them to be met in any satisfying manner. He had vowed that he would be the respectable Bonaparte. That he would live up to his mother's ideals of who he could be, though she had fallen far short herself. And he had held his grandfather's example of dignity and moderation above all else.

None of that went hand in hand with the kind of sex he liked best.

Valentino also knew that a great many men on this earth had allowed themselves to be brought low because they were controlled by their sexual urges. He did not intend to become one of them—though her comment about hair shirts just now cut deep, because that was precisely how he'd thought about his marriage.

He and Francesca had never had any chemistry, though he thought she might have attempted to manufacture some, at the start, because it was expected. But he had not wanted that from her. It had been easy to tell at a glance that she was not the kind of woman who would find the games he liked to play at all entertaining.

Valentino had assumed that he was done with them. That he would sacrifice those things on the altar when he made his vows. He had been planning to get married that day not knowing if he and Francesca would even have a sex life. There were other ways to have heirs, after all. At best he had expected something dutiful and rare, and otherwise had expected they would go about their lives as they pleased.

Then the princess had appeared the way she always did. The Carliz storm, sweeping into his bedroom, and making a mockery of every vow he'd ever made to himself.

And then to discover that on top of all the other ways that she had ruined him already, it turned out that she was the kind of very special, very unusual woman who could meet every need he had…

She had wrecked him.

Again and again.

He had woken so early that morning that he wondered if he'd slept at all. He had felt not simply replete, the way anyone could after a release such as that. He'd felt something else. Something he wanted to call *recharged*, though it had felt something far more than merely physical.

Valentino had not wanted to accept that feeling at all.

He had rolled out of bed, telling himself that he absolutely would not look back at her, but then he did.

Breaking one more vow where she was concerned—and that had been the part that had pricked at him. To him, Carliz was nothing more than an addiction. That was her role in his life. He'd had one taste and she might as well have been heroin.

The way he had *hungered* for her.

When he'd looked back, he could muster up his own outrage. Because she'd looked more beautiful every time he looked at her. And never more so than on that morning, curled up in his bed with smudges of exhaustion beneath her eyes as she slept—because she had met him no matter what he'd thrown at her. She had exceeded expectations he hadn't even known he'd had.

He was very much afraid that she had ruined him for all other women.

That was unacceptable.

He had left his rooms, like a ghost. And he had built this place himself, a monument to the family he'd never had and the legacy he'd hoped to build, though his brother had always called it a mausoleum.

So perhaps it was not a surprise that he found himself in the gallery he kept because all great houses had galleries, featuring portraits of his family. Never his father.

But his mother sat there, looking regal and lovely, whole and almost happy. And the next portrait, his grandfather stood behind a chair where his grandmother was perched, the two of them smiling just slightly. As if they did not wish to get too overwrought in the presence of the artist.

And he had seen where passion led. He had watched it play out in real time, to desperate and terrible ends. If there was one promise that he could keep in his time on this earth, it would have to be that one that he'd made when the truth about his family had come out.

He would never, ever allow himself to become a slave to passion.

Valentino had watched it rip his mother apart. Because she had loved his father despite everything. And it had not made even one bit of difference.

His father, for his part, had only shrugged, or laughed, and asked what a man could be expected to do? *Passion always wins in the end*, Milo had told them all.

Valentino had sworn it off then and there.

So that was what he did when he next saw her. He had sworn Carliz off, because it was the right thing to do.

But now she was walking determinedly out of his life, while carrying his baby.

And he was forced to recall that there had always been one thing that he'd held far above passion. His duty.

And his family legacy, whether he cared for his current family or not.

He caught up with her one final time, standing there on a sandbar while the sea closed in on two sides.

This time, she only glared at him.

"We will fly to London," he told her. "I wish to have

my doctors there run every test there is, to make sure that both you and the child are well."

"Because, obviously, I have failed to do that myself."

"You're not the only one who requires peace of mind, Carliz," he bit out.

But she studied him. "And you'd also like a little blood test, I imagine. Just be sure."

He neither confirmed nor denied that. "Either way, there is no need for you to hike back to the mainland. We'll be leaving shortly."

"To what end?" Carliz demanded, and she really did yell that out then. To the sea. To the sky. To Italy in the distance, where it had sat for millennia. Where they would be nothing but a wisp of memory, one day, like everything else. Valentino did not find that thought as comforting as he usually did. He did not like the thought of Carliz disappearing. Even while she continued to yell at him. "No matter what you discover with that testing won't admit you're going to do, what does it matter? I've already told you—"

"I will need to confirm that the child is mine," he told her, as dispassionately as he could. "Not because I question you, but because my legal team will, and so will anyone else who tries to contest my will and testament." He expected her to argue that, but she didn't. Because, of course, she was a royal. She knew all about contested wills and the importance of a documented trail of bloodlines. "Once I do, Carliz, we will be married."

CHAPTER SIX

THE COLD RAIN in London was a shock after the island with all that bright, golden light, the sound of seabirds wheeling about overhead, and the sea itself, there in the corner of every glance, every look.

Carliz found a certain comfort in it, however. She had always loved London. She'd spent a great deal of time here, over the years, and there was something about the muted colors and the layers of gray on gray. There was something about the bright pops of color, here and there, and the busy rush and tumble of an ancient city in modern times.

Not to mention, the bleakness suited her mood.

She had not expected Valentino to react this way. It wasn't that she hadn't hoped that he might—she had, she could admit, if only in the darkest part of the night when she couldn't hide even from herself—but she'd thought that hope was foolish. In the light of day, she'd been certain she was kidding herself.

And now she felt strung out between those two extremes. What she'd braced herself for when she saw him versus that tiny little spark of hope she had tried her very best to extinguish. While the truth of things seemed strung out in the middle with her, since it didn't seem as if she was really getting either one. Whatever this was, it seemed to be some sort of…uneasy compromise and she'd spent the entire flight from the island brooding about it.

She had the time and space to brood on forever, as it happened, because it certainly wasn't as if Valentino spent any time talking to her. He had shown her to her seat, then removed himself to a different compartment of the plane, where he had conducted a number of extremely terse calls. She had been able to hear the sound of his voice in three languages, but not the words.

Maybe that was just as well. Carliz had stared out the window vaguely wishing that she might find herself a parachute and leap out when she saw the mountains, even though they weren't the right mountains. They weren't *her* mountains.

It was silly to yearn for home, but she had far bigger problems than a little bit of loneliness. Like that infernal little bloom of hope that she felt was deeply unworthy of her. It was sheer foolishness to let herself believe, even for a moment, that this man who had treated her so shabbily might somehow, magically, have gotten over that in the interim.

Right when she appeared to tell him she was pregnant, imagine that.

She already knew that he was happy to marry for convenience—why not for a child? It had nothing to do with her.

But still, there was that tiny hint of spring, down there in all that gray she'd been lost in since July. Even if it seemed to her a cruel trick of fate that all the time she tried to convince herself that she was getting over him, that she was moving on with her life, fate had been making sure she couldn't.

It didn't help that she knew too well that there had been that part of her that wanted to go back to the island all along. That had wanted to see him, once again, just to make sure that nothing had changed.

You mean, to see if something had *changed*, a voice inside challenged her. *Despite everything.*

Now, as she sat in the back seat of a sleek car that cut through the London traffic like a knife, she felt awash in too many competing emotions to count. While he sat beside her, typing on his phone and rolling calls as if he didn't have a care in the world.

In her next life, Carliz thought, she would very much like to come back as a man who could compartmentalize so many things he might as well be a stack of tiny boxes masquerading as a person.

Eventually, the car stopped and Valentino led her into a listed house in a nosebleedingly expensive part of Central London, and that was saying something when one was a literal princess who had grown up in an actual palace. The house had its own entrance round the back, past a mews house that her security was dispatched into by a simple nod of Valentino's head.

Carliz made as if to follow them, but was stopped short when Valentino merely lifted that brow of his.

She felt…chagrined, at once. Because her body reacted the way it had that night, long ago now. As if his command over her was absolute—but worse than that, as if she *wanted* it that way. Immediately, she could feel that telltale slickness between her legs. It made her want to wail out in a deep kind of grief that she refused to entertain. Not now.

Wailing would be too dramatic for a rainy afternoon. Instead, she simply followed him. As if her body was in control again, when it had already gotten her into a mess of vast proportions. Really, it shouldn't have a say.

He let her in the back door of a very old house that was small compared to his stark little fortress on the island, but impressive all the same in London. Inside, there were beamed ceilings, uneven floors, and a sense of history with every step. The building itself was so old that it somehow made perfect sense that he had furnished it so minimally, so that the history itself was the centerpiece. It had a slightly richer feel than the more popular Scandinavian and midcentury American look that was all the rage everywhere, and felt cozier for it.

Carliz decided that she hated the fact that she liked *both* of this man's homes. She would have fared much better with him if he'd brought her to some hideous corporate flat, all chrome, flash appliances, and the ubiquitous *fitness center*.

"You must have an excellent interior designer," she said as she followed him through the built-out kitchen, all greenhousey and skylit. Perhaps, she could admit as she heard the words hang in the air, a bit accusatorily.

She expected his staff to come bustling in, but no one appeared. Instead he stalked before her into his surprisingly bright and airy kitchen, where he began moving around as if this really was his own space. As if no one was around to cater to him at all.

These insights should not have curled in her the way they did, like a soft heat all its own.

"I have never consulted an interior designer," he said over his shoulder. He turned to look back at her, all arrogance. "I'm not particularly interested in the opinions of others."

"How foolish of me not to intuit that from your whole…" She eyed him, and chose not to finish the sentence. "My mistake."

"It is not that I think others should not have opinions," he said, and she felt the touch of that faded blue gaze. As intense on hers that it felt like a physical caress. Her body reacted as if it was. "But I rarely let them affect me."

She felt chastised, and that did not sit well. She turned away from him, crossing her arms over her bump, the brightness and unexpectedly welcoming feel of this house of his suddenly grating on her. "I thought you would be marching me into some kind of clinic. The better to poke and prod me so that other people can tell you things I already know. And I think you know, too."

"Carliz."

She hated the way he said her name like that. And hated far more that her body could not resist it. Could not resist *him*. Even now, when she knew what would happen. When she had lived through the ecstasy of that night—and the three bitter months that had followed.

Yet she found herself turning back to him anyway. Despite her ferocious desire to do the opposite. She wanted, desperately, to walk off. To leave him here, surrounded by stark walls and cozy beams. To show him that he had no power over her.

But that would be a lie.

Valentino was watching her with a certain glittering intensity from the other side of the kitchen, the long, central counter block between them. His gaze searched hers for a moment. A breath.

Carliz felt vulnerable in a way she did not like at all.

"I have always done my very best to do my duty," he told her then, as if he'd come to some kind of heavy conclusion, and it was a dizzying thing to have what she'd thought she'd wanted all this time—Valentino finally *talking to her*—only to find she didn't want it after all. Or not like this. Not when the light outside was nothing but a bright gray and in here she was feeling more raw by the moment. "Sometimes what is dutiful comes down to the details. It can be a tedious matter of crossing *T*s, dotting *I*s, and documenting it all, but that does not make it any less of a necessary duty."

She blinked at that, not sure why it made her feel hollow inside. And after a moment, when it was clear she wasn't going to respond, he turned his attention back to the mail that had been left on his counter. Stacked neatly in a way that suggested there was some staff, somewhere. If not the butler, housekeeper, and many housemaids scenario he used on the island.

But the longer the silence stretched out between them, the more Carliz wondered if that had been… Not an apology. Not precisely. But an explanation, perhaps, which she supposed might be the same thing to a man like Valentino.

It was as if he was telling her that it wasn't that he thought she was lying. But that he had to be sure all the same.

Or maybe, came that tart voice within, *you are desperate to believe anything good about the man. No matter what he does.*

She didn't realize she let out a sound, some sort of sigh, until she found him looking at her yet again. And everything was raw. The sky above them, through the glass, was the same sort of gray that had been pressing into her for months now.

His baby was inside her. And now he knew.

Nothing was ever going to be the same. Everything had already changed, and they only had six months left to play catch-up before the *real* change came. Had she truly grasped that when she'd set out for the island this morning? Because right here, standing in a lovingly restored and cleverly remodeled kitchen in Central London, a world away from the palace in Las Sosegadas or his own island castle, she couldn't believe she'd been so determined to hurry that change along.

"Carliz," he said again, though his tone was different this time, as if he felt the rawness as much as she did. "I—"

And though her heart pattered about foolishly, almost too foolishly to bear, he never finished.

Because there was a knock on the door and then it opened almost immediately. And as a small crowd marched inside, it took her moment to get her bearings. Again.

By the time she did, she had been escorted into a small reception room and ushered into a seat while various medical personnel buzzed all around her. There were tests, a small interrogation dressed up like a medical exam, and within an hour there was no more doubt. *I*s were dotted and *T*s were crossed.

Carliz was now *officially* having Valentino Bonaparte's baby.

"I have my people working on this," Valentino told her, his voice grave.

She couldn't read him at all. Everyone had left again and it was just the two of them, sitting across from each other in a very old room with entirely too much information between them. *This* could mean anything. There were the years they'd played games around the truth of what had happened in Rome, a lightning bolt out of the blue that had never made sense, but was real all the same. There was the memory of the night they'd shared. And there was now the proof—to his satisfaction, apparently—that they had made a child out of all of that.

"Which part of *this* do you mean?" she asked, as if she had mistaken this for a charming garden party of some sort.

He stood and it made her heart hurt, then, that he was dressed so formally. That he had been dressed like that earlier. When he could not have known that she would descend upon him the way she had.

Meaning he needed that formality. That austere uniform of his.

She watched him cross to the fire and stand there, as if gathering his thoughts.

It poked at her, that he did not seem to have a casual setting. That there was only this. Valentino Bonaparte, the dutiful heir. Picture-perfect in every way.

Oddly enough, though she understood all the pressures that could lead to living that way, watching him wear the weight of it made her want to weep.

"These are the things that will occur," he told her, in a quiet voice that was a lot like that voice he'd used on that dreadful morning after. So certain. So terrible. "We will marry, and quickly. It is regrettable that there will be inevitable speculation about the nature of our relationship these past few years. There already has been, as I'm sure you're aware, following the wedding."

"I have spent absolutely no time at all following anyone's thoughts on what happened that day," Carliz said, sharply. "It might surprise you to learn that your wedding and what happened after was not something that I wish to relive."

Something flashed across his stern face and the ache in her intensified. But when he shot her one of those dark, compelling looks of his, she did not falter.

"What astounds me," he said, sounding more and more as if he was actually having a feeling by the moment, "is that I go out of my way to live as blameless a life as possible. I have tried in every arena to act with honor, respect, and dignity. And yet, through no fault of my own, I am consistently and repeatedly dragged back down into a mud not of my own making."

"Yes," Carliz murmured with entirely false sympathy. "Poor little billionaire. What a tragedy it is to have even one moment of one day that is outside of your express control."

The look he shot her then, all affront and astonishment, might have made her laugh on another day. But she was too churned up inside. There was too much happening, here in this quiet room, where she wanted more than anything else to scream.

But she locked that away inside, because she didn't want to give him the satisfaction.

Or maybe she was afraid that if she started screaming, she wouldn't stop.

It began to occur to her that maybe she had not been getting over him the way she'd thought she had been. That maybe all of that gray listlessness had been grief and mourning, not simply a new state of being.

But none of that mattered now.

"In any case," he said, biting off his words, "we will get married here. I will not add an illegitimate child to the list of—"

"The list of what?" she asked, maybe a little sharply. "Slings and arrows thrust upon you, not of your own making? Because that's not how I remember that night, Valentino."

She was certain that she had intended to be civilized. But there was something about the fact that he was mad that wrecked all of her good intentions. If there'd been a heavy enough object nearby, she rather thought she would have flung it straight at his head.

"The doctors say you're in your second trimester. But all is well." His jaw tensed. His nostrils flared. "I am glad."

"Yes. Noticeably glad, I'd say. The kind of gladness that fills whole rooms."

"We will have to fashion the appropriate contracts," he said then, sounding almost bored. And when that opaque mask settled onto his features once again, she felt it like a hand around her throat. Choking her. Leaving her feeling claustrophobic. Her fingers twitched with the urge to go stick her fingers into that mask, like maybe she could peel it away. As if it was made of a hard plastic and not simply his will.

"Yes, naturally, there will be contracts," she agreed. "I'm sure you will have a great many offensive clauses for the palace's legal team to object to. But there is another wrinkle." He only stared back at her, as if daring her to continue. For some reason, that made her feel… Almost merry. "I am a princess of Las Sosegadas, as you know. That means that I cannot legally marry anyone without the permission of the sovereign."

"That is archaic."

"So are monarchies. Literally." Carliz shrugged. "Mila has always assured me that she will give me no quarrel in this area, but then, you are a special case. I suspect she already dislikes you."

"I have never met your sister."

"No, but I am her baby sister. And according to all the tabloids, you broke my heart. It's possible she holds a grudge." She sighed as if, upon consideration, she liked his chances even less. "She is a just and fair-minded queen but she does hold a wicked personal grudge, it has to be said."

"Everything I have ever heard about your sister suggests she is eminently practical," Valentino replied, in that tone of great authority, as if the things he'd heard were more correct than her lived experience as Queen Emilia's best friend and only true confidante. "I doubt very much that she is interested in the kind of scandal that will ensue if her sister to have a child out of wedlock."

"Maybe," Carliz said airily, because that was more likely to annoy him than if she exploded in temper the way she wanted to do. "Then again, it might make me more relatable. That's of great concern to the palace these days. *Relatability.* Mila is forever weighing how to appear approachable, yet iconic. All at the same time."

"Then I suggest you call her right now," Valentino said,

in that silken threat of a voice. His pale gaze moved over her like fire. "And explain to her that she has two options. She can cheerfully approve your marriage or she can oppose it. If it is the former, felicitations will abound on all sides. If it is the latter, you will be legally married in every single country on the planet…except hers."

He let that sink in, in case she was tempted to misunderstand what he meant.

"I'll be sure to make her well aware that you said that," Carliz told him.

And in the end, that wasn't even necessary. Mila laughed when Carliz called. "I knew it," she said with the sort of glee she never showed in public. "And I'm not even going to ask you about complicated timing, overlaps with previous brides-to-be, or any of the rest of it. The heart will do as it pleases."

"I hope that's how you explain it to Mother."

Her sister laughed again, and Carliz almost felt as if things might be all right. At last. "Absolutely not. I am not taking that bullet for you, my darling sister. You will have to tell her yourself."

"Or she can find out in the papers like everyone else." Carliz laughed too, and it was if surrendering to a little levity changed everything, even the sullen British weather outside. She could see a bit of sunshine out there, trying wanly to illuminate a hedge or two in the garden. "I can't wait to hear if she finds Valentino Bonaparte *appropriate*."

"No one will ever be good enough for you," Mila said, her serene voice uncharacteristically absent, then. She sounded fierce. She sounded like a big sister. "Such a man can never and will never exist. So what I hope is that this time, Valentino has taken some time to reflect on his good luck that you will have him. And how little he deserves it."

"I will be certain to let him know," Carliz whispered.

Then she sat there in the reception room over the garden where he'd left her to make her call, staring about sightlessly. Because Mila had undone her. Effortlessly.

Her sister had not used or breathed the word *scandal*. She had not reminded Carliz of her promise never to embarrass the crown. She had acted as if this was all… perfectly reasonable and worth being happy about, even.

It made Carliz want to lie down somewhere and cry.

But she had no time for that, because she was in this strange old house that felt stuffed full of Valentino's presence even when he wasn't in the same room. She stood then, feeling far shakier than she'd like. For a moment she thought she might swoon like some overset princess of yore, felled by nothing at all, but then she remembered. She'd flown into Italy the previous night so she could catch the early tide and walk out to the island. She'd been so agitated, or what she had chosen to call *determined*, that she'd merely gulped down a few biscotti and set out.

She was starving. Not swooning and fainting because she was overcome by emotion.

Not yet, anyway.

Carliz put her hand over her belly and massaged the little bit of roundness that seemed obvious and prominent to her. It told her there was a baby in there, as odd as that seemed to her.

Though the oddness didn't keep her from that fierce rush of love she'd felt the moment she'd known. Before she'd let herself think about the practicalities.

That love grew stronger by the day and fiercer by the minute.

"Don't you worry," she murmured to her bump. "It doesn't matter if your father is terrible. He will do his duty by you." She shook her head at that, hating the bitter way that the words sat in her mouth. "But I will love you enough for both of us, I promise."

And she felt somehow cheered by that, no matter her emotions. They were buffeting her like one storm after the next and had been since that grotty toilet stall in New York. The reason she felt shaky *now* wasn't those emotions. It wasn't that she was in Valentino's presence, because she had been all day.

This was pure physiology and that felt a bit like a reprieve. She was a pregnant woman who needed food, the end.

She picked her way through the house, back to the kitchen, and slowed as she entered. Because Valentino was there. He was dark and tall and gorgeous, and aggressively male simply because he was *him*. But the truly astonishing thing was that he appeared to be…*cooking*, though she found her brain could not accept that as a possibility.

"You must be hungry," he said gruffly. Almost angrily, as if she was being hungry *at* him—

But she stopped herself from that train of thought. She had a sudden memory of her father from back when she'd been nothing but a naughty teenager. Her group of friends had gotten in a little bit too much trouble at boarding school and Carliz had been called before the king to account for herself, which she had done. But in a manner far too flippant for his taste.

He had shouted at her. And while he was not averse to expressing his disappointment in her in as many ways as possible, always hoping she might listen and shape up, he had never been the kind of man who *shouted.* She had been stunned into silence.

The king had sighed and pressed his fingers to one temple. *You could have been hurt*, he had said quietly. *And it is easier to be angry about that than to accept the fact that sometimes, Carliz, your disregard for your own safety terrifies me.*

She couldn't get that out of her mind. She watched Valentino's crisp, economical movements as he chopped things and then swept them into a bowl, moving around this kitchen as if he spent a great deal of time preparing food for himself here.

Maybe he wasn't angry at her. Maybe he was simply scared, as anyone would be. Of the future. Of this new life they were going to have to do their best to raise well. Or of the two of them together, for that matter. Married to each other. Somehow figuring out how to build a life from all these bright, painful scraps of *almost* that they'd been running from for so long.

Maybe he didn't know how to speak of these things.

And could she blame him? Neither did she.

Carliz went and slid onto one of the stools set on the other side of the counter, blinking when she needed more room than usual. Then smiling at that, because it would not be long before her belly impeded her from sitting in all kinds of places in the way she was used to.

It would be only one of many changes, one right after the next, resulting in the birth of a small human who would change everything even more, and irrevocably.

The truth was that it was impossible to really imagine. It was impossible to speculate on the magnitude of that change.

So instead, she said, "I'm very hungry, as a matter of fact. Thank you."

He had taken off his jacket and rolled up his shirt sleeves to cook, and there was something unbearable about it. Something so beautiful and poignant in the sight of his exposed forearms. All of those astonishing muscles coming together to do something so parochial as cook a meal.

"Someday I will take cooking lessons," she told him, as if she was making a confession. "I've always wanted to. I cooked a very little bit when I lived in halls at university. I can make a mean Bolognese, I want you to know. But I've always wanted to be the sort of person who can open a cupboard, scan the available ingredients, and come up with a whole meal. All of it delicious and bordering on gourmet."

"I was taught that cooking for oneself is a life skill," he said, though his voice…changed as he said that. As if he hadn't meant to say anything.

"I'm surprised to hear that." Carliz sighed happily when he slid a pair of dishes in front of her. One plate sported a fluffy omelet smothered in bright, cheerful vegetables. On the other was a stack of buttered toast. "I would have thought you had nearly as much staff as I did, growing up."

He stood across from her, bracing himself against the counter, but it was his expression that stopped her midbite.

"Our housekeeper made it a game," he said quietly,

though not in that controlled quiet way he had. This was much rougher. “When I was young, I often played in the kitchens. I learned how to cook and to clean, all skills she assured me would serve me well no matter my station in life.”

“She sounds like a wise woman,” Carliz said, but carefully, because there was a stillness about him that she didn’t understand. And a kind of bitterness in his gaze. “For here you are, capable of producing a fine meal at the drop of a hat, all on your own. I promise you that I cannot do the same.”

“Ginevra made me think that she taught me these things for my own good,” Valentino said, and now the bitterness was in his voice, too. “But she did not. It was all a part of the sick games I did not even realize were being played all around me. So yes, Carliz, I can cook. But what I taste is betrayal no matter what spices I use.”

She thought he would turn and stalk off at that, but he didn’t. He pushed back from the counter, shifting back until he could lean against the cupboards and cross his arms.

Carliz had seen him stand like that before. It never boded well.

“I take it your sister was amenable.” It wasn’t really a question.

Carliz returned to the task of eating, though she could no longer taste the food. There were too many questions whirling around in her head and more, she *felt* for him. She wanted to go to him and offer him comfort for the childhood that still brought him pain—but she knew he would not accept it. Not from her, not from anyone.

That made her feel for him even more deeply.

She forced herself to take a few bites, then picked up the linen napkin he'd placed by her plate and pressed it to her mouth. "Mila was lovely about the whole thing," she said as she lowered the napkin. "She never mentioned the scandal of it, though I know that must be a consideration. And I know that is your primary consideration. But I think there are other things that we should consider."

Carliz could sense his disapproval, though that closed-off expression didn't change. "Such as?"

"Maybe, Valentino, just maybe, I don't want to marry a man who doesn't like me at all," she said quietly. "A man who has spent the bulk of what can only loosely be called our relationship doing his best to get away from me. Why would I want to marry a man like that?"

To her surprise, he smiled.

It was a dark thing, a hard curve of sensual and stern lips.

But it was hardwired deep into all the parts of her she'd been so sure had frozen into disuse over the past three months. She'd been so sure it would never again be a factor, having learned her lesson at last.

She had been wrong about that. Very wrong. Because one little smile, one little spark, and she was engulfed in flames once again.

"I can think of at least one excellent reason to marry me, *Principessa*," Valentino said in that low, stirring way of his. "Do you need me to remind you what that is?"

CHAPTER SEVEN

VALENTINO MARRIED PRINCESS CARLIZ in the front room of his house in London.

It was an excessively well-appointed room, but it was not the famous cathedral in her kingdom that her sister would marry in, one day. It was not the lovely old chapel on the island where he had been set to marry last summer.

Carliz wore a quiet dress in a pale hue that was not quite white and did not smile. He wore a suit and presented her with a spectacular ring that had been his mother's, which, upon reflection was perhaps ill-suited for a union that he did not intend to let fall apart the way his parents had.

But when he kissed her, sealing their union, it was an unremarkable brush of lips and yet still that dark thrill rushed through him. That same insatiable need.

He already regretted that he'd had no choice but to make this decision.

"Will we be taking a honeymoon?" Princess Carliz, *his wife*, asked in that tone she'd taken with him over the past fortnight that they'd stayed here in London, sorting out contracts and wedding arrangements. It was edgier by the day. Too sharp, and that dark look in her usually gleaming eyes. "I can't wait to sit somewhere lovely in this same towering fury. It's love's young dream, I dare say."

"We will return to the island," he told her in freezing tones, and not because she was being provoking. But because all he could think of was that laughably quick brush of their lips. How could something haunt him when it had barely happened? "And we will iron out the contours of this bargain we've made."

"What a marvelous idea," she murmured dryly, holding her wedding flowers before her like a shield. Or a weapon designed to make him feel small, and he did not like that the happy little blossoms managed it when no one else had since he was, in fact, small. "Thank you so much for asking my opinion on the matter."

"We will leave in the morning," he gritted out.

Then he left her there to spend his wedding night in his club, fully aware that she had been his wedding night once before. At least this time he'd actually gone ahead and made the damned vows.

The Diamond Club was the sort of place where he ought to have been able to shrug off his cares and worries alike. That had been the point of it, in the beginning. It was exclusive and elite, invitation only, so that only the ten wealthiest people in all of the world were allowed to hold membership.

He liked everything about the place. The clubhouse itself was on a discreet and quiet street not far from his house in London. He kept a suite there, for he had often stayed at the club when he did not wish to be tracked by the paparazzi or anyone else. The staff was almost supernaturally excellent, capable of anticipating every whim almost before it was formed. Though Valentino had found the place had lost quite a bit of its luster once he realized that his brother was also a member.

He'd preferred the days before he'd known that, when he'd simply come and gone by helicopter, in and out of his private suite, never setting eyes on anyone but the fearsomely well-trained manager, Lazlo, who made everyone he encountered feel as if he worked only and ever for them.

Tonight, however, he did not wish to be alone in his suite. He tried to tell himself that he had removed himself from his house because his marriage was a sham and he cared nothing at all for the woman he'd married or anything else involving her, but that was how he'd expected to feel three months ago. Should he have actually married Francesca.

Had he felt that way tonight, he would have seen no reason to leave the house.

He had left because if he didn't, then that pounding, driving need inside him would take him over. It had already begun. He had stood there in the aftermath of their small ceremony, vowing to himself that he would not touch her again.

But what was he trying to prove? What new hair shirt was this, when he thought he was well used to the closetful he already knew too well—and could identify now, thanks to her.

Especially when he had shamelessly used the fire that always burned between them to get Carliz to marry him in the first place.

He assumed she would have married him one way or the other, eventually, or she wouldn't have gotten on his plane back in Italy. But he hadn't needed to mount any arguments. He hadn't had to offer her an object lesson in why they needed to get married in the first place. He had simply raised his brow and waited.

She had sat there in his kitchen, her cheeks getting redder and her eyes getting brighter.

He was sure that the whole of his house smelled of cinnamon, now.

I will marry you, she had said solemnly, as if there had ever been any doubt.

Valentino had told himself that the triumph he'd felt then was a simple thing. That it had nothing to do with any primitive need to possess her in any and every way he could, because he refused to accept that need existed in him.

It was simply the pleasure of a good deal well negotiated, he'd told himself.

But if that were true, there was no reason why a simple brush of lips at their wedding should haunt him out from his house and into the streets of London. There was no reason why the clatter and roar of the city should fade as he walked, because all he could seem to think about was the way she'd looked at him, those eyes of her like ancient treasure, as she'd recited her vows.

He could not see how more time alone in his head would help.

Once he got to the club, he went to one of the club's main rooms and nodded at a few familiar faces, though he did not stop to talk to anyone. It was enough to have his favorite drink waiting when he took his preferred seat. It was enough to page through the *Times* like some or other duke from centuries past.

It was enough to sit in the place, a monument to a certain kind of power, and remind himself that he was the one who had it. His wife—*his wife*—was a princess, true enough. But only one of them did the kneeling—

Stop, he growled at himself, outraged that even here he was not free of her. That nowhere was safe.

And when someone sat down in the chair beside him, despite the many empty and available spots around the soothingly lit room, he scowled.

Then all the harder when he realized it was Aristide.

It was all very well for someone like Aristide to speak of change. To pretend it was possible.

That did not mean it was.

Or that Valentino might wish to take part in it.

"I do not recall inviting you to sit," Valentino said after a baleful moment. "But then, you have never needed an invitation to intrude upon me, have you?"

There was a time when his brother would have taken that bait, but tonight Aristide only smirked. "Surely you must exhaust yourself with all of the expected snide comments, brother. Besides, it is all very boring. If you must insult me, is it too much to ask that you come up with something new?"

"If I had wanted conversation, I would have addressed my mirror," Valentino replied coldly. "That would have provided me with far more opportunity for reflection and honest interchange than whatever games it is you think you will be playing with me tonight."

And they stared at each other, all of that tangled history between them.

"I thought you should know," Aristide said after a moment, in a sort of deeply calm voice that Valentino did not associate with his reckless brother at all. There was a certainty there. A *settled* quality that made no sense, but that Valentino could see all over him. It was even in the way he sat. “It is early days, but Francesca and I are expecting a child.”

Valentino stared back at him. “Why are you telling me this?”

“I appreciate your congratulations.” Aristide shook his head. “In the past, you have had a tendency to assume the worst, so I thought you should know. My wife and I are having a baby. It is not an assault on you, or your position as heir—whatever that means with a father such as ours. I merely thought you should hear it from me.”

Valentino studied his brother, his fingers clenched tighter than they should have been around his drink. “It is funny, is it not, that you have anointed yourself the messenger of all of these things. That despite the reception you must expect from me, you consider it your duty to fill me in. What does that say about you, I wonder?”

“Perhaps nothing,” his brother said quietly. “But then, I am the one who trusted you to remain my friend no matter what happened. You are the one who broke that trust.”

But there was not any of the bitterness there that had been, once. Valentino could not account for the difference. It made him…uneasy.

“Your mother taught me to cook and clean as a child,” Valentino said instead, abruptly. “Do you remember?”

“Of course I remember,” Aristide said, and when he shifted in his chair he was the lounging, reckless creature he had always been. As if Valentino had imagined the change. Or as if this was a mask his brother wore, not unlike his own—but he dismissed that. “I was there.”

“Why?” Valentino asked, aware that he sounded much

more fierce than necessary. "Why did she do such a thing? Was it…did she get some amusement from this?"

He detested himself for asking. But then he didn't know why the only thing he could think to do after receiving the report from his doctor—the confirmation that Carliz really was having his baby, which *he* knew meant she would not be walking away from him—was cook for her.

Just as he couldn't understand why he'd told her about Ginevra and her cooking classes in the first place. About a period in his life he did his best to pretend had never occurred. Because he remembered all too well when he and Aristide had been friends. And how that had ended, when he'd discovered that most of his family had been lying to him all along.

He expected his brother to scoff. To toss off one of his trademark witticisms.

Maybe he wanted Aristide to do exactly that. To remind him that no matter the few good memories he had of his childhood, they had always been lies. That Aristide's take on that time would only be a part of those lies.

But Aristide only looked back at him with a curious sort of look on his face. For the life of him, Valentino could not interpret it.

"Cooking and cleaning is how my mother loves, Valentino," Aristide told him, a little too kindly for Valentino's taste. "It is how she shows her love. Not quite the villain in your story, I think. Just a woman in love. For her sins."

Something within Valentino seemed to crack wide open at that. He stood, leaving his drink untasted.

"I commend you on your ill-gotten marriage and all the many moral lessons it will teach an impressionable child," he said. And then, "As it happens, I have also married. And I'm also expecting a child."

Something flashed in Aristide's eyes, though it looked a lot like resignation. "But of course you are."

Valentino stood. "May the cycle continue."

He had said such things to his brother before. This was nothing new. But for the first time, he didn't feel the usual sting as he walked away. Usually there was a level of outrage, but it was always held up by his absolute certainty that he was in the right. That he was the good one. That he had always behaved as he should.

But if cooking and cleaning were how Ginevra showed love, and it was not simply her job… If she had taught Valentino this language as well as her own son…

He did not care for the direction of his thoughts.

It was as if something in him was shifting, changing against his will, and he did not like it.

He took his time walking through the streets of London with the wet in his face, as if that might sort him out. It was late when he shouldered his way into the tidy old house and started for the stairs, somehow unsurprised when Carliz appeared at the top of them.

As if he'd summoned her.

Dressed in nothing but a chemise because she clearly wanted him mad and desperate, and it worked.

"I thought you were out carousing," she said coolly, down her nose and down the stairs. "The way all bridegrooms traditionally do on their wedding night as it sets such a delightful precedent for the marriage, I am sure."

"It is still our wedding night, *mia principessa*."

And he released himself from the vows he'd made after the ceremony in that moment. Because he and Carliz had made their own vows today, had they not? And who was Valentino to deny the power of an ancient ritual?

With my body, he had told her, *I thee worship.*

He thought it was about time he started.

"Is this a wedding night at all?" she asked dryly, but there was a certain glimmer in that burnished gold gaze of hers. A knowing spark. "How would I be able to tell?"

He started up the stairs toward her, something dark and needy taking him over more and more with every step.

"Never fear," he told her. "I'll show you."

And so he did.

He advanced upon her, his heartbeat a match for the fire he could see in her gaze. By the way her eyes widened as he came ever closer, and best of all, the fact that she did not move out of the way. Not by so much as a hair.

When he got to the top of the stair he simply hauled her to him, set his mouth to hers, and carried her, once more, to the nearest bed.

That was where he took his time, unwrapping her like the gift he undoubtedly did not deserve.

It had been a long three months. And she had been a virgin, which meant that he, who had never claimed any kind of ownership over any of his lovers, was the only one to have ever possessed her.

That knowledge worked in him like something mad, impossible, overwhelming. Some kind of virus taking over each and every cell and bone and organ. He could feel the way it infected him. He could feel it rush through him, making him feel near enough to unworthy that it was as if he was someone else entirely.

Someone he doubted very much he would like on the other side of this spiral down into sheer madness.

But he couldn't stop.

He didn't *want* to stop.

What he wanted was to make that sense of possession real.

Valentino reacquainted himself with every curve, every sweet plane. He found that thickening at her waist, her newly rounded belly, and felt something shake in him—deep.

If anything, the new intensity of her curves made her even more beautiful. The fact that she had married him, that she was carrying his child—he didn't have to like how those things had come to pass, and he didn't have to have the faintest romanticized notion of how things between them would go.

He was a man. She was a woman. And they had created a life between them.

Valentino would have to be the kind of monster his own father was, the kind of monster he'd dedicated the whole of his life to *not* being, not to care about something like that.

But this was not the time to think of monsters. This was a time to remind Carliz not only who he was, but who she was. And who they were together.

This was a time to find his way back to that glazed, bright glory in her gaze when she looked at him. The way her lips parted as if she was too oversensitive to breathe. The way she obeyed his every command.

Not, he knew, because she was somehow incapable of standing up for herself. Had she not proven that already?

"You like it when I tell you what to do," he said, his voice a low growl, when he finally moved her to sit astride him so he could gaze upon her as if she were something like a fertility goddess.

Because she was. She was *his* fertility goddess, and he nearly lost himself then.

"I promise that I will always do what you tell me to do," Carliz whispered throatily, a knowing little smile on her lips. "Just as long as we are naked."

He laughed, a low, dark sort of sound, and then he drove into her. She shattered at once, throwing her head back and crying out his name, and he knew.

She had given him the key to this puzzle.

He would make this work, after all.

This most unlikely of unions, which should surely have led him straight to disaster, would be all right.

All he needed to do was keep his princess wife as naked as possible.

CHAPTER EIGHT

THE SECOND TRIMESTER was much better than the first. Carliz felt like herself again.

Though it was hard to say if that was the simple benefit of being in a different part of her pregnancy, or if it was all to do with the marriage she'd somehow found herself in.

It was as if their wedding night had pried the lid off at last. She'd woken up the next morning, convinced that he was going to do the same thing he'd done after their first night together. They had started off in one of his guest rooms, because it was closest to where she'd stood at the top of the stairs when he'd come in. And then, because he'd been in that sort of mood, he had declared that they might as well introduce the rest of the house to its new lady.

So they had, until dawn.

She'd woken up in what he'd told her was his bed when he was in London, and there was no particular reason that she should feel such a thrill at that. She was married to him now. *Married.* It was likely going to be her bed, too.

Or maybe not, something in her whispered, because it had dawned on her that it was happening again. She was alone, again. He had left her to wake up without him, *again*.

That had not gone well the last time.

She had taken her time getting ready in the clothes she had sent on from the hotel she'd intended to stay in down in Italy, licking her wounds and planning a different life.

Naturally, instead, you married him, she'd muttered to herself.

Carliz had taken great care with her appearance that first day as his wife. If he was going to turn into stone again the way he seemed to do come morning, she'd intended to make it hard for him. She'd intended to make it hurt.

Because one thing had become abundantly clear during the long hours of the night. There hadn't been any spankings this time, but that was not to say that he'd gone any easier on her.

She would have been disappointed if he had.

Valentino Bonaparte was the only man alive who had ever treated her like she was *strong*. Not just pretty. Not just pedigreed. But fully capable of taking anything he chose to give her, then giving it back to him so that they both could benefit.

It was the loveliest cycle she'd ever been a part of.

And she'd understood, at last, that this was what he'd seen in her when they'd first met in Rome. This all-consuming hunger. This specific need that could only be doused for a little while, and only by surrendering themselves to each other again and again and again.

It had no longer been a surprise to her that he had walked away from it. That was likely the smarter path to take. Not the one she took, however.

When she'd dressed herself, done her hair, and fixed her makeup so she looked effortlessly sultry, she'd started down the stairs to face him anyway. Because the most important things she'd learned over the course of the night was that she hadn't made up a single thing that had happened between them. Not one thing. He had felt everything she had. He had experienced it all the same way that she had.

The only difference was that he had chosen to walk away from it. Then had acted as if he'd had no idea why she might want to rush straight in anyway.

Carliz had known better, at last. It didn't matter what he said. It didn't even really matter what he did, not while he had all those clothes on, all those bespoke suits that were really just deliciously tailored armor against his feelings.

The only truth that mattered was the truth they made between them, tangled up in each other, skin to skin.

She'd vowed that she wasn't going to forget that again.

Yet when she'd marched into that kitchen where she was still amazed that this man of all men actually *cooked for himself*, she'd stopped dead.

Because he had not been wearing one of those suits that morning. He had been standing there at his counter, wearing nothing but a pair of deeply fascinating boxer briefs that molded to one of her favorite parts of his body. He had been typing into a slick laptop that he'd cracked open before him. And he'd spared her a short, thrilling glance. "You should eat, *Principessa*," he had told her with only the faintest hint of admonishment. "You must think of the baby."

Then he'd indicated, with a tilt of his head, the plates of food that had waited for her on the table out closer to the garden.

Even weeks later and in a different country, remembering that first morning of their married life made her break out all over in happy little goose bumps.

There had been somewhat less giddy conversations with the palace. Her mother had been torn between outrage that Carliz had essentially gone off and eloped, histrionic concern at what that would *do* to the royal family's *image*, and obvious, unadulterated delight that *one* of her daughters had actually taken that step into matrimony.

Though the fact that the baby would come much too early, by even the most casual calculations, about put her over the edge.

No longer so heartbroken, I hope, Mila had said, on one of the occasions that the two of them spoke privately.

Hearts are amazing organs, Carliz had replied, which wasn't answering the question and they both knew it. *So much hardier than they seem. And somehow able to thrive in the most complicated scenarios.*

Just remember, her sister had said with that serene smile of hers. *If you bring him back home, I can throw him into the palace dungeon at will.*

The team that had been put together to find Carliz a husband were clearly less delighted, but the head aide spoke to her politely enough.

In the end, the woman said after a lengthy interrogation about the actual nature of her relationship with Valentino, including dates and hard truths, *you will be far more likely to behave if you're happy.*

I'm sure that's true of everyone, Carliz had replied. *And just as unlikely.*

Your sister does not require happiness, the aide had said. *She will behave no matter what. So you see, in our office where we dislike surprises, this is not so bad.* The older woman had leveled a look at her and though Carliz braced herself, she had not rolled into a lecture. Instead, she'd smiled and looked…kind. *And for all your mother's clucking, this is also not the Dark Ages. Congratulations on the next prince or princess of the realm, Your Highness.*

And it had surprised Carliz how much that had affected her. How much it had meant and continued to mean.

Just as it surprised her that now, when her duty to the crown was both assured and no longer a pressing issue, she felt something like homesick. Not for the grayness or the heaviness of those first three months, but what she missed were those nights with her sister. Getting to spend time with Mila the way they had when they were little girls, and even then, only rarely. Because Mila's destiny had always been assured and silly games with her sister had never been part of her studies.

Carliz knew that she would never regret those otherwise sad months for that time with her sister alone.

Living on a private island off the coast of Italy, of course, was not exactly the worst thing she'd ever had to endure.

Especially because Valentino kept right on treating her like dessert. And it turned out that the man had a sweet tooth that only Carliz could assuage.

He found her wherever she was. Sitting with her feet in the pool, wandering the gardens, reading a book. He was insatiable and better still, he was uninhibited in the extreme. He took her everywhere, in every possible way, until her days were shot through with sensuality like burning red threads that held everything else together.

His days were always filled with work, so he would call her into his offices and conduct whole calls while she stood there, naked before him. Sometimes he made her pleasure herself in the chair before his desk, her feet propped up so he could see everything while she tipped back her head, slipped her hands between her thighs, and did as he liked. As he commanded.

Other times he had her kneel before him and pleasure him while he tended to what he called the most tedious part of his life, his paperwork.

Her job was to keep him just on edge enough that he could continue to work. Just close enough so that he was not leveled by the need to make love to her mouth with that same inexhaustible self-control that made her shatter apart without him having to even lay a finger upon her.

She failed every time.

And she rather thought that was the point.

Carliz had been in Italy for near on a month when the rest of her things arrived, sent with love and courtesy from the palace. And it felt strange all over again to see her belongings hanging in the dressing room that adjoined Valentino's. It was odd to have a whole sitting room allocated for her use with its pretty little terrace that looked out toward the sea, and now the tables held the small trinkets she'd picked up in her travels.

It was an odd thing indeed to no longer be Valentino's assumed affair, his dramatic estranged love, but his wife. She wasn't sure she knew how to take on the role of a wife. She'd been much better at manufacturing the story of the first version of them.

Possibly because, for all the ways she knew this man as well as she knew herself, there were a lot of other ways she didn't know him at all.

There were rules about where she could walk on the

island, for example. She was not to stray onto his brother's property, ever. Much less visit his father.

"I will take care of that unpleasant duty when I must," Valentino told her. "I'd prefer it if he never laid eyes on you at all."

But he had told her that in bed and she'd still been addled by the number of orgasms she'd had. The pure magic that man could work with his fingers and his tongue. So she hadn't argued.

She liked to think that had he told her at a different time, she might have.

At a dinner in her second month on the island, he waved the subject of his father away.

"The man has nothing to add to anything but malice," he said dismissively. "He is a poison, nothing more. The only way I know how to deal with him is a campaign of failing to react no matter how outrageous he becomes. I'm not sure that I'll be able to do that if I'm also protecting you from his usual snide barbs."

That sounded so reasonable. But Carliz couldn't help noticing that his punctuation to that statement was to take her there, across the table, in a blistering rush of passion that left her panting, a little bit dizzy, and with her concerns unaddressed.

She began to put those things together. If she looked back, ever since their wedding night, he had responded to pretty much everything in precisely the same way. Sex.

When she had asked him what, exactly, was the root of his dispute with his brother—a rivalry so intense that the whole world knew of it—he had said something offhanded, then commanded her to strip. When she had asked about his mother, having seen a portrait of her in the gallery, he had swung her up into his arms, carried her into one of the nearby rooms, and tied her to the sofa.

In fact, she thought when she woke one morning after a typically long and glorious night in his arms, she could not think of a single real conversation they'd had.

Not one. And it made her feel foolish. Which she supposed she was meant to feel. Because that was what he was doing. He was playing her for a fool. He was doing it deliberately.

She wasn't sure how she had failed to notice.

Carliz swung out of the bed and snatched up the little silk wrapper that she wore, because he liked it. That annoyed her too, and she was frowning as she stalked out into the rest of what she supposed was *their* suite. Though now that she was paying attention, it was clear that the room set aside for her use was as far away from his as possible.

Another thing she hadn't noticed, because all she really cared about was where he was at any given moment and how quickly he could be inside her.

She left the suite and walked as regally as possible down the stairs, smiling in the best approximation of her sister's serenity as she passed staff members who she usually did not appear in front of in nothing but a silk wrapper. She marched herself across the house and straight into Valentino's office, standing there before his desk until he deigned to look up at her, one dark brow already aloft.

"Do you need me to teach you some manners again, *mia principessa*?"

She might be mad at him, but that did nothing to change the way her body reacted to him. It was as if he flipped a switch in her. As if that was all it took. One ly suggestive statement and her whole body was ting like a tuning fork.

"You're avoiding me," she accused him.

"How can this be so?" he asked idly. "We are always together."

"I don't mean physically."

"My dear princess wife," he said, and suddenly everything was silk and heat, and his gaze crowded into her like he was already thrusting home between her legs. "You are standing much too far away from me."

And it felt almost like an out-of-body experience, because she was aware of what he was doing this time. It was as if she was watching it from somewhere else. The way he rose and came around his desk to take her in his arms. The way he kissed her, so deep, so stirring, that there was nothing she could do but kiss him back with all she was and everything she had.

Carliz was both there and not there as he brought her down with him into that thick rug before the fire in his office, took his time stripping that wrapper from her body, and feasted on her until she had her fingers sunk deep in his hair and was sobbing out his name the way she always did.

And then again, louder still, when he set her before him on her hands and knees in deference to her growing belly and took her from behind, reaching up to pull her head around so he could kiss her in that same deep, restless way.

Until there was nothing to do but surrender as he took her apart.

But in the aftermath, she came back to herself, and this time, remembered. So she turned to him as they lay there and traced the stern lines of his face with a fingertip.

"It's so hard to believe we get to be together like this after all those years of running away from these feelings," she said.

She was close to him, and she was watching for it, so she saw the way he stiffened. It was almost imperceptible, but she saw it.

Carliz pushed on. "Do you know, when I first laid eyes on you, I don't think I ever truly imagined that this could happen. That we would get this day in and day out. Husband and wife, falling more and more in love—"

There was a part of her that wanted to tell herself that she was only testing him by saying that word, but he'd been fooling her quite enough. She didn't see why she needed to fool herself. Carliz had been in love with this man since the moment she'd laid eyes on him.

That was simply the way it was. The way it always had been.

But he sat up, disentangling himself from the heat they'd made. And the stern way he looked at her was not in the least bit sexy.

"I will thank you," he said, very quietly, "not to speak about your feelings in my presence."

"I will speak about whatever I want, Valentino," she replied in the same deceptively soft way. "I'm sorry if my love offends you. But I feel fairly certain that, given the fact you've been running from it since that night in Rome, you've been fully aware that it's been here, all along."

"I want you to hear me, Carliz." He stood then, leaving her sitting naked on the floor, surrounded by a wrapper of silk. And she couldn't seem to move as he dressed, quickly, betraying absolutely no emotion when she was certain she could feel it coming off of him in waves. "I know you have a tendency to hear what you wish to hear. And make up scenarios to suit the ones you already have in your head."

"Yes," she agreed dryly. "I'm clearly delusional. That's why I'm your wife. I hallucinated my way here."

"The chemistry between us is off the charts," he said coolly, and she hated him for that. Quantifying it seemed to cheapen it, and she didn't want *chemistry.* She certainly didn't want *off the charts* chemistry. Not when she knew that this was so much more than that.

And that he was only saying that because he was trying to diminish what it *really* was.

"I think what you mean is that you're in love with me," she said, because she knew he was. It was the intensity between them, she supposed. It was the fact he'd told her they could never be anything and now they were married. It could be because her life had always been glossy, but empty, and he had felt like the only real thing in it since Rome. It was because she was there when he held her close. She was there when he stared at her as if no one but them existed. She was here, now. She could feel what was between them and she wasn't afraid to name it. But that didn't make it easier to say. Because it certainly wasn't something he wanted to hear. "And that doesn't have to be scary, Valentino, because I'm in love with you too."

"I am not in love with you," he told her, and was all the more brutal because he looked…patient. Perhaps slightly pitying. There was no flashing in his gaze that she could cling to and call denial. There was no flare of temper in his voice that she could tell herself was the truth of how he really felt.

She thought it would have hurt her less if he'd backhanded her.

Instead, he slipped his hands into his pockets. "I can see that this is distressing you, but I thought we understood each other. I'm happy to have sex with you all day, every day, Carliz. I like sex. I particularly like it with you."

"If you say another word about sex or chemistry," she said, though her throat was tight and her voice sounded strangled, "I will not be responsible for my actions."

Again, that pitying look. "This is what I had hoped to avoid. But I suppose it is better to come to an understanding before our child is born. There will be no scenes in my house." And at least, when he took on that stern, formidable look again, it was better than pity. Anything was better than pity. Though she had to remind herself that he didn't know any better, not this man who'd built himself a mausoleum to reside in while he was still alive. Anything to avoid those feelings he didn't think he had, or the childhood that had made him this way. "Perhaps you have not noticed that everything in this house is precisely calibrated to soothe."

"Like a crypt," she said, and somehow without anything like a sob in her voice. Though she felt like a sob personified, all the same.

"I will not have chaos," he told her, something urgent in the way he spoke. The way he looked at her, even the way he held himself. All those feelings he didn't want, filling him up. *Love*, she thought, and she knew she was right because it hummed in her, deep. "I want the home that I live in to feel like an upscale art gallery, Carliz. Not a bar, filled with drunkards, broken glass, and puddles of regrets on the floor."

She decided this was not the time to break the news

to him that babies were not typically mindful of upscale gallery rules.

"You're describing an excellent Friday night," she shot back instead. She had the urge to wrap herself up again, to hide herself from his gaze, but that served him, not her. So instead, she stayed where she was, sitting there like a goddess on a half shell with every bit of royal blood inside of her pumping, hard.

Because she was her sister's heir, like it or not. She could give regal for days.

And she knew perfectly well that for all his talk about chaos and crypts, he didn't have any more control at the sight of her nakedness then she did when she beheld his.

In case she needed more proof that this man who could control everything, and believed he could control his own baby, could not control his heart around her.

"My fear has always been that we are fundamentally incompatible," he told her as if that had weighed heavy on him just moments before, when he had been losing himself between her thighs. "Sexual attraction without shared values is cancerous."

"Or it's fun, Valentino."

"How would you know?" he asked her softly. "You acted the part of the party princess, but it was a lie. A role you played to get attention, and now you have mine, don't you? But you don't want it."

"I do want it. That's what I've tried to—"

"What you want is a person you've made up in your head," he said, a quiet devastation that swiped hard at the confidence in this, in love, in *them* that she was trying so hard to cling to. "And what I wanted was a biddable, quiet wife who would bear no resemblance whatsoever to the black hole of attention-seeking behavior that was my mother."

If he really had slapped her, she didn't think she could have been more startled. "I have never heard you say a bad word about your mother before."

"Because I never speak of my mother," he bit out, something in his gaze that told her that whatever else this was, this was Valentino without a mask. She'd claimed she wanted that. She did want that. "What would be the point?"

"She was your mother. You don't need a point."

"Tell me if you see the similarities, Carliz." His eyes were blazing now. "She was a happy-go-lucky creature, everyone says so. Renowned for her beauty and vivacity. This is why my father pursued her. Then, as men do, he took her back to his island and turned her into a ghost of herself." His smile was hard. Brutal. "I did not witness this. I only saw the aftermath. The mother who raised me was the woman he made, not the woman he married. And that woman was jealous. Insecure. She was not pleasant to be around, and then, once the truth was out—confirming what she had suspected for years, only to be told she was mad—she supplemented the worst parts of herself with pills. Alcohol. Whatever was to hand."

"I'm so sorry," Carliz whispered. "You didn't deserve that. She didn't deserve it either."

"Do you want to know the overwhelming feeling that I grapple with day and night?" And now his eyes were flashing, but not in a way she liked. "Guilt. With a healthy dollop of shame. Because when my brother told me the information that should never have been kept secret in the first place, information he knew I should have had already, I wanted to leave. This place, my father, all of it."

He didn't say *and Aristide.* The brother he had clearly been close with, once. She wondered at the omission.

But Valentino was still talking in that same brutal manner. "My mother refused to go. And I watched her wallow in the feelings that had already bested her. For years. Until she finally made herself so ill that she needed a hospital. And my father refused to call for the boat or the helicopter that could have saved her. And I didn't know any of this until too late, because I was tired of her nonsense and sleeping in the old chapel at the base of this hill to get away from all of them. Those, Carliz, are the only feelings I have."

With every word he seemed to loom larger, so he was towering over her now, though he hadn't moved. And his eyes had gone nearly black with the force of what he was telling her. With the force of all those things she could tell that he kept inside him all this time.

"You were a child," she said, trying to sound calm. Centered. "It wasn't your responsibility to care for either one of your parents."

"Once again, how would you know?" His eyes blazed. His mouth was a flat line. "Nothing has ever been expected of you. You were never called upon to do anything at all but smile prettily and keep to the background. What responsibilities have you ever had?"

There it was, she thought dazedly. That backhand she thought she'd like better.

Turned out, she didn't.

"I can appreciate what you're doing now," she said then. And it was harder than anything else she could remember doing, even coming here to tell him about the baby, to remain calm. Or to sound calm, anyway. "You might want to remember that you've already spent years being unkind to me, Valentino. I'm used to it. I don't believe it any more now than I did then."

She had never believed it.

What had bloomed between them had been that strong from the start, like a chain linking them together, but also making it impossible for them to lie to each other no matter what words they used.

But there was more than that.

It was the way he had held her on the dance floor in Rome, as if she was precious. Made of spun glass and wonder. His hands had been so big and yet so gentle at the small of her back. It had been the way he moved with her, smooth and easy, as if he had been holding her in his arms his whole life.

There was the way he had tended to her after their second round that first night. He had carried her into his bath and washed her with his own hands, gentle once again. He had spanked her and she had still been processing how much she'd liked that. He had taken her virginity and she had still been wild with longing and passion and all of that shattering.

Yet he had treated her as if he cherished her.

It had made the next morning all the more devastating.

For a long time—those long three months—she had told herself that the truth of this man was in his hardness, but now she shared a bed with him. She knew the melting softness of the way he held her in the dark. She knew the kisses he brushed over her brow when he thought she was asleep.

She knew the hardness was an expression he used. But

Carliz was more certain by the day that the real Valentino was the one he hid.

This only confirmed it.

Though she had to keep telling herself that.

"That doesn't make you heroic, *mia principessa*," he said from between his teeth. "It makes you masochistic."

"But that's what you like most about me," she shot right back.

And this time, she knew that she dared him to put her over his knee. That she wanted him to, if only to prove yet again that they fit each other perfectly.

That she could earn his softness by taking his hardness.

That maybe she was the only one who could.

He met that dare and then exceeded it, spanking her until all of these things she felt about him came pouring out. He spanked her until she sobbed out her pleasure in that sharp, delicious fire, called him names, and then shattered into pieces with his fingers plunged deep inside of her.

Only to feel it all over again when he carried her to that chair, settled her astride him, and gripped her hot, red bottom with his deliberate hands. He built that fire in her back up, then held her there, sobbing for him all over again for what seemed like a lifetime.

And when he finally relented, threw her over the cliff and then followed, she leaned forward and bit him.

Hard enough to leave a mark, right there above his collarbone.

Valentino's eyes glittered as he pressed his fingers to it, some while later. He was watching her closely.

She could only hope she looked as unrepentant as she felt.

"That is the only scenario in which we will discuss *feelings* in this marriage," he told her. "Do you understand?"

"I understand what you said," Carliz replied. "That doesn't constitute agreement."

"I am leaving on a business trip," he told her. "Originally I intended to take you with me, but I think it is best if we put a little space around this, you and I."

She was curled up in the chair and when he handed her the wrapper from the floor, she didn't bother to take it. He hung it on the chair's arm beside her. "Naturally," she murmured in agreement. "You need to get those defenses nice and high again."

"Carliz." And she inhaled, quickly and deeply when he leaned over her and took her chin in his hand, tilting her head back so she had no choice but to fall straight into his gaze. Everything in her melted, the way it always did. Her body wasn't conflicted about him or their marriage at all. Or perhaps it simply wasn't afraid to follow things it wanted, even if it hurt. "I suggest that you spend your time in this house finding something to do with yourself that does not involve poking at me. Because that approach will get you spanked, yes. It will lead to scenes like this one, which are the only scenes I intend to allow. But it will never get you what you want."

But he had said things like that before, hadn't he? And here she was all the same.

Only when she swallowed, filled a powerful sort of sadness—for him, for her—that she couldn't seem to shove away, did he step back. Then she watched him pull himself together so easily. So quickly.

She really did wish she could believe that he was truly that cold, and hate him.

Carliz thought that maybe she could talk herself into it—but in that moment, the strangest sensation took her over. She clapped a hand to her belly, looking down in wonder.

"Is something wrong?" Valentino's voice was gruff. Not that stern, remote detachment that made her want to claw at him, just to see if ice could bleed.

"I think..." It happened again, and she smiled. And she knew. "I think he kicked."

They had found out they were having a son only the week before. In typical form, Valentino had only nodded curtly. Carliz had started singing the baby songs, because now she knew that it was a boy. A baby boy. Her little boy.

That was the sort of beautiful that hurt, but she liked it.

She held her breath as Valentino squatted down beside her. He reached out a hand but stopped before he touched her, looking up to her as if for her permission. And she felt...ancient. As if some deep, wild femininity that she hadn't known until now lived there inside of her. Because in so many things, she was more than happy to follow this man. But this was something she knew. Their future was *inside* of her.

She took his hand and she spread it out over that belly of hers that seemed to grow bigger by the day. By the hour. She watched his face change as that telltale little kick bubbled there beneath his palm.

"He knows his father," she whispered.

And for a moment, she saw a Valentino she had only ever dreamed about. He looked...shattered, but with joy.

His eyes changed and there had never been a blue that color, she was sure of it.

He looked down at her belly with wonder, and then he looked at her—

And Carliz watched as he remembered himself. She couldn't seem to breathe as he turned himself back into stone and ice.

Though it seemed to take him longer than it usually did.

"I will be gone ten days," he told her, so matter-of-factly it hurt. "It is my hope that you will use this time wisely. Explore the house, Carliz. This is the place I made to reflect who I am. It is all perfectly obvious. Every single thing I keep in this house is calming. I hope that you can be one of them."

He still had his hands on her belly, and he tightened them, just slightly, as if he was trying to hug his son.

She thought she might cry, but that would be worse. Instead, she forced herself to say nothing. To sit there with the baby they'd made kicking inside her for the first time as Valentino did what he did best and walked away from her again.

But this time, she did not cry. This time, when she stood—her sore bottom reminding her of him with every step—she decided to do exactly what he'd asked.

After he left, she wandered around the house, looking at the whole of it sternly, the way he must.

She saw every bit of minimalism, as if he'd wished to diminish the very things he chose to display. She saw bare walls, likely chosen with that same deliberate hand, that she remembered from London, too, though London retained the character of the original building to give it a cozier feel. This place had been built for starkness. Everything was very spare, which she knew she was meant to find sophisticated.

But she had been raised in a palace, filled with ancient artifacts and national treasures, all of them crammed in so that no era was left out.

And her country was a cold, snowy place. The winters were long and dark.

They liked color in Las Sosegadas. So did Carliz.

So the next morning, she went into the little study they'd set up for her and she took some time to arrange all of her half-finished canvases, replacing the soporific paintings that were already hanging in the suite. Then she gathered up her paints and stepped out into the hall, finally feeling completely at home in this place.

Then she did what she'd been yearning to do all along, and decorated.

Every wall. Every ceiling.

And when the staff begged her to rethink, she simply chose bolder colors.

Carliz worked feverishly, night and day, and when she was done, she had completely transformed Valentino's austere little palace.

She had made it chaotic. Bright. Happy and more than a little whimsical, and in every possible respect, the exact sort of *scene*—attention-seeking in every way—that he hated.

And oh, would he hate this.

There were only two days left before he came back by the time she was done. So she settled in, enjoyed the bold, silly freedom of the place while she could, and tried to get ready for the coming storm.

CHAPTER NINE

AT FIRST VALENTINO thought that he must be having a stroke. A cardiac event of some kind. The first strange note was that none of his staff would meet his eye. He noticed it when his man met him in the drive, as he always did. And instead of exchanging the usual polite few words, he had simply tended to the luggage and hustled away.

But it did not take more than two steps into his house to understand why.

First he assumed he was dying. Or had died. He was not sure which was preferable.

Nor did he need anyone to tell him what had happened here. He could put it together.

She had transformed the house into…a cacophony. There was no other word for it.

"Yes," came her voice, and he realized that he'd said the word out loud, having followed the explosion of color on top of color, next to pattern and more color, all the way down the great hall and back. "It is a great, glorious cacophony of emotion. Behold it. Learn to love it. That's what it's for."

Valentino took his time turning to look at this woman. This madwoman who he had married, who was sitting on his steps like a wild creature someone must have dragged in from the sea. Her hair looked as if it hadn't seen a brush since he'd left. Somehow it looked redder and thicker and much, much wilder, an impression she was helping along by being barefoot. Though it was nearly December and despite the sunny days, it was not warm. She otherwise wore paint-splattered overalls and some kind of torn shirt beneath them. Like an urchin instead of the wife of one of the richest men alive and a princess in her own right.

But what he couldn't seem to look away from was that defiant look on her face.

"And what," he asked in as calm a voice as he could manage, which was perhaps not very calm at all, "did you imagine my response would be to this outrage?"

"I hoped, of course, that you would see it as the gift that it is," Carliz replied, almost *merrily*, to his ear. "But if you can't, then I think it's a reasonable enough trade." When he stared at her without comprehension, she smiled. "You do not wish me to express my emotions, Valentino. So you can look at them."

The strangest part was that he was not as irate, as awash in fury, as he should have been. He should have been cut straight through by this act of destruction when he had told her exactly what this house meant to him in its pristine state. This time he had been betrayed by his wife, who claimed to love him just as others had—and Valentino clearly needed to take a hard look at why there was such a long line of these betrayals throughout his life.

But as he stared at her, what he regretted was not that he had essentially handed her the means to strike at him like this by ordering her to fit in with the house. But that he had not taken her along with him on his trip.

It reminded him of that vow he'd made himself right after the wedding. He had wondered who, exactly, he had been trying to teach a lesson. Because Carliz was not only the one woman he could not forget, she was also the only person he could not tuck away into an appropriate compartment, never to think of again.

She was a curse. If his trip had been a test, he had failed it. Has he been as haunted by her in all the hotels he'd been forced to stay in, in all the cities he'd visited, as he was here.

Maybe that was why he did not react the way he might have even ten days ago. He did not lecture her. He did not attempt to order her to do this or that.

Instead, he looked at the colors. At the shapes and images. And it was a bit of a shock to see that she was actually a good artist when he'd thought her interest in art was that of a dilettante. If he was a different sort of man, he might consider this house a masterpiece and congratulate himself for giving her the perfect canvas.

But he was the man he'd been fashioned into right here on this island.

And it was time she understood that this was not a game he was playing.

"Very well done," he told her. The weariness of travel seemed to fall away the more he gazed at her, but there was a cure for that. He was about to show her. "If you're so visual that you felt the need to deface every surface of my home, then perhaps you should see for yourself."

She looked intrigued. He had known she would. "Tell me more."

He lifted a brow toward her…costume. "You will need to dress in something that does not make you look like a street urchin I swept up on my way back. Like some kind of dust mite."

"My darling man," she said, with that laugh he did not wish to admit that he had missed. But there the truth of it was. He had missed it. "I am the Princess Royal of Las Sosegadas. If I start appearing in public dressed like an urchin, everyone else will, too."

All the same, she went and she changed her clothes and when she came down she looked breathtakingly, simply sophisticated. Precisely as he'd known she would.

And that was when he took her to see his father.

It was faster to drive to his father's house, but he wanted to make all of his points as best he could. He wanted to make sure she fully understood him.

Because one thing he understood, now that he had seen what she'd done to his house—a perfect example of what she'd been doing to him, for years down—was that he had lost. Whatever fight this was, whatever strategy he'd imagined he could employ to gain the upper hand, it had all come to nothing.

She had won.

And so all that was left to him was to show her precisely what it was she could claim as her prize. What she had to look forward to. What would become of the pair of them, thanks to this insistence of hers on haunting him wherever he went.

He blamed himself. Of course he did. He had turned out to be exactly the kind of man he'd always sworn he would transcend.

But first, he walked with her.

"Many stories have been told about this island," he said as he led her out behind the house and onto a path that led away from the hill and its view over the water, up along the cliffs. "No one believes that anyone in my family is related to the most famous bearer of our surname, though there have been many ideas about who else we might have been. All that is known for certain is that the island was the province of goat herders for a long while, as it is of no strategic importance to anyone. And eventually, it came into the possession of one of my ancestors. It is said the ancestor in question was particularly beguiled by the island's pastoral charm."

"It is a rare island that does not have some or other charms."

Carliz walked beside him, seeming to keep pace with him effortlessly despite the increasing roundness of her form. She had gotten even bigger while he'd been away, and it amazed him that it suited her. All this *ripeness*.

When he glanced at her now, she wasn't looking at him. Her gaze was out on the water, watching the way the late fall light danced over the waves, silver and gold at once. She had tamed the bohemian he'd seen on his stairs quickly. Her hair was now twisted back into a knot on her head that looked nothing short of sophisticated. What she was wearing was not in itself extraordinary. A pair of trousers cut beautifully, boots that gripped the uneven path beneath them, and a sweater wrapped around her that looked at least as soft as cashmere, the better to keep out the chill of the ocean air.

Though all around him, the island smelled like cinnamon instead of salt.

"You are a chameleon," he said.

She laughed at that, and the look she shot his way was appraising. "I'm going to choose to take that as a compliment. I think."

"You seem to fit in wherever you go, effortlessly."

"Not effortlessly," she corrected him. "It's supposed to look that way though. I'm glad it does." Carliz seemed to feel his frown on the side of her face and when she looked over to confirm it, she made another low noise. "I was about to say that you should know this, but there's no reason you should. Your family has its measure of fame and notoriety, but it isn't the same as mine. Being a member of a royal family isn't the same thing as being famous. Or even notorious. We are public property, no matter what sort of monarchy it is that we belong to. And so every interaction requires public service, in one form or another. My sister and I were taught from a very young age that there was very little as important as making everyone around us feel comfortable. She is actually better at it than me, but you wouldn't know it."

"She's too lofty, then?"

Carliz shook her head. "That's not what I meant at all. It's only that she's the queen, you see. So no matter how hard she works to make people comfortable around her, what they see is *the queen*. Nonetheless, practicing being effortless is the bulk of what we did growing up. I think other children played. We practiced."

He walked on and the fact that they were next to a cliff with a terrible drop to the rocks below did not escape his notice. He thought it was fitting. He had spent the whole of his life vowing that he would not be like his mother. That he would not be like any other member of his family, in any regard. And here he was all the same.

Wrecked as surely as if he had tossed himself over the side.

A threat his mother had liked to make with regularity.

"There was only one person in my family who ever seemed effortless," Valentino said, though he had to force himself to say these words. He had spent so long *not* saying them. "And by that, I mean he was effortlessly cruel. He took pleasure in everyone else's pain. After my mother died, he only got worse. And over time, it became clear to me that my brother's reckless charm, as I have heard it called, was modeled directly on his. I vowed that I would be like neither of them. That I would honor those who came before me instead."

"You mean your mother?"

"I mean my grandparents, who deserved a far better son than the one they got." He blew out a breath, not liking that even talking of these things made him feel…not himself. All jangly and rough inside. "I have done my best to fill that gap, or so I thought. And then, instead, I allowed myself to get embroiled with you."

"Well and truly embroiled," she said, sounding perfectly cheerful.

"I'm trying to explain myself to you," he told her darkly, everything in him…in a terrible kind of pain he could not begin to name. "This does not come easily."

"What you are doing, Valentino, is walking along a cliff in late November, making dark mutterings that never quite come to the point," she said. Gently enough, though there was a thread of something like exasperation beneath, to his ear. "Remember, you didn't save me any pain these last few years. You caused it. Pretending this wasn't happening didn't make it go away. It just made it hurt more."

"That was not my intention."

"But it's what happened." She shrugged as if it was nothing. "Lucky for you, I love you anyway."

"Why?" he bit out. "Why have you been so certain, all along?"

She looked at him curiously. "Because I saw you," she said, as if it was simple. "I looked across a ballroom in Rome and there you were. I saw you. I recognized you. I knew you." She shrugged. "I can't explain it."

And she didn't even wait for his reaction to that, or look for it. That was how comfortable she was with the words. The sentiments themselves. He thought of all those bold shapes and bright colors, on every surface. Demanding that he see.

But she simply kept talking. "And now look. Despite all of that, here we are anyway."

"Yet I am the only one who knows where we really are," he told her. "You will understand shortly."

She did not reply to that cryptic remark. They walked further, just over the next rise, and then he pointed. Down below, down a narrow set of stairs cut into the side of the hill, was the stretch of land his father liked to call The Peninsula. It was a relatively narrow bit of rock and sand that stuck out from the top of the island, and it was the site of the first house. Now it was known as Bonaparte's Folly, which was an apt a name as any, Valentino supposed.

"Welcome to hell," he said darkly.

He did not mean that to be amusing. So he was surprised when beside him, Carliz laughed.

And she was still laughing as she started for the stairs,

gliding down them in a light-footed sort of way that made it clear she had no idea what she was getting herself into.

But that was the point of this, he reminded himself. His father was always issuing summons, Valentino only occasionally responded to them, and that was how they'd been banging along for ages now. Left to his own devices, he didn't think he would respond at all, but anytime he leaned in that direction, Milo had a terrible habit of showing up at the worst possible times. And for the express purpose of embarrassing his son.

His revenge, Valentino knew. Because he did not like to be ignored.

At the bottom of the stairs, Carliz was already marching for the house that stood there, dark and imposing like all the nightmares he'd had as a child. He had to hurry to catch up with her, and when he did, she only tossed him a look and kept going.

"I'm not afraid of your father," she told him.

Valentino ran a hand through his hair, a childhood tell he'd thought he'd beaten out of himself long since. "I'm not afraid of him either. But I don't underestimate how good he is at what he does, either."

"I understand." She kept her eyes on the house before them, a true antique building that had been updated only in parts—those parts being the bits of the house his father liked. The rest of the old pile could fall off into the sea for all he cared. Mind you, he still held on to every heirloom, every painting, every bit of the heritage the house contained, because he knew that worrying about how casually he might destroy it kept Valentino up at night.

"I don't think you do understand," he gritted out to Carliz as they walked. "But you will."

She stopped then, just short of the grand entrance. "My father was in no way the devil. I loved him dearly. But I was a disappointment to him and he told me so. And because he told me those things when I was very young, very impressionable, I have given them an undue weight over the rest of my life."

He only stared back at her, certain he did not know what she meant. And even more certain that he did not wish to know.

"But I have come to understand that all of us choose our own shadows," she told him, her treasure chest eyes locked to his. "Just as we choose our own pleasures. They are ours to pick through, discard, or carry forever. We decide."

"You will see," he told her, filled with prophecy and doom—and that same pain beneath. "There is a reason my father lives on an island, instead of in the center of a glittering city. He has a habit of repelling almost everyone he comes into contact with. It's better by far if he remains in seclusion."

"Excellent," she said, and her lips curved in a way that really made him wish he had not come here with her. It made him wish that he had expressed his feelings on the topic of paint selection and artistic license in the manner they both enjoyed most, but it was too late. The die was cast. He could already hear stirrings from inside. "I've always wanted to ask a hermit what exactly it is they do all day. Sort through their thoughts? Tell themselves stories, as if a stuck on a desert island? I've always wondered if they think less or more than other people while all alone."

"My father thinks of only one thing," Valentino told her as the locks on the door were thrown, locks Milo had ostentatiously put there to lock them all in when Valentino's mother's behavior was at its worst. He kept them, all these years later, as an immediate reminder of those turbulent years. The screaming, the fighting. Broken glass and sobbing into the morning. "How to be the center of attention in all things."

Then the door was thrown open, and there stood Milo himself.

Smiling affably.

Valentino had often thought that one of life's great injustices was that his father did not resemble the kind of person he was inside. Because if he did, he would be gnarled and pockmarked and ridden with marks, poisoned from the inside out. Instead, he stood tall, with a full head of thick, dark hair. He was a vain man, and policed the lines on his face, comparing his looks to anyone he considered an enemy—which was to say, everyone he'd ever met. He was also partial to staring at his sons and despairing, loudly, that they should have received the great bounty of his genes while giving him so little in return.

As if their mothers had not been involved at all.

Milo was not as tall as either Valentino or Aristide. Valentino thought he got shorter every time they met, though maybe that was only wishful thinking on his part.

Though he would have seen them coming from one of his many windows, Milo took the time to stare at Valentino as if his appearance was a surprise. His lip curled, and Valentino could see the spark that usually preceded one of his cutting remarks in the light of his eyes.

But he didn't say a word. He only turned his attention

to Carliz, because he thought that the only reason a beautiful woman existed was to admire him.

And because he was likely hoping it would provoke Valentino.

Yet what Valentino felt was what he had when he was young, when he'd *known* that it was somehow his fault his mother was trapped on the island. Forced to live with Milo because of Valentino. Because Valentino was born, she was imprisoned.

It was possible she might have said so herself on some of her less lucid evenings.

He had tried to put himself between his mother and Milo, so he could protect her. And it had taken him most of his life to understand that she had not wanted protection. Not his. Not anyone's. What she'd wanted was attention. Milo's attention, specifically.

But she'd never cared how she got it.

Nonetheless, he was grown now and Carliz was his wife, not his mother. And he knew too well that not only would his father take far too much of a delight in it if he betrayed his usual composure by trying to take fire for her—but Carliz herself would not like it.

Milo still stood in the doorway, blocking it, his gaze moved insultingly over Carliz's entire body. Up, then down, and then back again to focus on her round belly.

Valentino thought his jaw might break, he was clenching it so hard.

"Well, well, well," Milo murmured, making a meal of it all in that odious tone of his. It dripped like acid down Valentino's spine. "How nice of our famous party girl princess to drop by and say hello to someone so unimportant as her husband's only blood relative. Full blood relative I mean."

Valentino had made a mess of all of this. He understood that more keenly now than ever. He had let himself do the precise thing he'd known he could never do, not without ending up like his poor, lost mother—strung out on passion, destroyed by claims of love.

But he did not like the way his father was looking at his wife. Any more than he liked the way Milo made that distinction in their blood, as if Aristide wasn't Milo's full blood relation as well.

Most of all he hated the fact that he could see straight through his father, and yet the man's relentless nastiness worked all the same.

But before he could say or do anything, or haul Carliz out of here before she was poisoned too, she laughed.

That absurd confection of a laugh that she was rightly famous for. This was one of the ways she sparkled hither and yon, all over the globe, like a mirror ball.

"I'd be tempted to take exception to that," she said as the laughter faded, reaching out and tapping Milo on the arm as if he was standing there telling a set of jokes. As if they were friends. "But I'm not the type that takes against a friendly bit of hazing amongst family. Especially when I'm sure you know better, Signor Bonaparte."

Milo's eyes flattened. "I know a great many things, as a matter-of-fact."

She leaned in like she was telling him a secret. "Then you know. You can call me *Your Royal Highness*."

And it was the way she said it. As if she was extending an invitation—suggesting that he remember himself while also making fun of her exalted station. Nothing could possibly have fascinated and infuriated Milo more. It was masterful. And she wasn't afraid, this marvel of a wife of his. She was completely assured.

She was Carliz of Las Sosegadas and she knew her own magnificence.

He did, too. Because he had seen her, recognized her. He had known her from that very same moment in Rome. Valentino stopped trying to pretend otherwise.

Even though they were here, where that kind of thing was used for sport. To hunt down any foolish enough to show it.

Carliz let out that laugh again, as if she was gracing Milo with a joke of her own. She even gave him a conspiratorial smile, showing him nothing but what she likely wanted him to see—the Princess Royal in all her glory. As unafraid as ever. Of Milo, but also of Valentino. Of this thing between them he would still rather deny. "It has a much better ring, don't you think?"

CHAPTER TEN

MILO BONAPARTE WAS a pig.

There was no prettying that up. There was no lipstick that would make the man anything but what he was. Tiny. Venal.

And vicious, as men like him always were. He'd tried to put her down, she'd pulled rank, and now he would not rest until he found a better way to get that scorpion's sting deep into her flesh. She'd met far too many men like Milo in her day. She'd learned long ago that it was best to laugh along, never quite seeming to get that he wasn't joking, and then to beat a quick retreat as soon as possible.

"Spicy," Milo said, taking her arm and standing too close. "I like it."

Carliz laughed. "A little spice goes a long way," she said, and then launched into an artless anecdote about accidentally eating too many Pot Douglah peppers in Trinidad on a silly trip one year.

She laughed and she laughed and she put space between her and Milo, but her heart ached for Valentino, who could not have done the same kinds of things when he was a child. He must have felt trapped here, battered this way and that by his father's cruelties.

Because Milo, like all other men of his ilk, liked nothing so much as a captive audience. That much was obvious.

And he was making a meal of it today. He took his *new princess-in-law*, as he insisted on calling her, all around the old castle as if conducting a tour. What he was really doing, Carliz was aware, was sticking any knife he could think of in deep so that Valentino would squirm.

Valentino did not give him the satisfaction. Externally. But if she could see that he held himself more stiffly than usual, she was certain that Milo saw it too.

So she found herself going full social butterfly. After all, this was one of the things she had always been good at. Drawing fire so that the real target—usually her sister—could get some breathing room. Because it didn't matter what this man thought. She didn't care what he thought. To her, he was nothing but another small, disappointing specimen who had an undue influence on the man she'd fallen in love with.

"There used to be flower beds all along the side of the house," Milo said in his oily way as they passed a set of windows. "They were ugly. I had them removed."

Carliz suspected that the flower beds were a sore point, because Valentino's jaw looked like granite. "What a shame," she replied, with another laugh. "I've always thought that as flowers can only ever be lovely, any fault in them must be down to maintenance."

And before Milo could tell her what—who—he was talking about, she set off on a circuitous story about the year she'd spent wandering from one major flower show to the next, from Philadelphia to Melbourne to Singapore and to Chelsea. She raved on about orchids until Milo walked ahead of her, likely to drown her out.

"They were my mother's favorite flowers," Valentino said in a low voice, looking at her with an expression on his face that made her heart hurt. "They died from neglect, but he likes to pretend he took them down himself. In the end, I suppose it doesn't matter how he killed them."

"It matters," she whispered back, fiercely. "It all matters."

Eventually, after a tour through the portrait gallery in which Milo lingered over a portrait of Valentino's mother and Carliz had made certain to act as if she was incapable of taking any negative bit of the story on board, he led them into a sitting room. He insisted they sit. Then he rang for service.

With a malicious sort of glimmer in his gaze.

They all sat there in a fraught sort of silence, until a beautiful older woman arrived at the door. She began silently serving them coffees and biscotti. Home baked, clearly.

But what fascinated Carliz was the way the woman looked at Valentino. With something like longing. Or perhaps it was regret.

Whatever it was, Valentino did not meet her gaze.

Carliz knew this was the famous housekeeper—Aristide's mother, Ginevra—the one who would not leave Milo's employ. No matter what was said about her. Or him, for that matter.

The one who had taught Valentino how to cook.

Clearly pleased with the interplay, no matter how silent, Milo settled back with his coffee and beamed.

The visit did not improve from there.

By the time they left—by the time, that was, that Valentino shot to his feet in the middle of one of his father's sly, insulting monologues wrapped up in the pretense of an actual conversation, he had managed to cover a lot of ground.

"He managed to insult not only my sister and her reign *and* the whole of my country, but both of my parents, one of whom has been dead for some time." Carliz said it wonderingly as they climbed back up the steep stairs, both of them breathing deep as if they'd been slowly suffocating to death in that house. She wasn't quite laughing, but she wasn't *not* laughing, either. It was all so vile and relentless. "I was either so beautiful that it made me an automatic whore or not quite beautiful enough to keep the eye of a Bonaparte, I couldn't tell. It kept going back and forth. And I do believe, right there at the end, that when he started going on about the apple only falling from the tree if the fruit is rotten straight through, that he was actually propositioning me."

"He was."

Valentino's voice was grim, but Carliz was too busy climbing stairs and putting distance between her and that man to pay close attention to that. "Really, if you step back and think about it, the whole thing was a pitiful work of art. Such comprehensive and contradictory insults piled one on top of the next. I've never seen the like."

"You shouldn't have had to suffer through it now."

They made it to the top of the stairs and she pulled her soft cardigan closer around her, because it had gotten colder. She kept forgetting that it would do that, given the boundless sunshine of most days. It wasn't like the mountains, where the change of seasons did not require any interpretation. And it certainly wasn't as cold here as it would be at home.

But even she was not immune, no matter how alpine her blood, to the wind right off an ocean that cut straight to the bone.

Valentino seemed impervious to the cold because of whatever was burning in him. She looked at him, then stopped walking herself. Because he looked if something inside him had *ignited.*

And not in the way she liked best.

"I hope you see, now," he growled at her when he had her attention. "No matter what I do, no matter where I go, there's always *that*. I always come back to that room. That man. That psychodrama that we have all been playing our parts in since I was born."

She felt stunned by that. Winded. "Valentino. I don't know what you thought was happening. But it's not you who should be apologizing for any of that behavior."

"The better he knows a person, the worse it gets," Valentino said, as if she hadn't spoken. "He finds their weaknesses. He exposes them, and capitalizes on them. He is relentless. Day after day, year after year."

"He is the voice in your head," Carliz said softly, as it occurred to her that they had somehow found themselves on uncertain ground again. "I'm sorry for that."

And when he looked at her then, he looked wild and untethered. Not like the controlled Valentino she'd seen so much of, and something in her shook at that.

"My mother and my father together were a disaster," he told her roughly. "And I have dedicated my life to making certain that I will never reenact that disaster, Carliz. I told you. Again and again, I told you that this could never be anything. I tried to keep you safe from it. You would not listen."

She felt something begin to shake, deep inside her. She found herself wrapping her arms around her own body, as if she could keep it in. Or as if she could make it better, somehow, by not letting him see that any of this was upsetting her.

But even as she thought that, she thought that really, that was the problem. All this pretending things didn't hurt when they did. All of this pretending not to feel when that was about as effective as pretending not to breathe.

She had loved him from the very first second she'd seen him. She had acted on that ever since. He knew that she had. Why was she bothering to *pretend*?

So she blew out a breath, and she watched him take note of the fact that it came out shuddery. "No," she agreed. "I would not listen. And do you know why?"

"Because you did not understand what you are dealing with," he thundered at her. He swept arm out toward the peninsula. Toward that sad little house that stood there, weathering storms inside and out. "This is me being honest with you, Carliz. Brutally, totally honest in the only way I can, and you still can't accept the truth."

She studied him, something beating too hard inside her. Some kind of low, desperate panic, because she didn't like the sound of his honesty. She didn't like the look on his face.

"You mean more honest than pretending the only thing between us is sexual?" she asked.

"That is the only thing that we can indulge in."

He moved closer and then his hands were on her upper arms, pulling her toward him. And surely there was something deeply twisted in her that she should revel in that. Exult in it. Yet she had known, so long ago in Rome and with one glance, that this man could fit her so well. That he could speak to every single part of her as well as he did. Even now, that knowing was like a rock inside her, and everything else was built on it.

And she also knew that if she did not fight for what she wanted now, he would roll right over her in his determination to pretend none of this was happening between them. The way he always did. She lifted her hands and slid them onto his chest, not precisely to push him away. But it was not welcoming, either.

"I met your father," she said, evenly. Very evenly. "And he seems like a lonely, bitter old man, who like many lonely, bitter old men, thinks it a great laugh to antagonize anyone who draws near. I don't know why you would imagine that he has anything to do with you. Or us."

"Because this is my blood!" he cried out, as if in anguish. "This is who I am. I've done my best to be something else, Carliz. Anything else. You have no idea how hard I've tried. I've tried so hard to be a good man. To walk the path of the honorable in every way. To do my best to live up to my grandfather's example, with dignity. And instead I am reduced to nothing more than...*this*."

"Is *this* so bad?" she asked, softly. She searched his face, his hard jaw. "What do you think would happen if you stopped trying to hide yourself from me, Valentino? What would happen if you did something truly remarkable, like taking me out to dinner? If we sat in a restaurant, ordered food, and talked to each other as if we were simply...people?"

"Why can't you see?"

And he sounded so wounded. She felt for him, truly

she did. If she could have, she would have taken this pain away from him.

But there was more to think of here than his feelings, whether he would admit he had them or not.

Carliz knew a little bit about the things families passed down, one generation to the next, even with the best of intentions. Heirs and spares. Good ones and bad ones. The roles people played that had never quite fit them, but they couldn't seem to shed. The expectations that sat heavy, like the weight of crowns.

She wanted better than that for her child. Maybe every mother did.

Maybe, a voice inside suggested, *your mother does too. Maybe that's what all her picking and picking is about. Maybe you've been reading it wrong, all this time.*

"If you let this man destroy your marriage the way he destroyed his," Carliz said, as gently as she could when her heart was breaking. "Don't you see? Then he's winning. You're letting him win."

Valentino stared down at her and she could see all the different faces he had shown her, whether on purpose or not. That stranger she'd seen so unexpectedly in Rome. How startled he looked. How shocked, just as she had been.

That grief she'd seen on his face in that drafty old castle keep. The unbearable weight of it all.

Her stern, deliciously hard lover, who knew no boundaries he could not push and cajoled her into heights she could not even have imagined, before him.

The bleak look on his face now. An echo of the way he had looked at her at their wedding. And that morning in July when he'd told her that they would never see each other again.

But now, here, standing on top of the cliff as the wind got colder and harsher, she saw everything. What he had been trying to hide. What she had been letting him hide. Because none of this—nothing between them—occurred in a vacuum.

"My father was a monster," Valentino bit out in that same rough tone. "He let my mother die because she had ceased to amuse him. The only reason my brother and I are alive is because it entertains him to have us forever at each other's throats."

"Then why not defy him and become the best of friends," she asked, trying to sound cool and remote but failing. "After all, who has more in common with you than Aristide? Who but the two of you know how you were raised, what happened here, and what you must carry in the wake of it?"

He shook his head at that, as if she'd delivered a body blow. "You can't reason with a monster like my father, Carliz. And I have always known that I have the same monster in me. Look at how I treat you. Look at what I think passes for desire. For passion."

"You mean those things we do *together*?" This time she laughed in disbelief, and a sharper hurt than she would have thought possible. "Those things you taught me? That I treasure?"

"I'm as twisted as he is," Valentino intoned, handing down a pronouncement from on high. "And it does not matter how I try to compartmentalize this obsession I have for you. I know where it ends. I watched it end terribly once already. I cannot allow myself to do the same thing. Carliz. Please. Listen to me when I tell you that whatever poisoning him is in me, too. It's the same blood. It only ends up in the same place."

And they were both breathing too hard then. There were too many things swirling around in her head. All the things she could say. All the things she felt.

But instead, she moved closer, tipping her face up to his, not caring at all when the rain began to fall.

"We are standing at a crossroads, you and I. A literal one. If you look down to your left, you'll see your past. In a stone house on the end of a spit of land, waiting for the sea to take it back." It was almost as if they might kiss, wildly, impossibly. It felt like that, but darker, while they were so close. So still. So *ravaged* by these things that he thought owned him. "On your right is the house you built so you could control it. So you could keep it stark and cold, because you thought that would keep you safe."

"It was never about safety," he argued. And he wasn't lying. She could see that. He believed that it had been about those things he'd told her it was about. *Calm. No scenes.* He didn't understand that all of that was the same fear.

"But I have defaced it, Valentino," she said, low and urgent. "It is bright now. Filled with color and chaos, and surely you must know that soon enough, there will be a child there too. And he will not follow your commands. He will not do as he is told. He will cry and he will disrupt our sleep and he will not care who you are or what promises you made to yourself long ago." She tapped on the chest before her, not gently. "He will want his father, and so you have to choose. It's that stark. The darkness or the light, but the choice has to be yours."

"You think it's a crossroads. You think it's a choice." He was shaking his head, but he didn't let go of her arms. "But all these things are in me, all of the time. It doesn't matter what I choose, they will all come with me. And soon enough…"

"Soon enough, what?" she demanded, and maybe there were tears in the corners of her eyes. Maybe not only in the corners, but slipping out and joining the raindrops that gathered there as the winter weather moved in, but she didn't bother to dash them away. "What is the point of you going to such lengths to have control over everything in the world if you don't have control of yourself? If you're worried about snapping, Valentino, there is a solution. *Don't.*"

He heaved out a breath. "As if it's that simple."

"You forget that I've met your father," she countered, pressing her palms into the wall of his chest. "Do you really believe that he's faced with some kind of internal moral dilemma? He's not. I don't know if that makes it better or worse. He didn't *accidentally* become the way he is, my love. He likes it. He *wants* to be cruel. If you don't, if that's not who you are… *You don't have to be anything like him.*"

She was not sure she had ever said anything more intently in all her life.

"I want desperately to believe that," Valentino told her in a gravelly voice. "But deep inside me, a voice always reminds me—"

"That's *his* voice!" she cried at him.

Then she stepped back, because she was too close to using the one weapon they both wielded so expertly, and with such deadly effect. Because she knew that if she kissed him here, they would consummate this moment, whatever it was, out here in the rain, the wind. And it would be glorious. She would come apart so thoroughly that she would think for a moment that it was impossible she might ever be put back together.

She loved that feeling almost beyond reason.

But then she would come back into her body, hard.

And everything would be exactly the same.

So she backed away. And she didn't care any longer if he saw her tears. If he saw her shake.

She was either able to show what she felt or she wasn't. There was no sense hiding it.

"You think that this is an honorable thing that you're doing," she said then, though everything in her shouted at her to move toward him. To taste him. To hold on to him any way she could. It hurt that she didn't. "You think that if you cut yourself off from emotion, from feeling anything—even though you already feel it—you can avoid it. Control it. But that's a lie, Valentino. And you might be able to lie to yourself. But don't you understand by now? You've never been any good at lying to me. Because I know that what you feel is real. I've always known. I don't know how."

But she did. It was that same chain, linking them together. She could almost see it gleaming now, out here in all this wet.

He said her name, or she thought he did, but the rain stole the sound away from him.

Carliz kept going. "And pretending otherwise doesn't make you a hero. It makes you a coward. And if you act like this? If this is the life you choose?" She put one hand on her belly, and with her free one she pointed right at him. "Sooner or later, your son will see you for the liar and the coward you are, and then what will you be to *him*? Just another monster, like your father is to you?"

The rain came down. The wind whipped at them. She thought he might have made a noise, the sort of noise an animal might make while in pain. And she hated herself for causing him pain.

But that didn't mean what she said was in any way untrue.

So she stepped back, still holding his gaze, no matter it was rain slicked too.

"Your choice, Valentino," she whispered, and she knew he heard her.

The rain and the wind could only take so much.

Then she turned around, though everything in her protested. She forced herself back along the cliffs and then down into the house she'd painted all those bright colors. It seemed a lifetime ago.

And even now, even after she'd faced his monster of a father and come out none the worse for wear, he didn't want to love her.

Carliz had to look at it head-on. She took herself, dripping wet and rapidly growing cold, and toweled off. She wrapped herself in every blanket she could find and curled up on the chaise in her favorite sitting room.

She stared at the wall she'd painted bright yellow and blue, and hung with old paintings. And she asked herself what—exactly—she planned to do for herself and her child if Valentino couldn't love them the way he should.

Because she might have decided it was enough to know what she knew, to have that faith. But she couldn't ask the same of her child. And that meant she would have to leave him.

Carliz didn't know how she was going to make herself do that, again.

Or how she thought she was going to live without him.

CHAPTER ELEVEN

VALENTINO STAYED OUT in that storm for a long time.

Every word she'd said hit hard and pounded into him, like hail.

One stone after the next, each one of them hitting their mark with deadly accuracy.

Was that his father's voice inside of him, that dark sneering thing that was so quick to point out his failures?

He thought of his family's history and all of those things he'd always taken as fact. Because he felt them himself? Or because his father had known what he felt and had steered him one way or the next as it suited him?

Had his brother betrayed him? Had his father made it seem as if *he* had betrayed his brother?

Maybe Carliz was right to point out that the true act of defiance would have been to stay friends with Aristides. The only true friend he'd ever had. They had adored each other.

His father hadn't liked that, had he?

And something else occurred to him, then. Was it possible that there was something critical he was missing when it came to love, to feelings, that Ginevra showed every day—by choosing to remain in a place she could have left? By choosing to love as she chose, no matter if it was returned. No matter what anyone else thought.

No matter if it was love or penance or something more complicated, it was hers. And she did not shy away from it.

And Ginevra had been a good mother not only to her son, but to Valentino, too. Little as he might have understood that at the time.

He thought of the kind of mother Carliz already was, and how different that was than his own. Because she had been so fragile, so consistently precarious, his poor mother. She had been so unable to fight her own demons, much less the man who'd married her so that he could toy with them too.

She had never stood a chance against Milo.

Then again, she also hadn't tried.

That truth seemed to hit him like lightning.

Because there was no way that his father could have done the extent of the damage on his wife if she'd been a woman like Carliz. It simply would not have happened.

First she would have laughed. Then she would have left.

And she most certainly would have taken her child with her.

Something in him seemed to grow warmer and brighter at that thought. And then, the more he held on to it, it was as if something inside him began to melt.

And as it melted, he felt seized with what he could only call a tidal wave of the kind of emotion he never allowed himself.

Not openly. It had to be sex, and specifically the kind of sex he controlled. It had to be the rules he made. The life he lived.

That was his emotion. That was how he *felt*.

But she'd known all along, hadn't she?

And as it broke over him, he began to run. Through the rain, through the gathering dark. He catapulted himself down the side of the cliff and raced through the gardens, desperate to get there.

He made it to the door and threw it open.

Because inside, there was color. Inside, it was bright and warm and happy.

And Carliz was here.

Since the moment he had laid eyes on her in Rome, she had been a bright, hot light leading him home.

Little as he had wished to accept that.

He ran through the house, shouting her name, not caring at all that his servants looked at him in astonishment.

He shouted again and again, until she appeared wrapped once more in what looked like a selection of scarves—

Except these were not chosen to seduce.

These were blankets, and if he was not mistaken, she'd chosen them to hide.

Something about the notion of his vibrant, gloriously bright Carliz hiding herself away made him ache. This house was already a monument to her vulnerability, painted in bold strokes so there could be no mistaking it.

She had made his house into a masterpiece to show him her love, and he had delivered her to a monster.

It was time to rectify this situation, once and for all.

Valentino walked up the stairs, aware of every brushstroke as he passed. The color here, the competing color there. She had told him the story of her love, of their love, and he had rewarded her by telling her that a stone house of misery was their future instead.

When he got to the top of the stairs he stared at her for a wordless moment, and then he simply dropped to his knees.

She made a startled sort of sound, or perhaps it was a sob. The blankets fell all around them as she reached out to take his face between her hands.

Carliz gazed down at him as if she wanted to soothe him, even now.

"I looked up across a standard, boring event, and was hit by lightning," he told her, hoping she could hear that he was speaking from his heart. Hoping she could see it on his face. Or even hear the way his heartbeat was threatening his ribs. "You know exactly what my life was like. It was this house. Beautiful in its way, but cold. Deliberately empty. Stark and studied. And then there you were. With your hair too many colors and your eyes too wise and knowing, and you saw me. And I looked at you and I saw nothing but color."

She moved closer, and whispered something, but he knew he had to get these things out. Because he was tired, so tired, of the things he'd kept deep inside.

The things that had hurt them both.

"Later I would say you were a witch. That I was compelled against my will, but I wasn't. You are so *bright.* I wanted to get close to you. I wanted to see if it was possible that anything could warm me the way you looked as if you could, and then you did." He gazed up at her. "I think I started melting then, and I've been fighting it ever since, and Carliz, I want that love story I've been reading about in the papers for years. I want to love you so much and so well that strangers pick up on it in a crowded room that I wasn't even in. I want to make you happy, and I understand what an extraordinary thing that is to say. I don't think I have ever been happy a day of my life unless you were beside me. And even then, I did my best to ruin it. But I want it all the same."

"The good news," she managed to say, her voice rough and her eyes shining, "is that we did vow to stay together forever. So we have some time to practice."

Something in him eased then, little though he understood what she was doing. He had expected to find her packing. He had expected her to show him coldness. He had expected—

But he got it, then.

She loved him. This was love. She was forgiving him in real time. She was showing him what it was like when someone was truly in love with him.

It wasn't easy. It might even hurt. But the love never stopped.

The love was like that light of hers, and it shone on forever.

"You could not have made anything more clear to me," he forced himself to say, to keep going, because that must be love too. Because that was what she did, What she had done and was still doing. "Than when you told me that I was set to become to my own son the very father who has worked so hard to ruin my life. So this is my other vow to you, while it is still just us."

Though it wasn't. Not really. Their baby was there between them. He smoothed his hands over her belly, filled with awe and reverence, as always.

And love, he understood at last.

All of this was love.

"I will love you," he whispered to the child she carried. *His son.* "I will not use you as some kind of sick entertainment that only I enjoy. I will try to raise you to be a good man, freed from the kind of voices I carry around inside me. And I promise you, I will not be a monster."

Carliz winced. "I didn't mean that."

But Valentino smiled. "You did. And you were right."

He stood then, pulling her close so he could smooth his hands over that wild hair of hers, let loose again from the knot she'd tied it in. Then he wiped away the moisture beneath her eyes, carefully, as if every tear was precious.

"I love you," she whispered.

"*Mia principessa*, then there is no time to waste. We have already wasted too much time. You must know that I have always loved you. You have told me you knew it. And I intend to love you forever, as best I can, and I…" But he paused, then. His heart pounded against his ribs. "I want to start over. If, of course that is what you want." And he realized, in this moment, how strong she was. How courageous to paint her bleeding, broken heart all over this house When he could hardly bear to ask a simple question. "Is it, Carliz? Can we start again, you and I?"

And for a moment, she looked something like dazed.

But then a smile broke over her face, brighter by far than any of the paint she'd slapped on his walls. Better than the brightest, sunniest day.

"Valentino," she said, smiling so wide he found himself smiling too, as if that was something he did with regularity—though he thought perhaps he should, "I thought you'd never ask."

CHAPTER TWELVE

THEY DID EXACTLY THAT.

They started over, as if they were new.

As if both of them were ready to accept what had happened that night in Rome, then and there.

And it was good.

But it was one thing to thunder on to his wife and spend his days relearning every part of her so that he might love her better.

Other relationships required more care.

He met with his brother in the Diamond Club, some weeks before Christmas.

"It's almost as if you're stalking me," Aristide said in his usual droll way. "And to think, you had to come all the way to London to do it when, last I checked, we were neighbors."

"I'm having a son," Valentino said. Starkly. He made no attempt to dress it up, and because his brother looked taken aback by that, he continued. "I would like him to know his cousins. I would like him to have the run of the island, as we did. And play as we did. And know nothing at all about our father or what came before. I wish we could have had that longer than we did."

Aristide sat in the seat opposite Valentino, and gestured

for his whiskey. He waited for a staff member to produce a glass, tossed it back, and then sat a moment before he spoke.

"If I didn't know better," he said, mildly, "I might begin to suspect that this is your version of an apology."

Valentino smiled. Then he leaned forward, and held his brother's gaze. "I would like to think of it as a new beginning." But because he was no longer playing the role he had for so long, he smiled. "If that is something you would find yourself amenable to."

And he found himself something a little too close to choked up when his brother looked at him, cleared his throat as if there was emotion there too, and then nodded.

When he told Carliz the story, she cried.

She cried a lot throughout the rest of her pregnancy. They spent most of their time on the island, though he would often whisk her away to this city or that. He would take her out to dinner at the finest restaurants, where they would sit. And order food off menus. And talk of everything and nothing.

"Look at us," she said after one such meal, her hand threaded with his as they walked back through the lively streets of Barcelona. "We seem just like *people*."

"Or near enough, Your Royal Highness," he murmured.

Their son was born entirely perfect in every way, not that they were biased. And they liked him so much that they decided to give him a set of brothers, three in total. He taught them how to be decent men and kept them away from his father. Carliz taught them perfect manners and her own dry wit, and encouraged them to run like wild animals all over the island with their cousins.

Just the way he and Aristide had done when they were small.

Life was good, because they made it good. Valentino learned to splash about in color. And how to love Carliz the way she deserved.

That it turned out, was the easiest part of all.

It was loving himself, too, that took work. It was the mirror that intimacy held up to his own true face that gave him pause.

But then, there were cures for that.

His children's delight in him, so different from the fear he'd felt for his own father. Or the sick need he'd had to protect his mother when he'd been too young to understand what was going on.

And when they were alone, the games that he played with his wife when both of them were naked, that these days were all about correction, not control.

Life was good. They made sure of it.

As the years passed, even a monster like Milo could not talk his way out of mortality. And it was a truth worth learning early that people died how they lived. Once the old man was gone, the brothers came together and knew that neither one of them could or would ever live in that house again.

"I suppose we can't burn it down," Aristide said, regretfully.

Valentino was tempted to light the match himself. "It does have historic value."

So they decided to make it something far better than it had ever been during their father's lifetime. An orphanage, but one that would take care of children instead of degrading and diminishing them.

One that would lift them up instead of smashing them down.

And it turned out, despite everything, that Valentino

Bonaparte made himself into a good man instead of a monster. With the great honor of a life lived, if not always as well as he'd like, as fully as he could. With the legacy of mended fences with his brother and a set of cousins who would never know that there had ever been any distance between their parents.

Best of all, he had Carliz to walk with him all along the path, sharing it all with him. Every step. Every moment. Making it better simply because she was there. All of that laughter. All of that joy. All because of one night in Rome and the brightest light he'd ever seen, guiding him home.

A home they made together, from scratch and brand-new, every morning they woke up and started again.

Which they planned to do forever.

And did.

* * * * *

MILLS & BOON®

Coming next month

GREEK PREGNANCY CLAUSE
Maya Blake

'You have thirty seconds. Then I walk out,' Ares warned in a soft, dangerous murmur.

Odessa believed him. After all, hadn't he done that once, this man who was a world removed from the younger version she'd known. Or was he?

Hadn't he possessed this overwhelming presence even back then, only caged it better?

Now the full force of it bore down on her, Odessa was at once wary of and drawn to it, like a hapless moth dancing towards a destroying flame.

She watched, mesmerized despite herself as his folded arms slowly dropped, his large, masculine hands drawing attention to his lean hips, the dangerously evocative image he made simply by...*being*.

At what felt like the last second, she took a deep breath and took the boldest leap. 'Before my father's memorial is over, Vincenzo Bartorelli will announce our engagement.' Acid flooded her mouth at the very thought. 'I would rather jump naked into Mount Etna than marry him. So, I'd...I'd like you to say that I'm marrying you instead. And in return...' *Dio*, was she really doing this? 'And in return I'll give you whatever you want.'

Continue reading
GREEK PREGNANCY CLAUSE
Maya Blake

Available next month
millsandboon.co.uk

Afterglow Books is a trend-led, trope-filled list of books with diverse, authentic and relatable characters, a wide array of voices and representations, plus real world trials and tribulations. Featuring all the tropes you could possibly want (think small-town settings, fake relationships, grumpy vs sunshine, enemies to lovers) and all with a generous dose of spice in every story.

@millsandboonuk
@millsandboonuk
afterglowbooks.co.uk
#AfterglowBooks

For all the latest book news, exclusive content and giveaways scan the QR code below to sign up to the Afterglow newsletter:

OUT NOW!

Available at
millsandboon.co.uk

MILLS & BOON